The Color of God

"Grace E. Running-Nichols has woven an earthy, intricate, and masterful novel of communal and individual redemption in this tale of love, betrayal, forgiveness, and healing. *The Color of God* is sure to plant seeds of truth, hope, and courage in the heart of every reader!"

~ **Scott Harrison**, *New York Times* Best-Selling Author of *Thirst: A Journey of Redemption, Compassion and a Mission to Bring Clean Water to the World*

"From the start of this timeless story, you're hooked. A self-reliant florist with a rock-hard exterior needs the crash that comes to her life in the form of a small boy chasing an idea he had for his mom. Everything moves fast from there as you walk into the web of neighbors, nemesises, and lost souls that want to be found and healed. Everything about Grace's debut novel makes you feel the intensity of a loving community in everyone's business, the heartbreak of past choices that finally have a chance to be reconciled and the soft, whispers of a divine pathway you long to follow through every glorious page. You won't want to put this one down."

~ **Jonathan Morris**, Theologian, *New York Times* Best-Selling Author, Executive Coach www.MorrisandLarson.com

"*The Color of God* is a beautifully crafted story that engages one's senses and provokes sensibilities. The community of Stratford comes alive with a cast of characters who, like the rest of us, are broken but never out of reach of redemption. Lives intertwine as a diabolical mystery is untangled that will determine the fate of five precious children, leaving the reader's mind and soul encouraged by God's amazing grace."

~ **Joy Casey**, Founder and Director of NewLife Ethiopia

THE
COLOR
of God

GRACE E.
RUNNING-NICHOLS

NEW YORK

LONDON • NASHVILLE • MELBOURNE • VANCOUVER

The Color of God

A Stratford Lane Novel

Published in New York, New York, by Morgan James Publishing. Morgan James is a trademark of Morgan James, LLC. www.MorganJamesPublishing.com

Proudly distributed by Ingram Publisher Services.

To order additional books:
www.thecolorofgod.us

Morgan James BOGO™

A **FREE** ebook edition is available for you or a friend with the purchase of this print book.

CLEARLY SIGN YOUR NAME ABOVE

Instructions to claim your free ebook edition:
1. Visit MorganJamesBOGO.com
2. Sign your name CLEARLY in the space above
3. Complete the form and submit a photo of this entire page
4. You or your friend can download the ebook to your preferred device

ISBN 9781631958236 paperback
ISBN 9781631958243 ebook
Library of Congress Control Number:
2021949912

Cover Design by:
Rachel Lopez
www.r2cdesign.com

Interior Design by:
Christopher Kirk
www.GFSstudio.com

Editorial:
Inspira Literary Solutions,
Gig Harbor, WA

Morgan James is a proud partner of Habitat for Humanity Peninsula and Greater Williamsburg. Partners in building since 2006.

Get involved today! Visit MorganJamesPublishing.com/giving-back

To Frank, my mentor, who gave me the writing education I never had.
To Dennis, my beloved husband, who teaches me daily to live in the miraculous.

Acknowledgments

Have you ever seen the movie *Julie & Julia*? In it, Julia Child's husband offers her this toast, "You're the butter to my bread!" I hold my heart every time I experience that scene. Here, in this sacred space, where I have the privilege of acknowledging many who've closely walked with me for nearly a decade of writing, I'll add my own twist to his words, "You're the coffee in my cup!"

First, thank you Pamela Kennedy, author and friend, for your note on January 8th, 2012, challenging me to write more than just Christmas cards and Facebook posts.

Thank you, Mom, for your daily presence, and Dad (now in Heaven), for listening as this story bubbled out of my imagination. You eagerly read and loved everything, even the ridiculous, deleted scenes! Thank you to my siblings and their spouses: Edward and Amy, for encouraging the beauty that fuels me, and to Kristi and Joe, for your delight in the plot, applauding when the mafia barged in, then laughing as they hightailed it out. (And yes, Joe, I did check the trunk for stowaways!) Thank you, Mom and Dad Nichols (now also in Heaven), for always mentioning Debbie Macomber as a *Guideposts Magazine* inspiration for my writing.

Thank you, Paul and Linda Schroeder and Tiffany and Art Moore, for your refreshing friendship and simultaneous suggestions of sending my manuscript to Frank Peretti. Thank you, Paul, for texting me in church (!) to say you'd miraculously placed my work into Frank's hands, and for living your real life as the kind of loving shepherd Lars becomes. Especially, thank you Tiffany for every hour—only God knows how many—of encouragement, wisdom, sacrifice, endurance, and beholding God in the midst of my word wrestling.

Thank you, Joan Brown, for finding beauty in my writing and speaking it into my life, even when I sat weeping in my nightgown over a scene, while my then two four-year-olds ate Kentucky Fried Chicken on the floor of the master bathroom! And thank you, Hilary Hammett, for reminding me that God would continue to pour his promises into my obedient work of "turning phrases," words I hid in my heart.

Thank you, Damaris Caughlan, for your extravagant passion for life, reminding me to seize the day and that all words matter. Thank you, Lisa Harrison, for listening to every crazy thought I shared between our balconies and for valuing my own story and my fictional one. Thank you, Sarah Davis, for asking to read everything before it was even ready, then asking the best questions I answered through freshly written chapters.

Thank you, Rebecca Ellington, for equipping our children academically, then surprising me with your otherworldly wisdom over my fictional family.

Thank you, Dawn Omdal, for seeing us as beloved, and for your stalwart faith and friendship, for being a second mom to our crew, and for loving my characters even before meeting them.

Thank you, Andrea Anderson, for walking alongside me as my kindred spirit, the beautiful Diana to me as Anne Shirley, for more than four decades, always pointing my writing towards the real Author of it all.

Thank you to my gentle readers, cheerleaders, and technical wizards, Susan and Molly Chandler, Keely Villahermosa, Cathy (and David) Hillman, Noelle Knutson, Mike (and Missy) Meyer, Linda Groom, and Karla Morgan, wise friends whose valuable critique helped in shaping the book from the beginning.

Thank you, Cheri Wagoner and Lauren Cox, for inviting me to mentor on Mondays. Your contagious joy and tenacity transformed our Bible Study into a beloved sanctuary of healing. Karen Davis, Cheryl Nelson, Trinity Starr, Sandi Howard, Jess Stancikas, and Jenn Hostetler (also my narrator), your graciousness and steady prayers trickled through to my writing, inspiring me to stay the course and keep climbing over each mountain of deleted words. Your faithfulness as we read the sequel to *Prison to Praise,* even at my bedside when I'd busted my knee (Bible Study slumber party?), still ministers to me. And Josh Mann, the words "contend" and "indefatigable" will live in my mind forever. Bex, thank you for the stunning visuals of Lucy you contributed as I was pondering the cover design.

Thank you to my seven brilliant childhood companions who absorbed my angsty book texts and reminded me of my identity: Laura Gerard, Naomi Mizusaki, Jennifer Nyhan, Lisa Pitstick, Gina Trommlitz, Kathy Bristow Smith, and Madeline Ben-Shoham.

Thank you, Pastors Jim Fleming and Matthew Ayers, for modeling the joy of the Lord as your strength throughout the seasons of our lives, and in so doing, inspiring Pastor Lars to do the same. Rochelle and Amber, thank you for your constant encouragement.

Thank you, Valerie Cheyne, for your effervescence in guiding me through a crash course in quitclaims real estate.

Thank you, Carol Morgan, Doris Howe, Debi Musick, and Liane Wolbert, for modeling commitment in community in social work and adoption. The appearance of angels was no surprise to you.

Thank you, Leo Gonzales and your team, for transforming broken, tired things into my visions of beauty. Miguel came to life because you exemplified who he could be!

Thank you, Guide Dog Foundation of New York, for giving us the privilege of raising two puppies and then allowing us to adopt them. Luminous and Serenity exist in my fictional world because of your non-profit organization.

Thank you to the Morgan James staff: CEO David Hancock, Jim Howard, Courtney Donelson, Heidi Nickerson, Emily Madison, and each of you who worked diligently, believing my novel was worth publishing.

Thank you to my beloved editors, Arlyn Lawrence and Kerry Wade. Your intuition, wisdom, patience, and creativity transformed my novel into what it is today! Thank you, Krista Ostrander and Chelsea Greenwood, for your technical help along the way. And thank you, Dawn Morris, for guiding me to Inspira Literary Solutions.

Thank you, Joy Casey, Scott Harrison, and Jonathan Morris, for loving every sacred life you meet and for leaping into the miraculous realm of doing the impossible for those who deserve it most! And thank you for standing with me here.

Thank you, Frank Peretti, for embracing the first "syrupy sweet" version of my novel from the beginning. You offered your mentorship, simply saying you wished to give back in a field where you'd been given much. You knew the sacrifice of time you'd be making when I had no idea. It was a marvelous day when Sylvia made you laugh, then, when Florence and Montreal made you cry, I began to believe in my story as much as you believed in my potential. You taught me to respect the darkness, to accept that not everyone will embrace redemption, and to celebrate every detail of authenticity in each character. You opened the door for me to learn and love the art of writing. I am forever grateful to you and your beautiful wife, Barbara, "the butter to [your] bread"!

Thank you to my beloved children, in-law children, and grandchildren, the real canvases and novels of my life—not on which *I* paint or write, oh no—the ones I'm privileged to watch come to life. The tapestry of each of your stories, lived out loud, is exquisite! *Oh that the God of the Universe would choose to allow me the gift of motherhood!* Thank you, Gabriel and Line, and your sons, Karsten and Johannes, for your inspiration and love. Thank you, Elias and Elise, for your delight and creativity. Thank you, Magdalene and Hayden, and your son Paxton, for your compassion and presence. And especially to you, Magdalene, for your role as wonder-woman assistant, graciously forging forward in this new territory. Thank you, Malachi, for your enthusiasm and for asking the question in the first place, "Have you ever wondered the color of God?" Thank you, Salomé, for your kindness, Emmaus for your dependability, Zion for your strength, and Ezra for your grace. And Olena Deneychuk, thank you for coming alongside me during many of the homeschooling years, to help carry the burden, share in our joy, and provide writing time on the side. I LOVE YOU ALL!

And thank you Dennis, my loving husband of 32 years. Thank you for reading every word I've ever written and for courageously telling me the truth, if it moved you it stayed, if it didn't, poof, it was gone. In patience, you'd hear it again, hours later, without a hint of condemnation. Thank you for listening when I fell apart and for gently pulling me up to stand again when I was able. Thank you for modeling self-sacrifice and excellence every day of our marriage, saying every step is forward with God. The last part of the *Julie & Julia* toast I must borrow for you, "You're the breath in my lungs." I'm thankful that we belong to each other.

If you find I've missed mentioning your help here, I must confess, Magdalene had to chide me by saying, "Mom, you're not writing your memoirs." Nevertheless, I've likely unintentionally forgotten someone integral to this book. Please forgive me and know I value you dearly, even if my memory didn't serve me well here.

Now, finally, I thank my Savior, Jesus Christ, for redeeming my life with His own and for His lavish gift of storytelling, beginning with His own parables.

Foreword

When Grace's pastor first handed me her manuscript, I found a writer young at the craft, stumbling here and there like a newborn fawn, and yet there was *something* in those pages that captured me: a heart for all kinds and colors of people; an eye and ear for life's details; a direct knowledge of human struggle; an imagination that placed me right in the mix and amid the personalities of a whimsical, Capra kind of neighborhood. Grace was onto something.

We worked together via Skype for a few years, just going after her dream, and I would say we got there. Grace is now a writer on her own two feet. *The Color of God* is ready, an engaging, emotional, feel-good read, and I'm very proud.

Frank E. Peretti
New York Times Best-Selling Author of
This Present Darkness and *Piercing the Darkness*

Autumn

Noun. au·tumn : the third season of the year, from September to November in the Northern Hemisphere, when crops and fruits are gathered and leaves fall

Nestled between Greenwich and East Village lay the close-knit community of Stratford. On a Friday morning in September, the first rays of the sun had just begun to illuminate the New York City skyline. Lavender hues of daybreak silhouetted each shop between Stratford and Lowell.

Through a wall of stained glass, light dappled the floor of Stratford Community Chapel and found its way through the cracks of the forgotten tower. A starling flitted along the wall of the chapel courtyard and landed near the playground on the corner where sunbeams shimmered pale yellow.

Down the street, lights flickered on inside the sub shop, while the mirrored doors of the daycare reflected a hint of blue sky. Across the lane, sunlight seeped into the coffee shop, where whirring grinders rarely paused. From the bakery next door, delicious smells of cardamom and cinnamon wafted skyward. Shadows danced on the front step of the bookstore, disturbed momentarily by someone who'd just slipped in through the back door. A few paces away, clothed in leaves of crimson and yellow, a Norway maple lifted its branches in celebration of autumn.

Finally, the sunrise alighted on the fragile window of Lillian Rose Bloom's flower shop. A gust of wind sent colorful leaves fluttering down to the sill where an indifferent cat pawed at the glass from inside. Soon these maple leaves would rise into flight again, when the vibrant fall rhythm of the morning would come to a crashing halt.

1

Lillian

Name. Li-lee-un : Latin origin, meaning "lilium" (lily)

L
illian Rose Bloom awakened to a shrill chorus of house sparrows lining her bedroom window.

"What in the world?" she whispered, peering up through the dawn light at their stout silhouettes, flitting about in a frenzy.

Their raucous chirps intensified, echoing through the thin walls of Lillian's second story apartment. She threw off her comforter and stepped into her work clogs, then slipped through her narrow hallway and out the fire escape door. It slammed shut behind her. She shivered in bare legs as a gust of wind blew through her flimsy nightgown and whipped her hair across her face. The crisp autumn air swept a blush across her white cheeks and stung her lungs.

There, against the railing of her fire escape terrace, stood the large cardboard box Lillian had lugged outside the night before. It contained the carefully selected fall foliage for her flower shop. With its lid strewn aside, all that could be seen now were twitching brown and white feathered heads, bobbing up and down—a sea of feasting sparrows!

Lillian rushed at the flock of thieves, who burst from the box in a flurry. Their tiny wings fluttered past her face, blurring her eyes. As she sputtered and brushed away the disgruntled flock, she lost her balance, but grabbed for the railing. In the confusion, one of her clogs flipped off her foot and toppled over the edge of the fire escape grate. Helplessly, she watched it drop to the alley below, where it landed somewhere between her flower shop and the bakery next door.

"Seriously!" Lillian fumed, turning her attention back to the box. The sparrows had demolished every golden wheat stalk and ear of Indian corn. They'd even pecked pinholes in each bright pumpkin and gourd, the ones she'd saved for her autumn arrangements. How could these delicate creatures ruin an entire box of beauty before the day had even begun?

She scooped up her remaining clog and dragged the box to the door, calming her nerves with the idea of a hot shower. She turned the doorknob. It didn't budge. In her hurry, she'd forgotten to unlock the door on the way out and it had locked shut behind her, leaving her trapped on the fire escape.

She whipped around in horror at the rumbling sound of a delivery truck turning into the alley from the street. Familiar fumes drifted up through the grate below her feet, where the baker usually smoked his morning cigarette while waiting to load bread. For a split second she felt paralyzed, until her eyes fell on the slim frame of her open bedroom window, just at shoulder height. She popped out the screen and pulled herself up onto the sill, where she dangled from the waist. *If anyone's looking up at me right now . . .* she thought, feeling her face flush from more than just the cold wind. From there, she hoisted one knee over and then the other, then finally abandoned herself to a belly flop onto her bed.

Lillian sat up and breathed a sigh of relief. She wiped her tangled curls away from her neck, but when she pulled her fingers across her shoulder, she discovered a white fluid mess of sparrow droppings.

She ran to the bathroom sink to turn the hot faucet to full blast. She stared at her disastrous reflection in the mirror. "If this is how forty feels, I think I'll stick to thirty-nine!" It didn't matter anyway, she reasoned; she hadn't told a soul it was her birthday.

Lillian relished her steamy shower, slipped on some comfy clothes, then headed for the kitchen. The light drifting through her living room window and the promise of coffee on this chilly New York morning drew her mind to the tasks of the day.

She breathed in the restorative aroma of French roast from her mug as she tucked her one clog under her arm and headed downstairs to find the other. The familiar creak of the last step alerted Mr. Blue Suede Shoes, Lillian's Himalayan cat, to his mistress' arrival. He stretched, then rubbed his chin against Lillian's leg.

"You missed breakfast on the fire escape!" Lillian scolded, but her speech died on her lips. There on the pine table, where she always displayed beauty, a tantalizing wisp of steam swirled from a piping hot cinnamon roll. Underneath it, the words *Happy Birthday Lillian* danced across a paper doily.

"What in the world?" she whispered.

Tap-tap came a knock upon the sky-blue side door as if its vintage hardware could be locked. "Hello," called the voices of Birgitte and Hans, owners of The Dansk Konditori. They let themselves in as the wafting aroma of fresh bread mingled with the scent of flowers and greenery. Of all impossible things for which one could wish, a connecting door between a flower shop and a bakery might seem like a gift from heaven, but Lillian cringed. *Could they not wait for me to open the door?* Lillian forced herself to soften her tense shoulders and brandished a smile of thanks.

Hans gave an exaggerated bow and presented the wayward clog from behind his back. "Missing something? Landed by our delivery truck, Birgitte recognized it as yours. Tried it on myself, but no respectable Dane wears flowery clogs!" He roared with laughter. Birgitte smiled apologetically, but he gave one last jab. "I was waiting for you to join me for a smoke!"

Lillian felt her silent answer, a crimson flush. The couple wished her a happy birthday, then stepped back into their bustling business. She clicked the door shut behind them and leaned against it.

Lillian stepped into her clogs, then turned to the glass window at the front of her shop. It had been less than a year since she'd painted *Lillian Rose Blooms* across the glass of her very own flower shop. A circular patch of fog from her breath formed at the beginning of the swirl in the letter *L*. As she wiped it away with her sleeve, her thoughts lingered over the letters.

She'd had her doubts when she'd written this line to advertise her new business in *The New York Times: The ever-invited guest, my blooms speak the language of joy or sorrow or any emotion in between!*

Yet, after only a few months, business was booming and blooming. She should've been thrilled and she was, mostly, but that deep satisfaction she'd anticipated remained just out of reach, as it always did.

Mr. Blue Suede Shoes meowed from under the counter. His sleek, black paws tiptoed along buckets of lavender, huckleberry branches, mums, white roses, and corkscrew willow boughs. Lillian scratched her cat's uplifted chin. Tomorrow was the Winthrop wedding and there was so much to do.

Lillian nibbled the edge of the pastry; it melted in her mouth. "I'm stealing a moment, no scolding, and no treats for you!" she announced to the cat, who had leapt to the table to sniff at the delicacy.

A few minutes later, Lillian pulled on her purple gloves and climbed onto her faithful work stool. The cat had returned to his bathing in the center of the brick fireplace, now filled with bulbs sprouting in twenty-four vintage jars. A rap-tap hello at the back door startled him. The glass containers complained as he launched from their midst. Cringing at the thought of another birthday visitor, and her routine disrupted yet again, Lillian squinted to see through the minute windowpane of the back door.

Benjamin Meyer, the owner of Ben's Books, stood outside on the cracked cement steps, careful to avoid a fragile viola blooming up through the uneven edges. In his hands he held a worn leather-bound book, *A Season to Bloom*.

Lillian snapped off her gloves, plastered on a smile, and invited the elderly gentleman inside. He declined. "Thank you, but I've only come to bring you this. I've smelled the dust between the pages of this book for many years. For you, there is no better birthday gift than this treasure trove of words. I know Rachel would've liked for you to have it." As he placed the heavy book in her hands he studied her eyes, and asked, "Is everything fine?"

Lillian dropped her gaze, embarrassed by her unexpected reaction. She dabbed at her eyes with the back of her hand. "Yes, yes of course, must be the dust, thank you, Ben."

"The pleasure is mine," he said with a bow, then turned back into the alleyway and toward his shop with a gratuitous wave of his left hand. Lillian marveled at the thin gold circlet, loose enough to slip from the aged hand. Devotion had kept the widower's ring secure these thirty years since his beloved Rachel's death.

Lillian shut the back door, then resumed her task behind the counter as the day began to unfold through her window. From her quiet perch, she looked enviously into the ebb and flow of lives intertwining in community.

At 7:23 a.m., Bus 20 eased away from the curb in front of Ben's Books. It stopped again abruptly as the last commuter, a handsome black man, fought to free his coat, wedged between the metal hinges at the entrance. In the meantime, a youth, whose wild, red hair suggested she'd overslept, took advantage of the pause to slip inside the bus. She crossed herself as if God himself had parted the double doors.

Two children held to their father's hands as they scampered to keep up with his strides. His eyes stared forward, determined to maintain timeliness. They smiled and waved at Mr. Blue Suede Shoes, who pawed at the front window, attempting to catch a pesky fly.

A jogger, waiting at the crosswalk, leaned over to tie his shoe. Next to him, a Hispanic woman holding a purse the size of a carry-on moved to wipe the face of the child in her charge. As she shifted her weight, the bag swung over her shoulder and hit the jogger mid-shoe-tie, knocking him to the ground. Lillian wondered which hurt his pride more, falling or being righted by a little woman half his height and double his age. The woman appeared to lecture him in Spanish. He sped away while she and the child stepped up to the opposite sidewalk just in time to avoid a delivery truck barreling around the corner.

Down Stratford Lane, a homeless man trudged up to a bench, teetered, then braced himself on a large trash receptacle. From inside it, he withdrew a partially eaten breakfast sandwich. As if on cue, a well-dressed businesswoman handed him a fresh cup of coffee, then hurried away. Lillian thought she was perhaps the only person to notice that the woman never drank the coffee she bought.

Across the street, Miss Ruby, the owner of Learn 'N Play Daycare, held a baby over her ample chest. He sucked his thumb while she ushered her eager students through the entryway. She patted their heads with her free hand as if she were a shepherdess counting sheep. Clinging to her pink cardigan, a toddler stood on tiptoes and waved to his mommy, who was maneuvering her blue Honda back into the morning commute. The mother blew him a kiss and then fumbled for her glasses on the dashboard.

As she deftly worked, Lillian looked into the lives beyond her window. A lanky boy on an orange bike appeared amidst the tangle of traffic, racing in a zigzag motion. He fixed his eyes on the golden bakery sign and sped toward it. He jumped from curb to street and up again, avoiding the parking meters while expertly flitting in between obstacles. Lillian attempted to focus on her task, but couldn't concentrate on anything but the boy in fervent motion.

The bus lurched and the blue Honda slammed on its brakes, but a taxi took advantage of the open space and zipped blindly into the middle of the street. Lillian felt her heart rise in her throat as the boy raced on obliviously. She found she had risen from her stool and was standing at the window, flailing her arms in an attempt to warn him.

"Stop! No!" she screamed, before involuntarily dropping to the floor, her arms over her head.

The screeching of wheels gathered screams from all viewers as the bike launched into the halt of an ordinary New York City morning. The front wheel of the bike sailed over the sidewalk in silent abandon with its boy twisting above the handlebars. Shards of glass penetrated the air like bullets in battle. Lillian pressed her forehead to the floor where she huddled, just out of reach of her window, as bike—and boy—shattered all.

2

Montreal

Name. Mon-tree-awl : French origin, meaning "Mount Royal"

Montreal saw it all in slow motion. There was a bus, a car, and a taxi—and the street turned into deafening chaos. He was out of control. The bike was headed straight for the curb and the glass windowfront beyond. He was going too fast to brake, or maybe the brakes didn't work, or even more likely, in the chaos he had forgotten they existed as he held onto the handlebars for dear life. It all seemed inevitable now. He saw it before it happened. Bike. Window. Shattering glass. Screams. Damage. Blame. Trouble.

Montreal was soaring, his body flying over the handlebars and twisting around in an instinctive movement beyond his control. He saw every face. Mouths open in screams or disbelief. His body moved through the air, defying gravity and time.

Then . . . *crash!* . . . he smashed through the window, the bike behind and on top of him. Everything was suddenly so loud and happening so fast. His ears were ringing and it felt as if his body would never stop rolling. He only had one thought: *Run.*

3

Lillian

T he tiles were cold against Lillian's forehead as she huddled on the floor. With her eyes shut tight and adrenaline pulsing through her veins, the room felt loud, like waves pounding in her ears. *This isn't happening, this isn't happening.*

Cautiously, she lifted her eyes. What had been her beautiful storefront only moments earlier was now a sea of broken glass. Soil fell from the immense garden chandelier as it swayed drunkenly. Fallen pansies and scarlet caladiums lay in shredded clumps intertwined with jagged window remains. Mr. Blue Suede Shoes twitched his tail from under a mass of eucalyptus branches. The wind laughed shrewdly as it dashed around the shop, capitalizing on its unprotected state. In the center of the room lay the mangled bike.

As she scanned this newly exposed world, Lillian found no boy. He had vanished.

An ambulance shrieked into the chaos on the street as two police officers dashed into the shop. One of them righted a chair while the strong arms of a paramedic wrapped Lillian in a blanket and guided her to sit. She cringed at the feel of broken glass scraping the tile below her clogs. She couldn't quell the shaking or get a good gulp of air. All around her was broken glass, and there was blood on the glass near the bike.

A paramedic squatted on the floor beside her. He was asking her something. Lillian tried to focus on him, but his face looked so blurry.

"Ma'am? You're in shock, just sit tight for a minute. What do you think, Al; shall we take her in?" He directed his words to another paramedic who'd just run over to take her vitals. "Can you tell me your name?" He was back to Lillian now, holding her wrist and staring at his watch.

Lillian looked from one paramedic to the other, then willed herself to concentrate. She drew in a deep breath and blew it out slowly. "I'm Lillian, and thank you so much . . . Al and—"

"Joe, ma'am—Joe." Joe looked at Al then back to Lillian. Lillian felt her head begin to clear. She tried to stand, but Joe placed his hand firmly on her shoulder. "You're doin' great. Just wait a bit, ma'am; your mind's catchin' up to what just happened."

"But I'm fine. I'll be fine, maybe just a little water and my cat," she said as she strained her neck around to look. "My cat—where's my cat?"

"Um, a cat? Anybody seen a cat?" Joe called to those around him.

Just then Benjamin Meyer appeared, carrying her empty cat carrier that usually sat under her counter. He remained quiet, standing by the opposite side of the table.

Birgitte yelled something in Danish to Hans, who threaded through the mess with Mr. Blue Suede Shoes held tightly in his grip, as far away from his face as possible. He dropped the cat into the open carrier, mumbling under his breath as he wiped his hands on his apron.

Ben clicked the little door shut while Birgitte motioned for the men to get out of the way, giving a sharp directive to Hans in Danish. Birgitte disappeared through the sky-blue side door, returning momentarily with a cup and saucer. Strong coffee was her remedy to all life's problems. Her pale eyes searched Lillian's face. Taking the cup with both hands, Lillian tried to keep from trembling as she took a sip. Smile lines returned to Birgitte's eyes.

"We'll bring soup and bread and your cat back later. Don't worry; we're here." Lillian nodded weakly as her neighbor gently shut the door between them.

"Great neighbors," Al commented,"—and coffee's okay now that your vitals are good. In fact, is there more where that came from? Smells great!" He continued, "All this and not a scrape; you're a lucky woman."

Lillian nodded, but Al had turned his attention to the approaching police officer. She shifted in her chair; it teetered. She leaned over to examine the rungs and found that one had split. *Seriously? My French garden chair's broken as well?*

"—no idea Joe, completely amazing; we're all scratching our heads." The officer finished his sentence, then turned to Lillian. His jovial voice echoed inside her aching head. "Hello, I'm Officer Doug Jensen, so sorry for your situation. What's amazing is that you're not hurt, and the cyclist, well, its miraculous that he's not dead. Trouble is, we can't find him." He pulled out his phone. "We've gotten statements from the drivers and bystanders. Flew right through your window, you know. Did you see him? Can you give us a description?"

"Sure, yes—yes of course. He was, I mean *is*, young, like thirteen or something, slight. African American perhaps, grey hoodie, jeans . . . orange bike." Lillian looked at the twisted handlebars of the bike, lying only a few feet from her. Someone was taking samples of the blood smeared on a floor tile. She held her head to steady her dizziness.

Officer Jensen furrowed his brow. "I'm done. This must kill you, knowing that boy is wounded. Terrible, but don't worry, we'll find and help him. And your shop'll be back together in short order—not that that's your first thought—work crew's comin' any minute now."

Lillian tried to collect herself. "Of course, Officer, that poor boy." She dropped her eyes to the cup in her hand, remembering an obscure conversation with her brother, Johnny, when they were young. He'd said, *Never try poker, your eyes can't lie!*

For three long hours, Lillian endured all kinds of "help" that seemed only to make matters worse. Finally, onlookers lost interest, first responders finished their tasks, and well-meaning neighbors trickled out. Amnesia crept over the street and normalcy resumed for most. The anthill existence of life in the city left only a slim space for interference.

Raw wind blew through the cracks between the boards, newly placed over the gaping window. The dull roar of traffic echoed about the shop in an amplified voice. Lillian glanced at the clock, reminding herself that she had no time to waste. Twelve clay pots, packed with oasis foam bricks, sat on the floor. She drew her purple gloves over her shaky hands, then pulled moss and greenery up into her workspace, though her vision for each wedding arrangement seemed just out of mind's reach. If she acted as if all were well, perhaps she could convince herself that it was.

Where is that boy? Officer Jensen had left the bike in Lillian's care in hopes the child might come for it. Lillian had promised to alert the authorities if he returned. She cringed again as her thoughts slipped back to the terror of the morning. *Would he come back? Could he?* Whatever the case, as quickly as possible, Lillian would erase this event from her life. Perhaps an iron grate in a floral pattern would enhance the new window, once repaired, and ensure future protection from juvenile delinquents.

Mr. Blue Suede Shoes poked his paws out of the open carrier, as if he were sampling bath water. He ventured out, following closely behind Lillian, who stepped into the narrow pantry of the back room. She blinked in the sunlight streaming onto the farm sink. Then, she noticed tiny flakes of bird's-egg-blue paint scattered about, chipped from the windowsill. Lillian's eyes followed the flakes up to the high window, newly forced open. Its ripped screen flapped in the wind.

A throaty purr from the cat, followed by an urgent human whisper of "Shh!" broke the silence. Lillian spun around.

There, crouched in the corner, was the boy.

His blood-stained hoodie partly shrouded his swollen face. Several deep gashes oozed blood through a wad of paper towel he held to his forehead. Mr. Blue Suede Shoes pressed his whiskered cheek along the boy's limp hand and gave it a gentle wash. The boy rose with difficulty to a standing position. He picked up the paper towel roll from the floor and handed it to Lillian.

Lillian fought back the harsh words on the tip of her tongue. "Come, let's get you help," she said instead.

"No!" he blurted out. "I gotta get home. Mama's sick and today's her birthday—her fortieth birthday." His soulful eyes pleaded with her as his story gushed out. "My brother and sisters need me. I just wanted to get her something, one a' those cinnamon rolls from that bakery. I didn't see the taxi . . . sorry 'bout your window, real sorry, but I gotta go. I just need my bike. Can I please have my bike?"

"Excuse me?" Lillian stared at him, incredulous. "Your bike is not the main issue here. Obviously, you need help, but 'Sorry, real sorry'? Oh no, *my* window is destroyed! This is *my* shop we're talking about! And guess what, it's *my* fortieth birthday too—unless that's just a lie you made up to get your bike back." Lillian's cheeks flamed as she ignored her stinging conscience. "And we're talking about *way* more than cinnamon rolls here! You vandalized *my* shop! You should be arrested for recklessness!"

A crack appeared in the caked blood at the boy's chin as he tried to stand up straighter under her barrage. Fresh blood splattered onto his wrist. He wiped it off on his pants.

Lillian watched, feeling sick inside. She waited for him to speak, but he just stared at her. She swallowed hard, then continued in a softer tone. "The officers and paramedics that came earlier want to help—obviously *I* can't help you—they can, though, and they're waiting. You're still bleeding, you know."

He remained silent.

Her words tumbled out. "Regardless, I need you off my premises, so let's do the logical thing. My front window's destroyed, and now you've broken in through my little window—and stolen my paper towels." She held up the roll.

The boy looked from her to the paper towel roll. "You know I didn't break your window on purpose! I—I can't stay and get inta trouble. Mama's so sick and I don't steal stuff or vandalize stuff!" He searched Lillian's face.

Lillian couldn't bear his eyes, desperate for mercy she refused to give. She looked away. "Give me a minute to notify the authorities. They'll help you." She backed up and grabbed her cell phone. In the space between them, the boy leapt up to the sink with incredible agility. She panicked. "Wait! Just take your bike, seriously, just take it! I don't want it here and . . . I have insurance. So please wait—you must take it!"

The last she saw were his raw, bloody hands gripping the windowsill, and his soulful brown eyes turning away from her.

4

Lars

Name. Lahrz : Latin origin, meaning "crowned with laurel"

L ate in the evening, Pastor Lars Gundersen's booming voice paused mid-sentence as he was practicing his wedding homily. He stopped as the rehearsal dinner caterer called from the side door of Stratford Community Chapel.

"'Scuse me, sir," came the thin voice, "my boss and the family asked me ta ask you if you want this—leftovers from the rehearsal dinner. Kinda cold, but—" The teenager sank behind the doorframe as Lars approached.

"That'd be great, thanks, everything tasted delicious. You guys catering tomorrow for the wedding . . . Chip? Wasn't that your name?"

The young server raised his eyebrows as he laid the boxed food in Lars' big hands. "Yeah, that's me and yeah, we're here tomorrow too, so . . . see ya tomorrow."

"Thanks, Chip; anybody else left out there?"

"Nope. I drove my truck—well, my brother's truck . . . anyway, they're gone. So, uh, see ya." He pulled at his cap and backed up.

Lars tipped his chin toward the sanctuary. "Well, if everybody's gone, then come on—join me for a late-night bite?"

Chip shook his head. "Nah, can't eat on duty."

Lars strode over to the front pews, unfolded several napkins, and began unpacking the food. He asked the reticent teenager still lingering in the doorway, "Are you on the clock?"

Chip dug his phone from his jeans pocket. "Um, nope, it's 10:07—paid till 10:00."

Lars smiled. "Okay, then, you're good; this is my invitation. Let's see . . . a few spare ribs, chunky fries, salad—not too sure about that—and what's this? A turret?" He pulled apart the top twist of a canopy made of tinfoil. "Three slabs of lemon meringue pie? My favorite!" He set the third piece aside.

Chip ambled over, took off his cap, and slid into the pew on the opposite side of the feast. "Ya got me at 'slabs.'" He grinned through a mouthful of braces.

As they ate, Lars started up the conversation, "So, you have a brother—who's nice enough to lend you his truck, pretty awesome—any other siblings?"

"Yup, a stepsister, she's a lot older. That's it besides parents."

"Nice," Lars answered, handing Chip the last rib.

Chip eyed it, then asked, "Don't you wanna take any home?"

"Eat up. It's just me, and I often forget about the food in my fridge anyway."

Chip stuffed the last few fries into his mouth then licked his fingers. "Don't ya get lonely? Don't ya want a wife or something?"

Lars leaned back in the pew, studying Chip's earnest face. "Well, I guess I don't think about that too much. I did, long ago, but that's a rather sad story, full of boring details."

"I don't mind boring details," grinned Chip.

Lars handed Chip his pie slice. "Well, all right, truth is, my fiancée changed her mind at the last minute, and by last minute, I mean, in a white dress and me in a tux, with music playing—that kind of last minute. And, like any logical human, two weeks later, I took off for Africa and didn't look back."

"Man, that was rude . . . but I guess Africa must be a cool place."

Lars took a bite of pie and nodded. "You know, you're so right, that was rude, and Africa is extremely cool. Ethiopia to be specific. I loved it! In fact, I stayed for ten years and met incredible people in that amazing country, but sometimes you just have to come home. So, I headed back to the States, finished my theology degree, and got ordained. A couple of parishes later, and here I am, trying to figure out what God wants me to do next."

Chip lit up. "Hey, you should meet my sister; she's just finishing up college!"

Lars put up his hands. "Oh no, no—I mean what to do as in *ministry*. I'm thirty-eight and the single life works great for me."

"Me too!" Chip answered.

Lars frowned. "You too? What are you . . . sixteen, seventeen?"

"Nah, fifteen, but don't tell anybody. I only got my permit . . ."

"Oh, I see. You *do* have a nice brother, but be safe, friend; I can always offer you a ride. And don't give up on women," Lars chuckled. "Wedding stories like mine are rare."

"It wasn't boring, anyway." As Chip stood up to go, he hesitated. "Sir, I—uh, just wanna say, thanks a lot; no one ever invited me to church before."

Lars put out his hand. "I'm Lars, by the way, and just so you know, I've never eaten spare ribs on the front pew before and it's usually me who asks all the questions, so something new for both of us! You are always welcome here."

At 11:30 p.m., Lars set down his notes. He was as prepared as possible for the Winthrop wedding. The crisp, clear day had become a blustery night. He took the saved piece of pie, turret and all, grabbed his rain gear, and headed out. His destination, Lillian Rose Blooms, was just down the street.

5

Lillian

In the late hours of this never-ending day, Lillian had no idea that one last visitor was on his way. She had spent the past few hours frantically trying to get work done and there was still so much to do. She stripped several dozen white roses of every thorn and leaf. The unprotected blooms looked fragile by themselves until she slipped them side by side into the moss at the base of each pot. Rising from the centers, corkscrew willow branches stood as dancers on stilts with their curly tops intertwining. Lillian placed tufts of lavender below the roses while the mums offered a vibrant finishing touch to the edge of each wedding centerpiece.

A knock on the door broke her reverie.

A man stood in the rain to the side of the windowed door, where large droplets gathered along the edge of his hood. Lillian felt the color crawl up her neck. *Oh, please, please, not now.* She spun around, rinsed her hands under the faucet, and splashed water on her face to cool it. She tucked a stray curl behind her ear and brushed the clippings from her apron, trying to calm her frustration.

At the door, she met the preacher she'd heard so much about. He stood just under the black awning, where the water, running down his tall frame, was soaking her new welcome mat. She bit her lip.

"Hi there, I'm Lars Gundersen, the pastor over at the chapel. I came to check if you were all right after your terrible day. I'm doing the Winthrop wedding, too, so I assumed you'd still be working."

"Yes, hello, I'm fine. Thank you. I'm Lillian, like my window says—said . . ."

He glanced at the boarded-up space. "Well, yes . . . I'd hoped to meet you before today. I'm so sorry I didn't; I've only been here a month. But anyway, I wondered if I could help, not with the flowers obviously, but with the boy."

Lillian thought, *Please leave*, but said instead, "Thank you, I appreciate the offer. It's sad he just disappeared into thin air." She bit her lip again. "I'm not sure what you mean about help with the boy. He's not here . . . obviously." She opened the door a little wider to show him.

The rain streamed down either side of the awning. "Yes, I heard that, but do you mind if I just step inside for a minute to explain what I mean? It's pretty wet out here."

Lillian sighed as she extended a reluctant hand, sweeping across her shop. She answered under her breath, "Why not? Everyone else has today."

Lars stepped out of his boots, then transferred the paper plate from one hand to the other as he shed his jacket. He wore faded jeans and a white collared Oxford shirt, untucked. She wondered if his light blue eyes always twinkled as they did right now. His ruddy cheeks and the warmth of his smile made her feel the need to lean on something. He offered her the paper plate. She stared at it, but couldn't will herself to take it.

Lillian was spent to the core with hardly a single polite word left in her vocabulary.

"So . . . good to meet you, but I must be going. I mean, *you* must be going . . ."

Lars unwrapped the plate. "This is pie. The caterers left it after the rehearsal dinner. I thought you'd like it since you've got about fifteen more minutes left on the clock to celebrate your birthday. It is your birthday, isn't it?"

"My birthday? How . . . I mean, yes, thank you . . ." She took the pie, then looked up at him. That twinkle again.

"Don't you like pie? It's not every day someone offers you pie, especially lemon meringue. I'd tell you I made it, but you know, in my profession I can't lie."

She tried a stab at upbeat, but her voice sounded edgy in her ears. "How'd you know it was my birthday?"

"The owner of Subs 4 U heard from Officer Jensen. I think he heard from the bakery owners when the coffee ran out from all the people stopping by. I picked up a sub, then got an earful at the coffee shop. It's a newsy neighborhood, you know. I also heard that the boy's bike is still here, which leads me to how I can help."

Lillian stiffened. "Everyone's talking about this?"

"There it is." Lars strode over to the bike and picked it up. "My secretary's husband will repair it; he's a genius. Then, when the boy returns, it'll be as good as new." Lars paused and looked hard at Lillian. "I imagine it feels strange to have so many people involved . . . I should've called first; sorry I didn't."

Yes, she thought, *you should have.* But she said instead, "No, it's fine, but please take the bike, that's an excellent idea." She walked over to the front door. "Now I must get back to work . . . was there anything else?" *No, please, nothing else, just go.*

"Yes." The smiling blond minister stood the bike by the door and reached for his gear.

And now comes the invitation to church. Why'd I set myself up?

"I wonder if you'd like to have coffee, I'll call you—"

Lillian's eyes widened as she quickly interjected. "Uh, well, I don't really date." *What in the world, this is so weird, did he really just say that?* "But, um, thank you for asking me . . ."

He laughed. "I meant coffee at the church, to meet my secretary, Barbara, and her husband Bill. When the bike's repaired you can come, or . . . I can keep it until we find the boy. It's up to you." Lars backed out the door, still chuckling.

Lillian nodded meekly. He waved and twinkled one last time as she shut the door behind him. She leaned her head back against it and closed her eyes.

"I'm ridiculous," she whispered.

6

Estelle

Name. Ih-stel : French, or Latin origin, meaning "star"

The soft lamplight streamed onto Estelle's mahogany skin as she waited. She arched her slim back to adjust the weight of the baby inside her, and then settled back against the couch cushions. She appeared serene, this she knew, but her eyes' amber hue pierced the distance between herself and her oldest son, Montreal. Yesterday, she'd dressed his wounds and iced his swollen face, showering him with compassion. But today, her compassion—and patience—had evaporated.

Montreal swallowed hard as he approached her.

"Sit," Estelle directed.

She stared past him at the faces of his three siblings, peering out from the bedroom doorway, a three-headed totem pole of moral support.

"Out," she commanded.

Montreal's first word came out in a half-croak as he dropped to the cushion beside her. "Fri-Friday morning, I rode my bike to get your favorite pastry—to surprise you. I thought I could do it and get back before anyone woke up. I could've, I know I could've, it's just that . . ."

The embers of anger that lit Estelle's protective heart faded into tenderness. Montreal leaned in and let the story tumble out with twelve-year-old earnestness.

"So, I was racing to the bakery, and suddenly, outa nowhere, a taxi almost crushed me! I tried to pop a wheelie, but couldn't. It was like this . . ." With a whistling sound, Montreal arched one hand up and over the other. "Like a stuntman, flying, but still holding my handlebars. Then I smashed through a window—like an explosion. It hurt so bad. I kept thinking, *Am I dead? Am I dead?* Like I was someone else asking the question."

Estelle nodded. "Oh, yes, a miracle, now go on . . ."

"So, I got up and there was glass everywhere." Estelle put her arm around his shoulders as he continued. "Nobody saw me. I think they were too busy pointing and staring at my bike. But the cat, he saw me, and I think he saw me go to the alley to wait for everyone to leave. I tried to be invisible and hid in a trash can."

Estelle interrupted, "A trash can? Now how did you ever think of that?"

"You know how I always put Aurora in the trash can when it's empty, after trash day? When I wheel it back? I did that same thing." He looked up sheepishly and Estelle lifted one eyebrow. "So, when things calmed down, I climbed through a tiny window, at the back of the shop. But when she found me, I thought she was gonna be nice, but she was mean and wouldn't give me my bike unless I turned myself in! I told her that you were worried, but she didn't care."

Estelle admitted, "I was worried—worried sick, but right now I'm wondering who 'she' is."

"She owns the flower shop and I tried to say I was sorry and explain. The cat was there licking me. But she said I'd be arrested, so I ran away and hid in the shadows to get home." His voice quivered as he let out the last, most important words. "It was awful, Mama, and I didn't get you anything for your birthday." He blinked back his tears.

Estelle pulled him close and kissed his head. "God has his hand on you, son; never doubt that. You were kind to remember my birthday, but you acted foolishly, too—not because of the accident, accidents happen—but by running away." She drew back to face him. "No matter how mean this woman seems, you broke her shop window. We must do something to make amends."

At 7:00 p.m., ten-year-old Florence set five bowls of macaroni and cheese on the table. On a serving platter, she laid the pieces of two oranges cut into boats along the edge. In the center, she arranged carrot sticks, fanned out like the spokes of a wheel. The slightest hint of dimples appeared on her cheeks as she placed it in the middle of the table. "Tonight we celebrate the color orange," she announced.

Five-year-old Aurora, who'd fallen asleep on her mother's disappearing lap, sat up and rubbed her eyes while Estelle fastened a stray hairclip to one of her braids.

Sebastian plopped into his chair first; as usual, he was starving. Though he was only eight, he stood an inch taller than Florence.

Estelle placed a hand under her swelling belly and pulled herself up. Gathering around the dinner table each night was of utmost importance, though even the idea of food nauseated her.

After grace, Aurora, with a mouthful of macaroni, sputtered, "Why is that baby in your belly makin' you so sick?"

Florence interjected, "You're a lady, not a wild animal; don't talk with your mouth full!"

"Wild animals don't talk, they grrr-owl!" growled Aurora.

Estelle held up her hand to still the brimming clash of sisters. "Well, my love . . . this baby is doing exactly what babies in bellies do. I'm sick for another reason."

Sebastian stared at his empty bowl. His shoulders trembled. "Mama, Florence says it's cancer . . ."

Florence glared at her brother. Estelle laid a quieting hand over her daughter's.

"I'm glad, not upset, that you told him." She looked around the table. "Yes, I have breast cancer. Now Sebastian, did you have something else to say?"

"At school, Emma said people with cancer die. She's goin' ta her aunt's funeral 'cause she died of cancer. Are you gonna . . ." He choked on his last word, covered his face, and ran from the table, knocking Estelle's water glass as he went. Everyone stared at their mama. She dropped her napkin over the spill, and followed him to the boys' bedroom.

Later that evening, as sleep settled over most in the tiny apartment, Estelle called Montreal to her side and resumed their earlier conversation. "Monday after school we'll take the bus downtown to the flower shop."

"We?" Montreal furrowed his brow. "As in you, me, *and* Florence, Sebastian, and Aurora?"

"*We*," repeated Estelle. "You'll introduce yourself properly to the proprietor of the flower shop, apologize for the damage you caused, and begin working for her voluntarily until you've paid the debt she incurred from your accident."

Montreal exploded. "Work for her! Mama, she's a witch; she's horrible! I can't go back; punish me any other way. Please don't make me!"

Estelle shook her head. "You didn't mean to destroy her window, but you did. How she treated you has nothing to do with your accountability. You must make things right."

Montreal muttered under his breath, "It's not fair."

Estelle put her hand on his. "You're right, life's not fair. We can't know the struggles to come, but we can choose our response. When you choose the humble way, eventually, in God's economy, he'll make good of it. Just wait and see."

Montreal dropped his head in frustration. He pulled his hand out from hers, then stared defiantly into her eyes. He hurled his words, "So you never answered Sebastian—how come you didn't? Are you? Is that why we're still here in this dump? Are you going to die?"

"I don't know," she answered quietly. Montreal tried to blink away angry tears, but Estelle just pulled him close. "It's okay to feel afraid; I do sometimes too. But God has a plan; I'm asking for him to show us what it is."

7

Julius

Name. Jool-yuhs : Latin origin, meaning "youthful, downy-bearded"

From the corner of Stratford and Lowell, past Ben's Books, Lillian Rose Blooms, and The Dansk Konditori, stood A Cup of Grace. The vibrant aroma of coffee invited many brisk-paced walkers to pause and contemplate a break. It was Monday, just after the morning rush. Julius, one of its two owners, checked his reflection on the side of the stainless-steel roaster. He drew on his coat, holding to the cuffs of his cerulean sweater so as not to snag the fine yarn. He called to Stuart, his partner, "I'm off to Lillian's to order flowers!" Stuart did not look up.

Julius walked across the room fluidly. A ring of keys had fallen from a patron's purse, these he laid beside her mug. He then unhooked an elderly patron's cane, which had slid between the slats of his chair. The jingle above the door gave a cheerful goodbye.

As he approached the flower shop, a gruff-voiced man in a hard hat stopped him. "One moment, sir!" Two additional workers, wearing hard hats and orange vests, steadied a wrought-iron bench as it swung from a pulley. Staccato beeps sounded from their vehicle as the men lowered the bench onto freshly poured cement.

"Wow," Julius commented affably. "How does Ms. Bloom earn special treatment from the city? Shouldn't our coffee shop have dibs on outdoor seating?"

"City? This is from Mr. Mullenix. Says he's sympathetic to the woes of the people, small business owners, says he," answered the gruff-voiced foreman. "Huh, fellas? Woes of the peoples is us!" He spat on the ground between himself and Julius. "We installed a bench, 5:00 a.m., 'fore business hours, but that bench—plain ole city bench—wasn't good enough for him! This here's the *second* bench, but NO overtime!"

Julius held up his hands. "Sorry, guys; I feel for you, but looks as if you're almost done. I'm curious; what's so special about this one?" Julius leaned over to examine the new one. "Looks the same as every other bench in the city, except for the brass nameplate."

The foreman took off his hard hat and bowed before the bench. "Hey, fellas, man's a genius—that *is* the difference, the nameplate."

Julius read the engraved words out loud: "*Building community begins by valuing every individual ~ Anthony Mullenix.*" The foreman spat again and Julius jumped to the side. From there, he caught sight of the flower shop window where Lillian's name had been painted in the same beautiful arch of scrollwork as before. Julius whistled low. "Like magic!"

"Magic? We had ta stand around and wait for the glass installers ta finish before we could switch benches. Breakin' our backs before sunup for nothin' except ta do it twice! Lucky as this here business lady's been real nice—coffee, doughnuts, smokes, real nice. But Mullenix, who does he value? Not us regular people. No respect!"

"Rumor has it Anthony Mullenix might run for mayor. Must be buttering us up with fancy fare like benches," suggested Julius.

"Fair? Bribes for the city built on our backs? Ain't backin' that!"

"Regardless, my friend, you're a street poet."

While the foreman was distracted in conversation, one of the men lost his footing, leaving a boot mark in the cement. The bench careened precariously. The gruff voice unleashed a string of profanity as Julius slipped by him and through Lillian's door.

Lillian lit up when Julius entered.

"How are you? Exhausted, I imagine," he said.

"Oh, did my new friends tell you about our installation party? Set up at 4:00 a.m., then a bench redo!"

Julius chuckled. "Since when does the city work in the wee hours?"

Lillian shrugged. "I know—odd, isn't it? I said I needed my window done by business hours Monday morning. At first my insurance company said impossible. Then, last night, I get this call that their work order was expedited and that a bench would be installed as well, so to expect two work crews. I hardly believed it, but they came."

"They seem fairly taken with you. Food and smokes, not bad, and they even let you paint your own letters!"

Lillian stifled a yawn. "Oh no, the window guys were arguing about who would do it, when the foreman pushed everyone aside and just took over. Did it freehand and it's prettier than my original lettering."

Julius scoffed. "Tell me it wasn't him! I thought spitting was his forte."

Lillian laughed. "The very same guy!"

Julius examined his Italian shoes for spit droplets, then said, "By the way, I'm sorry I was unavailable to help after Friday's fiasco. I was across town interviewing a potential supplier."

"That's fine. It was chaotic, but not all bad, I met tons of people, potential for me as well—as in customers," Lillian answered matter-of-factly.

"Really? That's what you're thinking?" Julius laughed. "Ruthless!"

"Well, no, of course not—not just that. Obviously, you heard about the, uh, sad situation with the boy?" She looked away as he tried to catch her eye.

"The coffee shop's been buzzing with talk of it all morning—the mysterious boy! Have you heard anything else about him?"

Lillian grabbed a pitcher from the counter, splashing a little water on the floor as she went. "Let me see if the guys are thirsty, real quick." She swept past him. "There's not much to tell yet. Everybody's hopeful for his safety."

Lillian returned to the counter, as did her poise. "Now, what else did you come for—certainly not just with questions?"

Julius answered, "You're right, there's something else. Our little Hope is arriving Thursday, according to the adoption agency. "Will you create something in every shade of pink for the coffee shop tables? Something delicate, perhaps orchids?"

"My pleasure," answered Lillian. "How old is she again?"

"She's three, been in foster care since birth and what a beauty!" He withdrew the toddler's picture from his coat pocket and laid it on the counter. But, instead of a smile, Lillian gave a look of concern.

"What's wrong?" Julius asked.

"Oh," she shook her head, "she—she just looks so sad."

"We'll fix that!"

Lillian frowned. "Aren't you even a little nervous about being a dad?"

"Not an ounce. Stuart is, though, and he can worry enough for both of us. In fact, he's so anxious, I've taken to sleeping on the couch until he's less irritable. I, however, am exuberant about the details of our daughter's homecoming! I'm also planning on filling the display case with pink cream cakes made by Birgitte and Hans. I'll meet with them this afternoon." Julius ran his fingers through his thick brown hair and caught his reflection in the vintage mirror on the wall. "And hey, maybe I'll ask your friend to paint our news on our window!"

Lillian shook her head. "Sorry, it'll cost you: coffee, doughnuts, and cigarettes."

"And probably it wouldn't be the same for them—not coming from a lovely blonde."

Julius slipped out the door, with a million things on his mind, but glad to have shared his news with his dear friend.

8

Lillian

Finally, with a farewell tip of his hard hat, the foreman jumped onto the truck while his men clung to the side. It lurched and jostled in hiccups down the street.

The new bench settled in like a long-awaited friend of the stoic Norway maple, now quickly losing her flaming cloak of leaves. Apart from its cape of caution tape, one might imagine the bench had always lived there, a calm presence in a frantic world. There was one detail, however, that bothered Lillian. *Why is it facing out and not in?*

The shop felt quiet. Lillian brushed her hand across the edge of Hope's picture. In his haste, Julius had left it behind. She gazed again at the hazel eyes, deep brown skin, and tight curls of the tiny girl.

That age, age three, had been such a joyful time in Lillian's life. It brought to mind her first memory, a conversation with her mother. Lillian had run into the kitchen from the yard, barefoot and dirty. Her mother had pulled her close, then taken her little hand and drawn it across her belly.

"In the spring, you'll have two baby brothers. They're growing inside me right now, just like the tomatoes in the garden." Lillian remembered imagining vines in her mother's belly with two babies connected by green stems on their heads, like the hats in her book of garden fairies. She'd left smudges of soil on her mother's apron. How happy and carefree her childhood had been with two squirrelly brothers and loving parents.

9

Julius

At the coffee shop, Julius' partner Stuart, a rugged, muscular man with a well-trimmed beard, rinsed foam from a pitcher. Across the bar, Julius chatted with an indecisive customer over the unique flavor of Brazilian beans. He stepped behind the counter to offer a taste and caught sight of Stuart's anxious expression. After finishing the transaction, he moved over to Stuart.

"What's up?"

"Just thinking."

Julius knew what Stuart was thinking about, what he was always thinking about these days.

"You're not your father. Stop worrying."

"What if I choke?!"

Julius shook his head. "You're not like your father at all. You don't abandon the people you love or blame them for your weaknesses. You're a wonderful man and a great dad-to-be."

Stuart pressed his palms on the edge of the counter and stepped back. "Julius, listen to me! What if Hope's pain is too much to handle? I'm thirty-three, and—let's face it—I know I'm selfish. She's not an experiment—what if we fail?"

"Fail? That's impossible. Of course, we can't fail; we're an incredible team. You're compassionate and intuitive, and I'm everything else. She'll forget her past as soon as she arrives, and you'll see what an awesome family we'll be."

Just then the interior designer for Hope's nursery entered the coffee shop. He held a stack of decorative items in one hand and the door with the other. "A little help here," he called out, "Leaning Tower of Pisa coming through!"

Julius hurried to assist. He caught two lace pillows as they tumbled, along with a box of mini shades, but couldn't save the recycled wooden sign that read *Hope lives here.* It hit the floor, splintering into several pieces.

At four o'clock that afternoon, Bus 20 deposited a family of five on the curb outside Lillian Rose Blooms at the same time as Julius was exiting the bakery. Julius could see Lillian through her pristine window, staring at them. First off the bus was a stunning pregnant woman, whom he assumed was the mother of the brood that followed her. The last child to disembark, a lanky boy, turned around and disappeared back into the bus. He reappeared holding a stuffed animal. He dropped it into the arms of the youngest girl, whose pixie face lit up as she embraced the toy. The lanky young man lifted his face and looked through the flower shop window.

Julius followed his gaze. Lillian was in a flurry, flushed and erratic, as she seemed to be trying to look busy, a very different Lillian from previously.

Julius saw the little girl, who appeared to be the wayward caboose of the family, slip out of line. Instead of tromping with the others into the flower shop, she made a beeline for the bakery window. He liked her immediately. She pressed her hands against the glass, enthralled by the array of delicacies.

Just then, an older girl turned back to circle the little one, like a border collie on high alert. "Look at the smudges you left on that window!" she barked, wrangling her charge back in line.

The woman, clearly their mother, held the door to the flower shop open as she smiled disarmingly at Julius.

Julius exclaimed, "I know you! You're Estelle Delacroix! Long ago, I heard you sing jazz at Zazoo's. Your voice is marvelous. I'm delighted to make your acquaintance. And these are your children? Please, may I treat them to pastries?"

Estelle touched Julius' outstretched hand. "Thank you for your kind words. Yes, this is my family. Currently, we're on an errand of restitution, so you will have to accept a rain check."

Julius peered into the little sister's forlorn face, raised his eyebrows, and pursed his lips. Giggles rippled through her. Julius winked at her and said in his thick British accent, "Your mum said definitely next time!"

The older daughter crossed her arms and aimed a disintegrating look at Julius. To her mother she whispered loudly, "Estelle Delacroix?"

"Remember, love," Estelle whispered back, "that's my stage name."

Estelle nodded to Julius, who tipped a pretend hat and smiled at the little girls. He watched them disappear into the flower shop, curious as to their connection with Lillian. Lingering in his mind were her words: "stage name" and "restitution."

10

Montreal

"**D**ay number two, hour number two, and minute number . . ." Montreal checked his watch and continued, ". . . seventeen." He grabbed the broom he'd laid aside and began again to sweep. A ribbon of ants swirled up the Norway maple, disappearing in and out of the grooves in its silver-hued bark. Montreal stopped to examine them.

The flower shop door jingled. Lillian called out, "Sweeping or botany?"

Montreal spun around. "Excuse me, Miss Bloom?"

Lillian met his eyes coolly. "Botany—the study of plants."

Montreal lit up. "Oh, you mean these ants? Come see! Look at their tiny marching legs." The broom dropped to the sidewalk.

Lillian shook her head. "I was *kidding*. I just want you to finish sweeping." The door banged shut. With a sigh, Montreal retrieved the broom.

"I'd choose botany," a warbly voice interjected, "or entomology, in your case."

Montreal jumped.

Up from the bench, *like Dracula from his coffin*, thought Montreal, a white-haired man appeared. Out from under a tattered fedora, two bloodshot eyes peered at Montreal.

"Hello, young sweeper," he said, raising a tremulous hand in greeting. "I'm Sinclair Lewis Obermann III; pleased to meet you."

Montreal steadied the hand in his. "Hello, sir, I'm Montreal. How are you?"

Sinclair drummed his fingers on the back of the bench. "How am I? Hmm, how *am* I?" He looked up as if considering different answers. "Truth be told, I'm wretched! I haven't had a drink in three and a half days and I'm mighty thirsty." He dropped back down and let out a fake snore.

Montreal laughed. "You're funny. Maybe I can help?"

The old man sat up again, his placid eyes suddenly frantic. "And what would you propose?"

"I could buy you a—a soda," explained Montreal, holding more tightly to the broom handle.

Sinclair began to drum his fingers again. "Oh that," he answered without much interest. "How much do you have?"

Montreal dug into his jeans' pocket and pulled out a crushed dollar bill, two quarters, and a dime. "This'll work in a vending machine."

Sinclair sighed. "You're nicer than most, you know." He squinted his eyes at something across the street as he pulled on the scraggly hairs at the tip of his white beard.

"Watcha looking at?" asked Montreal, following his gaze.

"Oh, uh, nothing in particular. Now back to work! It's not wise to chit-ter-chatter with a drunkard." He pulled his fedora over his eyes. "Now go away and let me sleep."

"Can't be a drunkard if you haven't been drinking." Sinclair ignored this.

Montreal reached for the door handle, but Lillian had beaten him to it. Their eyes met. "Are you giving that bum cash?"

"No, just thought I'd get him a soda, said he was thirsty, but . . ."

Lillian bit her lip. "Hold on," she disappeared behind the counter, then came back with a ten-dollar bill. "Here, get him a sandwich too. There's a sub shop down the street. But remember, this is a one-time deal. No more talking to strangers!"

Montreal grinned. "Really? Thank you, Miss Bloom!"

Immediately Lillian dropped her eyes and straightened her apron. "Never mind, just be quick. You're on the clock."

Montreal addressed the bench. "Heard that didn't ya, Mr. Sinclair, sir? Just keep snoozing; I'll be back in a flash!" He took off running, but yelled over his shoulder with a grin. "But watch out for those million ants crawling up your pant leg!"

Sinclair leapt from the bench and brushed wildly at his dirty coat.

Montreal ran backward just long enough to see Lillian laugh before she slipped back into the shop.

A few minutes later, Montreal breezed through the door of Subs 4 U. He leaned over his knees to catch his breath before examining the menu posted above the counter. His mouth began to water as he contemplated the money in his hand. *If I buy the least expensive sandwich, I'll have enough for two, but Lillian didn't say to buy two.*

"Everything but the Kitchen Sink" was a twelve-inch masterpiece of salami, ham, turkey, cheddar, jack, cream cheese, red onions, and banana peppers on sourdough. Iceberg lettuce was optional, but Secret Sauce was not. It came with a soda for exactly $10.00. *I'll get that, then get myself a small soda,* he decided.

A Chinese woman in platform shoes clip-clopped from behind the counter. She stood eye-to-eye with Montreal. "Sub for you?" she asked in a sharp staccato tone.

"No, ma'am, it's for the old gentleman on the bench down the street."

"Pastor Lars send you?" she asked.

"No, ma'am, I work for Miss Bloom. She sent me."

"I am Bangji!" She examined him from head to toe. "You are too skinny," she announced, and then instructed him, "You buy one sub for man; I give one sub for you."

Plucking the ten-dollar bill from his fingers, she whipped out two Kitchen Sink orders in lightning speed, as if she'd read his mind. Narrowing her eyes to slits, she dangled the red onions above the second sandwich. "No onions for you?" She dropped the onions back into the bin. "Got it. You not like onion, but vegetable good for growing boy!" With that she shoved a handful of lettuce into his sub. Special Sauce oozed out the ends.

Montreal ran the back of his hand across his salivating mouth. Bangji acted stern, but she couldn't hide her pleasure. He liked her.

After wrapping the sandwiches, she placed two extra-large root beers and a pink lemonade into a drink carrier. "Pop for old man and you, lemonade for lady!" Bangji trilled. Lastly, she plopped a sprig of mint and a strawberry into Lillian's drink.

As Montreal thanked Bangji, the door chimed and in strode Lars. Bangji clapped her hands and gripped Montreal by the shoulders, steering him toward Lars. "You know this boy?"

"Not yet, but word travels fast around here. Hello, are you Montreal by any chance? I'm Lars." Montreal grinned but didn't move, finding it impossible to duck out from Bangji's vise grip.

"Got time to create one more famous sub?" Lars asked, hiding a chuckle from Bangji. She hurried to fulfill his request. He addressed Montreal again. "I hoped to find you today because I have your bike at the church. It's shipshape and ready to ride. Shall I bring it to you now?"

Montreal stared in disbelief. "My bike? It's fixed?" He swallowed hard.

Lars took the drink carrier from the counter, paid for his sandwich, and gave Bangji a hug. He led Montreal out the door. "Hey, how about we walk to wherever you're taking these, together, then I run back to the church to get your bike for you?"

Montreal found his voice. "Oh yeah, that'd be great. Thanks, sir, Pastor, sir, I . . . um . . ."

"Later you can thank Bill, my secretary's husband. He fixed it. I just get the best job of delivering the good news and the goods."

At the bench, Lars and Sinclair met. Immediately Sinclair yanked his hat from his head as his eyebrows sank in repentance. "Father, I have sinned."

Montreal stifled a giggle as he met Lars' smiling eyes. Lars answered, "And so have I. That's why we need Jesus. May I join you for lunch?"

Sinclair didn't miss a beat. "By all means, let's eat!" He spread the napkin over his knees, bowed his head in silent grace, then bit off a tiny bite. Montreal noticed his genteel manners; Estelle cared *very* much about manners. He took note of everything to tell her when he got home.

Montreal stared at the lemonade. Sinclair leaned over.

"Dragon Lady thirsty?"

Lars looked from one to the other. "Oh, I see how it is—guess I'd better deliver Lillian's drink."

"Oh yes, please!" Montreal almost flung the drink at Lars, then began unpacking his own meal. He could hardly get to it fast enough.

"I'll be right back." Lars hopped up to find Lillian in her shop.

Sinclair and Montreal ate with murmurings of satisfaction for several minutes. Then Sinclair glanced over his shoulder. "Long drink delivery—what do you think, smitten?"

Montreal's eyes widened as he snuck a look himself. He grimaced. "Sure hope not!"

11

Lars

The little bell attached to the door jingled as Lars walked into the flower shop. He spotted Lillian with her back turned toward him, lost in the creation of one of her simple but elegant bouquets.

"I'll be with you in one moment," she sang over her shoulder. He smiled as he took in the heavenly fragrance of the greenery and heady rose blooms peppered around the shop in their artful assignments.

"No hurry," he quietly said back, instantly regretting the sound of his own voice as he watched the peace of Lillian at work abruptly halt. She turned quickly toward him with a surprised look. A fresh wave of light pink, matching the flowers in her hands, traveled up her neck to her cheeks as her eyes met his.

"Oh, hello!"

"Here's a fresh lemonade, compliments of Bangji, I assume. Um. Unless you ordered it, then, here you go. Everything looks so . . . beautiful here. You are an amazing artist with a rare gift, Lillian." He watched the color in her cheeks grow brighter.

"Thank you." She took the lemonade and set it down on the counter between them and looked like she was trying to think of something else to say. Lars searched his mind to help her, but it was blank as well.

So, he just burst out with a laugh.

And so did she.

Lars rejoined Sinclair and Montreal for their last bites of sandwich, then zipped across the street and through the park to retrieve the bike from the chapel. Shortly thereafter Bus 20 arrived and the men helped Montreal, whose work was done, load up his bicycle to bring it home.

Montreal's face shone through the bus window as he waved an enthusiastic hand to the men. With the other hand he held to the handlebars of his gleaming bike.

Lars turned to Sinclair. "What do you say, shall we take a walk?"

"Preacher, I'd be much obliged," Sinclair answered, lowering his voice, "I have something to confide, couldn't share it when the lad was here." They walked along the sidewalk past Ben's Books. "A man I don't recognize—I'm certain of it—was taking photographs from across the street. Stopped while Montreal got the sandwiches, but then again while we ate. Did you notice?"

"Not at all, please continue."

"I'm always around, you know. I know everybody around here, everybody who's anybody, yet I've never seen that individual. I've been paying close attention to that boy, and this just doesn't sit well with me. What's the purpose of these photos?"

12

Montreal

M ontreal waved to the driver as he hopped off the bus. He plowed through the shop door then plopped his red backpack onto the counter.

Lillian held a pink orchid spray in mid-air.

"Here you are! What's up with the backpack?"

"Yup! I'm here," he announced through mischievous eyes, "and I got something to show you!" Out from the backpack he pulled an item, hastily wrapped in newspaper. He handed it to Lillian. "What do ya think of this?"

Lillian paused.

"This'll just take a minute, right?"

"Oh sure," Montreal said casually as he reached for his apron, but kept his eyes glued to her.

Lillian withdrew a framed photograph. It was of Elvis Presley surrounded by three gorgeous back-up singers. The inscription read:

To you, Fabulous Regina—
Thanks for everything,
from Elvis Presley

"What's this?" Lillian asked, with the slightest hint of a smile.

"My grandma!" beamed Montreal. "Right there." Directly beside Elvis was a radiant woman in a body-skimming gown with laughing eyes. Elvis was leaning over toward her with his head thrown back and his eyes shut. "My grandma was really funny. She told me that just before the cameraman shot this, she whispered a joke to The King. That was the thing she did when he got stressed; she made him laugh. She said helping him be happy was almost more important than her singing."

Lillian set the picture between them and leaned on her elbows. "Your grandmother was Regina White? I know her voice! My parents were huge Elvis fans and I remember your grandma's voice; it was big and beautiful. My brothers and I knew every song he'd ever recorded and used to give my folks concerts. I was always Evelyn, standing right there by your grandma." Lillian's fingers brushed across the languid blonde with bouffant hair.

Montreal scooped up Mr. Blue Suede Shoes, meowing from the floor.

"Me and Mama thought you'd like it, seeing as how you named this cute dude after Elvis."

Lillian stared up at the ceiling. "Blue, until you . . ." she sang softly, "made me new with your song, all the day long, then we swooned in the glow of the moon . . ."

Montreal dropped the kitty. "Yup, that's the one they did on the old TV show, the one where my grandma did the long jazzy ending!"

Lillian put her hand to her forehead. "I haven't thought about that song in so many years! My brothers did that Elvis guitar thing, where they threw it back around and did these funky dance steps and twirls."

Montreal popped up on his toes. "Like this?"

Lillian's smile widened. "Yes, exactly!"

Montreal leapt over with both feet and gave a twist, grinning back. "My mom taught me this. How many brothers do you have?"

Lillian froze. Her eyes clouded over as she answered. "Two—I had two—only two." She pushed the picture to the side. "Here, put this away, please. We've got lots to do."

Montreal stopped mid-twist and looked at Lillian with his soulful gaze, but she had already looked away. Slowly, he shoved the newspaper back into his backpack and dropped it to the floor. He set the picture to the side of her laptop then squared his shoulders and waited for direction. Lillian tightened her apron tie, then slipped the pink orchid spray into a silver vase.

"This is the last bouquet for A Cup of Grace; I'll get something to load them in. I'll need you to deliver them shortly." Lillian disappeared into the back room for boxes.

At 6:20 p.m. Montreal hung his apron on the hook and called to Lillian as he threw his backpack over his shoulder. "See ya."

"Don't forget this," she called out as she hurried toward him with the photo.

"Nope, that's yours. My mom wanted you to have it. You know, since I told her all about Mr. Blue Suede Shoes, she thought you'd love it."

"Absolutely not! That's a precious heirloom. I won't take it."

Montreal shook his head. "Sorry. My mom might not look so tough, but let me tell ya, if she says do something, I do it. No way I'm sassing Mama!"

"Oh please, that's ridiculous. Take it."

The mischievous look reappeared. "You want it returned? You'll have to do it yourself, sorry."

"What in the world?" Lillian glared at him. "Okay fine. I will!" She ripped off her apron.

Montreal's eyes widened. "You mean now?"

"Of course, lead the way!"

13

Lillian

As Lillian followed Montreal into Silverstone Apartment 7A, the warm lamp glow mirrored Estelle's expression. She rose from the couch in greeting. "Oh my, you've come! How lovely, welcome!"

Florence stood up from the floor, leaving her math book, then disappeared into the kitchen, calling back, "I'll start some tea."

Estelle added, "And of course you'll stay for dinner."

Lillian dug into her bag for the photo. "Oh no—thank you so much, such a lovely invitation—I couldn't possibly." The bouquet of lavender she'd brought for Estelle fell from her arm just as she grasped the picture. Sebastian scrambled to retrieve the flowers from the floor, but broke more stems than he saved. Lillian let the photo fall back into her bag as he dumped the salvaged blooms into her hands.

Sebastian smiled, saying, "Can I take your stuff? 'Cause it's my job." He cupped his hand to the side of his lips and lowered his voice. "So, will ya please come in, so I can hang it up, to give it back to you later?"

She furrowed her brow. "Oh, well, just for a minute. I'm only returning what your mother sent over. It's not mine; it's your mom's."

Aurora slipped her hand into Lillian's and led her to the couch. "Do you like reading? I do!" She rummaged under the couch and found the book *Miss Muffin's Blueberry Day*. Snuggling up beside Lillian, she began to recite the memorized story in a grand voice. Lillian tried to straighten the lavender stalks while still paying attention to the orator.

Montreal, who'd also gone into the kitchen, returned with a vase and a coaster for her teacup. "Plain tea, right, Miss Bloom?"

Lillian's bewilderment met his laughing eyes. She'd momentarily lost her bearings. "Oh. Yes—yes, please—I guess you remember how I like it."

At the end of a cozy evening, Estelle whispered bedtime instructions to Montreal as she wrapped a shawl around Lillian's shoulders.

"Oh, please, Estelle, I'm fine; the bus stop is just across the way."

Estelle tucked her arm into Lillian's as they walked. "I'm so glad you came and I'm happy to wait with you until your bus arrives." She smiled up into the cool night air. Dim light from a single reluctant street lamp sputtered at them, but as the clouds parted, moonlight enveloped the path the women shared. "Doesn't this feel delicious on our skin?"

"I guess so; it's certainly a beautiful night," Lillian answered.

"Yes indeed, we won't waste a minute. My father used to wave from our porch until the last lights of visitors' cars had disappeared. As a little girl, I vowed to value people just as my father did, to the last minute."

"I had a kind father too."

"We're blessed then, you and me. I wish my children knew that kind of love from their father. It's been a long road, but God has been faithful through every single hard day."

The bus doors swished open, interrupting everything Lillian wished to ask.

Lillian wiped away the grime on the bus window, giving her a clearer view of Estelle, who waved until she was out of sight. What a rare woman she was: both serene and vibrant, gentle and strong. She seemed to always find creative ways to handle the tender emotions of her children. What had she said of the broken lavender to Sebastian? Lillian tried to remember.

After tea, she'd watched Florence carefully set each teabag on a napkin-covered plate to dry for a second round. Estelle had then asked Sebastian to bring her the broken blooms. "These we'll dry to enjoy in our tea. Don't you worry; they'll be useful after all." Sebastian's face had lit up.

The simple dinner of potatoes, sautéed with onions and ground beef, had smelled marvelous after Florence had added fresh oregano. She'd snipped it from a clay pot in the window. Each plate was decorated with two tomato wedges and a sprig of celery stalk: the simplest meal, beautifully made.

Sebastian had set a candle in the center of the table. "I get lighting privileges tonight!" he'd announced proudly.

As Montreal cleared the plates to the sink, Estelle had chopped apples and simmered them in a pan with cinnamon and brown sugar. More often than Lillian could count, Estelle would catch her children's eyes, respond to something they'd said, or laugh at their antics. Her laughter trickled like a spring of refreshment to the soul. Lillian couldn't remember many details of the happy chatter around the table, only that she'd felt welcomed and valued amidst the loving family. And thankfulness. She remembered it as a characteristic every family member possessed.

She found she was still wrapped in Estelle's shawl when it dawned on her that she'd missed her stop. She wasn't even sure of which direction she was going when she finally awakened from her daze, still sitting on the bus, far from home.

It was only she and a solemn man dressed in grey who remained. The same man had been on the 6:30 bus as well. *A coincidence*, she decided, and brushed the thought aside.

Mr. Blue Suede Shoes complained bitterly when she finally returned to the shop. He meowed all the way up the stairs as they walked side by side to Lillian's apartment.

She placed the laughing Elvis picture on her nightstand and sank onto her bed. "Regina, that daughter of yours is clever, and your grandson too. How else could I end up with your photo? Guess you're stuck with me, Fabulous Regina."

And with that she fell asleep singing the old melody in her head. *Blue, until you, made me new with your song, all the day long, then we swooned in the glow of the moon . . .*

Early Thursday morning, Lillian made herself breakfast. She laid a cloth on the table and lit a candle—*lighting privileges*, she mused. She buttered Birgitte's grainy bread, then lined her plate with thinly cut cucumber wheels, evenly salted. *Perhaps I need tomato wedges and a celery sprig*, she found herself thinking. Espresso steamed as the timer beeped for her egg. She lifted her spoon to crack the eggshell, but jumped when a loud banging from her shop below startled her.

What in the world? she thought, throwing on her robe as she raced down the stairs.

Julius stood at the door, pressing his forehead and fingertips to the glass.

"What's wrong?" she gasped, rushing to unlock it.

"Wrong? Nothing at all!" Julius was brimming with delight. "Today we get our daughter, and suddenly I realized the social worker needs flowers! Ebony Scott is her name—lovely name, don't you think?"

Lillian tightened the silk tie on her robe. "Julius, it's six o'clock in the morning."

"Really? Wow, early mornings aren't usually my style, but I'm sure you don't mind. Got some doughnuts and smokes?"

Lillian bit her lip. "Hold on, let me just . . ."

Julius relocked the door. "Come on, I'll join you upstairs for breakfast. We can chat about the bouquet and everything else. It's one of the biggest days of Stuart's and my life together! Hope will be so happy."

"Julius, please don't come up. Let me dress and quickly get ready."

Julius brushed past her. "Don't be a prude. You're not naked, and it's not like I haven't seen naked women before anyway. What, worried about someone watching us?"

Watching? Lillian glanced through the window before following.

In the kitchen, Julius eyed the sparse meal. He pulled up a number on his phone. "Hello, yes, you can . . . Mexican breakfast chilaquiles for two, please . . . delivered to the shop and residence of Lillian Rose Bloom . . . yes, I'll give you my card in just a sec." Lillian opened her mouth to protest, but Julius held up his hand to silence her. "Want a Dos Equis to go with that?"

"A beer? Now?"

"And just one Dos Equis, thanks." He finished the transaction, then hung up and turned to Lillian. "It's done. No complaining; you were about to eat boredom on a plate."

"Who'd you call?"

"That hotel, the Garden Hotel. My family's been trying to buy it for years. Haven't you been there? It's a tiny gem of a place, with amazing food!"

Lillian shook her head. "Fancy breakfasts are fine, but lately I prefer simple food."

"You? You're joking. Simple is boring; beauty and perfection, that's you, and it's all about the pursuit of the next thing!" Julius took a cucumber slice from her plate and popped it into his mouth. "We're a lot alike, you know." Lillian frowned as Julius licked the salt from his fingertips.

14

Jesse

Name. Je-see : Hebrew origin, meaning "the Lord exists"

"Hideous."

Jesse Taylor looked at her reflection in the window of Lillian Rose Blooms. At six feet tall, with long red hair, kelly-green eyes, and the slightest dusting of freckles on her nose, the world would call this twenty-one-year-old beautiful, but she knew better. She shook out the lace edges of her blouse, then tugged at her mercilessly tight pencil skirt. Rumor had it that the businesswoman, Lillian Bloom, had a heart. Her name was on the tip of every tongue these days. Jesse needed a job—a *legitimate* job, and if Ms. Bloom could hire the boy who broke her window, perhaps Jesse had a chance herself.

Before she could twist the doorknob of the shop, the familiar scent of cheap cigars and body odor accosted her nose. She spun around.

"Finch! What's your deal? Did *he* send you?" Jesse stared down at the hardened face. His eyes, threatening malice, took stock of her as she pulled again at her skirt. She shifted her weight from one foot to the other while scanning the street.

"Are you spying on me for him or for yourself?"

"Shut up! I do what he says," snarled Finch. "And you'd better too, if you know what's what."

"Get out of my business. I finished what he forced me to do at Stratford Law. I did what he said, for as long as he said. I'm done! I'm nobody's property; he promised me freedom after this last job!" Jesse's voice became shrill as she tried to shake the choking sensation crawling up her throat.

Finch sneered. "He doesn't care, not when Judge Rolland likes you; did too good a job, that's your *deal*. Seems you're the judge's *private property*."

"No one's anybody's private property. You shut up!" Jesse raised her hand to smack him, but he caught it midair. She wrenched it away. "I'm done. He's got nothin' on me."

"Last job? You don't decide!" With shaky fingers stained yellow from nicotine, Finch pulled out a wad of cash. He pressed it into Jesse's hand. "Listen, he's mad—real mad, somethin's up. Finish favors with the judge, just do it."

"Forget it!" Jesse threw the cash to the ground.

Finch pulled up his thick stature, grabbed Jesse's wrists, and pinned her to the brick wall. "Finish, then lay low, quiet like, and stop flarin' up. 'Cause he says so, got it? Don't be an ass, you know what I'm saying—this warnin's from me!"

Finch dropped her wrists and backed away as he dug into the pockets of his grungy trench coat. He shoved a cigar stub between his teeth, then vanished into the rhythm of the morning commuters.

Jesse shuddered as she slid down the wall, leaning against it with her arms stretched over her crouched knees. She stared down at the money on the sidewalk. The subtle numbing took hold. After searching the street for observers, she snatched up the bills and tucked them into her blouse. She ignored the self-loathing whispers in her mind as she rose to compose herself.

15

Benjamin

Name. Ben-juh-muhn : Hebrew origin, meaning "son of my right hand"

From the sidewalk outside his shop, Benjamin Meyer watched the red-headed beauty pick up the money from the street, then slip into Lillian's shop. He was amazed she didn't see him, though his bookshop was right next door.

How long had he been rearranging the half-priced bookshelf outside? His knees complained bitterly as he straightened them. Recently, he'd seen a man taking pictures of the boy, and now this shady character accosting a young lady. It was definitely time to share his concerns with Lillian, along with the thought he'd had while eavesdropping.

Benjamin entered the flower shop. Lillian looked up from handing the young woman a job application.

"Ben, hi! You're early this week, but I'm ready with your bouquet; be right with you."

Lillian tucked a stray curl behind her ear as she focused her attention back on the young woman. "Well—Jesse Taylor—my business is thriving and I imagine I could use some help; it's just, I'm not sure if you'd be a great fit. But I'll consider your resumé and let you know."

"I have a lot of skills, and I'm real efficient and a great learner. I can do anything you ask; never make the same mistake twice. You wouldn't regret hiring me."

Jesse held the application tightly in both hands.

Lillian dismissed her. "Well, we'll see. Thank you."

Jesse backed away.

"Sorry to sound desperate—I'm not—actually I kind of am, but I'm sure I'd be good at this . . . okay, thanks." And with that, she disappeared out the door.

Lillian gave her a fleeting glance then headed to the cold room. She came out with a bouquet made of orange Asiatic lilies, purple chrysanthemums, and yellow alstroemeria. She'd also tucked in a few pale yellow leaves from the Norway maple.

"In a hurry to get to the cemetary, Ben?"

Benjamin admired the flowers. "Nice as always, but no, I just wanted to offer my opinion. That young woman would make a very good assistant to you."

"Why do you say that?"

"I saw her outside, she's . . . interesting and in need of guidance. The world is full of all sorts of unwholesome situations for young people."

Lillian laughed. "Interesting, sounds about right, and she's edgy too. I can't imagine her as my employee; too much extra work to train her."

"That's only at first. You'd do so well with an apprentice, and clearly, she needs a mentor. Perhaps on a trial basis?"

"Trial basis? Ben, mentoring isn't my thing. I need an asset, not a hindrance."

"I never consider people in those categories, but I can explain my reasoning more thoroughly—"

At that moment, the sky-blue door swung open and in rushed Birgitte.

"Sorry to barge through; I must pull the rest of the pastries out of the oven, and Hans is off having a root canal!" She dropped Ben's lunch on the counter, then disappeared in a flurry, back the way she came.

Benjamin placed the rye and sauerkraut sandwich, along with the pastry, in his bag beside a red thermos.

"I make the tea; Birgitte makes the rest."

"A beautiful ritual, bringing flowers and lunch to Rachel's grave each week."

"Setting stones on her grave is the Jewish way. Flowers because she adored them in life."

Lillian wrapped paper and twine around the bouquet.

"Then we would've had something in common."

"Yes, dear Lillian, more than you know; she was a florist as well," he smiled.

Lillian stared. "Seriously? How on earth did I miss that?"

"Well, there's little time to talk of such things. You're a woman in a hurry. Perhaps you have a spare minute now?"

Lillian paused, then reached for a stool and brought it around to Benjamin.

"Yes, yes I do." She tapped her lip. "I guess I'm in a hurry, sometimes . . . most times. All right, what is your other reason to hire her?"

"Well, there's something else. I observed a ruffian bothering her outside your shop. I've also seen someone taking pictures of Montreal."

Lillian waved her hand. "I'm not responsible for taking care of everyone outside my shop. I don't know her, or her story, from Adam. And as far as Montreal goes, I'm sure you're mistaken."

Ben adjusted his glasses and leaned in. "What if I'm not?"

A few customers strolled in laughing and chatting. Lillian took a deep breath and straightened.

"Listen, Ben, this is Stratford—safe, modern Stratford—not the heart of the city. Nothing extreme ever happens here. You, my friend, need not worry."

"I do worry, and so should you," he said with a heavy heart.

"Thank you for your advice, anyway, on Jesse Taylor. I promise I'll consider her."

As the customers approached the counter, Ben turned to go, saying, "I believe her, and I don't think you'll regret hiring her. Thank you again for the bouquet!"

As Benjamin stood on the sidewalk outside of the flower shop, he checked his bag for everything, including Rachel's favorite book of sonnets. Usually, he felt great peace as he headed to the graveyard, but today his uneasiness remained.

16

Ebony

Name. E-buh-nee : Greek origin, meaning "deep black wood," a name given to a very unique and original female

Later that afternoon, in the waiting room of Stratford Community Social Services, Hope clung with one arm to Beth, Ebony Scott's assistant. In her other arm, she clutched a stuffed bunny and her tattered blanket. The toddler's clothes were clean but faded. Under tight ringlets, her wary eyes searched the unfamiliar space.

In a plum-colored suit, with sculpted braids piled high on her head and tortoiseshell glasses, Ebony Scott looked like a high-powered attorney. It was the very image she wished to portray in her dismal workplace. The mint-green linoleum and vinyl seating certainly came from an era before Ebony even existed. She told Beth, "Keep hold of this precious girl a little longer. I've got something I must say to those gentlemen first."

Ebony entered her office, just as Julius whispered to Stuart, "This place is so behind the times, desperate for a makeover. Wouldn't those fiery maples on the street come alive behind white linen curtains?"

Ebony Scott cleared her throat.

The men rose; obviously surprised to see her empty-handed. She waved them back to their seats.

"Gentlemen, Hope's waiting with my assistant. I have something to say to you before I bring her in." She leaned up against her desk. "You might as well know; I think a baby needs a daddy *and* a mommy. I've never placed a child with a gay couple before. Nevertheless, your home study was good, and I believe that you want to love and care for this baby well. Hope is one of so many. We desperately need families and don't have enough. I commend your willingness." She looked from one man to the other. "However, Hope is a fragile toddler. She's had a tough life like her birth mother before her—attachment and trust will be an issue. Your lives will turn upside down. Are you prepared?"

Stuart's grey eyes remained fixed on Ebony's. He nodded.

Julius leaned back with one elbow over his chair and his ankle on his knee. He fought back a yawn.

She took a step toward Julius. "You must promise me two things: that loving women will be in her life, and that you'll seek settings and friendships where she is not the only person of color. Do you understand me?"

Stuart answered in a husky voice, "Mrs. Scott, I know what *not* to do . . . and I'll do my best to be a good dad. I've thought about women for her life. I talked to Miss Ruby; she runs a daycare by us. She'll help."

"You did?" Julius reacted. "Wow, excellent!" He squinted up at the ceiling. "Let me think, there's also Lillian—loves kids—and then there's a fabulous new black family I just met, the son works for her—"

Ebony interrupted him. "Miss Ruby, I've had a bit of contact with her, but Lillian? Single, white woman, right? What does she know about children? Was she the one with the window accident?"

Julius answered, "Yes, oh, and I just realized, I forgot the bouquet I had her make—anyway, I owe you one—her window's fine now, yes. And the oldest son in that family works for her."

A crease between Ebony's eyebrows marred her nearly flawless features. "Excuse me?"

Suddenly, the buzzer commanded everyone's attention. Beth spoke through the intercom, "Mrs. Scott, Hope's having a bit of a meltdown. Shall I take her out walking?"

"No, bring her in; these men believe they're ready and I do as well—at least I think I do."

Before Beth walked in, Julius glanced around the room, then quickly added, "This space is too uninteresting for what you do, Mrs. Scott. Shall I renovate it for you? Something airy and bright, like the Garden Hotel perhaps?"

Stuart grabbed his arm. "Focus."

But Ebony felt her stomach churn.

Ebony watched through the window as the men waited for a taxi down at the curb. Stuart was doing everything in his power to calm the crying toddler while Julius fumbled with the car seat. Ebony held her fist against her stomach to quell the tumult. *Airy and bright like the Garden Hotel . . . the Garden Hotel.*

Beth buzzed in. "Mrs. Scott, your next client is here."

Ebony hurried to grab a bottle of Tums from her drawer.

"Give me a minute," she answered. Her eyes fell on the framed photo on her desk. There was her mother, holding Ebony's little hand with her baby brother on her mother's hip. They were standing in front of the Garden Hotel.

17

Julius

J ulius hopped out of the taxi, then turned around to help Stuart unbuckle Hope from her car seat. Stuart, seated beside her, had already undone each strap. Hope, however, wouldn't budge. He drew her blanket down from her sweaty head, but she jerked it back with her tiny fists. When Julius tried to slip his hand behind her back, she jammed herself against the side, refusing to move.

A horn screeched from behind the taxi. Their driver stretched his head out the window yelling, "Shut up! Sensitive situation here!"

He spun back around.

"Hey guys, for another ten bucks, I'll give ya two minutes. My heart bleeds for adoption and all that—but you're puttin' my professionalism on the line here!"

Stuart wrenched the whole car seat up and out through Julius' side. Hope sat perfectly still, clinging to her bunny under her blanket.

"Sorry, Hope," he spoke softly, re-buckling her front clasp, "I'm getting you inside, then you can climb out on your own time."

Julius fished a ten-dollar bill out of his billfold. Stuart swiped it from Julius' fingers. The taxi driver glared at Stuart, who dismissed him flatly. "That thirty seconds was free—Mr. Bleeding Heart!"

The taxi sped away.

"Jerk!" Stuart fumed, then turned toward the coffee shop. "Why are the blinds down?"

"You'll see," announced Julius, stepping ahead of Stuart. He imagined the sheer joy of what was about to happen would transform his partner's fierce mood. He unlocked the door and flung it open.

"SURPRISE!" came a roar of celebratory voices from the packed room decorated with pink balloons and streamers.

Hope drew up her legs and whimpered from under her blanket. Stuart held the car seat in one hand, while yanking down the streamers that ran in front of his face and stepping on them.

"Thanks for coming," he announced, "Julius will take care of drinks, on the house. Hope's not up for a party." His stony eyes met Julius', ". . . though Julius always is."

Stuart headed for the apartment, but Julius stepped in front of the door begging, "Please just stay a minute; everyone's so excited for us."

"Us? As in Hope and me too? Or is this just about you? Look at her, Julius!" Hope's tiny frame shook with quiet sobs. "Get a grip and get rid of this crowd."

He pushed Julius aside and headed upstairs.

Success for the afternoon and evening was measured in three minuscule ways. Hope finally crawled out of the car seat—after she'd soaked it. She ate Cheerios in chocolate milk—from a bowl on the floor. And she bathed—in the tub—like a submerged cat, scratching and scrambling for dear life. The exhausted toddler finally fell asleep on the couch, where she huddled under cushions. As he carried her from the living room to the bedroom, Julius stole her blanket and bunny—sticky and smelly from the liquids of the day. He washed, dried, and slipped them back into her arms before she even noticed.

Serenity, the Golden Retriever, watched patiently from under the coffee table, cautiously observing the new family member.

At 1:00 a.m., Julius was jolted awake by a bloodcurdling scream from Hope's bedroom. He ripped off his eye mask and threw off his covers. Stuart had already leapt from the bed and was running for Hope's bedroom.

Julius stopped short behind Stuart, who froze in the doorway. There stood Hope, in the center of her bedroom, her head lifted and eyes clamped shut, screaming a single note of terror. Serenity crept from under the bed to sit beside Stuart, nudging his hand with her head.

Julius pushed past Stuart and the dog to kneel on the floor and enfold the frantic toddler in his arms. Hope clawed his face and recoiled from his gentle hold. He spoke softly and tried again to comfort her with his touch, but her screaming grew even louder as she tore away from his grasp and rolled to the floor. She cowered in a heap with her arms and legs pulled tightly in and her head bowed to her chest. She looked like a little turtle, trying to shield itself from danger. Julius sat back on his haunches. He looked over at Stuart, clinging to the doorway.

"What do we do?"

Stuart choked on the words in his throat. His eyes welled up.

"It's me," he whispered huskily, "after my dad beat me, I was that—that heap on the floor. She knows the hurt, she's so hurt."

Stuart knelt and crawled toward her. He tucked his head between his arms and folded his knees in, mirroring Hope. And the man became the boy who'd also lain on a floor thirty years earlier, a turtle with a flimsy shell, hiding from the harsh world. He kept his body bent beside her as tears soaked his sleeve.

Stuart had tried to explain his past, time and again, but Julius had never digested the story until this moment. These were their scars of abuse. It was Julius now who sat frozen against the wall, watching the private grief they shared.

In the wee hours of the morning, there at the side of the room, Julius finally fell asleep.

He awakened to a grey morning, rubbed his aching neck, and unfolded his bent legs. Hope and Stuart were now sleeping peacefully on their sides, no longer as two separate entities, but as a father cradling his daughter. Julius stretched and got up to place Hope's comforter over the sleepers. Stuart opened his eyes.

"I'll get us coffee," Julius whispered.

A few minutes later, Julius returned with steaming espressos. They drank them in silence on the floor of Hope's room.

18

Lillian

At 6:00 a.m., Lillian slipped an envelope containing Hope's picture into the mail slot of A Cup of Grace. She'd remembered it as she headed out on her run. *Exactly twenty-four hours ago, Julius was at my door,* she thought. *I wonder how they're doing?* She bent down to tighten her shoe lace. When she arose, she was startled to see the despondent face of Julius through the glass. He opened the door. She handed him the newspaper lying on the front mat, but he didn't take it or even seem to see it. She began to back away.

"Horrible night," he mumbled. "I couldn't help; she was so unhappy." He stood there in pajama bottoms; his usually sleek face looked rough behind morning stubble. "Coffee?" he offered flatly.

Stuart descended the stairs from the back of the shop behind the counter. He set a baby monitor on the counter, then cracked his neck.

"Morning, coffee?"

Lillian shook her head. "No thanks, guys, just here to—"

"Check on us?" Stuart crossed the room and gave Lillian a hug. "Thanks, means a lot. Julius mentioned you yesterday; now I get why."

"Well, there you go . . . neighborly me."

A faint whimper sounded through the monitor. "How about chai? Julius, get chai lattes going—and muffins—muffins sound good, Lillian?"

Lillian backed out the door. "None for me, thanks. I'm fine; I'll just sneak out," she called softly.

Stuart waved as he took off up the stairs, but Julius just stood there, lifeless as a stone.

The Norway maple shivered as an icy wind whispered through its naked branches, where only a few dry leaves still clung. Looking out the window as she flipped her sign to "Open," Lillian saw something, or rather someone, stir on the bench. *He's here again,* she thought. Ever since Montreal had befriended Sinclair, the homeless old man seemed always to be around.

She hurried to the counter, discreetly making sure there was nothing he could easily steal.

"Hello!" Sinclair sang out from the threshold of the shop, removing his hat. "I've been resting on your bench waiting for you, up with the birds, you see."

"Yes, I do see." Lillian hesitated, surprised at the clear intensity of his eyes and his smell—he smelled of laundry detergent. "Sorry I haven't time to chat or buy you food. Maybe you can head to the soup kitchen, though I don't know if they serve breakfast."

"Oh, you don't? So, you've only been there for a light lunch?" he chided.

Lillian's cheeks flushed. She wasn't sure what the man wanted.

Sinclair continued, "I've actually already dined, thank you. Lars invited me in as if I were his long-awaited guest. Bet you've noticed how kind he is, even to the least of us."

Lillian filled the watering can, avoiding his smiling eyes. He went on, "That dear secretary, Barbara, percolated coffee. We three partook of a delectable dough-nut stack and chatted over foreign affairs. The world looks different when one hasn't had a drink in many days."

"Congratulations. Now if you don't mind, I've work to do."

"Point taken, but before I go, I have three thoughts." Sinclair followed her as she began watering plants around her shop. "First, we've not been formally intro-duced; I'm Sinclair Lewis Obermann III. I already know you since your name is splashed across your window. Mine was usually on the door, after I passed the bar, unless I passed *a bar* and stayed, that was how I always found trouble, but never mind."

Delusions of grandeur, thought Lillian. "If you don't need flowers, then I'm afraid I must get on with my work."

"Oh, but I do . . . yellow roses, please," Sinclair answered, with a wave of his hand toward the bucket of miniature roses standing by the sink. "Secondly, thank you for the sandwich the other day; it was a generous offering. My third piece of information involves young Montreal. I think someone is watching him." At this last remark, he rose to full stature and suddenly Lillian could imagine the man he used to be. Reluctantly, she grabbed a handful of roses and some greens, then deftly arranged a bouquet.

"Strangely, I did hear that from someone else."

Sinclair replaced his hat. "Good. That means the moon and stars to me that you believe me. Liking me is unnecessary, but we can unite to ensure the boy is protected."

"I—I don't think that's the approach. I'm sure if it's an issue, the authorities will handle it, if it gets to that."

"Ms. Bloom? Is that how you choose to engage? By stepping away from the good you could do? Well, that's not my way—not anymore." He turned abruptly to go.

"Your bouquet." Lillian knew he hadn't really intended to buy it.

He pulled some bills from his pocket. "The bouquet is for you. I did want to be your friend." He yanked the door open, then disappeared down the street.

As she watched him go, worry over Montreal began to grow in her soul. She stared absently at the flowers in her hand and realized it was the first bouquet she'd ever been given.

Just before closing, Jesse Taylor, wearing a navy suit, walked through the flower shop door. She stood at the window, patiently waiting while Lillian finished with her last customer. *Timely, well-dressed, respectful . . .* thought Lillian.

Jesse smiled at the customer and opened the door for her.

"Why, thank you. You certainly have lovely red hair," the woman commented with a smile.

"And you have lovely . . ." Jesse faltered as the woman stepped over the threshold, ". . . greyish, brownish hair." Jesse cringed and looked over at Lillian.

Lillian stifled her laughter until the customer was out of sight. "Thankfully, Mrs. Thompson is slightly hard of hearing. But she will always compliment you, so be ready next time."

"Next time? So, I got the job?" Jesse's stunned voice filled the room.

"Yes, absolutely," replied Lillian, surprised at her own confident answer. "You can start at the beginning of the week."

Jesse dabbed around her mascara as tears instantly appeared in her eyes. "Thank you, thank you! I promise you won't regret it!" She paused for a few seconds to compose herself. "So, should I stay . . . or go?"

Lillian beckoned her over. "I'll show you around now, but I'll be training you for at least a week before I expect you to understand my way of doing things." Jesse pulled at her cuffs and unbuttoned the lowest button of her jacket as she approached the counter. Lillian continued, "And by the way, though the suit is a nice touch, casual dress is fine with me."

Jesse undid the remaining buttons of her jacket and let out the breath she seemed to be holding, then blurted out, "Oh, good, I grabbed this from my mom's closet and she's like two sizes smaller than me!"

Lillian turned to lead Jesse to the cold room and thought to herself, *At least I'll never have to wonder what she's thinking!*

Winter

Noun. win·ter : the fourth season of the year, from December to February in the Northern Hemisphere, between autumn and spring; an old Germanic word meaning "time of water," referring to rain and snow

From the spindly tips of the Norway maple and along its uplifted branches, layers of powdery snow glistened in the late morning sun. Even the grooves in its silvery trunk glowed, like a veiled bride of winter. A fresh batch of snowflakes poured from the sky, as if ladies-in-waiting twirled around her.

Across the street at the daycare, giggling children bundled in bright coats leapt into snow mounds or sputtered with mouths full of snow from well-aimed snowballs. Fastidious squirrels raced from tree to tree, leaving puffs of white behind them.

At the sub shop, a heap of snow cascaded over the awning, burying a lonely rake. A passerby slipped under the flurry, but regained his footing on the well salted sidewalk. Soaring high in the sky, a pair of red-tailed hawks spun in their winter romance, while down below pigeons cooed, sheltered under the eaves of shops along Stratford Lane.

From the bench at the playground up the street, a silver-haired woman placed a carrot and a few raisins into the hands of a little boy. Then, suddenly, his misshapen snowman came alive with a happy grin. With sticks for arms raised in praise, the snowman seemed to say, *Welcome, glorious winter; Stratford has been waiting!*

19

Lillian

L illian hadn't even noticed the transformation of the Norway maple or the magnificent morning sky; she'd been far too focused on the tasks at hand. In her pursuit of efficiency, she scooped up Mr. Blue Suede Shoes and kissed his soft head. "Come on, you've been complaining all morning; up to the apartment you go." She glanced around the empty shop before sprinting upstairs.

The cat leapt from her arms to the living room couch. Lillian stayed momentarily rooted to the spot, captivated by the glorious scene outside her window. She cranked open the side window, the one with the missing screen, then did what she'd not done in thirty years. Leaning as far over the sill as possible, she stuck out her tongue to taste the icy flakes.

From her perch, all of Stratford sparkled, blanketed under the first snow of the year. She closed her eyes, lingering for a moment longer, to let the snowflakes flutter onto her lashes. She thought of Estelle's children. *Will they be tasting snowflakes today? Is there a patch of yard close to the apartment to make snow angels?* Perhaps she'd find lemon and raspberry syrup to send home with Montreal for homemade snow cones.

"Helloooo, Rapunzel, anytime you're ready . . ." came the laughing comment from a customer waiting on the stoop below.

"Oh, my," she yelled down to him and the two others staring up at her, "be right there!" She shook the snowflakes from her long curls and shut the window, sending a dusting of white onto the rug at her feet.

20

Montreal

Outside the flower shop a few days later, Montreal was attempting to string twinkly lights through the window boxes. Keeping the lights untangled while somehow making them look neat semed impossible, especially since he kept getting distracted! When he heard the sound of a car pulling up next to the sidewalk, he turned around. At the sight of the Lincoln Town Car idling at the curb, the lights fell to the ground in a heap at his feet.

An aged chauffeur, in white gloves, stepped out from the driver's seat. The man had just enough scraggly hair to slick neatly over his ears, like fenders over tires. Moving at a glacial pace, he reached to open the passenger door, but it flew open before he could touch it. An eccentric-looking woman appeared. She wore pearl earrings, large sunglasses, and a white speckled fur jacket, with her white hair swept into a French twist. Montreal thought she looked like a snowy owl.

The woman peered over her glasses into Montreal's face and said, "Now, you must be the benevolent provider of sodas and fetcher of sandwiches. How pleased I am to meet you. I'm Ms. Sylvia Obermann, Sinclair's sister." She thrust out her hand. "And you are?"

"Montreal—my name's Montreal," he replied, shaking her hand.

"Montreal, yes, Montreal what?" Sylvia waited impatiently for his answer. "You certainly have a last name, do you not?"

"Yes, Ma'am, well . . . my mother is Estelle Delacroix."

"Estelle Delacroix? Now that name sounds familiar, but I can't recall. My brother tells me you work for Lillian Bloom."

"Yes Ma'am, for nine and a half more days!"

Sylvia threw her head back and laughed. "I, too, have had miserable projects where I counted the hours and minutes until I finished. I know the feeling."

Montreal grimaced, "I didn't mean—"

"Not to worry; your secret's safe with me. Now, let's find that fierce employer of yours." She followed his lead through the front door.

"She's not exactly fierce," Montreal tried to quietly interject, but the woman ignored him and entered the shop.

Sylvia reached out to shake Lillian's hand. "Hello, I'm Sinclair's sister. He is the gentleman for whom you bought a sandwich. It's a pleasure to meet you. Now I need a large bouquet for the secretary of Stratford Community Chapel. Any flowers you have on hand will do just fine. I'll be back in five minutes." She glided out and turned toward the bakery.

Lillian stared. "That's his sister? Five minutes?" She turned to Montreal. "Tell Jesse I need her now!"

Montreal slipped into the back room where Jesse was studying flower and supplier lists. "Lillian needs you!" It was Jesse's first day at the shop and Montreal was ecstatic to have a work buddy.

"Me?" Jesse jumped up, then hurried to the counter with Montreal close at her heels.

Lillian bit her lip. "Okay—do you think you can handle grabbing a few things from the cold room?"

"I can help!" Montreal volunteered, worried for his new friend.

"Okay, here goes: grab seven maroon roses, nine golden mums—I can't remember which ones are there—five of something pinkish, pine foliage, and those lemon cypress clippings, if I've got any left from planting the window boxes."

"Come on!" cried Montreal, happy he knew exactly which flowers she meant. In the cold room, he pointed out everything, then zipped back to the front to help. There, Lillian was searching the shelf where vases normally stood. He saw the rising panic in her eyes at finding it empty, so he grabbed a white pitcher from under the sink and set it before her. "Is this okay?" he asked hesitantly.

"Oh, yes, that'll be perfect, thank you!"

Montreal filled it with water as she clipped velvet ribbon and twine from rolls under the counter and tied them to the handle. Snapping on her gloves, she turned to see Jesse hastening toward her. Though Jesse left a trail of leaves and stems, she had already arranged the flowers beautifully.

Lillian's eyes brightened. "You're a natural!"

Montreal felt like applauding, but then the handle of the sky-blue door rattled. Montreal swept the scattered greens, Lillian held out the pitcher, and Jesse dropped the bouquet into it. *Like a slam dunk at the final buzzer,* Montreal thought.

Sylvia emerged through the adjoining bakery door and her eyes fell on the bouquet.

"Impressive, ladies. Abundant thanks!" She handed Lillian a handful of cash, then walked out the door. Outside the window, Birgitte handed a loaded pink pastry box to the chauffeur.

Montreal followed. Luckily, the twinkle lights still needed hanging, because then he could soak in every detail of the impressive woman to share with his family when he got home. As he headed for the front, Jesse gave him a high five, saying exuberantly, "We're a great team!"

Instead of slipping into the back seat, Sylvia turned to Montreal and said, "By the way, you're impressive too." She lifted her finger to her chauffeur. "Now, Charles!"

Charles stepped up to Montreal, opened the pastry box for a quick look, then handed it to the boy. On top, Sylvia had scribbled in her spidery script, *To Master Montreal and His Family.*

Montreal stuttered out a few thank yous and would have hugged the old chauffeur if the box weren't so heavy. He'd never seen such a delicious assortment of pastries in his life!

21

Sylvia

Name. Sil-vee-uh : Latin origin, meaning "spirit of the woods"

Sylvia found Sinclair shivering on the bench in front of Stratford Community Chapel. She smiled at him. He was clean, clear-eyed, and coatless.

"It's remarkable! So many wonderful changes. But, of course, there's still that belly. And I suppose you gave your new sheepskin coat away?"

"Too many of my fellow nomads need coats; next time buy me ten." He smiled slyly and then added, "Or increase my allowance!"

"Not yet, dear brother, but if you stay sober, I do believe the time may come soon. Unless you've gone back to gambling." The last sentence was harsh, dropping all pretext of pleasant banter.

"It's been twenty years and you know it." He stood up and offered his arm.

Sylvia slipped her arm in his, and cleared her throat. "I'm sorry, that was uncalled for. I don't know what came over me."

"I do. Fear, fear and bossiness . . . alas, the bossiness will never cease, but it's definitely time to leave the fear behind. I certainly have."

"Maybe, for once, you are right."

"For once? Generosity becomes you," he chuckled, poking her in the side with his elbow.

At the door of the chapel office, Barbara thanked them for the flowers, then directed them out into the garden.

"Last I laid eyes on him, he was headed out, armed with hedge clippers. Should be on this side of the forgotten tower . . . I mean North Tower. Pastor Lars said it needed a proper name."

Just beyond the garden gate, they found the clippers abandoned beside a broken A-frame ladder. From behind a monstrous hydrangea, Lars could be seen dusting himself off.

Sinclair called out, "Lars, been swallowed?"

Lars answered, "Sinclair! Yes . . . testing rusty clippers and ladders is one of my new skills."

Sylvia peered over her sunglasses at the pastor in faded jeans and rolled-up shirtsleeves. For a split second, she doubted the wisdom of her errand.

Sinclair laughed. "I've taken a few dives when tipsy, but rarely when sober—you *are* skilled!"

Sylvia glared at him, but the merriment in his eyes—again, those eyes, clear without a hint of glassy drunkenness—restored her resolve.

Sinclair brushed debris from his pastor's hair, then gave him a hug. It was evident that these two men shared the same unsinkable joy. Lars' face lit up as he reached for Sylvia's hand.

"Hello Ms. Obermann, great to finally meet you. I'm Lars."

Over mismatched mugs of peppermint tea and packaged shortbread cookies, Sylvia began the speech she'd been practicing. "Pastor Gundersen, forty years is a long time to wait. Alcoholism has stolen at least two-thirds of my brother's life and that's an ugly fact." She sat perched on her seat, clutching her handbag in her lap. "I've not seen him survive for more than a few days in decades without a drink. It's been bleak, bleak indeed. For the first twenty years, he held it together, but after a rough patch between us, he ended up preferring the street." She coughed into a handkerchief pulled from the cuff of her sweater. Sinclair took her hand, but she snatched it away. "I don't understand your methods. In fact, I can't even decipher if you actually know how to counsel in any classic manner. Yet, my brother is a new man!"

She glanced at Sinclair, and suddenly he was her brave little twin brother again. A memory overtook her: the two of them, seven-year-olds, sitting silent as church mice at their mother's funeral. He'd taken her hand then, too, and had dared to whisper in the echoing cathedral, "It's okay to cry; Mother said so. She said be kind, kind and strong together." And they had been, until he left, forcing her to be kind and strong on her own.

"As children, we stuck together until alcohol tore us apart. When he decided to live on the streets, it was as if our mother died all over again. Except for Charles' devotion, I've been alone, alone until you brought my brother back to life." She couldn't keep the tears from spilling over. No light coughing or dabbing of her eyes could hide her emotion now.

"It isn't me who's done it, Ms. Obermann," Lars explained gently. "Sinclair chose to stop drinking—"

Sinclair interrupted, "—it was guilt at first, and a cash-flow issue, but then Montreal offered me a soda, and Ms. Bloom, a sandwich, and Pastor Lars invited me to dine and listened . . ."

Lars grinned. "It was God in the details sorting us."

Through darkened eyes, Sinclair added, "And I've a plethora of sorting and confessing still to do. You, of all people, know that, Sylvia."

Sylvia straightened her skirt. "Oh, diddle-daddle. You're forgiven for *that*; I told you years ago."

"But there's more . . " Sinclair hesitated, looking from Sylvia to Lars.

"No matter, brother, what's done is done." From her handbag she withdrew a crisp envelope. "Since Sinclair insists that submarine sandwiches and drinking root beer have paved the way to sobriety, I wish to encourage you. This is the beginning, seed funds for more of that—there's plenty more. Thank you, thank you, abundantly!"

Lars beamed. "Well, Ms. Obermann, Sinclair is my good friend. Every one of God's creatures has a battle. On any given day we're either champions or wounded warriors. My method is: trust God and love the face in front of me." He held up the sealed envelope. "As for this, there's lots of needy folks. Sharing meals of sandwiches and root beer are a great way to begin building community."

Sinclair broke in, "Okay, then we'll call it the Sylvia Obermann Sandwich and Soda Fund, the S.O.S.S. for short!" With that announcement, he kissed his sister smack on the lips and embraced Lars.

22

Lars

It wasn't until Sylvia and Sinclair had left that Lars popped open the wax-sealed envelope. Inside he found five crisp hundred-dollar bills along with a scribbled note. Barbara, who'd been sitting at her desk, wheeled her office chair over to listen, as Lars read aloud.

Dear Pastor Lars Gundersen,

Please find within a token installment of funds for your community-building ministry. As my brother progresses in his life of sobriety, I'd like to add to this initial sum. In time, if all goes well, there will be ample funds for the restoration and renovation of Stratford Community Chapel. I'll expect financial estimates for the work to be done as soon as possible.

Sincerely,
Sylvia Helen Obermann

Barbara clasped her hands together.

"Oh, Pastor Lars, I knew God had big plans for you in this place! I knew it from the first Sunday Bill and I heard you preach!"

Lars laughed and hugged Barbara, careful to avoid jostling her well-trimmed perm.

"Well, that's the best news. Especially since you were the *only* ones there that first Sunday. Praise God!"

23

Lillian

At the end of the day, Lillian wrapped twine around the pink pastry box Ms. Sylvia had given to Montreal. Jesse then asked him, "Hey there, want me to ride with you on the bus to help protect your pastry treasures?"

"That's okay, I can make it," Montreal answered, looking up at Lillian.

Lillian smiled. "Pastry treasures, that has a nice ring to it. How about if I take you? Jesse, will you join us?"

"Wow, that'd be great!" exclaimed Montreal. To show his excitement, he set down the box and jumped into the air, clicking his heels to the side.

Jesse replied, "Sure! And guess what, I can do that too!" She pushed Montreal toward the back door, calling to Lillian, "Want to film us?"

For a split second, Lillian had no idea what she meant, but then she saw the two of them practicing their heel-clicking jumps. She grabbed her phone and followed.

"Yes, of course, coming!" Standing against the back door, with her phone poised on video, Lillian counted down, "Three, two, one, and go!"

Montreal and Jesse tried five times before they could click their heels in the air in unison, but they did it! And by then all three of them were laughing hysterically. Lillian couldn't remember the last time she'd laughed so hard.

Benjamin Meyer, who must've heard the racket outside his bookstore, stepped into the alley with a warm greeting to Jesse. Then came Birgitte and Hans! After watching a couple of times, Hans announced, "That's nothing; Birgitte and I were skaters in Denmark! Watch this!" And without warning he swept his petite, robust wife up in his arms and swung her around; her shrill screams quickly turned to laughter. Lillian followed Montreal's lead and began to applaud them.

Birgitte brushed flour from her apron and announced, "Come on, everyone, we have so much leftover quiche and a few meat pies; dinner is on us! Besides, we haven't met your new assistant, Lillian."

Lillian felt suddenly shy at the attention all around and choked on her answer. Jesse stepped in and spoke for her. "Thank you, it's great to be here. You must be Birgitte and Hans. Montreal told me about you and all the great stuff you make, even before I saw it in the box. But we have to get this one and his treats home. We'll catch you another time, but thanks. See ya around!"

Finally, Lillian was able to speak, still flustered at all the commotion.

"Oh, yes, I must get Montreal home, but thank you anyway."

Ben graciously responded, "I would be delighted to share your delicious pies and quiche. Shall I save you some, Lillian?" But she shook her head.

After dropping Montreal off and chatting with Estelle for a few minutes, Lillian pulled into Jesse's driveway. "I'm sorry I didn't introduce you to Estelle, Montreal's mom. She didn't look like she felt well."

"No biggie, I get that. She's pregnant, so no wonder."

Lillian nodded but thought, *She seemed especially tired today, though. I wonder if something else is wrong.*

Jesse hopped out of the van. "Hey, thanks for the great first day. I'm so glad I've got a job and you and Montreal are really great. Whatever you need, I've got your back."

On the way home to the flower shop, instead of concentrating on the tasks of the coming day, Lillian found herself thinking of the people connected to it. *I've got your back.* It was such an odd phrase, but one Lillian decided she liked.

24

Sinclair

Name. Sin-clair : French, English, or Scottish origin, after the hermitess St. Clare or St. Clere; Latin clarus, meaning "illustrious, pure, renowned," and "clear pool"

Like he did most afternoons, Sinclair meandered down the street, this time in the opposite direction of Carson Memorial Hospital. Suddenly, before he even realized how far he'd come, he found himself standing in front of the very jewelry store he'd been avoiding for decades.

"This sober energy is taking over," he declared, but stopped short as memories flooded his mind. There at the window, rearranging diamond engagement rings, was the spitting image of his old friend who'd owned the shop. The young man, who now looked up with a friendly, indifferent smile, must have once been the seven-year-old who'd helped from behind the counter.

A snow flurry whipped up, blowing sharply into the side of Sinclair's face, as if his shame were screaming at him. He clamped his hands over his ears and stumbled backward over a trash receptacle.

He saw the young man rush to the door, then call out, "Sir, are you okay?"

Sinclair didn't answer. He clamored past a Norway maple then slid into an alley. As he waited for the coast to clear, his guilt washed over him. It was twenty years ago, but it could've been yesterday: the deceitful call to his friend, the plans made, then he'd never shown up, but the police had. Sinclair kicked at the rubbish at his feet and began to frantically pace.

"I'm sorry, Isaac! You died and I never made it right before it was too late!" He pressed his fingertips against his sweaty brow. *How can I make right all that I've done wrong? How can Lars' God ever see good in me when failure is always biting at my heels?*

He spied an empty beer bottle on the street by his feet. He scanned all around then picked it up and gave it a sniff—just a sniff—but it smelled oh-so-delicious.

25

Lillian

Lillian tied the plaid ribbon onto the pine bough wreath as a finishing touch and stepped back to the sidewalk to examine it. A sharp bark at her elbow made her jump.

"Serenity! You scared me to death! What are you doing out here on the street by yourself? Where are your dads?" She pulled off her gloves and scratched Serenity under the chin.

"Come on, old girl; I'll lead you home." But the Golden Retriever wouldn't budge. Again she barked, a single note of alarm. Lillian searched her urgent eyes. "What's wrong? Something at your shop?" Lillian peered down the street, seeing the usual morning line at the door of A Cup of Grace. "Hmm, something with Hope?" Serenity circled around, barking several times and wagging her tail. Lillian grabbed her hat and mittens from a basket by the door and called to Jesse, "Something's wrong, I'm going to follow Serenity!"

"The dog? That's totally weird but okay, I'm here." Lillian barely heard her, she was already out the door.

"Show me," Lillian directed, and Serenity took off in the opposite direction of the coffee shop.

They crossed at the crosswalk, then dashed past the dilapidated park and over the grass at the corner of the chapel grounds. Lillian waved to Lars and Barbara, who were examining the church roof from the steps. Lars called out, "Lillian, you all right?"

"Serenity's frantic and she never is. I think something's wrong!"

"Where are Stuart and Julius?"

"At their shop, I think." Lillian faltered, but Serenity urged her on.

"Got it, I'll head that way," said Lars.

26

Lars

Acouple of minutes later, Lars whipped into A Cup of Grace. He threaded his way through the line until he saw Stuart. Sweat framed Stuart's face, pouring down between his sideburns and ears. He was passing a latte to one customer as he called out the name of another while swirling cream on a Frappuccino. Julius was nowhere to be found; neither was Hope.

They're probably upstairs, Lars told himself, but couldn't swallow the worry welling up in his throat. Finally, within earshot of Stuart, he blurted out, "Serenity is out on the street acting anxious. Is everything all right?"

Stuart looked frantically around him. "What?—what do you mean?"

"Lillian's following Serenity, and seems to think something is wrong."

Just then Julius appeared at the door leading down from the upstairs apartment. He had a duffle bag slung over his shoulder, his hat and coat in hand, and was concentrating on his phone in hand.

"Where's Hope?" Stuart called to Julius, who looked up from his phone, confused. Stuart ripped off his apron. "Where's Hope?"

Julius threw out his arms. "I told you I needed space. You weren't even listening!"

Stuart glared at Julius, as he shoved past him. "Hope's not with you?"

Julius froze. "With me? No, I thought . . ."

"I told you to watch her!"

"What was I supposed to do? She only ever wants you!" Julius grabbed his bag and headed for the door.

Lars saw the veins on Stuart's arms pulse. His hands curled into fists but immediately he forced them to loosen. "*Cover*," his voice seared, "we'll talk about this later. Lars—" He threw his chin in the direction of the street as he held the door for Lars.

Lars turned to Julius. "I'm close by; come talk anytime." Then he hurried over the threshold, saying to Stuart, "First to the chapel. Lillian and Serenity ran from there; my secretary will know where."

They could see Barbara in the distance, standing on the bench, waving to them. She called out, "Lillian found Hope! Over there at that new shop." She pointed toward a crew of men hauling rugs from a truck parked at the curb. Arabic words flowed between them.

Lars outran Stuart to where Serenity sat at the feet of an affable man with a bushy beard. The dog was fully restored to her docile self. Lillian stood at the man's side, speaking to the feisty toddler, who dangled from his arm like a noodle on a fork. Her chubby hands hid her face, wet with tears.

Stuart rushed over, falling to his knees as he reached for her. "Hope! Oh, Hope!"

"No!" she yelled, through the slits between her fingers.

The man dropped Hope into Stuart's waiting arms, but she fought him and slid to the ground. "Thank you, thank you," breathed Stuart. "This is my little girl. My shop's down there. Thank you!"

Lars ducked under a carpet roll to stand beside Lillian. She looked up at him and he smiled down at her before putting out his hand to the man.

"I'm Lars. We're all so thankful and glad to meet you. Welcome to the neighborhood."

"I am Rashid, owner of The Persian Rug. I am honored to make your acquaintance. We are glad to help. We say in my country, you cannot clap with one hand alone."

Lillian interjected, "I'm sorry, Stuart. I didn't see her pass my window. Mr. Rashid said that when Serenity saw Hope was safe with him, she came to get me. Amazing!"

Rashid laughed. "Ms. Bloom says she has no children—no experience. I have many, so I understand this tiny, bold girl. I'm always willing to help." A little face, surrounded by wavy black hair, poked out from the door of the shop. Rashid took her hand and drew her out onto the step. "This is my youngest daughter, Nazreen. It is she who saw your child through the window."

Lars smiled at her.

The little band dispersed with Stuart, Hope, and Serenity in the lead. Lars promised to come back again to Mr. Rashid to meet the rest of his family and Lillian offered to bring flowers for their grand opening the following week. Barbara said she could hand out their flyers to local businesses on her speed-walking route and wondered if his family ate broccoli casserole. It was her favorite welcome-to-the-neighborhood meal.

As Lars headed out late for an evening walk, he noticed light streaming through the windows of A Cup of Grace. Stuart, who was mopping the floor, beckoned to Lars to come inside. Stuart whipped up two cappuccinos and doused each with a careful portion of Irish cream as Lars settled into a seat.

"Brutal day," he commented.

Stuart delivered the mugs. "Brutal's the word. It's still hard to believe. How'd she get clear over there?"

Lars shrugged. "Amazing, like Lillian said. I'm sure God protected her." He blew at the frothy mug.

Stuart scoffed. "Well, if I believed in that sh—stuff, I'd agree. I'm just glad you were there." Here Stuart's voice failed him. He motioned to where Hope stood by the stainless-steel fridge. She was holding a pink mug. In her silence, Lars hadn't even noticed her.

Stuart took Hope's mug and filled it with hot cocoa. At first, she refused it, but then he set it on a napkin on the floor. She plopped down between Serenity's paws, as if they were arms of a lounge chair, and picked up the cocoa.

Lars smiled, then asked, "Where's Julius?"

Stuart pulled the dish towel from his shoulder and began to vigorously polish the counter. "Beats me."

27

Bangji

Name. Bàng-jí : Chinese origin, meaning "super" or "excellent"

On a grey day, a week later, Bangji was sweeping debris outside her shop. Snow was on the forecast again so she'd spent the morning getting more salt and shovels ready. The bright yellow-and-red awning of Subs 4 U welcomed guests in all kinds of weather. Bangji kept her store meticulously clean, even to the point of scrubbing the sidewalk when needed.

Suddenly, Hope crossed her path. She was holding tightly to Serenity's collar, yanking the dutiful guardian forward. Serenity would stop to bark, and then follow the three-year-old along, obviously torn between protecting Hope and going home.

Bangji dropped her broom, scooped up the wandering child, and almost bumped into Stuart.

"You didn't notice baby leave? You're a bad dad. You almost lost your baby."

Hope tried to wriggle from Bangji's arms, throwing her head back in angry protest, but the little woman was unmoved. Serenity surrendered to the admiral, flopping down at Bangji's feet.

"Thank you. Now will you please let her go?" Stuart begged. Bangji set the subdued child down, but planted her own feet in the center of the sidewalk, like a mini tank, blocking their passage home.

Stuart let out an exasperated breath.

Bangji blasted him. "In China, I was a judge! You and me in China, I'd be in charge, and I'd say, no baby for this man! You need help! Where's Julius today? Why did he leave?"

Stuart clenched his teeth and made a fist at his side. He shook his head and swore under his breath. "Bangji, I don't know. He needs time to get his head straight. You don't have to get it, but I'm doing my best. Thanks for stopping her, but we're going now."

"Lillian can help you. You ask Lillian?"

"Julius had that idea too. But now that he's gone, she's far from helpful." Stuart stepped along the edge of the sidewalk. Hope put her finger in his belt loop, grabbed Serenity by the collar, and followed him home.

Bangji watched, fuming. The world on this street was so different from the one in which she'd raised her daughter Ming, now thirty-four, in China.

Quon, Bangji's husband, appeared at the shop door, lifting his eyebrows in question.

Bangji turned to Quon and answered in Chinese. "That newly adopted child appeared at our storefront accompanied only by the dog. One of the men has left and the other is completely ill equipped to handle this responsibility! Adoption in America is an honorable undertaking, but in this situation, it's a tragic mistake!" She picked up her rake and snapped back to work, raking invisible leaves.

Quon disappeared back into Subs 4 U.

After a few minutes of mad raking, Quon called to Bangji from the open window, "Are you done scolding Stuart inside your head? I think the rake has been thoroughly punished." She chuckled at her husband's gentle chiding. "Is it time for a peace offering for the struggling family?"

She relaxed her shoulders and answered, "A twelve-inch Italian meatball sub and an extra small pink lemonade in a princess cup. I'll deliver!"

Quon laughed out loud. "Yes, Emperor!" he said, as she set her rake in the corner. "You've never fooled me, you know. Soft hands hold the string of your dragon kite!"

28

Montreal

Montreal held the shop door for Jesse, who slipped on her fringed jacket and swung her handbag over her shoulder. He was sorry to see her go.

"Thanks, bud," she smiled as she raised her hand for a high five. "See ya Monday."

He stuttered, "Uh, no—this is my last day, my hours are done."

"Are ya sure 'bout that? Maybe, maybe not."

Montreal stole a glance at Lillian, who nodded. "Jesse's right, there's definitely a *maybe* in the works. You work hard. Your attitude's great and you never complain." Montreal's eyes widened; he'd complained in his mind enough to last a lifetime! "So, do you want to keep working for me? Not as a regular paid employee, you're too young for that, but as a cat sitter, among other things."

As if on cue, Mr. Blue Suede Shoes rubbed up against Montreal's jeans, then flopped onto his back on the floor and stretched out his long torso.

Montreal squatted down to rub his belly. "You like that idea, big fella?"

Jesse watched from the door, no longer in a hurry to go.

Lillian continued, "I'd pay you ten bucks an hour plus bus fare, with a ten-minute break and sometimes a pastry on the side. How's that sound?"

Montreal gave a happy shrug but then his face clouded over. "Not sure I can be gone more in the afternoons, though—Mama's so tired—might need more o' my help. The cancer's making her sicker; she can't eat much and the baby's coming anytime . . . you know." He looked up to find both women staring intensely at him. Jesse dropped her purse.

Lillian's hands were at her mouth. "Your mom has cancer? What kind of cancer?"

Jesse leaned in, towering over Montreal, her voice shrill. "Anytime . . . like what's *anytime* mean? Like today?"

Montreal stepped back, accidentally treading on the cat's tail. His sharp cry startled Montreal. "It's, uh, breast cancer and Mama thinks—says—the baby's due in a few weeks, so anytime; I think that's anytime?"

Jesse put her hand on Montreal's shoulder. It felt like a lead weight.

Lillian ripped off her apron. "Jesse, I need you to stay."

"Absolutely!"

Lillian shoved one arm through her jacket sleeve and grabbed her wallet. "Montreal, I really want to talk with your mom right now. I had coffee with her the other day, remember? She said nothing. We'll grab coffee and a few other things now and I'll come with you. Is that fine?"

Montreal stared down at his feet. "Uh, you know, you could just wait and let Mama tell you herself. She—she didn't exactly tell me ta tell you." He looked up wishing his eyes had memory morphing rays like his favorite kids' adventure series, *Born in the Eye of the Eclipse*. He opened his eyes extra wide and stared at Lillian. *What if . . .*

Jesse met his gaze. "What are you doing? Stop foolin' around! Get serious!"

Montreal blinked away his imagination, finding tears in its place. "You have no idea," he whispered softly.

Lillian touched Montreal's shoulder gently. "Of course the baby's coming soon; your mom's belly is big, we know that. And anyway, I need to ask her about the work and explain your new job." Her smile looked fake. "Don't worry about telling us; I should've known or asked or just—understood." Lillian faltered. It was she who now looked at the floor. "I—I'm sorry about that. I'm sorry about a lot of things—I treated you so badly when I first met you and I was mean. Please forgive me."

Montreal shoved his hands into his pockets and scuffed the floor with his foot, not sure how to answer her. "That's okay; your pretty window's real important to you. I made a mess of everything. Wish I'd never broke it."

Lillian shook her head emphatically. "I don't."

29

Lillian

Lillian and Montreal stepped off the bus in front of Archie's Convenience Store, a block from Silverstone Apartments. There Lillian grabbed a box of herbal tea, a gallon of milk, blueberry bagels with cream cheese, the few wilted veggies she could find, and a cooked chicken. At the checkout she snatched up some floral paper napkins. Gum and sour candies dangled from hooks on a side stand. She hesitated, then directed Montreal to choose two of each as she spilled her armload of goods onto the counter.

According to the name tag pinned to his apron, it was Archie himself who stood behind the cash register. He scratched his belly and heaved up his sagging waistband as he waited for Montreal's candy selection. Lillian readied herself for a rude comment about her indecisiveness, but all he said was, "Ain't these purty?" as he examined the napkins for their barcode.

As the glass door swung closed behind them, Montreal burst into laughter. Lillian, who'd been concealing her own, let out that funny snort that sometimes escapes from stifled giggles. This made them both laugh even harder.

"In my house, that laugh's called a cap-snort," explained Montreal, when their giggles finally subsided.

"What?" asked Lillian, wiping her eyes.

"It's when something flies out, like a laugh or a burp. It's like a cap flying off a soda bottle when you shake it up and barely pop it off—pshew!" Montreal thrust his arms up into the sky. "The pressure explodes it!" Lillian's face was blank. Montreal chuckled. "You've never seen soda exploding from its bottle?" Lillian shook her head. "Oh man, you gotta see that; someday I'll show you!"

"Deal!" Lillian announced to her jovial companion.

Montreal and Lillian entered the apartment quietly. Florence shushed them anyway, pointing to Estelle, who lay sleeping on the couch. Montreal set the groceries on the kitchen table and dug out the sour candies from the bottom of the bag.

Florence snapped them from his hand. "Not before dinner!"

Montreal grabbed them back. "Calm down! It's fine. Relax, would you?"

Florence stared daggers.

Lillian pulled the tea and napkins from the sack, then whispered to Florence, "Can we share some tea?"

Estelle awakened. The big kids began to blame each other for being too loud, but Estelle put up her hand. Suddenly she clenched her jaw and clutched her belly. Florence ran to her side and Lillian joined her, kneeling at Estelle's feet. After a minute of what appeared to be agonizing pain, Estelle opened her eyes and slowly relaxed her shoulders. "Braxton Hicks is all—false labor. I still think I have some time to go."

"What does your doctor say?" asked Lillian.

"I don't have one. I thought we'd be back in Montreal by the time I'd need one," answered Estelle.

"Montreal, as in Canada?" asked Lillian.

"Yes, I'm from Canada, originally. We've been in New York for about a year. When our plans fell apart, we couldn't head back. So here we are, making plans as we go."

After supper, Lillian excused herself from the table and stepped outside to call Jesse. As she sat on the cement steps by the front door, she quietly unloaded her concerns. Jesse remained silent on the other end for several seconds. "Jesse? Did I lose you?" Lillian asked.

"No, no—not at all. I think I can get her help, give me a sec."

Jesse clicked off and Lillian just stared at her phone waiting. When it rang, she struggled to steady her voice, "So what help did you find?"

"I—uh—I called my mom. Did I tell you she's a labor and delivery nurse?"

Lillian almost dropped the phone. "What? No, you seem to have missed that little detail. You haven't really told me anything about her."

Jesse laughed half-heartedly. "Yeah, we don't talk too much. I'm, uh . . . anyway, she's a great person and everything. So, surprise! It's a good surprise, right?"

"Yes, of course, please go on!"

"So, she was pretty willing to help. Anyway, she had a slow day on the labor and delivery deck. She's on a twelve-hour shift and her fave obstetrician is in-house—Dr. Franklin—love him. He'll see Estelle pro bono tonight, as soon as she can get there. We'll just need to rally the troops."

"Fine, but what on earth do we do with *the troops?*"

"Bring 'em here. I'll watch 'em," Jesse answered matter-of-factly.

"To the shop? Are you still there?"

"Yeah, it's peaceful here. So bring 'em."

"My shop and apartment? These little guys have lots of energy. You're kidding, right?"

"'Course not, it'll be great. Estelle could deliver tonight—I know about this stuff; my mom's got stories. Better to have kids here, where I can manage the shop and them at the same time."

Lillian stammered, "Jesse, are you even a kid kind of person? I wouldn't be there to help. You're an only child! Did you babysit neighbors or work with children—ever?"

"No . . . but seriously, what could be so hard about babysitting?" She sounded like she was rolling her eyes. "So, what about the C-word?"

Lillian felt the cold seep up through the steps. "I haven't brought it up. With the kids right there and Estelle so exhausted and frail—it's like saying it out loud will shatter something sacred. It's like profanity. I can't."

Just then Aurora snuck out the front door. She was dragging a fuzzy purple blanket covered in pictures of hot air balloons. "'Scuse me," she whispered to Lillian, "this is my coziest thing in our whole room." She wrapped the blanket around Lillian's shoulders, and then snuggled up under it, right beside her. "I promise not to say a peep—I'll just sit here and pretend we're havin' a campfire—with marshmallows." She smacked her lips. "And you don't hafta tell anybody I'm here. I'm an itty-bitty mouse—that's me. Pretend I'm not here; just keep talkin'."

And with that, Aurora laid her head on Lillian's lap and squeezed her eyes tightly shut. "I'm sleepin'."

"Um, Jesse, seems I have a little squatter in my territory. I'll let you go, and see what I can do. Wish me luck."

"A what?" asked Jesse.

"A squatter—Aurora," Lillian clarified.

Aurora piped up loudly in self-defense, "I'm not squattin'—or listenin'. I'm sleepin'!"

The youngest three were finally asleep and Montreal was at the kitchen table hunkered down over his homework when Lillian explained Jesse's proposition. Estelle responded swiftly, "All's well for now. I know my babies and this one isn't coming for at least two weeks." She patted her belly as if talking to it. "I've been praying about an OB, so this is a great relief. I'll see him next week. I've got money tucked away for the birth, but if Dr. Franklin will see me pro bono beforehand, I'd be so grateful. Thank you; you're so kind." She sipped her tea with a quiet finality, then added, "And in regards to the job for Montreal? Love it. He'll be there Monday."

Lillian tried to quell her worry, but it welled up inside her until it spilled over. "But the cancer . . . I know you have breast cancer."

Estelle set her cup down and spread both hands protectively over her belly. "Yes, I do, and I'll deal with that next, *after* the baby." Lillian noticed Montreal's back stiffen as he shifted in his seat. Estelle had obviously seen it too and added for his benefit, "But I *am* glad you know, Lillian." Estelle took Lillian's hand and squeezed it reassuringly. Lillian stared down at their hands, not knowing how to respond.

On her way home, Lillian called Jesse back. "My nerves are fried, but Estelle won't budge tonight. She's gracious, but so stubborn."

"Like someone else I know," Jesse interrupted.

"What? That's more you than me! Anyway, can your mom reschedule an appointment for next week?"

Jesse answered, "Bummer she's waiting, but yeah, I'll get on it."

"In the meantime, you can brush up on the babysitting skills you've never acquired and I—well, right now I feel like I could run a marathon with all this bottled-up anxiety!" She thought about how Montreal would probably call her a human cap-snort.

On the cleared pine table at the front of the flower shop, Lillian smoothed out the blueprints of La Maison's banquet hall. She tapped her lips, thinking, *Of all people, Anthony Mullenix wants my flowers for his gala! Hotel tycoon, philanthropist, up-and-coming politician . . .* She loved his slogan written on the tiny brass plate on her bench: *Building community begins by valuing every individual.* Since his people had requested her services, she'd been dying to see the details of the setting. She placed an iron garden frog at each corner of the blueprint, then stood back to examine what she had to work with. "Hmm," she nodded to it as if in conversation. "Oh, yes . . . uh-huh."

The events coordinator, Dwyer Ignatius, set his hands wide apart across the other side of the table, and leaned forward. "Excuse me?"

Lillian looked up into his face and laughed. "Oh my, forgive me, Mr. Ignatius, I was lost in thought, you know. What an incredible place for a charity dinner! Of course, I realize it's Mr. Mullenix's own hotel. It's just such an honor for me professionally."

"Indeed. Hopefully you're up to the task." Dwyer lifted his brows in question.

"Of course, oh yes, of course!" Lillian retwisted a few strands of hair that had slipped from the bun at the base of her neck.

Dwyer pulled out his phone. "Mr. Mullenix keeps a tight schedule; be quick with your questions."

At Lillian's request, Dwyer had supplied the blueprints for the dining space and terrace for Anthony Mullenix's dinner event. She flipped back and forth between several colored pencils held in her apron pocket, highlighting areas as her eyes danced. It felt as if ideas came to life in her mind more quickly than she could word them.

She began shooting questions at him. "Walls, tapestries, paintings—what are they like? Or even the curtains or carpets? Give me an idea of what we've got going on in the color scheme. These windows and French doors, what's the view?" She pointed to each exit. "Are there evergreens in the garden? Christmas lights, hopefully white and not tacky blue or neon." She bit her lip, hastening on, hoping that comment had gone under the radar. "How many heaters on the patio? How about the fountain? I think it's inside the court area. Can I float votive candles in glass holders and strew petals in the water?"

"Ms. Bloom, as I stated to you on the phone, Mr. Mullenix has one preference: lavish. Since this is a charity event for the children of our community, no expense will be spared." He flung his hand in the air dismissively. "Just do whatever it is that you do."

"Well! I can do just about anything!" Lillian answered, indignant. "What kind of centerpiece bases does Mr. Mullenix prefer? Crystal, iron, glass, stone? Large and airy, tight and modern? Come now, you must have some direction for me."

Dwyer picked at something invisible between his teeth. "The direction is perfection. Encouraging his impressive array of guests to join his park project is imperative. Deliver something spectacular and he'll be satisfied." Dwyer placed a bulging envelope over the blueprints and stated, "He pays in cash."

"Well! How does Mr. Mullenix even know what I charge?"

"Believe me," Dwyer smiled cynically, "he knows people's price. Now, I assume we're finished here."

"Finished? Oh, my word! You've answered almost nothing. At least give me an idea of his taste." Dwyer straightened the lapels of his three-piece suit. Lillian noticed his simple wedding band was in stark contrast to his expensive gold watch.

"Please," insisted Lillian, "just one more question. Is it true Mr. Mullenix may be announcing his candidacy for mayor? Shall I insert a few vases containing red, white, and blue? Perhaps placed alongside some New York City history pamphlets at a table near the entrance? I mean—I know it's early and all—"

Dwyer cut her off. "Listen—what you need to know, I already told you. The purpose of this is purely philanthropic." He then strutted toward the door and almost knocked Jesse to the floor as she blasted into the shop, late as usual.

Jesse glared at him, but her angry eyes brightened immediately. "Iggy? What are you doing here . . . and in such fancy duds? You sure clean up nice! How's Maria and the kids?" She reached out to embrace him.

Dwyer stepped back. He shook his head ever so slightly. Stuttering, he shot a glance back at Lillian, who was very curious as to what was unfolding before her eyes. "Th-they're fine. This is business Jess, just business," and he shoved past her and out the door.

"What? Are you kiddin' me?" Jesse caught the door before it snapped shut. The face she turned back to Lillian was that of a pouty child. "That was totally weird—weird and mean! I totally know him—well, knew him, I guess. Some-thin's up." She walked to the back room to hang her coat and bag, shaking her head as she went. She stopped in her tracks to examine a plate on the counter. "Oh, that stench! What *is* this stuff?"

"Sorry, I forgot to get rid of it. It was supposed to be my high-protein break-fast," Lillian smiled. "Feel free to indulge. I thought I was spooning out canned salmon, but grabbed the wrong can—it's cat food!"

Jesse dropped her bag on the floor with such momentum that it burst open. She rushed past it to the bathroom where she threw up in the toilet.

Lillian frowned at the spilled contents of Jesse's purse. "Nice response—only don't let Mr. Blue Suede Shoes hear you. He might be offended."

Lillian knelt, half wondering if she needed a broom and a dustpan. She dumped wads of tissue directly into the wastebasket, then tucked a water bottle, a bag of chips (half-eaten), a candy bar, and a pack of mints back into the purse. She grabbed a lighter, an almost-empty pack of cigarettes (it too went right into the trash), a horoscope tracking notebook, and a star chart, and slipped them in as well. She picked up several lipsticks, a tiny tube of toothpaste, some blush, a few eyeliners, and a cracked mirror compact, dropping them into a gaping side pocket. Finally, she placed Jesse's overstuffed wallet into another side pouch. A broken zipper caught on the wallet's edge, however, and it burst open. "Seriously?" Lillian pressed the bulging wallet sides even and snapped it closed. A business card flipped out from the side.

Lillian drew in her breath as she read:

Abortion Appointment: Thursday 10:30 a.m.
Women's Healthcare Clinic

The toilet flushed. Hastily Lillian shoved the card into the wallet, along with the last random items back into Jesse's purse, then stood. She held up the purse, dangling it in front of her.

Jesse slipped out of the bathroom. "Aw, thanks for the cleanup on aisle one! I'm sure I've got a toothbrush in there somewhere." She dug around.

"You do," Lillian answered in a flat voice.

Jesse pulled it out, smiling weakly, "Thanks for that stinky beginning to my day. Ever tell you I get nauseated easily? But hey, then I fling my stuff and you clean it up. You always know how to help!"

"Hmm, not always." Lillian set the plate on the floor. Mr. Blue Suede Shoes sniffed it, then turned up his nose.

Jesse called from the bathroom, her voice muffled from brushing, "So, what was Dwyer Ignatius doing here?"

Lillian pulled her eyes away from Jesse's bag and the secret she'd seen. "He's Mr. Mullenix's events coordinator. Saturday night we'll be doing a charity banquet at La Maison Hotel. How do you know him?"

"Um—a friend—I, uh, well—yeah, he's a friend."

"Okay, so what does that mean? Friend or not?"

"Iggy was great. He cared. You know how some people see your crap inside and they don't leave or get all judgey? He was that." Jesse paused, nodding to herself while tying on her apron. She held her nose as she shook the cat food off the plate and into the trash can. "So gross . . . anyway, his wife was the same, plus they've got the cutest kids. Me and Iggy both worked for Mullenix. Guess he's been promoted. Fancy clothes, fancy attitude—looks like he's done somethin' right for the—Mr. Mullenix."

"Anthony Mullenix? The what?" asked Lillian.

"Huh? Oh nothing, we just call him some different nicknames, that's all . . ." Jesse's voice trailed off. "Iggy never used to care about being *in* with the crowd—not a pleaser, but so, so smart. He'd do the job, then, shoot outa there. Anyway, he acted bizarre today, *not* normal. That edge was really weird."

"Interesting, I didn't know you worked for Anthony Mullenix. He's a big deal. What was your job?"

Jesse stared blankly at Lillian. "Nothing, I mean nothin' important. You know, a dead-end job."

Lillian shrugged. "Well, this event for him is an excellent job for us, just a bit stressful with the time crunch."

Jesse nodded. "But you *do* know I took a personal day Thursday. It's on your calendar, but I'm just taking half a day, be back in the afternoon, no problem. " She averted her eyes, then paused to examine the envelope Dwyer had left on top of the blueprints as payment. "What's this?" She picked it up, then dropped it immediately, as if it stung her.

Lillian stared. "You're talking about Dwyer Ignatius acting strangely, now it's you. It's the cash envelope from Anthony Mullenix; your friend says that's how he always pays for services. Same as Sylvia, I was thinking—is that how he works?"

Jesse gave a visible shudder. "I—I have no idea."

30

Jesse

At the end of the day, Jesse barely made the bus home; its doors swished shut just as her feet hit the upper step.

"You're lucky," came the familiar gravelly voice of the driver.

"Lucky I've got you," came Jesse's standard answer.

The bus lurched forward. Jesse's insides churned like laundry in the quick cycle. She lowered herself onto the edge of the front seat. Out of the corner of her eye she caught sight of a man in a grungy trench coat at the back. It was Finch. Everyone around him leaned away, giving him ample room to air out. Jesse's hands flew to her lips; it was easy to feign sickness when she thought she really might be sick! She rose and motioned desperately for the door to open.

"Sheesh, Lucky Lady," griped the driver, but obliged.

Jesse leapt from the bus and over the curb, then turned back around and really did heave into a sewage grate. Through the bus window, she saw Finch hop up, but the bus lurched forward again before he could follow her.

The last person I'm talking to is Finch! She clutched her sick stomach as she watched the bus disappear down the road. "Get out of my life—all of you!" she fumed.

"Jesse, are you all right?" came a voice from the shadows. "Because I'm certainly glad to see you!" It was Sinclair, trying to get his footing on the slippery sidewalk. He was wringing his hat like a rag from a bucket.

"Seriously, Sinclair? Trying to give me a heart attack?" She leaned her head back. "Why're you glad? Need me to buy you a drink?"

"I beg your pardon? No, not at all. I'm mostly liberated from that habitual weakness. I've been waiting to tell you something, but you also appear distressed at the moment."

Jesse wiped her mouth with the back of her hand and shook off the sympathy that surprised her. "It's the flu, so you better stay away." She pushed her scarf up around her ears and set off at a quick pace.

"Wait," called Sinclair, "I just have one question. Did Lillian tell you someone's watching Montreal?"

"What?" Jesse spun around.

"I've noticed enough to be worried. I know things and someone is taking photos of the boy. And—well, nothing else, I just find it imperative that you know. You especially."

"Yeah, no kidding, I love that little dude." She tried to shake that fight-or-flight feeling welling up inside her. "But what's the deal with me *especially*?"

"Our first concern is for Montreal. I think you can find a way to help him."

"Hmm, sure I can, but not sure what you think you know about me. Whatever it is, you'd better forget it."

Jesse hurried away, slipping in and out of shadows. She continued to glance over her shoulder as she dialed a number on her phone.

"Jess, I can't talk to you now," came Iggy's stern voice on the other end of the line.

"Excuse me? Too bad, you've got a ton to explain! But my question first: the boy who works in our shop is being watched—photographed. What do you know about that?"

"I told you I can't—"

Jesse interrupted, "Listen to me! I was shocked to see you today, but you weren't so shocked to see me. Why? Are you spying on me?"

"No, the Boss picked the shop. He picked the florist, but I knew you'd be there. I was trying to get you to keep quiet."

"Why'd he pick my shop, my new boss? I thought you were getting out, but now you're his diva. A turncoat—is this about the judge?"

"No, this is something else. It's just handy for the Boss that you're there. He expects you'll inform him, obviously, but that's not why *I* was there."

"Inform him about what? I refuse. Lillian is a nice, normal person. I wouldn't hurt her, no way. And I owe him nothing, but tell me, is something happening to the boy? I'm freaking out here."

Only silence at first, then Iggy replied, "He's being watched. Montreal, Estelle, the other kids, it involves all of them, but it's complicated."

"You know his name? You know his family? Are you kiddin' me?"

"Jesse, steady, there's a lot to this."

"What's *this*? What do you know about them?" Jesse clutched her waist and forced down the bile coming up her throat. "How about an old guy named Sinclair? What do ya know about him?"

"Stop, Jesse—calm down!"

"You used to care about all the garbage Anthony does to people. What, you're part of it now?"

"Of course not."

Jesse's voice was shrill. "You've gotta tell me!"

"I will, just don't lose it! Breathe. Calm down. Are you calm?"

"Yes!" Jesse exhaled. "Yes."

"Just this now—you know the Boss is running for mayor of New York City. Remember his obsessive record-keeping? Now, he wants everything uploaded, but every potentially shady thing must be purged. My job was to make smooth transitions, filling in any missing dates. But he missed something—a single document—it's enough to bring him down."

"Don't do this! He's gonna kill you."

"No, I'll destroy him first! He's dug his own grave. I have the evidence; I put the document on a thumb drive. In a few days, when I've got everything in place, I'll tell you the rest. In the meantime, watch yourself and Montreal!"

"What do Montreal and his family have to do with Mullenix?"

"Everything," he said, and the phone clicked off.

On Wednesday morning, Jesse stood back, folding her arms and watching Lillian set an ornate urn, orange from rust, on the counter. Jesse tilted her head. "Hmm . . . running out of money, are we?"

Lillian laughed. "Don't you like my diamond in the rough? Found it on my Sunday thrift store outing. With a bit of elbow grease and a thin coat of paint over the iron, it'll make an excellent centerpiece for the banquet."

"At least you have an imagination!" Jesse had to tease, but couldn't wait to see the beauty Lillian would find in something everyone else deemed worthless.

"Want to help transform this aged beauty?"

"Yeah, I can do that," replied Jesse, bracing herself at the wave of nausea churning her insides. At only a few weeks along, she was amazed at how horrible she felt.

"Okay, but it's heavy, I'll help you—"

"Of course not. I'm assuming you meant in the back alley." Jesse knotted her apron and twisted her hair up. She dropped a wire brush in a bucket and hauled the urn up under her arm. With her elbow, she pressed the door handle down and sidled out. She yelled back before the screen door banged shut, "Got this, no problem!"

Jesse squatted near the trash cans to arrange her workspace by the spigot. She unwound a small section of hose, then realized she'd forgotten soap. She rose abruptly and plowed straight into Dwyer Ignatius, who appeared more familiar to her now, dressed in street clothes. She pushed him back, saying, "You've gotta be kiddin' me, Iggy. How is it that I don't see you for six months, then twice in a few days you almost knock me to the ground!" She started to smile, but one look at his face and she felt her smile melt away. She gasped.

Iggy's left eye was swollen shut and there was a deep gash along his chin. He pulled Jesse over to the wall and laid his hand lightly over her mouth. "Shh, Jesse, it didn't work—the other night, word leaked out. Boss' guys gave me the once-over but couldn't find the thumb drive. I told Maria to hide it somewhere at her work, then I put her and the kids on a plane. They're headed far away, where no one can find them. Once they've safely arrived, and I've worked out a few more things, I'm out. Only, if he finds I've lied . . . you know how it goes. I'm dead."

"What? Are you crazy? We'll get help!"

"No, Jess, I just need you to keep a couple of things for me now." He pressed a key hanging from a chain into Jesse's hand. "It belongs to a safe in a room at the Garden Hotel." With that, he slipped his wedding ring onto her finger, where it hung loosely. "And take this; it's proof you know me."

Jesse slipped the chain around her neck, then whispered emphatically, "What is going on Iggy? This is crazy. It's time for the police! Jensen's a good guy; he'll help."

"I know, but it's too risky." Iggy leaned against the brick wall with one arm outstretched and the other on his hip, as he stared down at the asphalt. "I don't think the Boss knows what I found yet, so I have a tiny window. Help by doing what I say."

"We can figure this out together," pleaded Jesse.

"No! I'm not risking your life too! Just keep these things safe until Nolan West finds you. He's from the Boss's inner circle; he'll find you. Give him the key and ring *when* he asks, not before that."

"When will he find me?"

"Soon."

"So, what do Montreal and Estelle have to do with this?" she asked, holding her hand to her chest.

Iggy checked his gold watch, stroked her cheek softly and backed away. "Time's up. You don't need to know any more. If we get this right, they'll be safe, and so will my family and you. That's my biggest concern now, the people."

"Wait, wait! So, I get this to the guy, Nolan, then what?"

"I'm not sure yet, but he'll figure out something. Just be careful. Eyes are everywhere." And he ducked out of sight down the alley.

Jesse dared not watch him go.

She closed her eyes and breathed in deeply. "God help him," she whispered.

"Yeah . . ." came a slurred voice amidst the haphazard array of trash cans. ". . . 'Spose if there's a God, he's right confused too."

Jesse jumped and whipped around. Her eyes widened in horror at the presence of an eavesdropper. Then they narrowed in a flare of temper. She leapt to action, heaving trash and canisters aside. "Who's there?"

A toothless woman, wearing feathers in her matted grey hair, grinned up at Jesse from a position of repose, slumped against a pile of trash bags. She held up an empty bottle and sighed. "I'd clink your glass if you had one and if mine wasn't empty." She peered into the bottle longingly. "Judith. You can call me Judith unless you're my best friend, then you wouldn't call me anymore. . . but you're too pretty to be her. She was pretty. I was too, then I lost everything and everyone left, but then I left too . . ."

Jesse shook herself free of the drunken monologue just in time to fling a trash lid down and vomit into the can.

Judith chuckled. "Had a bit too much, missy?"

Jesse wiped her mouth on her sleeve and glared at Judith. Then yet another interruption jolted her.

"Jesse!" came Sinclair's jovial voice as he appeared from around the corner and came into the alley. "We meet again. If I'd known your lovely self was joining our happy celebration, I'd have requested coffee for three!"

Now it was Judith's turn to glare. "Coffee? You told me you were going to get me a drink. Coffee ain't a drink. Coffee's coffee."

"Yes, but coffee's what you need," Sinclair looked from Judith to Jesse and back again. "And so nice that you two have met."

"We're celebrating what now?" asked Judith in an irritated voice.

"Sobriety! This is the first minute of the rest of your life." He settled into an overstuffed garbage bag as if it were a beanbag chair.

Jesse gathered her wits about her, looked around, then stooped down confidentially. "Listen, Sinclair, your friend here, Judith, she's been talking crazy, seeing things—said she saw some beat-up guy talking to me. Seriously, I'm scrubbing this urn and I've tons of work to do. Could you take her and her hallucinations somewhere else, please?"

Judith chuckled and elbowed Sinclair, who juggled the hot cups and barely missed spilling coffee all over her. "Yeah, hallucinate that gold band right there! Was that beat-up dude proposin'? I've seen some strange stuff on the street, but that was the worst proposal ever . . . didn't even get on a knee. Then the bum left—like they all do."

Jesse looked at the ring on her hand. Sinclair raised his eyebrows.

"Shut up! You're out of your mind!" Jesse blurted out as her voice rose. Judith and Sinclair stared. "Sorry . . . just leave, leave me alone," Jesse searched for some semblance of composure, then grabbed the urn and fled back into the shop.

She startled Lillian, who was working at the sink. "Are you all right?" said Lillian. "Scared me to death!" On the counter beside her sat a sea of pedestal vases.

"No, I'm not. What's the deal with Sinclair's snooping?" She set the urn down on the counter with a thump, dangerously close to the delicate containers, and began to pace in the narrow space. "And now he's on some mission to rescue every drunkard in New York City! He's all rosy and righteous—like his drunken past doesn't exist anymore." She stopped to face Lillian. "Well, it's gonna bite him back. He'll take that drink, just watch, and everything'll come crashing down. Mistakes never disappear." Jesse clenched her hands into fists. "They just grow deep in you and dog you night and day. Life's cruel . . . and he's gonna fail. Just like the rest of us!" Jesse swiped the urn from the counter and stomped over to the back door.

Lillian followed on her heels. "What are you doing?"

"My job! And if they're still out there, I'll hose 'em down!"

Lillian grabbed at the urn. "You'll do no such thing; calm down!"

The fragile handle of the antique broke off into Lillian's hand. Jesse stopped her tirade and stared at the handle. She wilted as she spoke through her own lament. "Oh, Lillian . . . I'm such a maniac. I'm so sorry."

Lillian set the urn down and met Jesse's eyes with kindness.

"So, I must tell you, I know what's going on and why you're so pent up with anxiety. I was trying to find a way to say this gently. A card slipped out of your purse Monday and, well, I know you've got an abortion planned for tomorrow morning. Talk to me about this, please."

Jesse felt the color drain from her face. She grabbed her coat and bag, took three angry steps toward the front door, then turned back around. "Frankly, this is none a' your business!"

She stalked out the door, hesitated, then swung around and came right back in. "Lillian, this all makes me crazy! It's—it's been a horrible day, I know you mean well, but I can take care of myself. I'll be here tomorrow and I'll be fine. I always am." And with that, she walked resolutely out the door holding the strap of her handbag over her shoulder, with her left arm swinging at her side.

31

Lillian

The day slogged by, dragging the minutes along. Lillian felt such relief when the wall clock finally chimed four. Montreal would soon enter the shop with his familiar whistle and some vivid story about someone he'd noticed on the bus. She smiled in anticipation as she set the broom and dustpan by the door.

Something shiny caught her eye. She bent down to find a thin gold band. Lillian examined it in her palm then held it up to the light. The worn inscription inside read *Maria* along with a date.

The bell jingled. Lillian quickly tucked the ring into the back pocket of her jeans.

Montreal's grin brightened the room. "Have I got a story for you!" he announced as he strode over to pick up Mr. Blue Suede Shoes, who immediately began to purr. "So, there was this toddler eating a messy banana in the second seat, and this stern woman, wearing a white coat in the front seat. She held a tiny poodle on her lap and the poodle was very hungry . . ."

32

Stuart

Name. Stoo-ert : French form derived from Old English and Middle English, meaning "household guardian"

I t was dusk on Wednesday. Inside A Cup of Grace, Stuart's new part-time employee, Kevin, accidentally left the steam wand on after removing the pitcher from under it. Scalding milk sprayed everywhere. He yelled as he jumped back from the machine. The startled faces of customers turned toward him.

"I'm fine," he stammered, red-faced.

Stuart seized the moment. "Yes, everyone please meet our new assistant, Kevin. And he's doing a *fine* job." He gave Kevin a friendly shoulder punch.

Muffled chatter resumed as Kevin dropped to his knees to wipe the floor. Stuart crouched beside him. "Dude, discretion is key. Mistakes happen—it's what you do next that matters. Screaming—uh, no—don't love when customers get alarmed. *Capisce?* You're getting it; don't sweat the small stuff." Stuart's eyes swept the room. "Speaking of small stuff . . ."

Just then Serenity appeared in the doorway of the stairwell at the back of the shop. She gave Stuart a one-bark explanation. He excused himself and bounded up the steps, two at a time. Upstairs in the apartment he followed Serenity through the living room, down the hallway, and into Hope's bedroom.

A whimper sounded from under the bed. Stuart sank to the floor to find Hope huddled on the rug with scissors beside her. The damage was done. Little clumps of reddish fur from Serenity's luxurious tail mixed with tight, black curls lay strewn across the rug. The dog placed her head on her paws, looking guilty, as if she could've intervened. Hope had been out of Stuart's sight for only a short time.

Stuart crawled into the tight space as Hope wrapped her hands around her shorn head. "Hope! Man! What were you thinking! D—" He stopped himself. In these uncharted waters, he mustn't capsize her fragile little lifeboat. She hadn't run away; she'd just run to her bedroom. He counted to ten in his head and then, with a calmer tone, began again. "Uh . . . let's see . . . I'm sure you're sorry you cut your hair and Serenity's fur . . . and it's gonna be all right and I'm sorry I left the scissors out. Okay? Are we both good?"

Hope lay still for several seconds, then reached out and touched his hand. He closed his over hers. It was the first time she'd touched him on her own.

Just then, Stuart's phone vibrated from where it lay on the floor. Julius' frozen face appeared on the screen; Stuart grabbed it.

"Hey, I'm sorry I haven't texted or called you back . . ." came Julius' aching voice.

"I know. Come home—your mom told me you were at the beach—*this* is your home." Stuart whispered insistently, keeping his hand folded over Hope's.

"I can't do it; I don't know how. Hope doesn't need me; you don't need me."

"Julius, did you bring your meds?"

"I don't need them anymore," came Julius' monotone answer.

Stuart wiped at his sweaty brow. "Julius. Get in a car and drive home. Grab the keys right now; I'll stay on the phone. We can talk about what's going on in your head when you get here. We'll figure it out here."

"You have no idea."

Hope pulled her hand away as Stuart tried to steady his voice. "I do; I know what you're thinking—don't do anything stupid—just get in the car. Grab your coat; grab your keys. I'm right here, Hope's here, we love you."

"I can't. I just can't—" Julius hung up.

"Julius! *Julius!*"

Hope crawled out of her hiding place and stared up at Stuart. "Sorry, Babe, not meant for your ears—none of that was."

Frantically Stuart texted Kevin:

close now

clean and lock up

I gotta go

He then texted Julius. He could feel the sweat dripping down his face and neck.

sit tight

on our way

take out fish crackers and peanut butter

I'll see what Hope wants :-)

stop pacing

play your grand

see u soon

An hour and a half later, Stuart veered off the highway at the neon lights of Mel's Truck Stop. The car needed gas and they could use some fuel themselves. Hope's constant fussing and Houdini-like escape attempts from her car seat had left his nerves shattered.

In the line, Hope wriggled as Stuart eyed the menu. A little boy stood behind them, between his parents, and said to Hope, "That's not your daddy. You're not the same. He's white and you're black!"

Stuart was in the midst of ordering as Hope began pulling off her shoes and socks. Sweating profusely, he scrambled to stuff her purple socks into the sparkly white tennis shoes he held in one hand as he fumbled with his billfold and her in the other.

Hope stuck her bare feet straight into the little boy's face and said, pointing to the pink skin on the soles of her feet, "Same!" Then she pointed to Stuart and said, "Daddy!"

33

Julius

Julius barely noticed how dark it had become on the shore of his family's beach house. He huddled on the damp ground just out of reach of the lapping waves. They thumped in hypnotic rhythm, forward then back, forward then back.

A soft light appeared in the distance, swinging steadily as it neared. It was a lantern held by his sister, Gwyneth, who also carried blankets. *Of course she brought blankets*, he thought. The twelve years between them allotted her extra motherly clout. The lantern light spread out in a circular patch as she sank down beside him.

"Hey. Mom called. Said you've been here a week. What's up?"

"I'm all right—same old, same old," Julius answered dully.

"Really? Oh good, because I thought something was actually wrong. That's reassuring—same old—sounds just like you." She forced a laugh.

"I'm fine. Leave please," he muttered.

"Since when do I follow orders? Especially from one of the few people I love, who actually loves me."

Julius wiped his tears with the back of his hand. "I want to be alone."

"Too bad, Mr. Drama. I'm staying because I love you."

LEAVE! LEAVE ME ALONE! he screamed inside.

"A clue here?" She thrust out her hands. "Did Stuart ask you to leave?"

Julius shook his head. "Never! It was me. Remember, people are *disposable* to me."

Gwyneth sighed and looked out across the water. "You got me. Once, ten years ago, I said that, but you've proved me wrong a hundred times since."

"No. You were right. Hope hates me, stares at me accusingly, like she knows my past. And Stuart? Angry all the time. I can't do anything right. They treat me like I'm worthless. Even the social worker demands more of me than anyone, as if the whole adoption rides on me! Why? Why keep trying? I'm done."

"Julius, children are hard; they feel our stress. Stuart can be rough, no doubt, but with Hope, *you* have to soften *her* heart, not the other way around. Stay the course; it'll get better."

"I don't know how to love people; no one ever gets me." Julius buried his head in his arms. All this talking, yet he'd already decided what to do.

"That's not true. Relationships are painful. You can't expect everything to make sense. You've loved me through my pain of three—four—failed marriages."

"Four?" Julius looked up from his hands to see his sister's lips quiver. "Oh Gwennie, not Hugh?" Julius fought the urge to hug her. He'd always tried to comfort her, ever since they were kids. Yet she rarely shed a tear, no matter how much she hurt.

"He left me, but I'm not here for your help, believe it or not; I'm here for *you*. Besides, I'll find another loser." She tried again to laugh.

"Gwennie, sorry, but as far as losers go, that's me. I have a record, starting with Lucy."

"Lucy?" Gwyneth screwed up her face. "Isn't this about Stuart and Hope, in real time?"

"Of course, but it started with Lucy, ten years ago, then business after business, now adoption—on and on. No one gets me. I give everything that's in me, then I have to save myself. But I'm so done with that."

"Please! Facts here. When you stay for the time necessary, you leave good things thriving! Theater—fabulous and still running. Photography for troubled teens, Philanthropic Investment of the Year—"

"Exactly, every single one is fine, and doesn't need me now. What is it worth to stay the course at all?" Julius interrupted, wishing to get away, but worried she'd see the gun.

"That's what entrepreneurs do! They work themselves out of a job—that's savvy. And you left everything *thriving*! But with Stuart and Hope, stay, please stay. This is your time to stay the course!" Gwyneth shook her head. "*You* have no evidence against *you* being worthless and there's nothing to support a necessity to go. And social workers must be suspicious, it's part of their job! Just be honest with her."

"I complicate people's lives, Gwennie. It all started with Lucy—"

Gwyneth swore. "Lucy again? She's gone—long gone. This is about Stuart and Hope—stay focused."

Julius tried to cling to his argument. "It's like Dad always said; I can't stick to anything. I'm worthless. I tried; he just never saw me." Julius felt the gun; it was cold, pressing against his side.

"Your worth is beyond measure. Forget Dad; my million dollars of therapy taught me that long ago. Truth is, you did sometimes leave in the middle of a project. That's my point, you can't leave now. The times you stayed, things and people were better because of you."

"You succeed—I fail."

"You're making zero sense. Is the coffee shop nothing? Your seed money into Stuart's dream—hottest espresso bar in Stratford. Stuart couldn't have done that without you."

"It's just money, Gwennie. It's not love."

Gwyneth punched his shoulder. "You make me crazy! My success has left me one thing—*alone*—but you have Stuart and Hope. Nurture them, press in, don't give up. And with Lucy, if you're so desperate about her, then find her; make the past right." Julius' head throbbed. He rubbed his temples. Gwyneth paused, "Oh, you already tried?"

"I'm so confused."

"Welcome to humanity. That's why we need each other. Now listen to me—reality here—as a lawyer, I say you have no right to take your own life."

Julius stared down at the light on the sand, as hot tears slipped down his cheeks. "You can't tell me that professionally; there's no law about that, Gwennie."

"Too bad! There should be!" She grabbed his hands. "You have no right to take your own life because you'd be taking it from me—me and Mom, Stuart, Hope, your neighbors, all of us. And you think the pain would be gone? Maybe *you* wouldn't feel anything in death, but we would, and the pain of losing you would kill us—a slow, lifelong death by anguish."

He looked into her face and saw tears; he blinked back his own. She put her hands up to his face.

"Keep loving people; don't give up. Have you made mistakes? Yes, you're human just like everybody else! Yet, I'm learning how to love through you. You have a depth of love I'm trying to understand. I need you—so do Stuart and Hope!" Gwyneth picked up the lantern and pulled at his hand. "Now come on. All this yapping has made me cry and I don't do that. Besides, I'm starved. I bought chowder from The Lighthouse."

Julius wasn't ready to go, but suddenly he wasn't so sure what to do either. He'd stay to decide—alone.

34

Gwyneth

Name. Gwi-nuhth : Welsh origin, meaning "blessed, happy"

O n a table next to a blazing fireplace, Gwyneth set bowls of creamy chowder with sides of thick-crusted sourdough bread. There was even Julius' favorite: English hard cider.

She checked the clock again, then sat down at the grand piano. A stack of old sheet music lay piled in a basket, all Julius' pieces. She plunked out an old melody, one she used to love, something about sunshine.

The front door opened slowly.

Gwyneth let out a sigh of relief. "Finally, I was really starting to worry again. Please play this for us, play this one or we can eat first, then you play, since the chowder's getting cold—"

Stuart's weary face appeared around the door, with Hope asleep on his shoulder. "Chowder? Definitely goes with fish crackers."

Gwyneth's eyebrows went up. "Oh, Stuart, it's you . . . I had no idea you were—"

But she never finished her sentence. From out beyond the massive glass doors, along the deck, there was no mistaking the sound. A single gunshot broke through the blustery night.

35

Lillian

A gust of blustery wind moved down Stratford Lane past A Cup of Grace, then up against Lillian's window. Lillian neither heard nor saw the real storm pass.

She was wandering in a field in her dream—a field of ribbon-like rows of silver-green tulips. At first the rays of sun stretched over the field, but then the rumbling began, always the same. She braced herself. The ground underfoot began to shift as the sky darkened. Lillian fell to her knees as the tulips erupted out of the dirt and withered against hardening soil. The trenches between the rows disappeared as the parched earth flattened out to become asphalt. The mounds of dead tulips melted into double yellow lines. Four shadowy figures appeared, walking rhythmically in her direction along the center of the road. As Lillian's heart raced, their steps beat to the pounding in her chest, ever quickening. One of them held a baby.

Thud.

Lillian woke face down on the floor beside her bed. She lifted her aching head, then dragged her body up to a sitting position. She let out a long sigh and rubbed her aching neck and shoulders.

I thought I was free of this. Why again? she asked herself, pushing aside a mess of morning curls.

Her room seemed too bright; perhaps it was just the throbbing of her head. She glanced at her nightstand where a sleeping pill package lay open. *That's right, how many did I take? One, two? Two—two pills at 3:00 a.m.* Thirsty and groggy, she reached for her water glass and bumped her cell phone. The screen lit up.

What! She sprang to her feet. The numbers announced the unthinkable: it was 10:00 a.m. Thursday.

"Jesse!" she cried.

36

Jesse

At 10:37 a.m., Jesse stepped through the automatic doors of the Women's Healthcare Clinic. Subtle strains of music floated through the expansive, pale-green room filled with soft yellow chairs set around coffee tables. Behind the reception desk, a pleasant woman invited Jesse to sign in and help herself to some water. "I'll be with you very soon," she added, motioning Jesse to sit.

Jesse lowered herself onto the edge of a chair, trying to keep from jostling her nauseated stomach. She didn't know if it was morning sickness or something else. Her hands were sweaty and she felt faint. Two sentences played in her head: *This is my decision. This is the best solution.*

Dry heaves welled up in Jesse's throat. Her hands flew to her mouth and, with her chin down, she rushed to the restroom. A man caught her elbow just in time to direct her away from the swinging door through which a woman was exiting. Jesse dashed inside the restroom, barely avoiding a collision.

When she returned, the man had settled into a chair beside her things. "Kept an eye on your valuables while you were . . . busy," he explained.

"Thanks," she answered, concentrating on the magazine selection.

He reached for the magazine farthest from him, and in so doing revealed a loosely fitted gold watch—a watch she remembered. She opened her mouth in shock, but he glanced up at the camera in the corner of the room. His hair was plaited in braids that fell to his shoulders, and he wore a suede car coat. His deep cocoa eyes, almost the same color as his skin, were intense, but not unkind.

"Who are you and why do you have Iggy's watch?" she whispered, clenching her teeth both from agitation and nausea.

"The watch is actually mine—it's my proof from Iggy to you," the man whispered. "I'm Nolan West." He did not extend his hand or even look up from the magazine he was thumbing through. Jesse sat down beside him.

"The Boss has me watching you—making sure you follow through with this appointment—but I'm really here for Iggy."

"I don't care what the Boss thinks or does. This is my body, my decision."

Nolan gave her a knowing look. "Right. And all the Boss's guys are just here to make sure you're making your *own* decision. Got it." He nodded toward the main clinic entrance. "That door's guarded, side one's guarded, but at the end of the hall, inside the exam area, there's a way out. No guard—just sayin'."

Jesse's head swam.

"You think I'm being forced and need a way to escape? I choose this. You're a snitch for Anthony, that's all!"

Nolan's face hardened. "No, we're a team—me, you, and Iggy. The Boss thinks I'm here 'cause he sent me; it's a perfect cover for us to meet. You gotta trust me." Nolan laid the magazine down and checked his phone. "I'll find you again, to get what Iggy gave you." His last whisper was barely audible. He looked up. "Ready? The nurse is coming. Not my business, but if you're not sure, don't—it's your life, yeah, but it's your baby's life too."

With crisp steps, the receptionist approached Jesse.

"Please come with me."

Jesse stood. She looked back at Nolan, but he ignored her, feigning fascination with a headline on the newspaper.

Suddenly, a commotion drew all eyes to the front. A frantic woman rushed into the clinic. By pressing against the automatic doors, she'd stumbled forward. Falling headlong in her own momentum, she bumped into a potted bamboo. It wobbled on its stand. Dripping sweat and out of breath, the woman steadied the pot, then pushed back her mass of tangled blonde hair in search of someone. Pinpointing her target, she called out.

"Jesse!"

It was Lillian.

"I'm so sorry, I'm late! It was ridiculous; the bus broke down. I ran all the way from Hunt!"

Jesse could hardly think. This frazzled woman breathing hard beside her was somehow Lillian. All eyes were now fixed on the two women. In a hushed tone, Jesse begged, "Lillian, I don't know what's wrong with you, but please, just go . . . this is hard enough without you here."

"I had to catch you before you went in. Please don't do this!" Lillian panted.

The receptionist stiffened. "Ma'am, if you'd excuse us." She took Jesse by the arm and steered her toward a technician, who stood in the passage leading to the exam rooms.

Lillian maneuvered herself between him and Jesse.

"Jess, I'm sorry to surprise you, but I overslept! I just needed to tell you—I, I did this at your age. My pregnancy was unplanned, and I thought it was the right thing to do. But I've regretted aborting my baby my whole life. This is your *baby*. Don't do what I did!" Jesse watched the receptionist raise her hand, to motion the security guard at the door. Lillian continued pleading, unaffected. "Jess, I'll help you. Please don't do this; it'll break your heart. It's your baby."

Jesse backed up. "Stop talking. This is my decision. This is the best solution." She bumped into the receptionist, whose eyes had become stormy.

A guard approached and took Lillian by the arm.

"Ma'am, I'm escorting you out."

Lillian twisted her arm free and inadvertently whacked the clipboard out of the technician's hand. The metal clip at the top of the board flew off and hit the guard in the eye. He yelled and gripped Lillian's hand tighter.

"Nice work, woman—assaulting a security guard and disruptin' the peace—now you're in for it. The police'll take it from here."

Lillian fought him answering, "I don't care! We're talking about a life here!"

Jesse covered her face and began to sway. Iggy, Nolan, Lillian, the baby—her baby—the Boss, nothing made sense except the deep pleading in her soul to flee.

The receptionist steadied Jesse, then directed the guard, "Get that woman out of here."

Lillian searched Jesse's face. "I want what's best for you, Jess. Whatever you decide, I'll support you."

Jesse faltered, "I'm so stupid. It's my—"

"Mistake, yes, but we'll fix that," the receptionist interjected.

"It—it doesn't matter. Nothing matters; it's my mistake."

The guard pointed to one of the exits, then fumed at Lillian, "You are coming outside with me. We're gonna wait for the police. They're always circlin', waitin' for disrupters like you."

"You matter," Lillian whispered to Jesse, "you matter very much to me and you're not stupid." The guard tried to get between them as he corralled Lillian toward the door. She called back in a clear voice, "No life is a mistake!"

The receptionist pulled a bottle of orange juice from the fridge and gave Jesse a sip before leading her, once again, to the technician. Jesse turned just in time to lock eyes with Nolan West, whose affirming look gave her courage.

37

Julius

From the beach house breakfast nook, Stuart had been staring out the window at the rippling waves. Gwyneth was passing Cheerios to Hope, who ate them one by one from under the table.

Stuart stood up, making a loud scraping noise with his chair as he pushed it back from the table. Perched on a stool at the counter sat Julius, an empty coffee cup in his hand.

Stuart turned to Julius. "What did you say earlier? Courage?"

Hope popped her head up to see what the ruckus was. Gwyneth leaned down. "Hey, sweetie, let's put on our boots and go build a sandcastle; morning fog's all clear." Hope clapped her hands and ran for the door. Gwyneth grabbed their coats and swept the little one outside.

Julius reexamined his empty cup. "Yes, courage. I've been trying to explain it all morning; I wish you'd try to understand. I didn't have the word last night, but today, I do—it's courage."

"Oh, let me *try* again to understand! You were going to commit suicide—didn't—shot into the sky anyway to show *courage*. Right?" Stuart's voice began to escalate. "Because scaring us all to *death* has something to do with courage?" He shoved the chair back against the table and began clearing plates.

Julius half expected Stuart to aim a plate at him as he answered, "I told you, there's something complicated in my past that you don't know, but you're too angry to hear it now."

Stuart dumped the plates into the sink with a loud crash. One of them broke. "Why should I care? The past is the past. You forget it and move on."

"Please, just calm down! You may be able to forget and move on, but I can't. I won't. But now I choose you and Hope, and making my past right." Julius approached cautiously. "And I want to say I'm sorry. Sorry I didn't believe you needed me." Tears welled up in Julius' eyes.

Stuart turned away clenching his fists. "Stop crying!" he yelled. "I don't care if you're sorry!" He grabbed the one remaining plate from the table and threw it into the sink, shattering it completely. "I thought you'd done it—thought you were dead. I thought you'd abandoned us. How could you do something so horrible, then think you could just explain it away?"

Julius ran his fingers through his hair, struggling for words that felt just out of reach. "It was wrong. What else can I say? There at the brink I decided to live—to face things—even when it'd be easier to just disappear." He searched Stuart's face. "When I heard our car drive up, I didn't want to leave anymore, so I shot into the darkness—I don't know how else to say it, but I was choosing courage. I was choosing to stay." Julius reached his hands out to Stuart.

Stuart just stood there. "You're so strange, but . . . I accept your apology." He threw the towel onto the counter. It slid across it then landed on the floor. "And I believe you. Just *never* do that again, or anything to separate us. I just can't handle it—I can't and I won't!"

Julius let his arms fall to his sides, deeply stung by Stuart's rejection. "Yes, I know. I'll do my best."

38

Lars

With determined steps, Lars pressed through the tall weeds and thick brush at the back of the church property toward a tarp-covered heap. He needed transportation and Barbara knew where to find it. In the early nineties, an elderly widower had gifted a vehicle to the parish. Lars had heard that the only remnant of the 1972 Ford's former glory was its name; otherwise, it belonged in a scrapyard. He was about to find out if this was true. He lifted the tarp and let out a low whistle. "A Gran Torino."

To his initial relief, turning the ignition sparked the muscle car to life, but only to sputter and fume for a brief moment. Yet, where horsepower was lacking, prayer power was not. Lars popped the hood and bent his head over the engine.

"God, please give me a way to help Lillian, in this car or by some other means. She needs me! Amen."

With his head still bowed, Lars opened his eyes. There in the dirt stood two sets of well-worn work boots and a gas can. He looked up to find two sturdy men in coveralls. One of them stretched out his hand. "Miguel Ortega, and my brother, Gabriel, here to work!"

Lars shook their hands heartily. "No way—and named after angels? Are you mechanics?"

Miguel said a few words to Gabriel in Spanish, who flipped his hat around and dug right into the engine. He too whistled the sacred words, "Gran Torino."

Miguel nodded his head. "We love cars, so yes, we're mechanics, but building renovation is our specialty. We stopped by the church to find work and Mrs. Barbara said we'd find you here, and that you might need this." He held up the gas can. "Do you think you have some building work for us too?" He motioned to the roof, void of shingles in many spots. Lars assumed he'd also seen the dilapidated windows warped from water damage, the crumbling stone walls, and, of course, the overgrown grounds. The church was in a sorry state.

"Wow, what an opportune time to stumble across our church looking for work. Yes, the church is a wreck! But right now, I just need to fix this car," replied Lars.

Within ten minutes, Gabriel clamped the hood shut, wiped his hands on the rag in his pocket, and motioned for Lars to get into the driver's seat. With a burst of exhaust, the engine roared to life as Lars started it up.

"Thanks so much! You both came at the perfect time!" he exclaimed. "Walk the grounds while I'm gone; Barbara will be delighted to show you everything on our list. Then come up with an estimate for repairs—we'll talk soon."

"Thanks, Father, we will . . .and we can restore the Gran Torino too," said Miguel as he backed away.

"Wonderful!" Lars yelled over the engine, as he threw the sports car into gear, leaving a trail of black smoke behind him.

39

Lillian

"You have a visitor, Ms. Bloom," came the voice of a female guard. The cell lock clicked open and the door grated along the track.

Lillian followed the guard and entered a blank room. She sat down in an aluminum chair and exhaled, seemingly for the first time in hours. She expected to see Lars enter from the outer door. She didn't know why, but he was the first person she'd called after her arrest. The anticipation of his peaceful presence, even here in the police station, filled her with hope. But it wasn't Lars who entered the room.

"Why, hello, Ms. Bloom. What a pleasure to finally meet you. Am I not who you'd hoped to see?"

"No, not at all . . . but, hello!" Lillian leapt to her feet. Before her stood Anthony Mullenix. She'd seen his picture plastered everywhere of late—in newspapers, magazines, in every corner the eyes of the city looked. It was as if she'd already met him. And yet, in real life, towering well over six feet, he was beautiful, a word she'd never used to describe a man. His eyes were cinnamon brown, framed by dark lashes and expressive brows. They were full of soul—soul and something else. He had dimples in his cheeks, accentuating his wide mouth and easy smile. Was he Hispanic, Middle Eastern, Polynesian, black? Was he thirty, forty, fifty? He appeared to be a man who could slip through the doors of any company or the borders of any country and call it his own. Add his chiseled features to his charisma and confidence, and Lillian wished that back in her cell she had prepared herself to meet such a man.

"Hello, Mr. Mullenix. I'm glad—glad and privileged to make your acquaintance." She reached out in greeting. He stared at her hand indifferently, leaving it hanging in mid-air. She quickly withdrew it as her cheeks flushed. "I—I imagine you're concerned about your party Saturday evening, but I can assure you—"

"I'm here because I always know the chessboard and who's in the game." He spoke as if she were his confidante, then motioned for her to sit, which she did promptly. "But you imagine correctly as well. You're a floral master and a genius in design, a wonder to confound the ordinary mind." He sat down opposite her, tipped his chair back, and motioned to the guard. "Get us something from the vending machine." He flipped her a ten-dollar bill.

Lillian marveled as the guard hurried to obey. She tried to get her attention, blurting out, "Oh no, oh gosh, you don't have to serve us, that's not your job." But the guard ignored her. Lillian turned to Anthony and said, "It's illegal for her to leave us alone."

Anthony placed his hands flat on the table and rose to look down on her. "We only just met, and you think it's dangerous for us to be alone? Or is it just that you're so wise to the world?" Lillian scooted her chair back, but he closed the gap between them as he came alongside the table. "Not your first offense? Or is it just something you made up to impress me?"

Lillian felt a shiver run up her spine. "My only offense. And no," she swallowed hard, "I'm not trying to impress you. I'm a professional woman."

"I'm sure you are." He settled back into his chair and placed his leg over his knee in a relaxed pose. His linen shirt revealed the silhouette of his muscular frame. "Well, you'll also be glad to know, as a professional, that I've posted bail and cleared your name, as well as this entire incident from the record. Neither your reputation nor your business will suffer. I've saved you."

Lillian digested Anthony's words in silence.

The guard reentered. On her wrist hung a bag with Lillian's clothes and in her hands she held a tray. On it were the drinks and a small lockbox of Lillian's personal items. Anthony winked at the guard, then turned his attention to Lillian as he held up their sodas. "Cheers to you and sweet freedom! Now grab your things and change; we're going back to your shop."

Lillian opened the box and found her purse, watch, and earrings. She hesitated as she picked up the gold engraved ring. She must've forgotten it in her jeans, after finding it on the floor of the shop. The ring had stayed buried in her pocket even through the wash. She picked it up and said, "I think this belongs—" but stopped herself when she noted Anthony staring intently at the ring.

He reached his open palm across the table. "What's that you have there?"

"—to my . . . friend, my friend—I must get it back to him—her—them." Lillian snapped her hand shut. "I'll change and be right back!" She jumped up to follow the guard to the locker room. When she rejoined Anthony, the ring was safely hidden away in her pocket.

Anthony strutted through the door ahead of Lillian, then led her toward the exit through the main office and lobby. The people in the room seemed frozen in awkward silence, averting their eyes as Anthony and Lillian passed.

Anthony directed Lillian to his black Corvette parked on the street. She climbed in and Anthony shut the passenger door. Just then, the Gran Torino roared up to the curb with Lars in the driver's seat. Through the tinted glass, Lillian saw Anthony give the car a sideways glance and hesitate in his smooth stride. His chiseled jaw appeared to have a sharper edge as he slipped into his driver's side without acknowledging Lars. Lillian tried to open her door. "That's my ride, actually. He's come for me—thanks, anyway." The door wouldn't budge.

"Your ride? I paid your bail. I'm your ride." Anthony shoved the car into gear and they sped away.

The black Corvette purred up to the front of Lillian Rose Blooms. Anthony pressed a button that unlocked Lillian's door. "Voila!" he mocked as he pocketed his keys and sauntered into the shop, with Lillian close at his heels.

Why is the shop door open? she thought.

To Lillian's surprise, there was Jesse, working steadily, placing long branches into a new silver urn. Twelve pedestal vases lined the counter beside her. Newly delivered assortments of blooms in deep, rich hues stood in large buckets on the floor. Jesse looked pale as she peered up from her work.

"The appointment went well, I take it?" Anthony asked, pulling a cigarette pack from the pocket of his blazer, lighting two and handing one to Jesse.

"Why wouldn't it?" countered Jesse, flipping her hair from her face and slipping the cigarette between her fingers.

Lillian eyed the exchange.

Jesse stared coolly into Anthony's face and placed one hand on her hip as she drew a deep drag. The embers grew bright at the tip of her cigarette. She examined them, then flicked some ashes to the floor. There was silence for a moment as Jesse and Anthony locked eyes. "Anthony, would you like to watch us work?"

"Tempting, but I think I'll pass." He cupped Jesse's face roughly under her chin and raised his eyebrows to Lillian. "Keep an eye on this wild thing. And by the way, Ms. Bloom, though there's no need to worry about your arrest records. I've got my own copy, for safekeeping—I keep a copy of everything. Now you girls kiss and make up. See you tomorrow."

As soon as the door shut behind Anthony, Jesse stomped out the cigarette, smashing it to smithereens as if it were a deadly spider. She shook out a shiver, saying, "Ugh!"

Suddenly her eyes welled up with tears. "I tried to get to you, but he beat me to it—I saw his car at the jail, knew what he was gonna do. I've got you all involved. I made a horrible mess and you were right—right all along." Jesse hugged Lillian, clinging tightly as she spoke. "I didn't do it; I couldn't. I kept my baby."

40

Julius

Early on Friday morning, Julius blew into his icy hands as he walked out of the coffee shop. The bitter cold of the beach mornings seemed to have found its way to Stratford Lane. Julius stepped into a circle of light cast by the flower shop lamppost and paused, wondering if Lillian was awake. Warm light from above drew his eyes up to her living room window. He picked up a pebble and tossed it against the slim side pane.

Lillian appeared looking surprised, and then happy when she saw that it was him. "Just a minute," she mouthed as she strained to crank open the window.

"Julius," she called softly through the screenless frame, "you're back!"

"I am." He forced a smile. "But sorry for throwing a rock at your window—bad form."

"Seriously, I'd be mad if I hadn't been so worried; you just disappeared. We've all been worried."

"I did disappear. Bad form again, so sorry. Feel like talking? How've you been?"

Lillian sighed. "So, you don't know? I'm fine . . . now." She leaned over the narrow sill and swept snow from a branch of the Norway maple. "Yes, I have time to chat. Do you have something new to celebrate, like on our last breakfast rendezvous?"

"Celebrate? You mean like courage and homecoming?" He immediately regretted his odd response.

Lillian's eyes widened. "You *do* know about me being in jail?"

"Well, I, uh . . . did you say jail?"

"Oh gosh, did Jesse tell you yesterday? I didn't realize you were even home or I would have stopped for coffee." Lillian smiled weakly. "Oh well, you always know things. I guess I'm glad I don't have to tell you myself."

Julius pushed the hair back from his forehead. "Exactly, so, uh, you're fine—obviously out of jail and Jesse . . ."

"Fine, yes, I mean she's nauseated, which I've heard is good in pregnancy, good for the baby."

"So . . . uh, if you want to tell me about the jail situation, and Jesse, that'd be great." Julius lied, wishing he could freely say his true thoughts, which ran along the lines of, *No, please no, I can't even process my own head, much less this right now.*

Lillian shrugged; even in the dim light he could see her flushed cheeks. "Nothing to tell, I just overreacted, but—apart from the jail thing—it was wonderful in the end and more like something you'd do. I stood up for a vulnerable life. Maybe I'm more like you than I thought."

Julius stiffened, suddenly finding himself in a conversation he didn't want. Everyone seemed to see him as something he was not. "Okay, well, good then, everybody's good. I'll just keep walking." Julius pulled up the collar of his coat and shoved his hands in his pockets. "Hey, that window looks precarious. I'll get you a new screen and fix it for you."

"It's fine; I rarely open it. Now, if Montreal saw it, I imagine he'd have some delightful tree-climbing story." She brightened.

Julius backed away. "Okay, so bye, have a good morning . . ."

"Wait, what about you? These have probably been tough days, I'm sure. I'll just run down and unlock the door. We can order breakfast from your garden place, or you can eat a cucumber off my plate." She laughed.

"No, I'm great, the dad thing's just exhausting. I saw your light and it looked inviting, but now I need to walk. See ya." He hurried away, afraid of his own tangled thoughts about suicide, about everything. He had no idea how to even begin.

Julius walked and walked for more than an hour, past many familiar places, as if he'd never really seen them. Finally, he found himself back on Stratford Lane, on the steps of the chapel where, again, warm light welcomed him through its windows. He ran his hands down the heavy wooden doors, then grasped the iron rings and pressed. With a great moan, the towering doors gave way, drawing him into a stone vestibule. Along the floor, a faded red runner beckoned him through a second set of doors, propped open with stacked bricks. The vast sanctuary enveloped him in amber light that glowed from crystal sconces lining the walls. One massive chandelier illuminated a stained-glass window of Jesus, with his arms stretched out on the cross.

From the balcony came Lars' rich voice.

"Julius, is that you? I've never had anyone join me so early. Oddly enough, I was just thinking of how I wish I had a cup of your coffee." He held up the mug in his hand. "This cup's disgusting."

Julius pulled at the collar of his coat as he strained his neck to see Lars. Suddenly he didn't want to be at the church anymore, much less talking to a pastor. Thankfully, Lars had given him an out.

"Perfect timing, then, and your favorite is Ethiopian Harrar; I'll get Kevin to make it. He's opening. I'll also include one of those almond pastries you like." He turned to leave.

"Oh no—no, my coffee's fine, my fault it's lousy. I heated it up from yesterday's pot. My secretary, Barbara, is very thrifty and saves it. Please don't go."

Julius stopped short. "Tell me you didn't do that. Did you? Old coffee is tar. They use it to pave the streets of New York City."

"Good to know. I've tasted worse drinks since getting here, though. You should try the communion wine!" He gave a shudder. "Wait right there."

Lars disappeared before Julius could refuse, then reappeared through a side door, approaching with long strides. "So how are you? Want to talk? Or want some time alone with God, an oxymoron if ever I heard one."

Julius blurted out, "Am I . . . even welcome here?"

"Yes."

"Like, yes, right now—for just now—or always?" Julius couldn't mask the huskiness in his voice. "Because you see, I've been told to leave before."

"I'm sorry to hear that; that must've been painful."

"I was fifteen, a guitarist in a church band. Wasn't sure if I was gay, but when the youth director asked us to share struggles, I told the group. Next thing I knew, I was excused. God had no use for me; I'd be *a burden* to the ministry. I was *too lost.*"

Lars sighed. "Do you think that's how God speaks?"

Julius scoffed, "Why, do you think it was Satan?"

Lars slipped into the back pew and scooted over, motioning Julius to join him. He grabbed a pew Bible, flipped to Matthew 11, and read, "'Come to me, all you who are weary and burdened, and I will give you rest. Take my yoke upon you and learn from me, for I am gentle and humble in heart, and you will find rest for your souls. For my yoke is easy and my burden is light.' God's voice is always rooted in one hundred percent grace and one hundred percent truth; no one is *too lost*, and burdens are what Jesus takes from us, at the cross." He set the Bible back down and leaned his forearms onto his knees.

Julius perched on the edge of the pew beside him. "Okay, great, let's talk Bible theology. So, what do you think of homosexuality, Lars?"

Lars placed his ankle on his knee. "Is that why you came so early? To discuss what I believe about homosexuality? That would be a deep discussion and I'd love to have it someday, but first you asked if you're welcome here. You are. God made you and He loves you to the core of your being." He put his arm along the back of the pew. "So, what's really hurting your heart? I think it's something else."

Julius slumped down in the bench, slipping his body along the curved base to rest his neck on the hard back. He stared up at the ceiling. High overhead, two birds flew in through one missing windowpane, swept along the length of the curved ceiling, then zipped out again. "Seriously Lars? It's like a dilapidated Noah's Ark."

"Yup, dilapidated, but a safe place to rest when the tumultuous waters of life threaten to drown us."

Julius shot a glance at Lars. "Nice intro. Tumultuous waters, right, okay, Noah, I'm diving in. I'm a fraud . . . I haven't told Stuart my past. I've got a ten-year-old son whom I've never seen." He waited for a reaction.

In the same calm voice Lars encouraged, "All right, go on . . ."

"No one but my sister knows he exists. It eats me alive. My guilt is like this dark shadow, and when Hope arrived, she was the floodlight I couldn't shut off. I'm a hypocrite! I'm a horrible person! Done with me yet? Is my welcome on thin ice?"

"Never, on both accounts. And 'horrible' isn't the word I would use. You are a person in pain."

Julius covered his face with his hands, feeling a wave of disgust wash over him. "So, what brilliant thing did I do two weeks ago? Come clean with Stuart? Get therapy? Oh no, I called her, my son's mom—Lucy—out of the blue—'Hey, Lucy, watcha been doin' for ten years?'—*ten* years, Lars! Tell me you're disgusted with me, or I'm leaving!"

Lars thrust his hand toward the door. "Then leave! And if you do, I'll follow you, because I'll never tell you that. Your heart's been broken over this for years, and you just took the first step of restoration. That's not cowering; that's courage—and your first step of faith. There's nothing God can't heal, Julius!"

Julius closed his eyes. Yesterday, he'd felt almost giddy; he thought the courage he'd wrangled would hold. He thought that a restorative conversation between him and Stuart would clear the air, opening a space to speak of Lucy and Storm. He was wrong. Stuart drove home in silence and Hope pinched her eyes shut when Julius tried to read to her. He'd envisioned a fresh start, but the same disappointment met him inside their apartment. In the wee hours of the night, his mind was fair game to all the old demons of self-loathing. They descended on him, wreaking havoc on even his good memories. It was the poisonous idea—back in full force—from which he'd fled, out to the street. It asked relentlessly, *Why don't you just end it?*

Lars spoke into Julius' pain. "The best way to unravel the tangles of life is to start at the beginning. Want to tell me about Lucy?"

Julius gave a deep sigh and began. "We were young. We were the best of friends, wild, living life by our own rules. She told me she was pregnant and I said it'd ruin everything. Abortion was obvious to me, but she refused. I gave her an ultimatum, but she didn't care—or maybe she did—whatever the case, she kept the baby. Later I heard it was a boy; she named him Storm." Julius stood up to pace.

"Great name," interjected Lars.

"After I called her, after all the time between us, I hated myself. I was aching to tell Stuart, but he wouldn't talk to me about anything. Hope hated—hates—me. So, I fled to our beach house. I planned suicide. I told myself that even my dad, who loved no one, never left us. Yet that's all I ever do, abandon people. So, ending it seemed best for everyone. I thought I'd found courage when I *didn't* kill myself, but now, I see it was another display of cowardice."

Lars stood up and leaned against the side of the bench. "Julius, your life is of utmost value and you live with courage every day. You see the good in people and even more than that, you see their need. Time and again I've seen your generosity fill another's need. Now you want healing in the relationships in your life. That's a new path and I'd love to help you with that. Maybe you can tell me what Lucy said when you called her?"

Julius threaded his fingers through his hair. "She said she'd be glad to see me, but needed some time to introduce the idea to Storm."

Lars put his hand on Julius' shoulder and looked at him squarely. "What? Wait, are you serious? She said she'd be *glad* to see you?"

Julius nodded. "But I have nothing to say to her; it was a ludicrous idea."

"Oh no, it's a brilliant idea. Meet her! Do it! And when you see her, first thing, ask forgiveness for what you asked her to do, and for the years you've missed. Then give her room to decide what she'll do next."

"No, I don't deserve forgiveness."

"No one deserves forgiveness Julius; forgiveness is a gift—a gift that gives us a clean slate, redemption. Jesus' light shines into our lives through forgiveness. Did you know 'Lucy' means 'light'? She's willing to see you; that feels like the first step in her forgiving you."

Julius put his hands over his face, overcome with emotion. Lars reached his strong arms around him, and Julius found that he couldn't hold back his tears.

After a while, still exhausted, but feeling lighter in his soul, Julius told Lars, "Thank you, thank you so much. It's definitely time for coffee now. Want to walk with me to our shop?"

Barbara entered the sanctuary as the men were leaving. She was carrying a tray with two steaming mugs of coffee. "Gentlemen, coffee?"

Lars smiled, but it was Julius who spoke. "Hello, I don't think I've had the pleasure of meeting you—Barbara, isn't it?" She beamed. Julius removed the tray from Barbara's hands and set it on a table. "I hear reheating coffee is the thrifty way around here—I'm impressed—but how about joining Lars and me this morning at my coffee shop, and I'll send you back with a month's supply?"

Barbara narrowed her eyes at Lars, who burst out laughing.

41

Lillian

"Miss Lillian, you should've seen the baby flopping around in Mama's belly last night. She moved under the tie on Mama's dress, like the knot was a beach ball rolling over waves." It was Friday afternoon and Montreal was tying his shoes, getting ready to catch the bus. Looking up, he said, "Mama says that if she's a she, she'll name her Lavender, because that's the first bouquet you brought her. You know, it's like she's naming the baby after you—like you're sharing our baby!"

Lillian was holding his backpack in her hands, ready to secure the straps on his shoulders. His words caught her off guard and she couldn't hide nor wipe the tears that sprang to her eyes. To hide her watery eyes from the boy, Lillian pretended to have a coughing fit, giving her an excuse to wipe her face on her sleeve. Montreal adjusted his pack, but instead of dashing out the door, turned back and stared up into her face. He wrapped his arms around her waist in a hug.

"Sorry I made you cry. You're bad at pretend coughing."

Lillian pulled his shoulder in, hugging him back. "It's okay, I know. And by the way, I'd like it if you'd just call me Lillian. Now get out of here or you'll miss your bus."

Through her front window she watched him race along the sidewalk, leap up the bus steps, and slip through the doors seconds before they snapped shut. He waved through the glass until the bus disappeared out of sight.

Lillian wondered how long she had been staring out the window at nothing. She finally turned from the window and wilted into the French garden chair beside her. It teetered under her, but the split rungs held. The tears began again. Jesse had decided to keep her baby and now Estelle was practically naming a baby after Lillian. It seemed like her past kept bubbling up and she couldn't keep her tears away. She fought to remember something. *What did Julius say? "I saw your light and it looked inviting." The light—so inviting.*

Suddenly she knew just what to do! Before she could lose her nerve, still wiping at the tears that refused to quit, she hurried upstairs to find something she'd saved. She found it, slipped the paper into her pocket, grabbed her jacket, and sped back down the stairs.

Flipping the sign to *Closed*, Lillian fumbled to lock the shop door while slushy rain pelted her back. She shivered as the ice-cold droplets found their way down the nape of her neck, but she ignored the impulse to grab her heavier coat. If she paused now, she might change her mind.

She reached the doors of the church within minutes, sweat mingled with her rain-soaked hair and tears. Slushy snow had soaked through the upper part of her work clogs. At barely a nudge the doors gave way, revealing Lars, who was opening them from the other side. She backed up, suddenly embarrassed by what must've been a frantic look on her face.

"Lillian! Um—here, hold on—" Lars bent down to yank out the corner of a wet towel caught in the hinge of the door, then dropped it onto a mound of several more. "Come in, you're soaked through! Sorry if I startled you. When snow melts, the vestibule becomes a shallow pool and my towel idea isn't exactly working." His face was covered in black smudges, as was a small raggedy towel he'd thrown over his shoulder. She tilted her head in question, to which he held up his hands. "Soot—hands, face probably too—I'll explain in a minute. Please, welcome."

She stammered, "You look too busy. I—I can come back later."

"Oh no, please come in. The soot project is done and the result is brilliant. I think you might love it."

He led her past the closed sanctuary doors, also stuffed with towels at their bases. Lillian eyed a random pile of bricks as she picked up her pace to keep up with his long strides. At the far end of the vestibule, Lars motioned to a slim passage with a door tucked in at the end. It was rather short and narrow—a door full of storybook possibilities. Lillian's thoughts turned momentarily to Aurora.

Lars' voice warmed the damp passage. "You're hardly going to believe this wonderful find. Let me run to wash up, then give me a minute while I get us some tea."

Lillian watched him head back the way they'd come. A heavily carved table stood along the narrow hall, right at her elbow. As she slipped by, she glanced into the mirror that hung over it. Her hands flew to her face as she thought, *What on earth?* Below her puffy eyes, smudges of mascara lined her face. She pulled off her non-waterproof jacket, which she hadn't even bothered to zip up. Her ears stuck out from her wet hair, plastered to her cheeks and, of all things, her white jersey was soaked in the front and had become see-through. "Ugh," she sighed, wiping her face with the cuffs of her sleeves, then trying in vain to fluff up her hair.

She pushed against the ringed handle of the little door. The dullness of the stone passageway vanished behind her as warmth and golden light drew her into a hearthside room. A blazing fire crackled from a magnificent fireplace. The toasty room glowed amber as light danced between leaded glass windows built into the curves of the wall. *This is the base of one of the old towers,* Lillian realized, feeling she'd been transported to a medieval castle.

Lillian curled up into one of the immense wingback chairs drawn up to the fire. It soothed her like a down-filled bed, but after a short time she climbed out— too afraid of dozing off.

Finally, Lars appeared, carrying a bowl of sudsy water with a sponge floating on top. Tucked under his arm was a dishtowel, a flannel shirt, and a blanket. "This was the best I could do. The tea tray is right out there on the table. I even found a box of doughnuts, maybe from another era. Could be boxed manna." He grinned. "I'll wait out here for you to . . . freshen up a bit. I'm afraid the women's restroom is flooded, and the men's is covered in soot—from me. Barbara, my secretary, found the shirt and followed me with the tray."

"Hi," Barbara's voice called faintly from the hallway.

"Thanks, Barbara," Lars called after her departing steps. Then to Lillian he added, "I asked her to stay late, so she's around while we talk." He set the tray in the room, then turned to go.

"Freshen up? I'm a disaster," Lillian muttered under her breath.

"Oh no, that's impossible," came Lars' voice, just before the door clicked shut.

A few minutes later, Lillian found herself dunking a stale powdered doughnut into her chamomile tea, while Lars explained, "I was wondering why we couldn't build a fire in this lovely inner sanctuary, so I poked a broom handle inside the old chimney shaft. Along with the burst of soot—which you saw—I found an abandoned nest, wedged along the flue, clogging the entire passage. Now that I've found a way to heat this room, our homeless friends will have a place for warmth. Perhaps some will even engage in a Bible study here with me. I just got the fire going, then you came—excellent timing!" Lars settled down on the edge of the hearth and took a sip of tea. "So, that was my reason for the soot. Would you like to share yours—your reason for the tears?"

Lillian pulled her legs up in the chair and blew on her tea. The cuffs of the plaid shirt covered her hands. "I—I have a sad thing in my past. Several actually." She swallowed hard then looked up. "But I wonder if I can tell you this one thing—the reason I reacted to Jesse's abortion as I did."

Lars nodded, and handed Lillian the box of tissues from the tea tray. "I may need those too, I imagine," he said, with a kind smile.

Lillian began. "Twenty-two years ago, my high school boyfriend Bryce and I were a formidable team: Class Couple, yearbook editors, all that. After graduating, Bryce expected me to follow him to George College since he'd gotten a full ride for basketball. His intellect almost matched mine—" Lillian stopped, and found Lars' smiling eyes. She hesitated. "Sorry, that sounded ridiculous."

Lars interjected, "Nope, you have a great mind; just confirms what I already know. Go on."

"I'd arranged to go to Lafayette University, since my best scholarship came from there. My dream was to own my own florist business. Lafayette was perfect for that. Too many details?"

Lars shook his head. "A good story always has lots of them."

"Our first year of college was okay; even with our long-distance relationship, we stayed fairly close. Then, I missed my period. It was halfway through the summer following our freshman year. I was terrified. Immediately I began to vacillate between an abortion and marrying Bryce, the only two options I thought I had.

"One night, as we walked along the dirt road behind my parents' house, Bryce was really sullen. I was trying to find the courage to tell him about the baby, but before I could explain, he blurted out that he thought things weren't working, and our lives were going in different directions. He said he couldn't handle our 'couple thing' anymore and thought that if I wouldn't follow him to George, we should split. He said I'd been acting strange, so I probably thought the same way.

"I wanted to scream, 'No! You have no idea what I'm thinking . . . I'm carrying our baby! I'm scared, overwhelmed.'" Lillian pulled a tissue from the box and dabbed her eyes. "Instead, I answered, 'Fine!' If that's what he wanted, then we should end things—right then." Lillian stopped to blow her nose and found Lars' own kind eyes welling up.

She continued, "The next morning I felt numb as I made the abortion appointment. But later, Bryce called. I didn't mean to, but I spilled everything: the baby, the abortion. I thought—just maybe—we could still be together and work everything out. Bryce was silent at first. I should've understood that. But then he reassured me of his devotion and promised to get me through the procedure with our great future still intact." Lars grabbed the teapot and filled her empty cup.

"A week later, we met at the clinic, but I wasn't sure I could go through with it. I had such an ache in my heart. Bryce smiled his charming smile and kissed me, said I was brave and wise and from here on out, we'd start fresh with nothing holding us back. Even though I dreaded the next step, Bryce would be on the other side of our 'setback,' as he called it, waiting. I believed him—he was easy to believe."

Lillian sighed, shivering a little, as the memories flooded her. Lars set another log on the fire.

"After the procedure, I remember I could barely walk to the door and almost threw up by the door frame. I hated myself for what I'd just done. The pain was horrible, the worst. I searched the room, but couldn't see him anywhere.

"The receptionist saw me and handed me a folded note in Bryce's handwriting."

Lillian reached into her pants pocket and handed Lars the faded yellow paper. He read the words silently, but she knew them by heart.

Hey Babe,

Good job, proud of you for getting this done. Nothing left for us, especially after this. Didn't want to sway your choice, but you were right last week. It was great while it lasted. Probably best you not tell anyone about this, don't want to ruin your reputation. You'll know soon enough, meant to tell you last week, but wanted to protect you mentally. I've been seeing someone else. She's great and probably the One. Hope you find the same.

Good luck,
Bryce
(P.S. Thought a note would be easier than a long, drawn-out discussion.)

Lars handed the note back to Lillian, his eyes full of sorrow. She went on, "That was it, left alone without a real goodbye, secretly replaced." She leaned her head back and briefly shut her eyes. "Bryce had been false, but the baby had been real. There'd been life growing inside me and every cell in my body knew it. I'd told no one else—no one ever knew. And the pain of it has never left." Lillian let the tears stream down her cheeks unchecked. Lars said nothing to fill the space. She was glad to sit in silence with him until she felt ready to finish her story.

While Lars poured the last drops of tea into her mug, she shared her last thought. "I can't blame Bryce. In the end, I chose to abort my baby. I caused my own greatest sorrow and regret—my greatest sorrow, that is, until five months later. But that's a story for another day."

Lillian wiped her eyes with finality; there were no more tears to cry. "Thank you for listening. I'm glad I told you. I feel kind of empty—empty but good."

"Free maybe?" Lars asked.

Lillian pressed her finger to her lips. "Yes, I feel better having told you, thank you, but not free. I'm the guilty one. And I still feel angry—angry at Bryce, even after all these years. It's been heavy on my heart for so, so long. I'm so weary of it."

"Lillian, he was cruel to you. He left you and persuaded you with deceit. He is accountable for what he did, but carrying unforgiveness is like a festering wound. Forgiving him doesn't make what he did okay, but it liberates your own heart."

Lillian nodded slowly. "You're right, I know. He probably never cared though. Why should my forgiveness matter?"

"Walking in forgiveness of Bryce liberates your heart, but only if you also decide to forgive yourself as well."

Lillian looked down at her hands. "Lars, I killed my baby and I'm so sorry I did. There's no way I can be free of that."

Lars went over and knelt beside her. "Lillian, listen to me. Your baby is with Jesus; there's no pain or suffering in heaven. You are forgiven. Receive it as God's gift to you. That's grace, you know—undeserved love—offered through Jesus. With forgiveness comes healing."

"That's what I truly want," Lillian whispered.

"Then receive it from Jesus," Lars answered.

By the end of the evening, the fire had burned down to embers and the second pot of tea was empty. Barbara brought Lillian a bag for her wet jacket, and a coat, saying, "I heard there was a need for coats for the homeless, so I bought every single one from the thrift store. Good timing for you!"

Lillian tried to refuse, but before she could, she was wearing the coat and it was fully buttoned.

Lars teased, "Barbara, you provide for our needs even before we know them ourselves."

Barbara beamed. "Job security!"

Lars locked the church doors behind the women. Barbara drove off, then Lars walked Lillian home.

"Thank you for this evening." Lillian smiled as she unlocked her door, then frowned as she looked down. "And thanks for the coat *and* shirt too. I forgot I was even wearing it!"

"Save it for a painting project. That sounds like something you might love to do. And who knows, you might find someone in need of a coat. Thank you, for your time and for your story." Lars backed away from the door as she waved goodbye through the window.

Upstairs, as Lillian undressed, she felt her pockets for Bryce's note, but it was gone. *It must've fallen from my pocket on our walk home,* she thought. She wrapped herself in her robe and sat on the edge of her bed. "You're free, Bryce," she whispered, "and so am I."

She slipped between her covers and fell into a deep, peaceful sleep.

42

Sylvia

"Charles! Charles!" Sylvia called through the intercom in her bedroom. Charles' muffled answer came back through the old machine. "Madam?"

From Charles' downstairs suite she could barely make out his muttering: "Blast it all, where are my glasses?" After several minutes, Charles finally arrived at Sylvia's door, fully dressed and wheezing horribly. "You called?"

Sylvia frowned at him over her laptop from where she sat in the center of her king-sized bed. "Charles, do you need your inhaler? Were you asleep? Isn't this your Sherlock Holmes series night?"

Charles straightened the lapels of his vest. "No inhaler, thank you, and yes, it most certainly was, Madam."

"Well then, why were you sleeping—" The chime of the Swedish clock interrupted her: *dong . . . dong . . . dong*! "Oh, Charles . . . can it possibly be three a.m.? Goodness gracious, I'm so sorry, dear friend, please go back to bed . . . or, now that you're awake, I've been sleuthing, you know . . ."

Charles blinked several times to focus. "Shall I make a pot of tea, Madam?"

"Oh yes, please, and bring up those lemon squares as well; that will be divine—simply divine."

Sylvia slipped from her canopy bed, careful not to disturb her computer and notes that lay across her coverlet. She pulled on her velour tracksuit and turned on every light in the room.

Charles returned with a silver tray. Sylvia peered over her glasses. "Muscat grapes and peanut M&Ms, delightful!"

Charles allowed the outer corners of his mouth a slight upturn. Sylvia smiled at her lifelong butler. He was as stoic now as he'd always been, probably since the very day Sylvia and Sinclair's parents had hired him at the ripe old age of twenty. His first week of employment had ended with the twins' christening. Four years later, he'd married his sweetheart, Martha, the nanny, who'd later stepped in as a second mother to the twins after Mrs. Obermann died. Tragedy struck again a decade later, when Martha died in childbirth along with their newborn daughter.

After Martha died, Charles had continued to work for the Obermanns, a career that spanned over six decades. The grief over the death of his wife and child never really left him.

Sylvia took a sip of tea and downed a few grapes, then asked, "Are you ready to hear the ideas swimming around my head?

Charles sighed as he pulled the desk chair up to her bedside.

"Oh, Charles, not to worry, you'll be thrilled with what I've discovered—well, thrilled is perhaps too strong of a word. Like—interested, rather—because you're as smitten with Montreal as I am. I'm inviting him and his family over tomorrow, by the way, and that will certainly be a thrill."

"Tomorrow as in today, Madam, or tomorrow as in day after today?"

"Tomorrow as in . . . today, yes, of course, that would be today. Thank you, Charles." Sylvia placed her computer between them. "Now for the business at hand. Here's Montreal's mother, the fabulous Estelle Delacroix. I recognized her name when he mentioned it." She began to scroll down the screen through a myriad of photographs of Estelle as a young starlet, onstage and offstage, surrounded by fans. Sometimes, when the pictures were taken at a distance, a tall, well-dressed man appeared at her side. "Watch for him," she directed.

"Might he be her husband?"

"That's the very question that's driving me! There is no record of a wedding anywhere, but there is this man . . . he's everywhere."

The first picture on which Sylvia intentionally paused was from a Canadian newspaper. There was Estelle cradling a newborn. The caption read: "Favorite smoky-voiced singer honors city by naming firstborn Montreal."

Sylvia smiled. "First things first, there's that delightful boy as a newborn." She lingered for all of two seconds then moved on, pointing to the shadowy figures in the background. "Now look at all these men, bouncers of some nature, ruffians all around, and there's the debonair one again, large and in charge. I wonder if he was her manager, secret husband, or lover? And if so, why isn't he close by her side with the new baby, instead of standing apart from her?"

Charles pointed out the hotel in the background. "Are they not staff, Madam?" Sylvia thought this was a foolish idea; she had no desire to waste time reading about the hotel. Next, Charles pointed to the woman and Frenchman named in a caption as grandparents, Regina White and Rousseau Delacroix. It was they who flanked Estelle, beaming on either side of their daughter and grandson. "Oh, I imagine the new father is just camera shy, or maybe he's a diplomat who needs security?"

"There's no good reason for him not being there—none at all—just wait; I think he's mafia." Sylvia picked up her teacup, then set it down again without sipping. "Mafia sounds so exciting, too theatrical perhaps. Yet, as manager, I suppose he'd need security guards . . . at least for his wife. See here? Fast forward two years to the Italian paparazzi's splashy photographs. She's gorgeous." The caption translation read: "Lovers' quarrel leads jazz phenomenon Estelle Delacroix to deliver baby early. Canceled appearances no matter, baby Florence and beautiful mama talk of the city."

Charles squinted at the attached article. "Madam, I believe this says something about a hotel opening . . ."

Sylvia continued, "Stay focused on Estelle, please, Charles. Stunning indeed. Marvelous dress, exquisite jewelry, even though she only just gave birth. Still regal and pleasing the crowd." She ran her finger across the sea of faces behind Estelle, who waved from the hospital balcony. "Same men with stern looks behind her, but no hubby, manager, whatever he is. But look, way back there. Isn't that he?" The lanky man stood against a wall, well behind Estelle, with men on each side. "And I ask you, what kind of lovers' quarrel leads to a premature delivery?"

"Oh Madam, perhaps that's gossip and the men are the hospital security staff?"

"Charles! You've been in Florence with me at the Ospedale Santa Maria Nuova, remember?"

"Who can forget," Charles commented under his breath.

Sylvia chose to ignore this. "You sprained your ankle trying to keep up with me on the hotel steps. Though I don't blame you—you were carrying all of my fabulous shoe purchases. But we had no fancy secret service attendants then."

"We might have, if you'd not been directing the hospital staff yourself, Madam," answered Charles dryly.

"True, true." Sylvia pulled up several more articles from other foreign papers to include one from the Johann Sebastian Bach festival in Germany in which a nanny held baby Sebastian. There, however, Estelle's face looked worn and stressed. "This is the last of the photo diary in Europe. There's one short article from a Montreal paper, with a fuzzy photo where she appears pregnant again. Then she disappears from the limelight completely."

Charles nodded slowly. "That makes perfect sense. She was invited to attract audiences to the openings of several grand hotels. Finally, it became too much for her, so she left fame to bear her fourth child and now leads a quiet life in the States. A noble choice."

"Or, she was forced to leave, threatened or abused, something to do with her controlling manager or husband who was committing crimes all over Europe!"

"Crimes? Madam, there is no evidence of criminal activity anywhere. What are you insinuating?"

"And he became jealous of her fame . . . though she was well sought after, he'd arranged the exposure for his own benefit. I'm just curious as to who he is, exactly. He's never named and never close enough to the camera to be truly identified." Sylvia added ruefully, "Now that I have this info, I must get the real 411 from Estelle herself. I'll tell you my suspicions once Estelle clarifies!"

"Madam, if I may be so bold, you watch far too much crime television . . . might you be meddling in Ms. Delacroix's personal affairs?"

"Me, meddling? Well, of course I'm meddling, Charles. How else can I help people? After meeting Montreal and hearing his mother's name, I had to do some detective work. One of my many questions is, why is money so tight after such a lavish life? Did she spend every red cent? Or purposely leave everything behind?" Charles removed his readers and rubbed his eyes. Sylvia moved closer to him. "And, that shadowy man who appears to be her companion, he may very well be the father of all her children—the children clearly resemble each other. Where on earth is he now? Obviously, she's seen him in the last eight months."

Charles sighed again. "I feel sorry for the woman who'll be on the other end of your interrogation. Sinclair tells us she's not well."

Sylvia touched Charles' arm. "Charles dear, I heard that also. Who would be well after so much stress in her life and baby number five in the oven? I think I can help. That's why I needed proof to back my questions."

Charles yawned as he leaned against the side of the upholstered headboard. "What arrangements would you like for me to make then, Madam?"

"Thank you, Charles. Please invite Estelle and her children to the house for tea tomorrow—I mean today. Better yet, let's do the mile-high pancake stack like Mother used to do and invite them for brunch. We'll have mounds of whipped cream, maple syrup, strawberries and—"

Sylvia stopped speaking. It had been too much for Charles. His head had flopped backward and from his wide-open mouth came the first of several whistling snores. She hopped out of bed and eased his long legs up onto the coverlet. She pulled off his shoes, then rolled him up like a burrito in a blanket. She turned off the lights and, with a happy hum, headed downstairs to make a pot of oatmeal.

As she passed through the foyer, she peeked out the side window of her brownstone, just in time to fling open the front door and catch *The Times* before it hit the welcome mat. "Strike one!" she yelled to the shocked paperboy.

As she trotted into the kitchen, she skimmed the front page. Her eyes lit up once again. "The gala," she said aloud, with a snap of her fingers. "That's it! Goodness gracious, this will be excellent!"

43

Estelle

The morning surprise, a pancake breakfast at Sylvia's brownstone, delighted Estelle's children. While the children enjoyed the lavish pancakes, Sylvia peppered, indeed almost interrogated, Estelle with questions about her past. After all these years and all the blurry photographs, Sylvia believed she'd connected the past with the present. Estelle felt almost relieved that someone had figured out her secret.

When Sylvia revealed her grand idea of Estelle attending the gala that evening, Estelle was hesitant, but finally agreed. There could be no more perfect setting to reveal her secret to New York City. Montreal, however, sunk into a worried mood. He understood the significance, while, much to Estelle's relief, his siblings were oblivious. No reassuring words could encourage him in the least, so Estelle gave him space while the girls flitted about, excited at the idea of dressing up their mother for the event.

Estelle slipped the final dress option, a white sequined gown, over her shoulders, then shimmied it down her body. It fit—just barely. She stood in front of the full-length mirror that was tacked to the inside of the hall closet and smiled at her own reflection. She looked over at Florence. "I'm like a white taffy, frills at each end—but bulging in the middle!" Florence grinned back as she disappeared into Estelle's bedroom.

Estelle had never seen a live performance of her mother with Elvis: he'd died a few years before her birth. However, she'd watched reel after reel of black-and-white films of them singing. Her favorite was of Regina in this very gown, with dangling earrings and her magnificent blue brooch. She remembered the screaming crowd pressing up against the stage in frenzied obsession. Regina White had been radiant with her full Afro, glistening ebony skin, and resplendent smile. She and the other two backup singers had danced in flawless unison as they belted out soulful harmony. When Elvis introduced his band, Regina tripped on her hemline, but Elvis caught her and spun her into a dip, as if it were rehearsed. Regina had said in later years, "For all of Elvis' extravagant gifts, his 'happies,' as he called them, his genuine thoughtfulness, playfulness, and kindness were what we loved best." Regina had taught Estelle the same generosity she'd seen in Elvis, but Estelle had desired the fame as well. She'd decided that, someday, the audience would cheer for her. Eventually they did, but at a great cost.

Aurora popped her face between Estelle and the mirror for closer examination, drawing her mama's thoughts back into the present. Aurora furrowed her brow. "What's a taffy? I think you look like a shiny white snake that swallowed a humung-io-sis bowling ball!"

Estelle laughed, "Oh yes, that's much better!" She then called to Montreal, who sat at the kitchen table, "Son, please phone Ms. Sylvia and tell her I actually found something to wear to the gala." She looked down at Aurora and smiled. "And tell her I'm going as a well-fed snake."

"Okay." Montreal peered over his math book. "But wait—as a what?"

Aurora's eyes lit up. "Oh, Mama," she giggled, then buried her face in the fake fur coat hanging at the back of the closet.

"Aurora, that's it—the cherry on top!" declared Estelle. "I forgot; I also kept Mother's flashy white coat."

Florence reappeared. In her hand she held Regina's brooch and one sparkling earring. "Sorry, Mama, I found the jewelry in the box where you said—and it's ever so lovely—but there's only one earring."

Aurora shot out of the closet, ran to the bedroom, and was back in a flash with the missing earring clenched in her soaking wet hand.

Florence narrowed her eyes. "Did you steal Grandmommy's earring? Just because we don't have much money, doesn't mean—"

Aurora lifted her chin, peering through haughty eyes. "Mr. Bubbles needed some fun. He's bored in that fish bowl. So, I got him some buried treasure. I just loaned it."

Estelle pulled Florence over to separate the girls. "Thank you for finding these." She secured the brooch and clipped on the earrings, then swept her long tight curls into a topknot. The girls let out sighs of adoration as they gazed at their striking mother.

Sebastian walked over from the kitchen, leaving a trail of cracker crumbs behind him. "Why did Grandmommy sing in a pregnant dress?"

Estelle reached her arm across his broad shoulders. "It's not a maternity dress, but because Grandmommy had your strong frame and lots of curves—it just so happens that I fit her dress now. Even with our baby about ready to pop out."

Montreal joined them to relay the message. "Ms. Sylvia says her car'll be here at 5:30." Then he added, crossly, "Why are you going? It's so weird!"

Estelle looked through the mirror's reflection into his eyes. "Because I must. Thank you for being protective of me, but this is to be our private conversation, one on one."

Aurora grabbed the book she'd dropped on the floor when her mama had appeared so dazzlingly before them. She held it up to Montreal's face. "Pleeease read me *The Princess and the Peanut Butter and Jelly Sandwich*?"

He shoved it aside and stalked away.

Aurora appeared to ruffle her feathers for a fight, but Estelle caught her arm before she could swoop in.

"Leave him," Estelle directed. "He needs space."

A little while later, Montreal stood in the doorway of his mother's bedroom with his arms crossed.

"Come in," she called softly. With a final sweep of ruby lipstick on her full lips, she turned from her vanity.

He slumped down on the edge of the bed facing her. "You look pretty," he admitted.

"Thank you, son; your thoughts mean a lot to me."

"Then why do you have to go to this stupid party? I don't think it's good."

"Because everybody will see me. They'll see who we are and I believe the publicity will protect us from being used. It's time to come out of hiding, before your father does something to expose us in a bad light. I have a plan. Will you trust me?" Montreal shrugged his shoulders. She kissed him on the head just as they heard a car driving up.

Florence opened the front door. To the joy of all three siblings, whom Montreal would babysit, Charles deposited two gourmet pizzas and a lemon tart on the kitchen table. Montreal remained solemn.

Estelle hugged each child goodbye. "Pray that all goes well," she whispered to Montreal. "Pray, but don't worry."

Sylvia, wearing light-blue chiffon, clapped her gloved hands as Estelle slid into the seat beside her. "You look ravishing, my dear! The dress, the jewelry, and that vintage fur. Marvelous, simply marvelous!"

Estelle blew kisses to her children as they waved at her through the sidelights of the apartment. "Thank you, Sylvia—all my mother's. Only an expert gemologist would know her jewels are costume—well, mostly. Now, my coat, on the other hand, looks like a bedraggled polar bear, but never mind. My mother had a knack for pulling off anything, even her best secondhand finds!"

"Well, your entrance will be that of a starlet! Are you nervous?"

Estelle closed her eyes, breathed in deeply then let it out. "No, I'm ready." La Maison was a blaze of light, welcoming guests in all their finery through its red-carpet entrance. Estelle and Sylvia swept through the wreathed doors and into the foyer, where Sylvia plucked the mink stole from her shoulders and dropped it into the hands of the waiting cloakroom attendant. Estelle followed Sylvia's lead. The attendant fingered the synthetic fur, yellowed with age since its purchase in the late sixties. She then winced, as if she'd caught a whiff of some horrid stench. Ms. Sylvia peered over her glasses into the attendant's face, pulled a fifty-dollar bill from her pearl handbag, and whispered, "Keep a sharp eye on that white coat, gift from Elvis—stripped the fur from his famous fur-lined room himself! Special present, you understand, worth a year's salary." The wide-eyed attendant bowed to Sylvia, then even more deeply to Estelle.

Once safely out of earshot, Estelle scolded merrily, "Sylvia, how could you! That coat—as you well know—was bought at a secondhand store by my thrifty mother. You already heard that story."

Sylvia waved her hand in the air. "I'm so thankful to have met you. This has been an incredible day. So let an aging woman embellish the light parts of your story. Lord knows there's enough heavy ones to sink my yacht!"

Estelle laughed in her beautifully melodic way. "Well, I'm deeply thankful to you, Sylvia. It's simply amazing that I could be your guest at this event—it's the perfect venue."

Sylvia continued, "I'm honored and excited! And just to clarify, you're the loveliest and the most important woman at this gala. I'll stand for no rudeness to you. Besides, that gal earns fifty extra dollars and we get a giggle—a necessary giggle, I say." They looked back to see that the attendant had placed Estelle's coat on a separate rack. She stood in front of it at attention, as if she were a guard at Fort Knox.

Sylvia and Estelle entered the banquet hall of La Maison. They stood in awe of the breathtaking blooms spilling from pedestal vases at every table and woven through vines in the chandeliers above. Water trickled down the terrace fountain, where floating rose petals encompassed votive candles. It looked like a natural pond of water lilies encircling dancing fireflies. Neither woman, in all her European travels or at any elegant party, had ever seen such magnificent flowers. "Lillian's work is stunning beyond measure," whispered Sylvia.

"Like no other," Estelle agreed.

Estelle stared at the photographers and reporters vying for the best views and stories of the evening. Suddenly, she faltered. She prayed silently, *Oh Lord, am I putting us in more danger? Is this right?* Her hands fluttered to her neck, then, as she forced her shoulders down, she fingered the brooch.

Sylvia peered over her glasses into Estelle's face. "Now, don't you lose your nerve, lovely lady; I see you fidgeting. We both know this is an excellent plan. You've performed all over the world; think of this as a belated encore." Sylvia grabbed a handful of chocolates from a candy bowl and slipped them into Estelle's purse. "Here, treats for the children."

Estelle took a deep breath. "Okay, but what I really need, before the big entrance, is Lillian. It's very important that she's with us."

"Oh, goodness gracious, she's probably completely unpresentable. What did she say to you on the phone at noon? She'd been at this since daybreak? Let's allow her to stay behind the scenes. I'm positive that's her desire as well."

"Sylvia, you're probably right, but please, let's ask her anyway."

"Of course, of course, we have about twenty minutes, but where to?" Sylvia squinted around.

Estelle took Sylvia's hand and drew her through the myriad of guests to the back of the room. "I think I saw . . ." She paused to look around. "Here we are; I saw staff entering right here."

The women passed through swinging doors into a bustling prep area where waiters zipped in and out, loading trays with hors d'oeuvres. Beyond that room, a back door led out to the alley where they found Lillian. She was loading her delivery van with remnants of foliage and items she'd used to set up the great hall. She dropped the bucket she held the instant she saw Estelle, and hurried over.

"What on earth are you doing back here? You look gorgeous, by the way—both of you—but go back in. It's freezing, and you don't want to miss your moment. I'm still trying to wrap my head around this. I'm in production mode—and in shock!"

Estelle embraced her. "Lillian, thank you, I feel beautiful in Mother's gown and jewelry, as round as I am! What an unbelievable few days you've had—everything with Jesse—incredible! I'm so glad we talked earlier, but I'm so sorry I didn't tell you everything before. And now we're here amidst all this beauty you've created, adding confusion."

"What? Never mind me and my week, you're exhausted." Lillian searched Estelle's eyes. "But, maybe you don't have to do this tonight. Maybe just wait, and another opportunity will come up."

Estelle clutched her belly momentarily, and both women looked alarmed. "Just a hard kick from Lavender," she explained, grabbing Lillian's hand. "I know this is right. We just came out to ask if you'd stand with me."

Lillian shook her head, looked from one woman to another, then ripped off her apron anyway. "Oh, my word. Okay, but only if I can stay out of sight."

Sylvia spoke in relief. "Good choice, especially since you look like a mixture between a mole and a forest fairy!"

Estelle smiled, pulling twigs from Lillian's hair. "Sorry, I hadn't even noticed."

Lillian tossed the bucket and remaining things into the van. "It's my favorite look. Now, let's go before I change my mind."

The threesome zipped through the door, weaving their way back through the staff. Sylvia almost toppled a tray of deviled eggs en route, caught one by accident, then popped it into her mouth.

"Why, thank you," she said to the startled waiter. "I'm absolutely famished!"

They reentered the room only seconds before their host. Anthony Mullenix, dressed in a silver tux, walked to the center of the hall and across a marble stage. Lillian stayed against a wall, half-hidden by a plant.

Sylvia whispered a quick instruction to Estelle. Then the music quieted as two spotlights centered their beams on a newly placed podium. Anthony Mullenix stepped up to it and the room erupted with applause. He thrust his arms out, then bowed and clapped in answer, back toward the crowd. Like a king on his dais, his rich voice commanded everyone's attention. "Ladies and gentlemen, I welcome you, one and all, to my charity extravaganza! Because of you and your incredible generosity, children throughout our marvelous city will soon experience the joy of delightful, safe, exceptional parks in ten locations. This is only the beginning of my campaign to restore our city for the most vulnerable among us. As you know, I am . . ." Suddenly, his words hung in the air.

All whispered chatter ceased as every eye turned from him to the stunning sight that had rendered him speechless. It was Estelle. She raised a water glass with a smile that shone out across the room. Anthony shifted his weight from one foot to the other, squared his shoulders, then raised his champagne glass to her and his silent guests.

He cleared his throat. "As I was saying, I am Anthony Mullenix—and I'd like for you all to meet the lovely surprise I planned for you this evening!" He paused until all eyes were fixed back on him. "Please welcome my exquisite wife, Estelle Delacroix Mullenix."

He crossed the room to Estelle, tucked his arm around her side, and whispered fiercely through a forced smile, "You will take your place beside me, be gracious, and dance!"

She smiled back, answering under her breath, "That wife is dead to you; this one is here only to be seen." Her words were bold, but they caught in her throat. It was all she could do to feign indifference and quiet the tremors of fear rising up inside her.

The camera flashes came alive as shocked guests clamored in for a closer look at the mysterious woman few had seen or even known existed. The press pushed forward, and Estelle slipped out of Anthony's hold.

Anthony tried speaking over the clamor as he hurried back to the podium. Sylvia took her cue and parted the crowd as Moses did the Red Sea and, with her arm tucked into Estelle's, paraded her around in a semicircle, waving. "Yes, splendid, isn't she? No comments, please."

Estelle smiled at every photographer, then locked eyes with Anthony one last time.

"Now you girls scoot," Sylvia said behind her hand. For a split second she frowned, but then added, "Not to worry, Charles will bring your fanciful coat to you later." She then stepped forward into the gathering with her arms out as if she were a vintage star waiting for her close-up. In her best theater voice, she announced, "My chauffeur is waiting."

Lillian pulled Estelle back toward the double doors.

"Lillian," said Estelle, as they hurried through the inner serving quarters again, "that last little part—Charles waiting to whisk me away—isn't true. Sylvia told me he'd be the decoy, while we take your van. Is that okay?"

"Of course! Good call!"

They ran out the back door with Estelle struggling to catch her breath. Lillian had to reach out to assist in pulling her onto the seat of the van.

They sped out of the alley just in time to see Charles zipping off in the opposite direction. Several curious photographers and journalists clamored into vehicles to follow him.

"Well done, brave accomplice," said Estelle, dropping her head back.

"How are you doing? Are you all right? You were amazing in there, so serene and elegant, but seriously, this stress cannot be good for the baby. What if you deliver early? Maybe even in the van!"

Estelle smiled, arching her back. "Not tonight; I'm praying not—and hopefully not in your van!"

Lillian hesitated. "Maybe this doesn't matter, but I overheard something while I set up—it felt disturbing. One of Anthony's staff said kind words about my flowers, so my ears perked up. Another then added that it was lucky for them that I was good, because I was hired for another reason. Why would they say that? What other reason could there be?"

Estelle stared out into the traffic, considering. "With Anthony, there's always connections—connections made for future use, for blackmailing. He's looking for a way to manipulate you, by drawing you in."

Lillian bit her lip. "And now he's paid my bail and cleared my name, while retaining my records for 'safekeeping.' He has blackmail as of yesterday."

Estelle sighed. "Yes, he does, but Anthony already believed you were a threat. Nevertheless, what you did for Jesse was wonderful and you weren't trying to hurt the security guard; anyone could see that."

Lillian stopped the van in front of the apartment. "It's disturbing. Why should he think of me as a threat? I'm not a threat to anyone."

"Lillian, don't you know? It's because the children love you and you love them. By that simple fact, you have the power to ruin his plans."

Lillian helped Estelle out. "What plans could *I* ruin?"

"I'll explain soon." Estelle hugged her, then lowered herself out of the seat.

"Got it?" asked Lillian.

"Yes, now you get back to the gala. Thank you," she said, then hurried up the apartment steps.

44

Lillian

Back at the gala, beyond the kitchen, Lillian stayed out of sight as she finished cleaning up her workstation. Her mind refused to settle as questions upon questions mounted. At one point, a server tapped her on the shoulder. She spun around with such fervor that the man lost hold of the four votive candle holders he was carrying. "Oh, my word! I'm so sorry," she said, reaching to gather them up. "I'm a bit jumpy; did these go out?"

"Yeah," said the frazzled server. "Can you hurry, please? Someone spilled their appetizers in the fountain and these sank—but I gotta clean up the floating food."

"Of course. I'll take care of it; you run back in!"

Lillian wove through the back garden to the fountain. She waited for the server to finish straining out the olives and soggy bruschetta before slipping the freshly lit votives back into the water. At the martini station on the other side of the fountain, lively laughter caught her attention.

"Why Ebony Scott, is it even remotely possible that you've never tried a dirty martini?" a familiar voice was asking. "Well then, tonight's the night!" Julius elevated his drink then offered it to the stunning woman, who politely declined. Stuart stood a few feet away, yanking at the collar of his shirt as he glared at Julius' jovial display. Lillian backed away silently, so as not to be seen. Nothing about this evening felt right.

45

Nolan

Name. Noh-luhn : Irish origin, meaning "champion"

Not far from the sparkly votives floating again on calm waters, Nolan West moved into the shadows of the terrace doors. In a dapper charcoal tux, no one would suspect that he'd just returned a wallet he'd pickpocketed out of boredom. Across the room, he could see Anthony engaged in conversation with a small group of celebrities, but he kept glancing over his shoulder. Through his false laughter, Nolan could hear the stress in his voice and knew Anthony was looking for him. To hide what he was about to say, Nolan wiped his mouth with his napkin, glad it was almost time to rendezvous.

He whispered into his wrist receiver, "Iggy, she stole the show. No idea what she's doing, but left a while ago with Bloom, in Bloom's delivery van. Iggy, ya copy?" But there was only silence on the other end.

46

Estelle

"Is everyone else sleeping?" Montreal nodded. "Well done. You make us tea while I find my nightgown and robe. Then I'll explain things a bit better, as I promised."

Estelle curled up on the couch and warmed her hands on her mug while Montreal nibbled the special chocolates Sylvia had tucked into her bag. As Estelle felt peace settle over her spirit, she began, "Here's what I intended to tell you earlier. When I brought you children to New York City, I thought your father's heart had changed. Moving us here was foolish, but I wanted so badly for your father to be who I believed he could be. I wanted us to be a family again after four long years. Is this making sense?"

"No, we're already a family without him."

"Hmm, well, true—but I thought our influence would open your father's eyes and soften his heart to us and to God's love, that first month on his Hampton property." She dropped her head back slightly and closed her eyes, trying to find the right words. "Yet, with everyone swarming around him day and night, and rarely a minute for us, I realized we were there for something else. I understood that he was keeping us away from everyone for his own ambitions, as his secret, for his own controlled timing. When we left, it was strange that he didn't come after us. I knew he wasn't just giving up, so I've been wary."

"What do you mean, ambitions?" asked Montreal, tensing his shoulders.

Estelle put her arm around him. "Political ambitions—and I was right; the extravagance of this evening proved it. He announced my arrival as if it were his own idea, but I didn't mind. My intention for tonight was to show *him* that we're not his pawns nor does he have authority over us. I am free to do as I like, and so are you children; he cannot control us. Now, as he runs for mayor, I will keep us out of the limelight. We have good friends who will help us. By attending his gala, I've shown New York City that Anthony Mullenix has, and has always had, a family. Tonight was my surprise appearance and I'm relieved to be known, even briefly, on my terms."

"Now that everyone knows, can we please just go back to Grandmommy and Grandpapa's old house in Canada? Can you just tell the people who bought it that it was a mistake?"

"No, son, that's their home now and we belong here where we've already found loving friends. I've surprised your father in whatever he was planning; Lillian and Sylvia helped me. Soon the rest of us will meet your wonderful Pastor Gundersen, and, surrounded by this new community, I believe God has a plan for us."

"You'll like him so much, Mama."

It warmed Estelle's heart to see Montreal's spirit lift, just in hearing the kind pastor's name. "I know I will," she said, stifling a yawn. "It's late; shall I tuck you in?"

"Yes," came his surprise answer.

47

Jesse

Sunday morning, Jesse shuffled through the clothes strewn across her bedroom floor. She steadied herself against the doorframe of her bathroom with a hand on each side, clenching her teeth to keep from vomiting. She groaned, then gave in to the inevitable. As she slipped off her T-shirt, she caught sight of her tattooed torso in the mirror. Even the brazen ink dragon, stretching from her breast to the tip of her hip bone, looked shrunken and weak. She stared down at her middle. "Are you in there, little person?" she asked weakly. "Can you hear me?"

"Who are you talking to?" Jesse jumped at her mother's voice. Roxanne was passing by the bedroom door, which Jesse had left ajar. "Laundry doesn't do itself, you know."

"I know—I've just been busy." Jesse threw on a hoodie and sweatpants, dumped a bunch of clothes into the hamper, and headed downstairs.

"Want some toast or coffee?" Roxanne asked, tightening a hair tie around her short, auburn ponytail.

"No, thanks," Jesse replied as she pulled a cola from the fridge and popped the tab.

"Were you talking to someone?" Roxanne persisted, wiping her glasses of smudges before putting them on, then vigorously wiping the clean countertop.

Jesse snapped, "No—I mean yes—myself, actually." She grabbed *The Times* from the counter where it lay. Splashed across the front page were grand photographs of the gala. But almost more intriguing than the event, she read, was the appearance of Anthony Mullenix's estranged wife, who disappeared almost as quickly as she'd arrived. Was this New York City's very own Cinderella story?

Lillian's texts from the previous night still seemed so unbelievable. There was so much more Jesse wanted to know and now it would be the latest buzz around the city. She thumbed through the paper as she nibbled the toast her mother had placed before her.

"I've got a twelve-hour shift today. Got plans yourself?" asked Roxanne, wearing her worry across the deep lines on her forehead.

"Yeah. This Estelle thing is bizarre, so I'm meeting up with Lillian later to hash it out."

Roxanne loaded her lunch into a paper sack and zipped up her sporty jacket. "Didn't you work for Mullenix at some point? Doesn't really seem like the family type. Are we supposed to believe all those kids are his? Seems more like a publicity stunt than anything else."

Jesse glared at her mother. "Estelle is the kindest woman on the planet! She would never do this for publicity! You think she's had children with random men? Mom, are you kiddin' me?"

Roxanne shrugged. "Women do that, you know." Jesse coughed as a bite of toast caught in her throat. Roxanne handed her some water and continued, with her eyes on her daughter. "Maybe you don't know her as well as you think. Everybody's got secrets, and being married to the man running for mayor is a pretty big one."

"Well, obviously I'm a bit shocked—okay, a lot shocked—but even with secrets, she's honest. I trust her; me and Lillian both do."

"Honest with secrets, huh? Strange, but if you trust her, that means something. Trusting's not easy for you." Roxanne looked as if she were wrestling to say something else, but turned instead to fill a water bottle at the sink. "Tell me the whole story when you know it, will you?"

"Yeah, yeah sure."

"'Kay, so, goodbye," Roxanne offered as she started to leave, but Jesse didn't look up. Just before the door clicked shut, Roxanne poked her head back inside. "You're way too skinny, by the way. Please eat, will you? Love ya, bye!"

Jesse stared at the newspaper without seeing it. She felt hollow. When did she stop telling her mom the truth about her life? Perhaps she never really had at all. When her dad left, ending all the years of affairs, fighting, and lying, Jesse had only been eleven. Roxanne had seemed a different person after that—numb, somehow. Protecting her mother from pain seemed more important to Jesse than adding her own complex issues to it. She was much better at deception than her dad had been. The clarity of that thought startled her. But how long could she hide her pregnancy?

Something in the paper caught Jesse's eye—a picture of the McPherson storage facility, destroyed by a fire the previous night. The caption read: "Five men lost in fire, arson suspected." It was one of Anthony's buildings.

The doorbell interrupted her thoughts; she jumped. She held her heart to calm it. Who would be ringing the doorbell this early in the morning? She whipped the door open and stepped out. There stood Nolan West. With his eyes darting to the left and to the right, he almost bowled her over as he stepped forward. "Jesse, get inside," he ordered, "I can't be seen with you."

Jesse put her hands on her hips. "What do you mean you can't be seen with me? Excuse me?"

Nolan pushed her back inside with the tips of his fingers on her shoulders and a wide berth between them. "Why's it always like head-to-head in the ring with you? I'd be proud to be seen with you—it's got nothing to do with that and you know it!"

Jesse stood against the inner wall as dread welled up in her spirit. "Why are you here? You said you weren't checking up on me for the Boss."

Nolan spun a chair around and sat facing her, his forearms resting on the back. "No, I told you, we're on the same team. Sit down. You gotta hear it sitting down." He pointed to the seat beside his.

Jesse lowered herself slowly onto the chair. "Hey, I don't like how you're looking at me. So, whatever it is, spit it out, 'cause I don't have all day. Lillian's—"

"Jesse, stop talking," Nolan dropped his forehead onto his wrist. Without looking up, he held out a hand to Jesse. She swallowed hard and took it. His cocoa eyes met her troubled gaze; he spoke through husky tones. "I'm sorry, Jess. I don't wanna say it, but you gotta know. It's Iggy. He was in the building, the one that burned down last night."

Jesse shook her head back and forth, whispering, "No, no . . . don't say it—*no*!"

"You have to hear it, I'm sorry, too, real sorry, but he's dead."

She held out her chin as tears burned her cheeks. "No, I'm telling you, no way, not Iggy! I don't believe you."

"You do, you know you do! And he is—he knew it was coming." Nolan rose and fished in his pocket for cigarettes. Instead of pulling one out, he shoved the pack away and drew Jesse up from the chair. She didn't resist, feeling like a rag doll who needed to be gathered in his arms. Her tears wet his neck as she silently wept. Placing his hand over her head, ever so gently, he rocked her. After a few minutes, she lifted her chin and stepped back, dabbing her cheeks with her sweatshirt sleeve.

"I can't stay," Nolan said quietly. "I'm so sorry I had to tell you. I'll let myself out. Keep the key and ring safe. I'll be in touch soon, when I'm ready for 'em." Jesse crossed her arms and drew up her shoulders. For a split second she looked away, fighting the wave of guilt that came over her.

Nolan frowned. "What? You don't have them?"

Jesse's voice quivered. "No, not both. I lost the ring. I've searched everywhere. Gone. I've blown it; he's dead because of me."

"No. He gave 'em to you 'cause he knew he was being hunted. Best you can do now is find the ring. You gotta find it!"

"I will," sniffed Jesse miserably. "Wait—does Maria know?"

"Not yet, that's where I'm heading next, to contact her. I've got a number, Mexico maybe. Once I tell her and know she's safe, I need the key and ring."

"Back door's that way," Jesse directed.

He looked over his shoulder. "Gonna be okay? 'Cause I'll stay a few more minutes if you need me."

"No—but yes, I always am okay, eventually." Jesse stood up.

"You don't always have to be strong, you know, at least not alone."

"It's gotten me through life, until—until the appointment. Nolan . . . one thing. Friday, I took the back door; I didn't do it. So, thanks."

"I saw you. I see everything, you know," he said. "It was brave. It was right." His hand was gentle as he gripped her shoulder. Then, with a tip of his chin, he slipped out the back door.

48

Lillian

The wind blew straight through Lillian's thin coat as she stepped off the bus in Central Park. Jesse, who'd already arrived, sat shivering on a bench. Lillian hurried over, gave Jesse a hug, and arm in arm, they began to walk.

They approached a vending truck advertising hot dogs, hot pretzels, and hot coffee. "One of each hot thing and a cola, please," Lillian ordered from the scruffy teenager listening to music through earbuds. He spun around and, swaying to the beat in his head, began to prepare their order. Lillian was surprised he'd even heard her.

"Hungry?" asked Jesse.

"No, but you are. Coffee's for me, food and cola for you two." She smiled. "And one more thing I've arranged—if it's fine with you." Lillian paused to examine Jesse's face; it seemed so solemn. "I just talked with Estelle and she wants us to stop by later in the week. Since we've got a full work week and the kids have school, I suggested Friday. And I think Lars will be there as well."

"Yeah, sounds okay. I'd rather hear everything straight from her. It's all so weird." Jesse rubbed the back of her neck with her hand.

Lillian continued, "I'm really glad to have this time alone with you—not working, I mean. Everything's been so intense lately; you need a breather. And Jess . . . I'm really proud of you."

Jesse gave her a flat look. "Proud? No. You have no idea."

"I can be proud of you if I want to—I am. And I think you're brave."

"I just heard that from someone else. It's just—just . . . no one has any idea." Jesse shook her head. "How about the father of my baby; know who that is? There's so much bad happening, I can't even start to tell you."

Lillian dug into her pocket. "Anything to do with this? I found it on the shop floor. I think it belongs to Dwyer Ignatius. I almost gave it to Anthony, but I had a strange feeling I should give it to you. You said Dwyer's wife's name is Maria, right?" She pressed the ring into Jesse's palm.

Jesse burst into tears.

The scruffy teenager, who'd just begun to hand the tray to Lillian, stopped in his tracks. One earbud fell out as he stared at Jesse. "Wow, you're, like, really sad. Sucky day?"

Lillian stared at Jesse as she quickly took the food from his hands. "No, she's fine, just fine. Just a tricky moment, thank you, that's all." She reached into her purse for cash.

"Dude. It's on me." He handed Jesse a wad of napkins, then straightened the plastic mustard container that fell over as he did so. For a brief second, he continued to stare into the awkward silence. Then he popped the dangling earbud back into his ear and resumed his seemingly oblivious dancing to the beat of his private concert.

After they'd eaten, Lillian cleared away the trash from their table. When she returned, she found Jesse absently twirling the lost ring on her thumb. Lillian lowered herself onto the bench. "So, feel like talking about why the ring made you cry?"

"No."

"Okay, well, that's fine. I suppose you don't want to tell me who the father of your baby is either?"

"Why? Want to tell me about the father of *your* baby?"

Lillian flushed, thinking, *Should I tell her? Does she actually want to know?* She searched Jesse's hard face, then gave up. "Let's go. I was thinking of using some of the leftover flowers from the gala for a new display."

Jesse didn't budge. "So, you tell me your stuff when it's convenient and then close back up so you can pretend like you don't have any pain. That makes perfect sense." She stood up. "Whatever. The ring's got something to do with Anthony Mullenix . . . and a judge, Judge Rolland. He's the father of my baby. He has a wife and three kids, the model family, only this one makes four. I was the other woman—just like my dad's other women, who I always hated! Glad you asked? Now guess what my job was before you hired me. Give up? Escort, everybody's favorite, especially the judge's."

Lillian looked down at her feet. "Oh, Jess . . ."

Jesse stood there staring at her, until finally she just shook her head and gave Lillian an immense hug. "You make me so crazy and so frustrated I could scream, but I still wanna be with you. You're such a dork of a boss. Am I fired?"

Lillian hugged her back. "No. But don't call me a dork, even if you think I'm one. I'm still your boss and, by the skin of your teeth, you're not fired."

49

Estelle

Friday evening, Estelle kissed Florence on the cheek. "Thank you for washing up. I'm just beat tonight and I don't know why." She lowered her aching body onto the couch, curled her legs up under her, and dropped her head back.

Florence folded her arms and tapped her foot. "You don't know why? Late night parties, four kids, baby coming, and—"

Estelle lifted her head and fixed her eyes on her eldest daughter. "Come on." She patted the cushion beside her. Florence stayed rooted to the spot, shaking her head as she fought back tears.

Estelle reached out her arms. Florence rushed to her mother and buried her face in the crook of her neck. "It's all right," Estelle soothed as she rocked Florence. "You're carrying all this worry on your shoulders and there's no need. God has never let us down and He isn't about to right now. This is hard, beloved, but we can trust him together."

From outside, a loud roar caught their attention. It was as if a jet were landing at the curb. Estelle lifted her eyebrow to Florence, who sat straight up, her worried eyes now wide with curiosity. Pajama-clad Aurora and Sebastian raced from the bedrooms, with Montreal at their heels. They threw the door open as Montreal announced, "The Gran Torino has cleared the runway! See? It's just like I told you guys!"

Sebastian helped Estelle up from the couch. "Why, thank you, son," she smiled. "I mustn't miss the stylish arrival!" He and Aurora ran to the front steps, but Florence hung back.

With a final burst of exhaust, the car jerked to a halt. Down went the driver's side window and out came one of Lars' lanky legs, next his backside, then the other leg. Finally, with a bit of a hop, the whole man was out of the window. Aurora clapped. "Again! Again!"

Montreal reached out for a handshake, but Lars pulled him forward instead and gave him a bear hug. The boy laughed. "Door jammed?"

"Yup! But don't ruin my entrance by announcing it," voiced Lars out of the corner of his mouth, though everyone could hear. Estelle laughed; she'd expected something delightful from the man who'd encouraged Montreal more than anyone. She pulled Florence by the hand to stand alongside her in the doorway.

Montreal introduced his family. Lars greeted each one by name, then addressed Estelle. "I've been so looking forward to meeting you and your beautiful family!" He held up his index finger. "Hold on a minute, I forgot something in the car—" From the back seat, he withdrew a huge jar of jellybeans. These he deposited into Florence's hands, saying, "You look like the wisest candy steward of the bunch!" Her furrowed brow softened. To Estelle, he handed a plush blanket with an embroidered lamb in the corner.

"You're early. I like that." Estelle smiled. Her heart felt full, seeing the joyful countenance on each of her children's faces in this moment. Winning Florence over so quickly was a feat few ever accomplished.

"Thank you for inviting me. If not early, I'm late—and tonight I couldn't miss a breath of your intriguing life story. I just realized, though—" He looked over Estelle's shoulder into the apartment. "I could've picked up Lillian and Jesse. They're not here yet, are they?"

But before she could answer, a puddle appeared at Estelle's feet.

"Oh my!" Estelle's eyes fell to the wet cement step below her. "Of all things!" she said to herself as her heart sank. "Pastor Lars, I'm afraid my water just broke. Can you get us to the hospital? My babies come fast!"

50

Montreal

Montreal, in the back seat of the Gran Torino, tried to keep his nerves steady. His mother, seated in front of him in the passenger seat, was breathing rapidly through spurts of pain. He saw the beads of sweat along Lars' forehead begin to slide down into his eyes. Though Lars held the gas pedal to the floor, the race car seemed only to lurch in slow motion. The highway to the hospital appeared too much for the newly repaired car.

Florence was squeezed next to Montreal in the back seat with their other two siblings. Her emotions erupted, and she cried out, "Pastor Lars, please—please step on it!"

Montreal had been silently pleading with Lars' cell phone for service bars, when suddenly he burst out, "Look! I see a police car! Should I flag it down?"

"Praise God, yes!" Lars answered. "I'm stopping. Grab the blanket and hop out—be careful! Watch for cars!" He pulled the car over to the side of the highway, where Montreal jumped out and waved the blanket frantically. The blue lights of the patrol car lit up as the vehicle spun back around from the meridian.

Montreal recognized Officer Doug Jensen, one of the small band of Stratford Chapel members, as he bolted from his car. Jensen called out, "Lars, is that you?"

Montreal rushed into him, unable to stop his momentum. "She's having a baby right now and the car won't make it to the hospital!"

"Hey there, Montreal! Your mom? She'll be all right, buddy," Officer Jensen's strong arms steadied Montreal, as he called back to his partner, "Rosie, a baby's comin', radio an ambulance! I'll grab the first aid kit from the trunk." Then to Montreal, he directed, "Go with my partner."

Officer Estevez ran with Montreal to the car. "Hi! I'm Rosie; it's gonna be okay. Those your siblings?" Montreal nodded, fighting back tears. "You've got a big family, like I hope for one day. Everyone's gonna be just fine."

Florence was hurrying Sebastian and Aurora out of the back seat like a mother hen. Montreal watched them step carefully down a slight incline and over to a tree a few yards away. There, Florence reached her arms around her siblings in a little huddle.

Jensen slid up to Lars, who was kneeling on the gravel, facing the passenger seat with a container of disinfectant wipes beside him. Montreal laid the little lamb blanket over Lars' shoulder, then leaned against the car as he peered at his mother. His fingertips hurt; they were raw from chewing his nails. Estelle's breath came in quick spurts as she lay sideways at the edge of the front seat. She held her knees clamped shut as she clenched her jaw and groaned from deep in her throat.

"Montreal," directed Lars, "hop through the driver's side window between the steering wheel and the seat. Your mom needs to lean against you to push."

Montreal froze. "To push?" With quick resolve and parkour agility, he leapt over the hood and onto the highway side of the car, then slid through the driver's window. He wedged his slim body behind Estelle, like a human pillow. "I've gotcha, Mama; it'll be all right. I think Florence and them are praying."

Estelle rested against Montreal. "Where—are—they—" she stammered breathlessly.

"They're by a tree, Mama. It's okay, they're holding onto each other."

Officer Jensen opened the first aid kit. "Hey, Pastor, what do ya need?"

Lars answered, "In Ethiopia, the midwife always sat where I am now; I've seen this before. I know the ropes, but I've never been in charge. Let's see, get me the gloves, throw the towel from the back seat at my feet, and hand me a clean cloth from the kit—see if there's a clamp—but also get the kids to a safer spot." He addressed Estelle, "Don't worry, we'll get the kids."

Doug looked over his shoulder. "Rosie's there now talking with them."

In the distance came the faint sound of sirens. Lars cracked his neck. "Estelle, can you wait, or do you need to just let her come?"

Montreal held his mama's shoulders up as she braced herself against his knees, but his eyes were closed. Estelle's breathing came fast, then subdued, fast, then subdued, until finally there were only the quick spurts. She bent forward. "I—I can't hold her! She's—she's coming!"

Montreal gritted his teeth as Estelle groaned in pain.

"All right. It's okay; I'll catch her. Let her come," Lars encouraged.

The seconds felt agonizing to Montreal; he almost felt like he was in pain too. Lars cried, "She's crowning!"

Montreal could feel his mother's tense body straining forward. Then she sucked in her breath and with a great heave, gave a final push. Montreal opened his eyes to see the miracle. It all happened so quickly! Like a slippery fish from the sea, his baby sister slid into the open air, right into Lars' big hands—expert hands that enveloped her, then wrapped her up in the blanket.

Lars let out a choked "Hallelujah!"

Tears stung Montreal's eyes as he tried to hold his body perfectly still for Estelle, though he wished he could flop back in utter relief. Then, louder than he expected, the night air filled with the most precious sound in all creation: the first cry of a newborn baby.

Estelle dropped her head back onto Montreal's shoulder. "Hallelujah," he whispered, in wonder. "Good job, Mama!" Estelle smiled up at him, then sank back, sighing deeply.

With shining eyes, Lars laid the precious bundle into her mother's arms.

"Welcome to the world, Lavender Blue; we've been waiting for you."

Montreal stared at the tiny, smushed face, feeling his heart swell. Lars pulled off one of his gloves and reached for Montreal's shoulder. "Well done, young man!"

Just then, paramedics appeared beside the car. Seamlessly, they loaded Estelle and baby Lavender onto a gurney. While one checked the baby, another started an IV on Estelle. Officer Rosie brought Florence, Sebastian, and Aurora to Estelle's side for a quick exchange before mother and child were placed into the ambulance. Aurora kissed the sweet bundle on the toes. "When I see you next, sissy, I'm gonna count those little toes and kiss every one of 'em for real!"

Estelle lifted her hand to touch each child on the cheek. When she came to Sebastian, he noted, in his husky voice, "Mama, I was just thinkin', now I'm right smack in the middle. I'm your exact middle child."

Estelle gazed at him. "Yes, son, I bet you're proud of that." He nodded.

Lars handed the cell phone he'd just borrowed back to the Officer Jensen, then stretched his wide arms around the children. "All's well," he said, "I just called Lillian and she'll be waiting for us at her apartment. She's invited you for a sleepover tonight, then I'll bring you to Carson Memorial Hospital tomorrow. That's where your mom and baby sister will go now."

"Mama, can't I come with you?" begged Florence.

Estelle squeezed her daughter's hand and, in a barely audible voice, explained, "Not now, beloved, tomorrow. I can't wait to hear about your cozy night with Lillian. I'd rather go with you than them." Ever so slightly she lifted her one eyebrow to the paramedic, who grinned. It gave Montreal a lump in his throat to see his mama so frail.

Florence folded her arms. Lars whispered to her, "Thanks for sticking with us. I'm not sure how I could handle getting everyone settled in at Lillian's without you."

Florence answered gruffly, "You just delivered our baby; you can do anything! You don't need me."

Montreal could see that Florence was fighting back tears. "Hey, Flo, Mama will be okay; it's okay. You don't need to worry." Pinching her eyes, Florence turned away from her brother, but there was no way of hiding her distress. Montreal shrugged, looking over to Lars for help, but Lars motioned for him to hug her. Reaching across his sister's shoulders, careful to keep a few inches between them, Montreal patted her. To his surprise, Florence buried her face into the collar of his coat and wept. He bit his lip as he leaned his head on her.

51

Lillian

At 3:00 a.m., in the living room of her apartment, Lillian slid her arm out from under Aurora. It felt tingly and her back ached. She'd fallen asleep in her clothes while soothing the anxious five-year-old. For a moment the slumbering child awakened and sat up, then looked at Lillian through glassy eyes.

Lillian stroked her cheek, saying, "Hush, all is well; sleep now, darling girl." Aurora flopped her head crowned in a dozen braids back down and snuggled into the cushions. Soon her breath came in rhythmic snores. Lillian smoothed the braids away from the beautiful brown cheek.

Darling girl, thought Lillian. It was the pet name Lillian's mother had called her so long ago, even up to the last conversation on the day she died.

"Oh, darling girl," her mother had said on the phone, even though Lillian was twenty at the time and felt she'd outgrown the "girl" part, "we'll miss you. Skiing just won't be the same without you. Must you study these extra days of Christmas break?"

Lillian remembered her impatient remarks: "I've just a bit more to do. The dorms are practically empty except for the international students. If I can just finish, only three more days, plus the forty-five-minute drive home, then I'll be there."

Her mother let out one of those long sighs Lillian knew so well before adding, "But what about Dad's birthday? You never miss that."

"For now, tell Dad happy birthday and that I can't wait to see his new truck on Tuesday."

In the background her father called out, "Tell me yourself when you get here! Come on, sweetie; we all expected you to come."

"I'm putting you on speaker phone," said her mom.

"I know, Dad. I'm sorry, I'm just too busy. Give the truck a test spin, then tell me all about it later."

Lillian heard her parents' muffled debate, then her father spoke. "Without you? Forget it. I told your mom the old car has enough life left for this ski trip. We'll wait to try out my new wheels together."

"Oh Dad, celebrate forty-five in style, with your new truck! Please?"

"Nope, my mind's made up; it'll just have to wait for you."

In the background she'd heard Jack and Johnny yelling something about getting her room if she stayed away any longer, to which she laughed. "Stay out of my room!"

"Okay, darling girl, car's packed, hot cocoa's in the thermos, but we'll all be singing, 'I'll have a blue Christmas without you . . .' Her mother's cheerfulness sounded forced, but Lillian vowed in her mind to make up for her absence as soon as she got home.

"I'll be home before Christmas, I promise," Lillian countered.

She remembered their happy banter from the other end of the phone, then her father once more. "We love you and I'm holding you to your promise; we won't be around forever, you know."

Jack had ended the conversation. "See ya, sis, I've gotta be the sign-off guy, especially since Mom started singing Elvis. We wanna leave sometime in this century. Love ya!" Then click.

These words stung in her memory; they were the last ones she'd ever hear from them.

She covered her face with her hands and shuddered, fighting the anguish of twenty years. She wiped her wet eyes and stuffed the memories down again. That sorrow seemed to suck the very life from her limbs. Lillian stood up, pushing the memories aside, and her responsibility for Estelle's children to the forefront.

She stepped past the coffee table and linen chairs, then crossed the length of the living room. To the left was her kitchen and to the right, her bedroom door.

She peeked in to see Montreal and Sebastian sleeping soundly in sleeping bags on the floor, and Florence curled up on her bed.

Relieved, Lillian returned to the snoring child. She approached the picture window at the farthest wall. It was identical to the one at the front of the shop below. The wrought-iron lampposts lining the street cast soft light into the room through the muslin curtains. Spindly shadows from the bare-tipped branches of the Norway maple spread up the fabric like beckoning fingers. Lillian drew her hand across the cloth to gaze down through the branches at the empty street—but the street wasn't empty. There, lying across the sidewalk, with one leg draped over the curb, was a woman. Her eyes were shut, but her mouth was partially open. She lay motionless in a pool of vomit.

While dialing 911, Lillian raced to the stairwell, down through the shop, and out the front door. There, propped up against the brick wall, was Sinclair. The slamming door awakened him out of a drunken stupor. "Buying our next round, are ya, Lillian?"

Lillian rushed past him to kneel beside the woman; feeling her wrist, she found a faint pulse.

52

Montreal

Montreal jolted awake to the ambulance siren's blare from a few streets away. Florence jumped up and found the light switch. Sebastian rubbed his eyes as he sat up. "Sounds like they're comin' here! Are they bringin' Mama and the baby?"

"No, no, of course not, don't be silly," retorted Florence. Sebastian frowned, then crossed his arms over his face.

"Oh, brother," sighed Florence as she slid off the bed to apologize.

"Hey, it's okay bud, we'll see Mama soon," voiced Montreal, patting his brother on the back as he went to investigate. He gave Florence one word, chock full of annoyance: "Nice."

Florence scanned the room. "Where's Aurora?"

"You guys wait here; I'll find her and see what's up," said Montreal as he threw on his sweatshirt and jeans and made a beeline for the living room. On the couch lay a white throw in a heap, plus one stray hair bobble, but no little sister. He peered down to the street below where ambulance lights illuminated the scene. Lillian was stroking the arm of a woman lying unconscious on the curb with one hand and patting Sinclair, who crouched beside her, with the other. Sinclair was sobbing uncontrollably.

Montreal ran through the apartment and down to find Lillian. "Lillian, what's wrong?" he called as he approached them.

Lillian turned to motion Montreal away, but Sinclair caught sight of him. "Montreal," he slurred as he staggered to get up, "it's Judith, my friend; she's in bad shape. We had a teeny-tiny drink," he said as held his two fingers up, an inch apart, and cocked his head, "but then, just a tiny, itty bit more. The evidence points to me, but it was just a teeny-tiny . . ." He staggered forward, then caught himself. "I'll be *rrright* as rain. I'm here for you, I promise." As sobs overtook him, he fell forward, but Montreal caught him just in time to avoid crashing into the paramedic, who'd leapt from the ambulance.

Lillian directed Montreal, "Please, run back up, and keep everyone calm upstairs."

"Okay, just wondering, is Aurora with you?" he asked, turning on his heels.

"Asleep on the couch," Lillian stated.

Montreal's words caught in his throat as he shook his head. "She's not there . . ."

"What?" Lillian rose just as the paramedic knelt at the curb to assess Judith. "I'll be back, Al!"

The other paramedic hopped out of the back of the ambulance with oxygen in hand, saying, "Thanks, Ms. Bloom; we've got her."

Lillian peeled Sinclair from Montreal and together they forced him to sit down on the bench, away from the rescuers. "Stay put!" she ordered Sinclair, then told Montreal, "Watch him and help the paramedics with any information Sinclair can give. I'll find Aurora."

Lillian plowed through the shop door, but then came back in reverse. Montreal winced at the near collision between her and Hans, who'd just appeared through the sky-blue side door. Montreal jumped up to hold the shop door open. "What on earth?" Lillian demanded, closer to exploding than Montreal had ever seen her.

"Got up for a smoke," explained Hans, through his thick Danish accent, "and heard someone crying for her mama from your shop. And now an ambulance is here? She must've followed you. You oughta keep a closer watch on this one." Out from behind the door came Aurora. The five-year-old clutched a slightly squashed doughnut in one hand and reached for Lillian with the other. Hans nodded at the sticky mess. "That was the best I could do to distract her."

Hans pulled a hand-rolled cigarette from his nightshirt pocket and slipped it between his lips as he squeezed past Lillian. "Montreal," he acknowledged, "what's this, Sinclair and . . . is that his woman?"

Montreal looked from the weepy man up to the one ready to help. "Judith—sir—they had a little too much to drink, I guess."

Hans shook his head as he pulled out his lighter. "Hans to you, no 'Sir' or 'Mister.' That's too American." Then he addressed Lillian. "Take the little girl up; I'll stay out with Sinclair."

Montreal, seeing that Aurora was fine, pleaded with Lillian, "Can I stay with Sinclair too, please? He's super sad and I think we need Lars. Can we call him?"

Lillian blurted out, "Montreal, oh gosh, you shouldn't even be down here, you shouldn't be seeing any of this, or you, Aurora, for that matter." She shifted Aurora from one hip to the other. "I agree. This seems to be another Lars moment, but I'm sure he's exhausted."

Hans sided with Montreal. "Good plan. We call the preacher." He patted his robe pocket in search of a cell phone.

"Thanks, Hans, but you be sure to keep Sinclair in your sights," Lillian urged as she lifted her worried eyes from Hans to Montreal. "And you stick close to Hans—got it?" They nodded as Lillian turned with Aurora. "Montreal, I'll be right upstairs waiting and listening. Call up through the window if Lars comes; otherwise, run up as soon as Sinclair goes with Hans."

Montreal nodded.

The paramedics loaded Judith onto a gurney. Montreal glanced toward Sinclair, then asked them, "Excuse me, sirs—er, I mean, well—sirs, can't he go along with her?"

Al frowned. "Sorry, he's too drunk, but someone could."

"Wait!" came a breathless voice approaching the scene from the street. It was Lars, still dressed in the same clothes as earlier. "Hey, Charlie; hey, Al," he waved to the paramedics as he stepped up to the curb to give Sinclair and Montreal hugs. "Not sure what's all happening, but I'll go!" he exclaimed. "Is this Sinclair's friend, Judith?"

"Hey, Lars, yeah, we're trying to figure it all out, but looks like alcohol toxicity. If you want to come, great; we can take two," answered Charlie, as he and Al secured a strap around Judith and loaded her into the ambulance.

Hans pulled off his robe and wrapped it around Sinclair. "I'll get him sober, thanks, Preacher. Exact timing. Seems this God of yours has you on speed dial."

Lars answered with a grin, "By way of falling asleep in the car. When I finally got it back to the church, I was too tired to get out, but woke up when I heard the ambulance."

Hans nodded and flicked the embers from his cigarette onto the sidewalk. "Birgitte said you delivered a baby tonight too? Like the Scandinavian fairy tales; the humble guy's smarts and hard work make him a hero."

Lars answered, "Thanks for taking him and thanks for that. Al and Charlie must be Scandinavian too." He winked at Montreal, adding, "And you too, since that's Hans' best compliment." Montreal felt immediately calm, steadied by Lars' very presence, like an anchor to his boat.

Sinclair grabbed for the ambulance door, but Lars redirected him. Hans waved goodbye as he led Sinclair to the bakery. "Let's get you a stool and some coffee. Birgitte can sleep through anything except problems in her kitchen—don't make problems inside."

"Lillian!" Lars called up to the second floor of the apartment. Lillian appeared and leaned through the open side window; her worried eyes softened as their eyes met. For a split second, Lars seemed to have no voice. "Can—can I take Montreal with me? After we get Judith admitted, we can grab breakfast, then find Estelle."

"Yes, with you beside him as our cheerful lifeline, I believe it'll be fine. Montreal?"

Montreal felt a little embarrassed as he looked from Lillian to Lars, then answered with an affirmative, "Yes—yes, please! Thanks, Lillian, and don't worry, we'll be safe, and I'll hug Mama from you."

"Okay, then, yes for sure," Lillian replied, "and keep an eye out for each other. I wish I could come along; you're certainly two excellent companions. Your mama will be thankful."

"We'll stick close. You take care now and get some sleep. I'll touch base later." Lars grabbed Montreal's hand and together they dashed into the ready ambulance.

53

Lillian

illian watched them go, feeling her jumbled emotions settle into peace. She held her heart as she sank down onto the couch beside Florence and Aurora. Sebastian came along, dragging his sleeping bag behind him. She reached her arms around all three children. "When we hear from Lars again, we'll ask when we can see your mama."

"Good," Aurora answered, then whispered, "but I'm scared for that lady."

Lillian stroked her head and replied, "Me too."

Aurora's lip began to quiver. "I wish Mama was here. I wanna see her."

Florence agreed, "Yup, but we know what she'd do now, right, sissy? She'd tell us to pray."

And so they did.

By 4:30 a.m., the children had finally fallen asleep once more, the girls on the couch and Sebastian on the floor. He'd found a cozy spot in which he nestled, between them and the coffee table. Lillian began to climb out from amidst the pile of sleepers. She'd not been able to sleep and by now she was desperate for a cup of coffee. Teetering in her attempt to avoid stepping on Sebastian, she set one foot down firmly on the carpet, then hovered for a second with the other. As she pushed herself clear of all the little sleepers, she realized she was standing in a sticky mass of smashed chocolate doughnut. The white carpet would never be the same.

54

Aurora

Name. Uh-raw-ruh : Latin origin, meaning "dawn"

When the dull grey morning finally arrived, one might have imagined that the sun had overslept. If anyone had peered out of the flower shop windows, the dark clouds brooding over the city would have looked ominous. But no one there, or in the apartment above it, was awake to contemplate the sunless sky, at least no one inside.

A vase of daisies and a cup of cold coffee stood on the kitchen table. Beside them, Lillian slept, with her head slumped over her folded arms and her legs tucked up under her on the chair. She slept as peacefully as if she were in her own bed. Mr. Blue Suede Shoes, who'd been hiding during the drama of hours past, now began his second morning nap beside his mistress.

In the living room, Sebastian had found his way up onto the couch, sprawling as he often did, with arms flung out on either side. Florence had climbed into his empty sleeping bag on the floor. With her face framed in the down cocoon, under unfurled brow, her dimples made a rare appearance as she snoozed. The stray hair bobble remained unclaimed.

Outside on the bench below, the thrift store wool coat landed from above with a thud. Next came the clink of the tip of a well-aimed umbrella. The final deposit from the upper floor side-window made a bumpity-bump landing; it was a box of cat-treats. The little person who'd mustered the courage to run away stared down at the borrowed items she'd thrown. Only a few pedestrians passed under her, but no one noticed anything out of the ordinary; everyone was in a hurry or lost in the face of a smartphone.

Perched on the windowsill and holding to its frame with one hand, Aurora reached for the closest branch of the Norway maple. It was cold, but the snow had disappeared from its branches, surrendered to rain and in anticipation of spring. She scooted onto the branch, then all the way to the trunk.

"Don't look down!" Montreal had drilled into her mind when he'd taught her tree climbing at the park. She remembered his advice now. She squeezed her eyes shut for a few seconds as she clung to the trunk, then inched her way down along the remaining branches and knots without a hitch, careful of the slick parts. She jumped from the bench to the sidewalk, then pulled on the coat and popped open the umbrella. With a bit of hesitation, she examined the cat treats, the only snack she could find in the kitchen; hopefully they weren't poisonous to human girls.

She peered up at the menacing sky, believing she'd make it to the hospital before the first cloudburst. The most likely place for a hospital was surely in the direction the ambulance had gone several hours earlier. Mama and Lavender Blue would be pleased—how lonely they must've been without their favorite girl!

The frigid air came in puffs of cartoonlike clouds from her breath. As she walked, she looked and looked, hoping to see the hospital any minute. After a while, she no longer recognized any of the storefronts on Stratford Lane. Then the drizzly rain became pelting drops, forcing passersby to pull up their collars and dash ahead, or duck under awnings for shelter. Aurora stepped up to a storefront and let the umbrella fall back, teetering on her shoulder. Panic stirred in her belly. *Am I lost?* she wondered. Turning to face the storefront, she pressed her forehead against the cold glass.

She gazed into the window, where huge rugs hung on horizontal poles. One had lines of ovals marching down deep red and black columns. They looked like elephant footprints. Another was shimmery with flowers and leaves flowing out of urns. The one in front was porcelain blue and the color of ripe apricots. Beyond the hanging rugs were massive piles of carpets, stacked like the bread from her favorite book, *The Princess and the Peanut Butter and Jelly Sandwich*. In it, the princess leapt onto a bed of layered bread, peanut butter, and "oh-so-strawberry" jam. How she would love to leap onto those soft rugs!

While lost in imagination, she'd steamed up her side of the glass with her breath, so at first she couldn't see that someone was watching her. But then, a smiling face appeared, with dark curls and a little gold ring pierced through one side of her nose. Her eyes were almond shaped and her dark skin mirrored Aurora's. Aurora traced a smiley face in the foggy place on the glass; the little girl traced it back.

Without warning, a hand tipped in fingernails painted the shade of cotton candy, landed firmly on Aurora's shoulder. A full-figured woman, wearing all pink, stared down at Aurora. "I recognize you, Little Miss," she said. "Is your mama close by? Or Lillian Bloom?"

Aurora yanked herself out from under the woman's grasp and backed way.

"Hey now, you come here. If you're alone, you're not safe." Rhinestone glasses dropped from the plump face as the woman looped her bejeweled purse around her wrist, dropped her Learn 'N Play Daycare book bag, and reached again for Aurora. But Aurora took off running.

Aurora couldn't believe that the woman could run like the wind, but she could. Aurora threw the umbrella behind her. The woman whacked it aside with her purse and into an alley it spun. Up went the cat treats as well. These, too, she avoided with another arm blow—*like Wonder Woman*, thought Aurora. The alley cats immediately pounced on the posh breakfast cast so irreverently their way. Finally, though the rain was now slicing sideways and thunder and lightning scolded from above, Aurora flung the coat over her head and let it fly.

Aurora was losing speed. She stared back at the child catcher with wild eyes a second too long and *wham*!—down she went, head over heels, on a white cane with a slight red tip. It spun like a game spinner across the wet sidewalk.

The blind owner of the cane grabbed the brim of his cap and pulled tight on the leash of his guide dog. The dog let out a single bark, then stood stock-still at his owner's knee. The woman stopped short and scooped Aurora up from the ground, holding her tightly like a rolled carpet at her hip.

"Little Miss," she said breathlessly, "you coulda killed us all. What a race! If ya hadn't been racin' against me, I'd a bet on you, but I've been chasing children for near thirty years, and I always win!" She turned to the blind man who stood under the awning of a music store. "Sir, I'm Miss Ruby from Learn 'N Play Daycare. My deepest apologies for my little charge crashing into your cane like it was home base! Can we buy you coffee?"

A forgiving smile alighted on the olive-skinned face. "Apology accepted. I don't drink coffee. Did my cane trip the runaway you're holding?"

Aurora stopped her grunting and wriggling. She tipped her head to look under his black glasses, wondering how he knew she was there. Miss Ruby chuckled. "What a gentleman you are." She directed a word to Aurora. "Little Miss, did the cane hurt you?"

Curiosity overcame Aurora, who whispered to her new frenemy, "Is he pretending to be blind?"

The man chuckled. "No, Luminous, my guide dog, can attest to that, but I hear things most people can't—and you are quite loud. Now, if you wouldn't mind handing me my cane, I mustn't be late for class." The man leaned his cane beside him, then bent down to pick up a violin case and slipped it over his shoulder.

Aurora asked, "What are you doin' with that violin? Takin' lessons?"

The genteel man, with his perfectly coiffed beard, turned his face in her direction. "No, I'm not taking lessons, I'm giving them." A repair tag attached to the edge of the violin case read *Dr. Raymond Dreyfus, Lafayette College*.

Miss Ruby said, "I've heard of you, Dr. Dreyfus. I've heard you also teach children!"

Aurora piped up, "My Grandpapa played violin."

"Who was he?"

"Rousseau Delacroix."

The man bowed slightly. "Interesting. I must be on my way, but I do hope we meet again." he said. Then he headed off at a brisk pace, tapping as he went, with Luminous trotting alongside him.

In the course of their short conversation, the rain had stopped and the clouds had begun to dissipate, as if they'd lost their money on the wrong horse and were gloomily heading elsewhere. The sun stretched out over the street and onto the unlikely twosome. "If I set you down, Little Miss, will you promise Miss Ruby you won't run? My arm's near ready to fall off."

Aurora gave a nod. "Can you promise not to lock me up?"

Miss Ruby dabbed her sweaty forehead with a tissue. Pinkish-tan makeup appeared against the white. She pursed her lips, then laughed in one-syllable spurts, with her mouth wide open. "Lock you up? Of course not! I chased you because I know kids. And you had that runnin' away look. Kids is my job, and it's far too dangerous for you to be by your lonesome!" She draped her hot pink raincoat around Aurora's shoulders. "Now you can tell Miss Ruby all about your troubles and runaway reasons and we can do some figurin' out together. Nothin's so bad that a friend can't help you solve it."

"I'm not going with you and I'm not s'posed to talk to strangers and you're strange. Besides, I'm going to the hospital, 'cause Mama just had our baby in a car last night."

Miss Ruby nodded. "Well I'll be! The hospital's not that way—so no matter what, you're headin' where I'm goin'. The Carson Memorial route is back the way we came. Can you tell me more about your exciting night?"

55

Nazreen

Name. Nass-reen : Arabic origin, meaning "wild rose"

Nazreen saw the woman and the mystery girl approaching, but they didn't see her. She had righted the woman's book bag, dried off its contents, and set it against the door to her family's rug shop. On top she'd placed the forgotten rhinestone glasses and a little bag of cardamom cookies, hastily wrapped in a napkin. With that, she had slipped back into the shop, watching from a hidden vantage point as the girl and the woman noticed what Nazreen had left. *I hope she'll be my friend,* she thought.

56

Aurora

Aurora held tightly to the napkin, crushing the cookies only slightly. She'd share the treats with Mama as soon as she could, and tell her all about the magical little girl. Miss Ruby had promised they'd go back to the rug shop one day, but first they'd get Aurora home to Lillian.

That's not my home! thought Aurora in answer. *Home is with Mama!* But she kept quiet, repeating the name "Carson Memorial" over and over in her head.

As they crossed the street near the shop, Aurora noticed a waiting bus. "Caaa-rrrr-ssss-oooo-nnnn . . . Meeeemmm . . ." she sounded out.

"Yes, that bus marquee reads 'Carson Memorial Medical Center.' Very good reading!" remarked Miss Ruby. "Wow! Another wonderful thing about you! You can sound out words. Did your—" As they stepped up on the corner, Miss Ruby stopped short and fixed her eyes on something on the far side of the street. Aurora followed her gaze. Two children stood at the door of Learn 'N Play Daycare, holding the hands of a man who seemed to be pacing in place.

Miss Ruby's face grew even rosier. "Lord, have mercy, I'm late! Little Miss, come on. I gotta get you to Lillian fast! Let me just get ahold of that dad." Instead of calling with her cell phone, Miss Ruby let out a shrill whistle. She waved her hands frantically getting their attention—as well as that of a couple of taxi drivers.

Aurora had her chance. In the ever-increasing morning bustle, Aurora caught sight of an elegant black woman adjusting her briefcase as she stepped up into the waiting bus. Aurora grabbed the flapping belt of the woman's trench coat and entered alongside her, pretending to be a daughter-mother duo. The preoccupied woman didn't notice the lone little girl. *Perfect!* thought Aurora. The bus driver clicked twice on the woman's bus card, but she wasn't paying attention as she answered her cell.

Suddenly the driver narrowed his eyes at Aurora, stating, "That's an odd pink coat for a girlie your size."

Aurora furrowed her brow. "No, it's not. I like it . . . and that's a big fat beard for an old bald guy."

A slight grin softened his cynical face. He turned to the front, snapped the doors shut, then gingerly slid the bus into traffic.

57

Ruby

Name. Roo-bee : Latin origin, meaning red, ruddy, or blushing, and "precious gem"

Miss Ruby gasped. "Aurora? Aurora!" She searched all around her, but the slippery five-year-old had vanished. Miss Ruby felt sick. The bus! She looked in all directions, but it too had disappeared. Miss Ruby hauled her book bag and purse up onto each shoulder, secured her rhinestone glasses, and took off running to the flower shop.

58

Lillian

Lillian awakened with a start to someone pounding on the flower shop door. She knocked over the cold coffee beside her arm. It spread across the table and onto the white carpet below. Her groggy mind went from spilled coffee to smashed doughnuts, from Judith to Estelle.

She raced downstairs.

To her surprise, Miss Ruby appeared through the shop window. "It's Aurora—" she panted, "—on a bus—to Carson Memorial!"

Lillian pulled her keys from her pocket and undid the locks. "What in the world? Aurora? Can't be. I kept the keys on me—look," she said as she dangled the keys between them, "everything's locked, front and back."

Miss Ruby clamped her hands around Lillian's arms and gave her a slight shake, staring through false lashes. "I know it was her. I nabbed her, but then lost her—slippery little weasel—she's tryin' to get to her mother!"

"Miss Ruby," Lillian wrenched her arms free as a rush of panic crawled up her neck, "no. NO! Not again. You're mistaken; she couldn't have gotten out."

From above their heads, an anxious voice called down through the open window. "Lillian? What's the matter?"

Lillian looked up and answered, "Nothing, Florence, just rest a bit more. Aurora's there with you sleeping, right?" Florence shook her head, pressing her lips together in a tight line. Lillian trembled as she clutched the doorframe, feeling lightheaded.

Miss Ruby addressed Florence, "Hi up there! Can you wait one teensy minute while we chat down here?" She turned back to Lillian. "That's a climbing tree if ever I saw one! Now if you run, that bus stops three times before the hospital. I've seen you run; you can still make it." She began to dig into her purse. "Phone the police; I'll take that child in the window to my daycare."

Lillian called up to Florence, "This is Miss Ruby, my neighbor, owns Learn 'N Play Daycare. She knows where Aurora went. Wake up Sebastian and you two can go with her. I'll come back for you after I find your sister!" Florence clasped her hands and nodded. Lillian hesitated, then asked Miss Ruby, "Can you wait and call the chapel number instead of the police? You'll get Pastor Lars directly. He's by the hospital and can wait at that end of the bus route."

Miss Ruby pursed her lips. "Not call the police? Whyever not?"

Lillian put her hands up to her pounding head. "I—I don't trust him—them. Give me ten minutes; if I don't get to her by then, I'll let you know." With that, Lillian grabbed her shoes and took off.

59

Aurora

Meanwhile, Aurora sat beside her "mother," several rows back from the front of the bus. She watched the rearview mirror above the bus driver's head and, as soon as he glanced through it, she gave him a hint of a wave.

The woman, who'd now clicked off her phone, applied a fresh coat of lipstick. From the top of the lid, Aurora sounded out the name of the color. "Ma-roo-n-ed."

The woman smiled, tipping the lid to look at it. "Correct. You're smart." She sized up Aurora. Suddenly her smile melted away as an acute awareness spread across her face. Aurora froze, fear took hold, and, with eyes wide as saucers, she stared straight ahead, trembling.

The woman spoke in a hushed tone. "You're alone, aren't you?"

Aurora ignored her.

"I'm a social worker. Just point to your family and I won't ask any more questions."

Aurora reasoned, *If I'm as silent as a mouse, she'll forget I'm here, then I'll run off the bus!* But the bus kept jostling along; the woman wasn't buying the silence.

"Quickly now, show me your family or friends, and I'll leave you be. I'm a safe person. I just want to see that you're safe right now."

Aurora covered her face, bent over her knees and, in fire hydrant fashion, burst into tears. "I'm by myself! I ran away from Miss—" she paused having forgotten Miss Ruby's name, "—Pink and I'm going to see Mama . . . she's at Carson's Memory Hospital. Please don't tell Lillian!"

The woman continued in soft tones. "Who's your mama and who's Miss Pink and Lillian? You can tell me; I'm safe and I'll help you."

Aurora sobbed into her hands. She was exhausted, hungry, and caught; surely her life was over! "Our Lillian, the bloom Lillian. I climbed out her window and Mama is Mama, and my baby is Lavender Blue, borned in the car last night, and Miss Pink's name isn't that, but she is pink!"

60

Lars

Only a few blocks away, Lars and Montreal sipped orange juice at Pearl's Pancake House, across the street from Carson Memorial. Through the window they noticed Ms. Sylvia standing on the sidewalk, waving good-bye to Charles, who pulled away from the curb. Montreal stifled a yawn.

Sylvia waltzed through the door of the restaurant like she owned the place: a given, since she did. She shimmied her agile body into the window booth beside Montreal asking, "May I?" He scooted over. She called to their server, "Delilah! Coffee and my usual, please." Then she looked from Montreal to Lars. "Wow, what a night you've had. Heroes before my very eyes, heroes indeed! Did you order, as I instructed on the phone?" They nodded, as she unwound her purple scarf, then reached for the mug Delilah handed her. When the dust of her entrance finally settled, so did the seriousness in her eyes. Lars felt she'd aged since last they met. "I'm sick—sick about my brother's behavior. And worried sick about his friend Judith. What more do you know?"

Lars replied, "Judith is still in a coma, but since I'm no relation I couldn't stay. However, when her caseworker arrives, I'll have the role of chaplain, so then we'll collaborate."

Delilah appeared with a stack of fluffy pancakes dripping in boysenberry syrup. These she handed to Montreal, then placed a cinnamon maple roll stuffed with bacon in front of Lars. For Sylvia, she brought a bowl of oatmeal piled high with raspberries, pecans, and a pitcher of cream on the side.

Lars laughed. "This sure beats soda and candy bars at the ER." His cell phone ring broke into the feast before anyone could take a bite. "Miss Ruby . . . yes, wait, wait . . . slow down—" A wave of concern enveloped him. "Thanks so much. Got it! Goodbye!"

He shoved his phone into his pocket and stood up. "It's about Aurora. She's on a bus, alone, trying to get to Estelle. Let's go! You two wait at this bus stop here in front. I'll run to check the stop at Lowell and Hunt!"

All three of them rushed out the door. Lars waved to Sylvia and Montreal and, with the deep-green Hunt sign in view, sprinted down the busy street, hurdling over small dogs and zigzagging around dawdlers.

He made it there just as the bus arrived, though several people stood ahead of him, waiting. The doors opened, but before anyone could disembark, a panicked person darted up the steps, into the bus from the street.

Like popcorn, remarks burst out into the air. "How rude!"

"What the—?"

"Get at the end of the line!"

"Excuuuuse me?"

"Ouch!"

But the person squeezed through the ranks anyway.

Then Lars heard a familiar squeal from inside the bus, beyond the disgruntled passengers. It was Aurora—Aurora and Lillian!

The commotion died down as they descended the steps, hand in hand. A stern woman followed behind them. Lars drew them away from the bottleneck they'd caused. "Aurora! You're here and safe, praise God!"

Lillian scooped Aurora up in a hug. "Aurora, I was so worried. Why do you keep doing this? My heart can't bear it!"

The woman stood to the side, waiting a moment before she addressed Lars. "I see that must be the Lillian of Lillian Rose Blooms, and are you Pastor Lars Gundersen? The chaplain, who I'm to meet?" Lars nodded as she continued, "I realized you were involved when Aurora explained last night to me. So, you delivered her baby sister in your car instead of the hospital? Am I right?"

"Yes, but I can explain—"

"No need. And Miss Pink? Is she going to come galloping down the street any second as well?"

"Miss Ruby, that'd be Miss Ruby; it's she who called me." Lars felt small.

"And the police, did she also call the police about a missing child? Because I see no police and Miss Ruby is the day-care provider, is she not?" Lars felt like he, and probably most people, wouldn't measure up under her steely gaze. He didn't care what Ebony Scott thought of him, but wished to shield Lillian from her condemnation.

Suddenly Lillian seemed to come to her senses. "Hi, hello, I recognize you. I'm Lillian and thank you, so, so much for finding Aurora! It was I who told Miss Ruby not to call the police because I thought I could sprint fast enough. And, I just didn't trust . . ."

A wry smile appeared on the woman's face. "Don't trust the police? Is that so. Well, Ms. Bloom and Pastor Gundersen, I'm Ebony Scott, and as a social worker I'm fascinated by your responses. As for Aurora, I'm taking her directly to her mother. Goodbye."

Lars found his real voice, "Mrs. Scott, may we take you to breakfast first? There you'll see Montreal, Aurora's oldest brother, and we'll arrange to see Estelle, and bring her other children, so as not to alarm her. I'm sure you're very concerned that she feels no extra anxiety and only peace during her recovery."

Ebony Scott adjusted her tortoiseshell glasses. "Why, yes, yes of course I am. What breakfast place do you mean?" She'd begun walking at an impatient pace; the others joined in with her stride.

61

Estelle

Estelle shifted in her hospital bed as Lavender awakened. "Hello, beloved," she whispered. The little face became still, listening to her mama's voice. "Welcome to your first morning." Lavender's tiny hand appeared, tightly closed, pushing out from the blanket. Estelle smiled, feeling the beauty of the moment pour into her soul. The words to one of her favorite hymns came to mind: "When peace like a river attendeth my way . . ."

The door opened and in stole a man wearing a white coat and a surgical mask. Estelle recognized him immediately and reached for the call button. "Wait," he urged, removing his mask, "hear me out."

She cradled Lavender close to her bosom, feeling the anger blaze through herself. "If you want to see me or any of us, do so in the open. Sneaking in like this sickens me."

Anthony stepped closer. "Babe, I do this to protect you. If anyone knew you were here, all of New York City would be clawing the walls for gossip about my New York Cinderella."

"Why are you here?"

"For you. Remember what the world said of us? He promised the moon and sun to the rising star. We were real-life poetry; we can be that again."

"A rehearsed speech? Shall I applaud?" She fought to stay calm, though fear welled up in her throat. "What do you want? I won't allow you to threaten us—we're not your pawns."

"Challenging me, are you? Your past speaks loud and clear: unfit mother. Out of obscurity, the nightclub addict arrives, but I can change those headlines waiting to appear. I can help, you know. You've backed yourself into a corner, so be careful not to smear 'The Benefactor of New York City.' I have a following few can rival." He laughed. "So, how many have heard that you gave birth in a beat-up car on the side of the road? None. I've already paid a small fortune to keep your neglectful choices out of this morning's paper. And this fifth baby—are we certain of paternity?"

"How dare you!" Hot tears stung Estelle's eyes. "We've been given this precious life and you know it. Let the paper print what it wants; I've never cared. Now, tell me, why are you here?" The room felt dark. She prayed silently, bracing herself.

He began again in a gentler tone. "I've covered for you, now it's time to stop fighting and give in. You know I only want a chance to love you; I get frustrated when you flare up. All I want is to help you and our children. I've missed you, even though you've been difficult. I still love you. Come on, babe, it's time to come home."

Estelle's stomach churned. "Stop lying."

"Come on, I've said I'm sorry. A year ago, I wasn't ready to show what I felt, but I am now; you just need to let me."

"Stop lying, Anthony," Estelle felt a wave of exhaustion weaken her. "I came, we came, willing to believe and forgive you, but you treated us as if we were worthless. You never even spoke to our children. Do you even know them? You always want what's just out of reach, without noticing who's reaching for you. You can't squander them, Anthony. I won't let you."

"I know; I know that now. That's why I'm here, risking everything for you! Just give me one last chance."

"Then what? You hold us hostage again? Use us? Crush your children's fragile hearts? I won't. You had your last chance. You can't hurt us anymore."

"I know you better than that, Estelle. I know you'll do what's right and be gracious. Only I can provide for you and here I am, but I won't always be this kind, and I won't wait much longer." Lavender let out a squawk. Estelle reached for the bottle, but it slipped from her fingers. Anthony checked his phone, then peered through the slats of the blinds. The bottle tipped back and rolled toward Estelle, where she could finally grasp it. Anthony turned back to her, his eyes now moist. "I'll give you all your heart desires. Please, must I beg?"

Estelle's voice rang out clear again. "Our hearts' desire? We have friends who see our needs and fill them. They love us unconditionally and our children love them."

Anthony fired back, "You mean the pastor of that empty church, that crumbling eyesore. And Lillian, of course, Lillian, who can't even keep track of our four-year-old?"

"Do you mean our five-year-old? She and the others are safe at Lillian's apartment right now."

"Haven't you heard?" he scoffed. "Aurora ran away. And Montreal's down there at the restaurant waiting with your pastor friend. He was up all night—because that's what teenagers should be doing! Calling these people your friends is just another sign of neglect."

"You don't even know your own children's ages. Montreal isn't a teen, he's twelve. And whatever's going on, there's a good explanation. I'm sure I'll find out soon. But as for need, it's you who needs us. It's all politics and power—it's in your best interest—that I've known for a long time. You're too cowardly and manipulative to say it straight."

Anthony's eyes flashed. "Their best interests are to be with their dad who will be New York City's next mayor. You can do this the easy way, Estelle, or you can fight me. You give in or I take custody. I'm their dad, an upstanding, stalwart citizen. You, my dear, are weak and pathetic. Someone who once was famous, and still thinks she's something. You're nothing but sick and impoverished, worthy only of pity. And what's more, you're a religious fanatic, more dangerous to our children now than you've ever been. When the pressure rises, those friends will leave. You'll find that your God doesn't exist. Then you'll lose everything."

"You're wrong." Estelle felt a deep calm come over her. "My friends are trustworthy and authentic, present and loving. But even when I didn't have a single friend, the Lord never left my side. He loves me and will take care of us. It's you I pity. You're surrounded by people, but alone in your striving. Do you have a single friend? Do you trust anyone? Can you shut off your fearful mind at midnight?" Estelle searched her husband's face. "There's still time to turn to God, Anthony.

Worth isn't in what others think you are; it's in who God is, in His love. You must pay for your crimes, but then your heart would be free—free of fear, of guilt, of torment. It's never too late for forgiveness."

Anthony narrowed his eyes. "You're even more of a fool than I realized!"

The nurse rang in. "Estelle? Your pastor, children, and Ebony Scott are here to see you—shall I send them in?"

Anthony put his hand on the door as Estelle answered the nurse. "Yes, please. And is my five-year-old there, Aurora?"

"Yes, she most certainly is," said the nurse, laughing a bit.

Estelle held the baby up to her cheek and closed her eyes. "Thank God. And please tell me, who's Ebony Scott?"

The nurse paused, "Um—she's a social worker."

Anthony smiled, his dark eyes dancing with malice, then slipped out the door without ever even glancing at Lavender.

A shudder passed through Estelle's weary body. "Oh God, please show me what to do next and please, protect my children."

62

Lars

The next day, Lars called up the stairs from the shop below, "Who's ready for an adventure?" A herd of feet clamored down the steps. Aurora came last, stuffing a folded paper into her sparkly purse.

"To Mama!" they exclaimed, in unison.

"But first, ice cream!"

The little brood groaned and waited for Jesse to hand them their coats.

"Hey, why the long faces? Are you kidding me? Pastor Lars always makes things fun! I've got twenty-four tulips to squish in between primroses for an auction centerpiece—tonight! So, I will meet you there!"

"Twenty-three," scowled Florence, pointing to a scrawny green tulip, "that one will never bloom."

"Nonsense," exclaimed Jesse, "haven't we learned anything from Lillian?" She set the mason jar in the window above the sink. "I'm sure in its own time, the sun will coax this little runt to bloom, you watch. Now off you go!"

Lars scooted them out the door and on their way.

After the troop of five ate ice cream for breakfast from a food truck, they headed along the street toward Carson Memorial. Montreal led the way, Sebastian at his heels, while Florence came next, distracted by worry. Lars kept the procession moving forward with Aurora in hand, happily skipping, as ice cream dripped down between her sticky fingers. Suddenly, she let go of his hand and raced ahead, then stopped short in front of a violinist and his guide dog.

Lars and her siblings hurried to catch up. Aurora beamed, "Look, this is my friend I met! The one I fell in front of."

Raymond Dreyfus finished his tune with a flourish and a laugh. "I know your voice. You are the little girl who accompanied Miss Ruby!" Lars fished into his pocket and pulled out some money, then dropped it into the open case. "Thank you," Raymond replied, "I stand here weekly to serenade the street. Your donation will go to The Guide Dog Foundation of New York."

"I'm Pastor Lars Gundersen, and I love that—I saw your sign—it's a pleasure to meet you. I'm here with Aurora and her siblings and I'd love to get your card. Perhaps when our chapel is renovated you can have a concert there!"

Raymond smiled. "Thank you, I'd be delighted."

"Is this Luminous?" asked Montreal. "Aurora told us about him too. I'm her big brother."

Raymond turned toward Montreal's voice and said, with a wry smile, "Yes, and he hasn't forgotten her either. Whoever could?"

Montreal burst out laughing. "That's true, Mr. Dreyfus!"

Lars peeked around the door of Estelle's hospital room. Lillian motioned him in. "Announcing the siblings," he sang out softly.

Estelle laughed as she placed Lavender in her lap then stretched out her arms as far as they could reach. All four of her children fell into her embrace on either side, careful not to smush their new baby sister.

Florence recovered herself quickly and demanded, "Wash hands, everyone! Then the order goes oldest to youngest for holding!"

Lars laughed. "Minus me, I'll happily wait at the end of the line!"

Lillian added, "And I already had my chance, and even learned how to burp a baby."

"Good job," whispered Florence.

"Thank you," said Lillian, reaching her arm around Florence's shoulders, who tucked her arm around Lillian's waist.

Lars caught Lillian's eyes, all misty with emotion.

"Come here, son, sit here at the edge of my bed," Estelle said to Montreal, then placed Lavender into his arms. He gazed lovingly into the tiny face. Lavender sighed and so did all her siblings in adoring response.

Aurora dug in her purse for her paper. She unfolded it and turned it upside down on the bed, then took a giant step backward.

Sebastian explained, "Today, Florence told Lars she felt blue. I said that if blue is the color of sad, then what is the color of happy? We decided that yellow is the color of happiness, so here is our picture."

Aurora flipped the picture right-side up to reveal the magnificence of the combined effort of all the artists who'd contributed. The entire page smiled with sunshine, flowers, boots, ducks, lemons, haystacks, and baby chicks.

"Beloveds, this is the happiest picture I've ever seen. Thank you." Estelle smiled.

Aurora encouraged her mama to notice the blob in the corner of the paper. She explained that it was a lemon meringue pie drawn by someone whose name she refused to mention, but said he liked pie best even though he wasn't so good at drawing. She glanced reassuringly at Lars.

Sebastian concluded, "So, we wondered, too—can our baby be named 'Lavender Blue Yellow'?"

Estelle pulled him over and kissed him on the forehead. "I don't see why not!"

Spring

Noun. spring : the first season of the year, from March to May in the Northern Hemisphere, between winter and summer, when new growth appears and gardens bloom

A t the tips of the Norway maple, tiny clusters of chartreuse flowers peered out from red casings. These corymbs, bursting from nearly leafless twigs, were like fragrant fairy bouquets announcing the arrival of spring. A newcomer to the neighborhood, a chattering chipmunk, burst up the Norway maple's silvery-brown trunk, zigzagging along its canopy of branches in search of a mate. But the tiny creature found only a fellow bachelor, a goldfinch, also sporting silky black streaks, flitting about under the bright blue sky.

The chipmunk hightailed it down to the sidewalk and zoomed past the bakery and coffee shop. At the corner, he skidded through arched forsythia branches awaiting their yellow trumpeting blooms. He didn't pause to see the start of magnolia blossoms or to sniff the sweetness of star-shaped serviceberries or early honeysuckle, but safely shot back across the street and disappeared into Shakespeare Garden.

There in the park along the walkway leading to the fountain, crocuses, lingering snowdrops, and daffodils spread like a Persian carpet of blue, white, and yellow. Delicate pink hellebores made room for tulip spears to erupt from the soil around the fountain. The pale grass had barely begun to soak in the sun, but soon kite flyers and plaid picnic blankets would accept its emerald invitation to joy. For now, the slightest hint of petals from cherry tree buds whispered in the breeze, *Awaken, Stratford, it's time to bloom. Spring is upon us!*

63

Lillian

On Sunday morning, Lillian leaned over the shop counter and tucked her slipper-clad feet under the rung of her work stool. She always did this when in deep concentration. She squinted at the blurry instructions for securing the new screen into the frame for her upstairs window. She drew the instructions closer to her face, but she couldn't focus. Dr. Franklin had advised an extended hospital stay for Estelle in order to gauge next steps for her cancer treatment. A breast biopsy was already underway.

"Then what? This waiting is making me crazy!" Lillian voiced to the open air.

The empty screen dropped to the floor with a *clinkity-clink* and the frame followed it. Lillian reached down for them. "Ugh!" she exclaimed, lowering the sheet of useless instructions. But then, she nearly jumped out of her skin. Directly in front of her, two puffy little eyes stared straight into hers. "Sebastian! You scared me to death! How long have you been standing there?"

Sebastian didn't say a word at first. He was completely dressed, down to his shoes. He'd skipped a button on his wrinkled shirt and a fresh jam stain smeared the edge of one cuff. Other than these small mishaps, he appeared ready for something. He cleared his throat twice then began in a shaky voice, "We need to go to church. I need to pray for Mama. She can't die, like Emma's aunt." The words overwhelmed him, and he covered his face with his hands to hide his tears.

Lillian pulled him close. In short order, the stifled crying turned into hiccups. "I hate it when that happens," she began. "It hurts way deep in your chest. Shall I turn you upside down and give you a glass of water?"

Sebastian peeked through his fingers. "You've done that?"

"Well, not exactly—I mean, it'd take a pretty strong person . . ." her voice trailed off.

"No, I mean cry so hard you hiccup," he said, wiping his eyes with his cuff, then pausing between hiccups to lick the jam stain.

"Why, yes, yes, of course, the time I—" her voice faltered as she looked into his trusting eyes. She began again, "Um . . . well, now that's a good question. No, I haven't actually done that, but lately I've cried a lot, so maybe I'll get there. Does it hurt like I said it might?"

His tears and hiccups had begun to subside. "I guess so, not sure. It hurts most on the inside of your inside, 'cause that's why you're cryin'." A few more tears ran down his cheeks.

"Yes, I think you're wise. Who's Emma?"

"My friend."

"Sebastian, some people die of cancer, but not everyone," Lillian handed him a tissue, but instead of taking it, he closed his eyes and leaned in. It took a split second to realize that he was waiting for her to wipe his tears. After she did, he stood up a little straighter and smiled a tiny smile through closed lips. Lillian felt a tightness in her chest as she realized how deeply she loved this tender boy. "Sebastian, if you feel that strongly about church, then yes—yes, absolutely, we can go, but I'm wondering if we could just pray here? It'd be a lot easier."

"Well o' course," he shrugged, "but Mama says a church is a family waiting to meet ya. If we meet 'em, they'll pray for Mama like she's their family too."

"Well, I never thought of that. Then church it is."

"I made you breakfast," he added proudly, "jam and bread."

Sure enough, on Jesse's stool sat a saucer with a scrawny heel of bread on it, almost lost under a mound of jam.

"Wow," was all she could say at first. "How'd you do this so silently?"

"I'm gonna be a secret agent when I'm big, so I'm always practicin'."

Lillian took a bite of the sickeningly sweet fare, trying not to cringe. "Good to know because you probably won't be a chef."

After some sleepy resistance from the other three upstairs, Lillian suggested, "Why don't I run over to A Cup of Grace for hot cocoas with cream and sprinkles?" Everyone agreed. Halfway down the stairs she hightailed it back and scooped up Aurora, who was still rubbing sleep from her eyes. "I'm not risking letting you out of my sight!"

At the coffee shop, Stuart finished the last whipped cream swirl just as the door leading to the apartment stairwell opened. Hope appeared, wearing her pajamas inside out, a yellow tutu and a kitten-ear headband on her emerging curls. She held a book, *The Teeny-Tiny Giant*, under one bangle-clad arm, and Serenity's collar in the other. Aurora looked at her, mesmerized. "Hi," she said, in a high-pitched voice. "I'm Aurora."

Hope scowled, dropped everything, and put her fingers in her ears. "No!" she hollered as she ran to hide behind Stuart.

Stuart added extra sprinkles to the cup he held out to Aurora. "Sorry, about that kid, she's working on her entrance."

Aurora scowled back. "A little bumpy, I guess." Then she brightened, "Where's Julius?" Stuart looked up at Lillian. "Seems he's, uh, headed to church."

Lillian pressed her fingers to her lips. "Weird. So are we. Did he say why?"

"Does he ever?"

64

Suraj

Name. Si-raaj : Sanskrit origin, Hindi meaning "sun"

At Carson Memorial, Dr. Suraj Anand tapped on Estelle's door in a light staccato rhythm as he always did, no matter how heavy his task. He was thirty-one, married, and had become a new dad exactly six weeks ago. His radiant smile could've sold cases of toothpaste if he'd chosen the field of modeling. Days like today, he wished he had. He entered at her soft-voiced invitation.

The fading winter sunlight illuminated Estelle's regal profile as she sat wrapped in a blue silk robe by the window, staring out onto the hospital grounds. Lavender slept, swaddled in her arms.

For a split second, Suraj remained at the door. Estelle looked over at him with her serene smile and nodded knowingly. He walked in, then pulled a seat close to her.

"Hello," he began, in his warm Indian accent. "I'm Dr. Anand. I'm a surgical oncologist. I'd planned to share your results tomorrow, but my call schedule gave me extra flexibility this weekend."

Before he could say more, she said, "Thank you. Is it because it's bad news you've come to tell?"

He wasn't ready for her bold question. "Well . . . uh . . . yes, perhaps it is."

"I'm ready," she said simply.

He looked down at his hands, hands that had often cut cancerous tumors and tissue, halting the deadly disease and restoring years of life to his patients. In India, his father had said of his gentle touch, "Someday, son, you'll be a healer." How he wished he could be one today.

He looked into Estelle's stoic eyes and said, "There's nothing I can do, Estelle. Your cancer is in both breasts and has spread to your lungs. I can't remove enough of the disease to propagate healing. It would only be an extra painful process, which would bring about no survival benefit. Dr. Franklin and I would like to refer you to a medical oncologist, where you can have chemo-therapy to slow down the progression of the tumor and metastatic disease, to give you more time."

"How many months?" she asked.

"I never say exactly, because I'm often wrong, but your prognosis won't likely allow for even a year. Your cancer is aggressive." He moved to stand but changed his mind. "May I ask you a personal question?" Estelle nodded. "Did you know how sick you were? In looking through your records from the past, there seems to be some steps you chose not to take."

Estelle looked out the window as if weighing her thoughts, then bent down to kiss Lavender's tiny brow. "Before I could follow through with the steps I'd initiated in Canada after my biopsy, we moved, and then I became pregnant. I knew an abortion, or taking medication that would poison my baby, would hang in the air as wise advice by some. But life is sacred." Her eyes seemed to ignite with passion at these words. "I wanted no part of that. I'd never choose treatment over my baby's life, so I didn't have any."

Suraj nodded and stood up. "Thank you for revealing that." Estelle's eyes softened. "Dr. Anand, do you have children?"

"Yes, a baby girl, as a matter of fact."

She replied, "Thank *you* for revealing that. Then you understand, don't you?" He gave a quiet nod, then left.

Instead of checking on his next patient, Suraj slipped into the stairwell down the hall and made a quick call to his wife.

"Everything okay?" she asked in a surprised voice, since he rarely called from work.

"Just wanted to hear your voice . . . that's all."

She chuckled, then soft coos filled the receiver. "And here's another voice for Papa's ears. Almost done with rounds?"

"Uh, yes . . . yes, very soon. I love you . . . see you in a couple of hours."

Suraj slipped his phone back into his coat pocket. He patted every other pocket, desperately searching for tissue, as tears streamed down his cheeks. Finally, he pulled off his white coat and rubbed his eyes on the sleeves of his scrubs. After a few more tears and a deep sigh from which he slowly exhaled, he put his coat back on, straightened his lapels, and went back to work.

65

Julius

The service came to a close with Barbara pounding out "Amazing Grace" on the old upright in the corner of the church. Julius sank down in the pew. Her rousing rendition sounded to him more like something from an old-time saloon than a church. He peeked around at the thirty or so congregants and Estelle's children around him and found that his contempt stood in stark contrast to their joy.

Sebastian tugged at Julius' sleeve. "If ya don't know the words, just make up your own. God won't mind."

Lillian reached her arm around Sebastian's shoulder and gave him a hug, then poked at Julius' shoulder before saying, "I'd love to hear your made-up lyrics."

Julius eyed the earnest child, then began to sing; he knew the words.

Lars' rich voice filled the echoey sanctuary with the benediction, taken from Numbers 6: "The Lord bless you and keep you, the Lord make his face shine on you and be gracious to you, the Lord turn his face toward you and give you peace. In the name of the Father, and the Son, and the Holy Spirit. Amen."

Lillian whispered to Julius, "I'm impressed. I don't know the words to anything. But it's all so lovely and I feel such peace when Lars speaks."

Julius let a smile spread across his face. "Peace, huh? Seems to me there's a lot more than peace you're feeling!"

Lillian flushed. "I—"

Aurora interrupted, "Lars told me we get doughnuts after!"

Julius laughed. "You are a sweets sleuth! I'll lead, you follow. I know right where that is." He extended his arm to Lillian and the rest of Estelle's crew. They filed out of the sanctuary, through the foyer, then in through the fellowship hall doorway.

The children ran over to the stack of pink boxes. Florence brought the pastries over to Lillian and Julius. He thanked her, then meandered over to a sputtering, forty-cup coffee percolator, circa 1970. There he nibbled his eclair as he waited for Lars, who was greeting each member of his congregation.

Julius saw the three elderly parishioners with blankets draped across their knees, reach frail hands out to their preacher. A no-nonsense nurse with salt-and-pepper hair and a name tag that said "Shirley" squirted each of their palms with hand sanitizer before they could greet Lars.

"Shirley from Blake's Manor. I know you," came Lars' jovial voice. "I see that you're taking excellent care of our favorite people." Her cheeks reddened as she straightened the disheveled cardigan of the man nearest her, not noticing he wasn't one of her elderly clients.

"Do you mind?" the cardigan-clad stranger retorted, to which Julius chuckled.

Finally, Lars was free to chat. Julius instinctively handed him a coffee cup, steadied his voice, then explained, "I'm meeting Lucy and Storm at the park in two hours. I—I came this morning because I don't know what to say."

"Oh man, so this is really happening. You are meeting your child! How can I help?"

"I just wonder, why am I even doing this? I'm sure they hate me."

"It's time," assured Lars, "and no, they don't hate you completely. If that were true, they wouldn't be coming."

"Great," Julius answered sarcastically. "So they don't hate me completely, only mostly? What do I do with that?"

"Ask forgiveness, be thankful—it's amazing they're even coming—and listen. That's a start."

"I don't know."

Lars paused, holding his cup under the spigot of the coffee pot. "You're a glass-half-full or half-empty kind of person." He tipped the empty cup forward.

"My youngest brother used to say, 'Don't even begin with what's *in* the glass. First be thankful *for* the glass . . . then, for a hand to hold it, and so on.' You can't anticipate what's to come; you can only be thankful for what's at hand." He poured his coffee to the rim of the cup. "Today, you've got a day brimming with possibility."

Julius chuckled. "Smooth. Do you always keep props around for instant sermons?"

"You handed me the cup." Lars grinned. "So, what did Stuart say when you told him?"

Julius' face fell. He teetered forward to the tips of his shoes then back onto his heels. "I—uh—didn't get a chance to."

"It'll only get harder."

"I know. I know. I started telling him, but I'd just come from lunch with a potential coffee supplier. He kept bombarding me with questions, suspicious about the meeting—just a business meeting! I finally gave up. If he can't trust my business decisions, how will he trust me in this?"

"Try again, then give him space to process. You have to tell him, Julius."

66

Montreal

After church, Montreal held the door of the shop open for his siblings and Lillian. Aurora ran through first and raced for the apartment stairs, followed by Mr. Blue Suede Shoes and an unusually quiet Sebastian. Florence put her hands on her hips, watching them go. "Aurora's brainwashed that poor cat!"

Lillian grabbed a plastic corsage box from under the counter, and slipped in the half-eaten doughnut she'd been asked to save. "Brainwashed? What do you mean?"

"She keeps cat treats in her pockets all the time and eats them with him. Didn't you see him waiting for her when we got here? I think he thinks she's a cat."

Lillian frowned. "That would explain the brown sludge in the washer. I don't know if those treats are even safe for humans. Flip the sign to *open*, would you, Montreal? It's just about noon. I'll be right back; I need to check on Sebastian anyway. He needs a little extra TLC and I have an idea." Before running up the stairs, she interjected, "In case someone comes, just be your kind self and help them. I'll only be gone a few minutes."

Montreal read Florence's look, then called Lillian back. "And Lillian—can Florence call Mama?"

Lillian smiled as she handed over her phone. "Of course, and you can talk in the backroom, Florence. I moved a cozy chair in there; thought it could be your reading or chatting nook." Florence was taken off guard and couldn't hide her dimples. Montreal knew that reading was her second favorite thing in life—second only to being in charge.

"Lillian, you're good at knowing what people need," he called after her as she ran upstairs.

Just then, a boy with a mess of wavy brown hair and laughing eyes opened the door for a woman. She stepped into the shop, laughing and exclaiming, "I didn't even see that yappy dog, but when that woman started yelling? You're right; they looked exactly like twins!"

"I bet they'll go to the coffee shop next, to get a ca-*pooch*-ino!" said the boy, with a grin.

"Oh please!" laughed the young mother, synching the tie of her red trench coat as they approached the counter.

"Hello," greeted Montreal, thrusting his hand forward to shake hands. The boy had a firm grip and so did the woman. Montreal liked them immediately.

"Why hello, what a friendly greeting, our first in New York City," she said.

"Oh, are you moving here?" asked Montreal.

"No way!" the boy blurted out.

Lillian appeared from the stairwell with Sebastian beside her. In his hands was a heaping bowl of popcorn. He sat down on the last step, content to observe the flower shop rhythm like a favorite movie.

The woman asked Lillian for a handsome bouquet for a man and one for a little girl. "Perhaps the one for the girl can be tucked into the arms of this." The woman withdrew a stuffed bear from her bag.

"I have just the thing," answered Lillian, reaching for a tiny vase.

"Montreaaal," called Florence, peeking around the doorframe from the back, "Mama wonders if you want to talk with her?"

"Yes, coming," Montreal called back, though he was sad to leave the boy. "See ya around—or not." Sebastian rushed to the back room ahead of Montreal; popcorn flew from his bowl like the wake from a jet ski.

The boy laughed. "Not likely!"

Before Montreal had finished talking with his mom on the phone, the boy and woman had left. Lillian and Montreal both agreed; there was something familiar about the boy.

67

Julius

Julius sat at the edge of the park bench, crossing and re-crossing his legs. From beyond the play equipment, he saw Lucy approaching, walking closely beside her son. Storm was a lanky brunette boy with wavy strands of hair that fell over his forehead. He was clutching a basketball.

Lucy's eyes were hidden behind large, teal-rimmed sunglasses. Her platinum hair hung in soft curls at her shoulders and behind red lipstick was a warm smile, one Julius didn't remember. The Lucy he'd known from the past would've been solemn, dressed in black, with spiked hair dyed jet black. In her arms she held an elaborate bouquet and a stuffed bear. Lowering her glasses, she locked eyes with Julius.

Julius rose from the bench, but didn't move toward them—somehow, he couldn't. They drew near, only a yard away, but Julius' jumbled thoughts left him wordless. Storm shoved his hand into the pocket of his jeans and held the basketball still in the other. His grey down coat looked remarkably similar to Julius'.

"Hey," Storm mumbled, then took off for the basketball courts.

Lucy set the bouquet and teddy bear on the bench as she watched him go. When he reached the court, he turned back to look at his mother, then shot a perfect basket. She smiled at him, crossed her arms, and turned toward Julius. "Shall we walk?" she asked.

Julius nodded and put out his elbow for her to take, but she declined.

As they walked along the paved path around the courts and playground, Julius' words felt like sawdust. He forced them out. "I feel . . . think . . . know, actually, I *know* that it must've been strange to get my call."

"How do you know that?" asked Lucy.

"Um. Well, I guess, I imagine that it must've been."

Lucy said nothing.

"Okay so, I imagine that my call was strange, after ten years—since Storm was born you haven't heard from me—since I told you what I thought about a baby . . . then left when you wouldn't . . ." Droplets of sweat accumulated along Julius' brow. He wiped them with the back of his hand. Lucy's face remained calm and cool. He attempted a fresh start. "I imagine that maybe it was strange to wait ten years, after our last conversation had been so—rough."

Lucy finally spoke, "Rough? You mean asking me to have an abortion was rough for you? I *imagine* that was the easy part. The rough thing was when I said no. Wouldn't you say?"

Julius clenched his jaw. "Lucy, I don't know what to say! You're making this so hard! It was all awful, and this right now is horrible. No words exist to make up for my selfishness and carelessness with life. Yes, ten years! Ten selfish, careless years. What can I say to you?"

Lucy pulled off her glasses and stopped short. "*I'm* making this hard?" Her blue eyes pierced him. "No! You chose what you chose then—I'm not making this hard now. You are. Hard, you say? Raising a child as a single mom at nineteen, that's *hard*. Storm being a fatherless child, that's *hard*. And if you think this conversation is also hard, then maybe we'll just go, because you sound ridiculous!"

Julius gripped her arm; she yanked it away. "Lucy, please—please don't go. I'm not trying to belittle you or compare my inability to communicate as a hard thing equal to your tough, tough things. I just don't know what to say! What do I say? Tell me!"

"We have a lot of years between us, a lot of choices, a lot of time you wasted not knowing your incredible son. But right now, you have one thing to say to me—and later, to him."

"What?" cried Julius, his voice despairing. "What?"

Lucy's eyes softened. "Do you really not know? Tell me you're sorry. Ask our forgiveness. That's the one thing you can do now. Through forgiveness there's a way forward."

Julius tried to speak, but was completely powerless to quell the flood of emotion that overcame him. He wept into his hands, loudly, like a child. Lucy stood still for a moment then silently put her hand at the nape of his neck and drew him over to her shoulder. He leaned his head down.

After a few minutes, Julius stepped back and wiped his face with his scarf. "I'm so sorry. I've been sorry for as long as I could remember, but I've been ashamed too. It's been eating me alive. How can you forgive me, even now?"

Lucy spoke softly, "Julius, I forgive you. I'd already decided I would, but I'm glad to hear that you care this much. I had no idea."

Julius shook his head. "I kept pushing thoughts of you two out of my mind, convinced you were better off without me. Besides, my lifestyle changed after you. But when Stuart and I adopted Hope, and she was more than just the idea of having a child, it was like a knife slicing open a deep wound."

"We both know we were disastrous together. At first, I only kept Storm out of stubbornness against you."

"And I thought you'd give him up for me. It was such a cruel thought."

She nodded. "But then, the little life inside me began to change my heart as well as my body. When he was born, it was like love came alive in my life . . . and faith too. There had to be a God to create my perfect baby." She took his arm and they resumed walking. "When you called, I felt ready to face you. I must've been ready to forgive you too, because here we are."

"I don't understand how you can forgive me so easily."

Lucy narrowed her eyes. "Not easily, of course not . . . and I'm still working through what that means. Forgiven, yes . . . repaired, no. That's up to you. But my dad has helped pave the way by never saying a mean word about you. He's been an excellent role model for Storm."

"So, Storm doesn't hate me?'

"He's never hated you, but you'll have to earn his trust. Dad encouraged us to come. But as far as a relationship with Storm, that all depends on what he wants. He's curious about you, but if after today, that's it . . . it's fine with me. It's all up to him."

"Just so you know, I'm certainly willing to pay up for all those years of child support I missed."

Lucy let go of his arm. "Stop! This sweet moment has nothing to do with money! Don't you dare spoil it!"

"I know, but . . ."

"Stop talking!" Her eyes became ice blue. "Your family's money won't control me or my child! You can't buy Storm's love like your father tried to buy yours. Someday we can talk of practical future stuff like college—with boundaries, maybe—but not today. Today is about you, me, and Storm." She pointed her finger at Julius. "And just to clarify, there's no weird *us* thing here either. Not that I'm your type anymore, and your lifestyle is complicated for us; I'm not gonna lie about that. Just remember the ball is in your court. We're inviting you into our lives. Don't blow it. You've got one shot!"

Julius watched as Storm aimed for the basket from far down the court. It was a steady, perfect shot.

Lucy's stern mood brightened. "Now I'm starved! A great start to making a good impression on a growing ten-year-old and his mother is through our stomachs. Feed us, please!"

Julius looked at her wide eyed. "You may see that I've changed, and you have too, some, but that instant mood change, *that* I recognize! You *do* need food!"

Lucy punched him in the arm. "Truth. Now what are you going to do about it?"

He smiled in relief. "That's the one thing I know I can handle. Does Storm like submarine sandwiches?"

"Ask him," she answered, pushing Julius toward the courts.

An hour later, Julius sat back with a feeling of deep satisfaction in his soul as he watched Storm finish the last bite of his Kitchen Sink Sub. Storm had acknowledged his apology with a simple shoulder shrug. It wasn't much but it was still miraculous, a tiny shred of light in the dark expanse of years. The day felt like a true beginning of restoration. Lucy wiped her hands and grabbed her coat just as the front door of Subs 4 U opened.

In walked Stuart with Hope on his shoulders. Immediately he spotted Julius, who stood, but was momentarily stuck in the narrow corner booth behind the table. Hope wriggled in an attempt to climb down from Stuart's shoulders.

"Papa," she called softly to Julius, but Stuart wouldn't let her go. He narrowed his eyes at Lucy then stared at Storm for several long seconds before glaring at Julius. He left without acknowledging anyone. Julius' own words died on his lips.

68

Lillian

Lillian sat on the broken French garden chair beside her shop door. All was quiet as she gazed beyond the street lamps and into the bright moon. "Blue until you made me new with your song, all the day long as we danced in the light of the moon," she sang softly to herself. She missed Estelle. What was taking the doctors so long to get the cancer treatment going? She fiddled with the edge of a Band-Aid. She'd struck her finger with a hammer while installing the new screen and security chain to the window upstairs.

Someone appeared on the front stoop. At first, she didn't recognize the slumped shoulders and gentle tap. *Is it Benjamin from next door?* she wondered, quickly unlocking the door.

There stood Julius. "Can I come in?" he asked.

"Yes, of course," said Lillian, drawing him inside. "You look like you need a hug and a shoulder to cry on."

Julius' voice was steady and soft, "A hug would be great, but I seem to have used up all my tears, both of joy and sorrow today, oddly enough." Lillian reached her arm around him as he continued, "Stuart's leaving me—well, I'm the one who must leave, but you know what I mean. It's his decision. I'll stay just until I find an apartment close by because I *won't* give up being a dad, not this time."

"I'm so sorry, my friend. Come tell me all about it."

She'd not noticed the bag at his side. He set it on the counter and withdrew the bouquet and the stuffed bear. Lillian reached for the bear and removed the tiny bouquet from its arms. Julius' voice was deep. "It's a long story, but the CliffsNotes are these: today you met Lucy and Storm. She was my best friend, and he—he's my son. I thought Stuart would understand, but I was wrong."

Lillian picked up the bouquet, then set it back down. "Seriously? Oh gosh! You—you have a son?"

"What? So I can't talk freely here either?"

Lillian searched his eyes. "Come on, of course you can. It's just a lot to digest. It's amazing. He's kind and handsome like you and I see why Lucy was your best friend." Lillian leaned on the counter and sighed. "Maybe Stuart just needs time to digest as well. This is a lot."

"Who knows. He gets stuck on every tiny detail; it's suffocating. Do you know what he said about the gala? That I was enamored with Anthony Mullenix; can you imagine anything so absurd?"

"I think your enthusiasm can make it appear that way, but talk to me more about tonight."

"Mullenix can be questionable, but he's only been courteous to me. I'm keeping our business relationship neutral for obvious reasons. Stuart doesn't get diplomacy; he doesn't get me. Obviously, he can't have a generous mind with Lucy either."

"How long has he been processing this—when did you tell him about Lucy and Storm?"

"I didn't exactly tell him . . . he saw us."

Lillian sank onto her stool. "Oh . . . you know Stuart has to sort things internally, a little more like me. Be gentle and patient with him. Give him time."

Julius frowned, "Are you like that? I thought you were more like me."

Lillian shook her head. "We're all so different. Who can tell? The children say I know what people need. I used to think it was enough with flowers, but maybe it's more about safe places to bloom. Anyway . . . want some tea? Sebastian might have left us some popcorn to go with it."

"Sure, upstairs?"

"I have a cozy chair in the back room now, and I'll pull up my stool. My apartment is full of sweet sleepers."

Later in the week, the phone rang in the flower shop. Lillian ran in from the alley where she'd been potting spring planters and called to Jesse who was in the bathroom. "Can you grab it?"

"You bet." Jesse hurried out then answered, "Lillian Rose Blooms, Jesse speaking. How may I help you?" Her eyes widened. "Yes, of course, just a moment." She pressed the receiver to her chest. "It's the principal's office!"

Lillian quickly washed her hands then grabbed the phone.

On a notepad, Jesse scribbled *WHAT?*

Lillian shook her head, then focused back to the caller as she tore off her apron and kicked off her work clogs. "Uh-huh . . . oh, I see—well, I'm so sorry you feel that way . . . are you sure?" Jesse put her ear to the receiver, almost touching cheek-to-cheek with Lillian. A pert voice on the other end brought the conversation to an abrupt close. Lillian hadn't finished speaking yet. "Goodbye? Okay, fine . . . you hung up." She grabbed her purse and said to Jesse, "You heard. Montreal's been in a fight—Sebastian's there too—hold down the fort."

Jesse nodded. "You know I will!"

"And Jesse, listening in, right up to my ear—"

"Got it! I know I'm nosey . . . I can't really help it, but I'm working on it." Lillian was almost out the door when Jesse called her back, "But wait, what about Bravo's? They need the table arrangements in two-ish hours."

Lillian eyed her watch. "I've only got seven minutes before Bus 20 comes, but show me what you've got so far." She paused to examine the scattered foliage and empty vases on the worktable. "Oh Jess, seriously? What've you been doing?"

"This . . ." Jesse turned the computer screen toward Lillian. "Your tech stuff. You told me you were bad at it, and you are. Like, disastrously bad! So, this is your new filing system, organization and tracking account payments, client info and ordering history, and flowcharts for future events. We'll advertise a month, a week, then two days before calendar holidays."

Lillian dropped her purse. "Oh. I, uh, oh. That's incredible." She picked it up from the floor. "Well, do the arrangements now—and next time, do them first—but that's really incredible, how'd you . . . ?"

"Been studying." Jesse feigned carelessness. "But I *will* finish the bouquets for sure. Take care of those little dudes and tell me *every* detail when you get back!"

Lillian slumped on the bench along the wall of the school office. Dirt still clung to her fingernails and a handful of shriveled petals bulged from one of her pants pockets, forgotten from the morning delivery. She'd never been in trouble in school—ever—but right now she felt she carried the little boys' guilt on her shoulders, like a thirty-pound bag of potting soil. She wished she'd called Lars.

A secretary with a pinched nose and squinty eyes seemed to consider a paragraph's worth of thought before speaking to Lillian. "And you are . . . ?"

Lillian stood to attention, trying to ignore a piece of ivy that fell to the floor from her disheveled ponytail. "I'm Lillian Bloom. Thank you. You called about Montreal and Sebastian."

"Why, yeees," answered the secretary, peering over her bifocals. "You're the friend mentioned by the Mullenix youngsters' mother. And she's off having a *fifth* child I understand?"

"Had one—it's a her—a baby girl."

"Humph, less apt to fight then, hopefully." She clicked open the locked half door, then directed Lillian through it. "Right this way, please."

In the principal's office, Sebastian sat like a heap on a chair, looking down from his tear-stained face. Montreal was beside him, seething, his fists ragged and bloody. Two other boys sat opposite them, holding ice to what soon would be matching shiners. Two well-dressed adults who appeared to be their parents glared at Lillian as she stepped inside. The sweaty-faced principal, in a tie that needed loosening, flung out his arm toward the only vacant chair. Lillian shrank into it.

Immediately, Sebastian rushed over to her and buried his pained face into the crook of her neck. She patted his head and made room for him on her seat.

The principal mopped his brow with a handkerchief and began reading a long list of discrepancies and the detention consequences required. Montreal glanced at Lillian through worried eyes. She gazed back through kind ones.

When the principal was finished, the other boys and their parents filed out, ahead of Lillian. She tried to speak apologies to them, but to no avail. She turned again to the principal, who'd plopped back into his chair.

"Close the door, Ms. Bloom, and stay a minute," he ordered. His stern face softened.

"Boys, you've got a rough situation. I know it. And I'd do anything to help, but Montreal, if you tangle with those boys again, I'll have to suspend you." He blotted his head and yanked at his tie, pulling it away from his damp neck. "And that would break your mother's heart. Those are bullies, but their families pour tons of money into this school, so my hands are tied." His eyes became more serious. "They'd have my job if anybody knew I told you that. But you're brave boys.

You've got your whole lives ahead of you and you'll make it through this rough patch, just don't make it any worse for yourselves . . . or me!"

"But, sir," pleaded Montreal, who'd stood when the others left and remained standing. "They were so mean. They said mean things to Sebastian about our mama and our baby. He just told the story about the car, Pastor Lars, and all the stuff he was excited about." He clenched his fists, then shoved them into his pockets, streaking blood along the edges of the faded denim. "It's not fair! They started teasing and Florence tried to pull Sebastian away, but they pushed her. She acted like it was nothin', but I'm sure it hurt her. I warned 'em, but they just kept on, so I decked 'em! I couldn't help it."

The principal rose and placed a heavy hand on Montreal's shoulder. He motioned Sebastian over too but spoke directly to Montreal. "Yes, you could! No, it wasn't fair, but violence is the last straw. There are days it seems the only way, but beatings pound out hope for reconciliation. Self-control is hard, but peacemakers make room for enemies to be friends. Abraham Lincoln said something like that." He looked from one boy to the other. "You're good boys. You'll be all right. Now get outta here. Go home with your nice friend and cool off. Have some ice cream or something." He turned to Lillian and shook her hand. "Keep up the good work. They need you."

As they walked out the door and across the school playground, Lillian said, "After finding the girls, we'll pick up some yummy food from Subs 4 U." Montreal took long strides ahead, his face solemn, but Sebastian held Lillian's hand, chatting happily about birds, swings, and Bangji's good eats.

69

Ebony

A few days later, in the heat of the coffee rush, Ebony Scott stepped out of the taxi and up to the door of A Cup of Grace. She clutched a stack of documents to her chest.

This is for you, Mom. Everything will be all right. This is justice. She glanced behind her to see if the strangers passing could read her mind. As if that were even possible.

At the counter, Ebony found Julius balancing a tray of steaming drinks while complimenting a toddler's crayon masterpiece. Julius spotted Ebony and mouthed, "Be right there."

In a few seconds, he was back with the empty tray. "Hey, on the house, what'll it be? And how's the new office? I hope you're pleased." As he spoke, he'd begun frothing milk with one hand while sprinkling cinnamon on an outgoing spiced latte with the other. "Leather sofas always shine with Persian carpets underfoot. Did you know that one came from The Persian Rug, down the street?"

Ebony cupped her hands around her mouth to be heard. "No, thanks; not here for coffee. I just need a quick couple of signatures. And yes, the office is fine, rug's nice, thanks so much."

Pausing mid-motion, Julius caught her eye. "Something wrong? Signatures from both of us—Stuart too?"

She shook her head. "No, nothing's wrong, just a few from you."

Julius called over to Stuart, "I'll be right back!" Stuart didn't look up. Julius led Ebony outside. "Hey, what's up? You seem annoyed. I thought you'd love the office."

"I do. And I'm not annoyed; I'm thrilled. I just need you to sign this."

Julius tipped his chin to the side. "Have you talked to Stuart?"

"No," she lied.

"I see," he said, wiping his brow, "then what's this?"

It's an itemized list of everything you provided for my office renovation, showing you've received no goods or services for your contribution. It's routine." *Am I talking too fast? Slow down, calm down.*

Julius scoffed, "This is completely unnecessary. Everyone knows I'd never give anything with strings attached. There's a lot going on right now. Do you really—"

"Oh no, *I* would never think such a thing," Ebony interrupted, "just give these pages a quick signing—a formality, really." Ebony held the papers out to Julius along with a pen. *Is my hand shaking?*

"You know that I've no time to look at these now. I'll run over later to read them, I promise." Julius said, backing up toward the door.

Ebony reached for his arm. *Don't look desperate—don't look desperate.* "Oh no, let's just get this out of the way. I also have one other page—it's just a few sentences really, and you already agreed to them verbally, regarding your adoption finalization. I'd like to get this signing over with now, then come next week, when the curtains are up, you can see the finished product!"

"The curtains *are* up—the drapery hanger left me a message yesterday."

"Right. I'd forgotten—lovely, just lovely drapes." She held the papers up higher. Her mouth felt parched.

"I thought you'd at least notice the changes, especially since it's totally different than my original Garden Hotel-inspired idea that you didn't like." Julius swiped the documents from her hand, pressed them against the brick wall to sign, then shoved them toward her. "It doesn't matter. Whatever," he sighed. Ebony gave him a weak smile.

As she hailed a taxi, she couldn't shake his hurt look. *This is for the best, for everyone*, she kept thinking. *I have no choice.*

A couple hours later, back at Stratford Community Social Services, the office manager Beth spoke nervously into Ebony's intercom, "Mrs. Scott, I have Anthony Mullenix here. He says you're—"

Before Ebony could answer, Anthony had pushed ahead through the door, with Beth following helplessly at his heels. He walked past Ebony's desk, then stood at her side. They locked eyes. She stood up slowly.

"Hello, Mrs. Scott," he whispered, as his eyes roamed over her voluptuous figure. "And how are you today?"

She sat down quickly, then answered, "Well, thank you. I've completed the errand. I've made the boundaries for Julius that you requested."

Anthony picked up Ebony's picture of her mother. She fought the urge to rip it from his hands. "I'm sure your mother would've been pleased with your commitment to remove Judith's 'legacy' from Stratford, drunkard that she is. When will the house go on the market?"

"As soon as I can arrange it. You do know however, with such a large house, your family will appear more stable in the eyes of the court, not less."

"You don't need to worry about what I know. My plans go beyond a simple purchase."

"But how do you know she'll buy it?"

He set down the picture. "You'll be sure no one else sees it's for sale, except the ones I've mentioned."

"It's a slim chance that only they'll know."

"You'll figure it out. I trust you, just as you trusted me when the time came for your mother to die. How tender those last moments must've been, in the arms of her daughter, by the help of her daughter."

Ebony shuddered. "I understand."

Anthony answered his phone as he headed out. Ebony closed the door behind him, shutting out his rising temper exploding over someone on the other end of the call.

70

Nolan

An hour later, across town, Nolan West waited in the parking garage of Anthony Mullenix's hotel, along with several of Anthony's men. He stood between the black Corvette and two sedans. No one spoke.

Anthony burst through the service door, accompanied by a bodyguard. The bodyguard shoved Nolan against the car as Anthony hissed, "I've just been informed of a situation. Dammit, West—you messed up!"

"Yes, sir." Nolan readied himself for a blow.

"Tell her that I know!" Anthony jerked his head at the men. They quickly dispersed between the two sedans. Only the single bodyguard stayed. Anthony's voice was now barely audible as he faced Nolan. "Tell her I find out everything. She knows better than to cross me, but there are other ways to get rid of baggage. She's safe only if she's of use to me. Right now, she's a liability." Anthony entered one of the cars. Nolan tried to follow, but Anthony pushed him back. "Judge Rolland's furious; I'm headed there to cool him off. Get her to change her mind."

The car sped off.

Nolan wiped the sweat from his brow, cracked his knuckles and shook out his hands. He left the garage on foot.

71

Lillian

Lillian watched Jesse take a huge bite of her egg salad, sweet pickle, mustard, caper, and anchovy sandwich on rye. With her mouth full she crooned, "Hmm, delicious; want a bite?" She held the dripping mess out to Lillian.

Lillian scowled. "Gross! Why didn't you just eat some of what we got at Bang-ji's? You know she'd be offended that you're getting sandwiches off Main instead of from her."

Jesse took another giant bite. "Think she'd make this?" Out spewed a piece of egg that dropped into Lillian's coffee.

Just then the door opened and in swept Sylvia in a white, fur-lined cape; she was holding an alligator clutch. Charles made it to the door just as it shut in his face. He repositioned his wobbly bifocals, then hobbled back down the steps to wait in the car.

Jesse whispered to Lillian, "What would Montreal say if he saw that—something about wearing a zoo?"

Lillian chuckled. "We're pathetic! That's exactly what I was thinking—something about a safari, no doubt. He could sure use a funny distraction today."

"Should I get him or let him finish his homework upstairs?" whispered Jesse. Lillian shushed her.

Sylvia set her clutch on the counter. "Girls, girls! Have I got a plan for you!"

"Lovely. Jesse, can you uh, finish your snack, please, and take order notes?"

Jesse, who'd been leaning over the counter munching her dripping sandwich, reached for the paper towel roll. "Oh—oh gotcha, right. Excuse me, Ms. Sylvia."

"Stop right there, young lady!" Sylvia peered at the sandwich. "Anchovies?" she sniffed. "Eggs, capers, mustard, and are those . . ." she sniffed again, "sweet pickles? Oh, my word, a fabulous creation. Can I steal your recipe?" Lillian gagged under her hand.

Jesse went to wash up. "I knew I liked you, Ms. Sylvia!" she yelled from the bathroom.

Lillian's cheeks flushed. "Please, I'm ready for your order."

Sylvia shooed the idea away. "No, no. This is businesswoman-to-business-woman advice. Your business is booming. Real estate is always a wise investment and there's a historic house for sale. With restoration, it could become your second flower shop. It's close to a quaint row of shops, and perfect for you to have a niche."

Lillian frowned. "Oh, thank you, but one flower shop's plenty. I'm not ready for another."

"Is your mind so limited?" Sylvia opened her clutch and withdrew a printout of the property. "It's not about you being ready, it's about the situation presenting itself and you having the courage to throttle it! Daddy always said—he owned Stratford Bank, you know, I have a photo somewhere—'Dare to invest in dreams today and your seed money will bear ample fruit for all of your tomorrows.' Perfect advice for you, a florist: fruit, blooms, and so on and so forth!"

She dug around in her clutch and found her wallet. Behind a vinyl pocket was a picture of a law school banner hanging below the bank sign. Under it stood their father, Sylvia, and Sinclair, surrounded by other graduates. "Daddy promoted success wherever he went and even celebrated accomplishments at the bank! Clout and inspiration combined!"

Lillian pushed the printout back toward Sylvia. "I—I thank you, but I'm fine with what I have. I don't need success like that."

Sylvia lowered her voice. "Listen, this is your chance. Take a business loan on your shop. I'll get you a fantastic interest rate. Buy the property and I'll help you renovate it. Then you can live there as well instead of your cramped apartment!"

Jesse, who was pretending to dust the windowsill, almost knocked over the tulip in the jar. It clinked against the window as she righted it.

Lillian tapped her lip. "Excuse me, but I must ask you—respectfully—Ms. Sylvia, why are you saying all this? I am perfectly content with my business and my lifestyle."

Sylvia's shrewd eyes twinkled. "To be honest, I see myself in you. Now, I can't reveal the details, but I've got the inside scoop and my brother is good friends with the owner . . . whose name starts with a J, U, D! The idea came to me when a very wise investor I know told me about the house and the social worker, whom you know, thinks it should be sold as well, and spoke with me." Sylvia's shoulders sank. "And to be even more honest, I'm too old to come alongside Estelle, but you're not. You girls need each other, and this is your perfect chance to help."

Lillian shook her head slowly. "So even if *Judith* owns this old house, I still don't think we need to take drastic measures. When Estelle's back on her feet, she might not want to live with me. Besides, this sounds risky. My own little shop, and life, are of great value, no matter how small they look to you."

"Small? No life is small. Every single life is of infinite value. I'd no intention to speak otherwise. Just don't be too slow to consider. We don't know the future, but I know real estate and this property will sell in a flash once on the market." With a flutter, Sylvia was out the door—out the door only to tap on the car window to wake Charles, who'd dozed off in the driver's seat.

Jesse kept dusting. Lillian asked, "What are you doing?"

"Pretending I wasn't listening . . . but look," she pointed to the tulip in the jar, "it was scraggly, you made it bloom, it's a sign!"

Lillian rolled her eyes.

72

Jesse

O n her way home from work, Jesse noticed a distinct silhouette just
beyond the flower shop. It was Nolan West. She followed him into the
alley, saying, "Why do you look like a wreck? I got the ring back."

"Good, but he knows you kept the baby. Sent me to rough you up. I just
need to get a thumb drive from the hotel, the Garden Hotel, then I can hide you.
Everything's gotta happen fast." He looked over his shoulder and all around.

"Hide me? Absolutely not!" She slipped the chain from her neck with the key
and ring dangling from it.

He grabbed it out from the open air and closed her hand back over it. "Keep
this under wraps. I can't take it yet—the Boss and the guys'll see it. Been walking
for hours; figured out a place to take you tomorrow, just till coast's clear."

"If 'a place to take me' means dinner, great, I'm starved. Anything else, forget
it. Read my lips—no!"

"The Boss is mad," Nolan hissed urgently, putting his hand on Jesse's shoulder. "He hasn't connected us—yet—and I can still get you safe. You gotta disappear for a while."

She pulled away. "Touch me again and I'll slug you!" Nolan stepped back, holding up his hands. She continued, "Sorry, it's just Anthony can't take my life away. I've got people now—people to love, who love me. And they think I'm smart and need me. I already decided; I won't go."

"Stubborn fool, keep it down." Nolan paced for a few strides while he searched his pocket, finding only an empty cigarette pack. "How 'bout this: fake an abortion at Lafayette Clinic to buy time."

"I'm not pretending to have an abortion for him, Nolan!"

"Jesse, do it 'cause I ask you and I care about you—then you won't have to hide. Make the appointment online when you get home. Then, meet me near the hotel tomorrow at shift change, five o'clock, and give me the key. My brother Darnell works at the car wash next door: he'll watch for you, then get you out of there."

Jesse held her fist to her chest. "All this for a thumb drive?"

"Connects the Boss to a crime involving that hotel!"

"He has hotels all over the world. The Garden Hotel is a mom-and-pop deal. It's got nothing to do with him."

"No, it isn't just a 'mom-and-pop deal,' but I can't figure out how it's all connected. The name changed twenty years ago, but I can't find anything about the owners. The thumb drive will tell us."

"This sounds made up, or like a trap. The Boss wouldn't waste his time on something so small."

"He would have twenty years ago! It's proof of extortion! Look, Iggy's dead. Who's next? I don't care about me—but I do about you, don't you get it? And that Lillian woman, Estelle, her kids—no one's safe till someone does something. Boss is nervous. This evidence must be big."

"A thumb drive is all you've got? This sounds like a joke. And besides, everything in the compound was under surveillance. If Iggy scanned documents to a thumb drive, wouldn't the Boss know?"

"It's enough—it's from the early days, when he was sloppy, working his way to the top. I'm risking it all because I don't think he knows about it—but it's dangerous—no doubt."

"This isn't gonna work."

"It has to. For now, we gotta calm him—distract him—show him you're listening to his demands. I've got an idea. Give me your blouse. I'll turn around, and you can wear your jacket without it until you get home. But I'll need your blouse as proof that I beat you up."

Jesse unzipped her jacket and slipped off her blouse, then ripped it before handing it to Nolan. As she pulled her jacket back on, Nolan nicked himself with a knife and pressed the white fabric against his bleeding arm.

"This'll be enough. Now get home, I'll watch till you're safe. Make that appointment!"

She slipped the chain with the ring and key back around her neck and tucked it away. "I will."

"He'll kill you and the baby, just to punish you, if you don't."

"I—I know."

Nolan stared at her, as he clenched the blouse in his hand. "I'm sorry for all this. I just want you to be okay—and to do what's right."

"We're a team, remember?" Jesse put her hand over his. "You and me . . . for Iggy."

Roxanne was in the kitchen when Jesse finally walked through the door. She stared at her daughter. "Something's wrong. What happened today?"

Jesse frowned. "Nothing."

As Jesse headed upstairs, she could hear Roxanne's voice trailing off. "Tell me you wore something under that thin jacket . . ."

Jesse yelled back, "Right, Mother, nothing. Don't you know I prefer to be shirtless?"

73

Lillian

At half past three, Lillian stood outside Silverstone Apartment 7A. Beside her, Aurora twirled in a princess dress. The school bus rumbled up to the curb, the doors swished open, and out tromped Montreal, Sebastian, and Florence.

"How was your day?" asked Lillian, helping Sebastian with his backpack.

"It was school," muttered Montreal, leading the way through the apartment door. "But Mama's coming home, right? Is she—"

Florence interrupted. "When is she coming? There's so much to do!"

Lillian reassured them, "Soon, but don't worry, we're ready."

Sebastian, who'd pushed past his siblings into the apartment, called from the kitchen, "You're not gonna believe this!"

They ran to see.

The kitchen table was draped in white linen with a pitcher of pale pink tulips in the center. On a platter lay strawberries, blueberries, and raspberries. Beside it stood a stack of heart-shaped waffles, a bowl of whipped cream, and a covered dish of bacon. Their mama's six china cups encircled a pot of tea with cream and sugar cubes on the side.

Florence turned to Lillian. "It's a feast! You're the best!"

"Aurora and I had to do *something* while you were at school, didn't we?"

Aurora piped up, "I got to pick—I picked breakfast!"

A few minutes later, the doorbell rang. There stood the shuttle driver, holding Estelle's things and Lavender in her car seat; beside him stood Estelle. She held out her arms and the children rushed into them.

Montreal took the car seat from the shuttle driver's hand, thanking him, but the boy's furrowed brow remained.

"You okay?" Lillian whispered.

"Mama's so weak, she can't even carry Lavender in her car seat—she's too weak." He barely croaked out the words.

"*I* can hardly pick up that car seat," Lillian smiled. "You're a great help to her. You children, her home, that's what she needs now. She'll be stronger in no time." Montreal's face remained somber.

The sun had only just risen when Lillian awoke to the subtle smell of chamomile tea rising from two mugs set on the coffee table. Estelle joined Lillian on the worn couch, with Lavender in her arms. "Thanks for staying the night," Estelle said.

Lillian drew her legs up under the quilt and extended her blanket over Estelle's bare knees. Lavender stared up at her mama, listening to her voice.

"Would you like to hold her?" Estelle asked. Lillian nodded.

Estelle placed the baby into Lillian's arms, then drew her mug up with both hands and sipped. She closed her eyes and dropped her shoulders as she leaned her head back against the wall. For a while she was silent.

Lavender pinched up her face and let out a squawk. "Shall I just keep holding her while I grab a bottle from the kitchen?" Lillian asked.

"Thanks, she'll like that. Seems she's a hold-me-and-move baby, like Sebastian was—most peaceful in the midst of action."

Lillian stood up carefully. "Isn't that just how he is? He sure radiates that kind of peace. We could use another one like him." Estelle sank into the sofa and smiled. Her eyes seemed so dark that Lillian could barely make out their familiar amber hue. "Rest, even for five minutes, and we'll be right back."

Lavender drank hungrily as Lillian settled back onto the sofa. Estelle poured fresh tea, keeping her eyes fixed on the teapot as she spoke. "I've been meaning to share something for several days—the reason I'm not having a mastectomy."

"I've been wondering," Lillian answered.

"I found out that it's of no use. Chemo and radiation treatment will lend me a little more time, but only a little. There's no need for extreme measures now. My time is short . . ." Her voice trailed off.

"Oh Estelle, please, I'm sure there's lots of time; you're strong—the strongest woman I know. You're just weak from giving birth, but you can fight this."

Estelle dropped her head back against the wall again. "I've been fighting for so long, for my baby's life, and my children. I've had more time than I expected, and I thank God for that, but my time is coming to an end; I feel it. I need to make a plan for their future." Lillian fought back the tears that stung as Estelle continued, "I must ask you, but don't answer right away." Her eyes became glassy. "Will you be their mother when I'm gone? Will you adopt them? They love you so much, and I see you love them."

Lillian faltered, "Oh, Estelle, I—I can't be you."

A smile brushed across Estelle's lips. "Of course; I'm not asking you to be me. You'd be the wonderful you that you are. There's a sweetness between you and them, a rhythm that's beautiful to watch."

"I've no idea how to raise them. There's no one like you—always calm, always brave."

Estelle let out a slow breath. "Oh no, raising children is a battle and we all need help along the way. Anthony calls me an unfit mother and I was. If not for my folks' help, and God's grace, all would've been lost." Estelle cocked her head as she heard wakeful voices from the back rooms. "Now, before they come in, I must make this clear. If you choose to adopt my children, Anthony will do everything in his power to undermine you. He wants them. He wants them because they're his ticket to political power."

Lillian frowned. "Surely not! How? They're just kids."

"I know it's hard to believe, but Anthony is a very, very dangerous man. You already know the power he wields. I'm sure he's already working on something. If you say yes to this, it will be a great sacrifice and a fierce battle. God will be with you, but it will be nasty!" In that moment, Estelle's eyes glowed, as if the amber embers had been stirred. "But love is more powerful than selfishness. And if you want to do this, God will strengthen you for what's ahead."

"I don't have your faith, Estelle. How could I do this without you?" The tears welled up in Lillian's eyes as she kissed Lavender's head.

"Faith is before you, within reach. Ask Jesus to show you who he is, and he will. He's who you need most, with or without my children."

For a few moments, the only sound in the room was the tick of a wall clock. Finally, Lillian said, "Lars would be better at this than me. He has a way of bringing out the best in everyone. His kindness and love—that's what the children need."

Estelle smiled. "Lars couldn't be the mother they need. I believe in you, Lillian, but you must believe too. This is up to you alone to decide. "

"Will you tell Lars?"

"I planned to tell him about the cancer spreading. I'll call him this afternoon, but I won't share what I've asked of you."

Lillian nodded, then glanced at the clock as it struck seven. "Shall I start breakfast?"

"I'll do it; you make lunches." Estelle smiled at the baby, sound asleep in Lillian's arms. "Just one more question: have I overwhelmed you?"

Lillian shook her head. "Your question hasn't overwhelmed me. Thinking of not having you here, that's what overwhelms me."

Estelle leaned her head onto Lillian's shoulder. "We have each other right now and the children; let's enjoy the day we're in."

At 8:00 a.m., a pajama-clad Aurora stood on a footstool pulled up to the counter as her older siblings grabbed their lunch sacks and headed for the door. With a crayon, she scribbled her name across an empty brown sack. "Lillian," she groaned, "you forgot me. Just 'cause I'm home with Mama . . ."

"Is that so?" asked Lillian in mock surprise, opening the fridge.

Inside was a bulging lunch bag with *Aurora* written in swirly letters across the front. Aurora embraced Lillian from her perch. "You remembered me!"

"Who could ever forget you?" Lillian clutched the tippy stool under the effervescent hug. "Now, come on. I've got to go, but that wonderful hug will last me all day at the shop."

74

Lars

B ehind Stratford Chapel and beyond an overgrown path, Lars searched along clumps of grass surrounding the North Tower. Standing apart from the main chapel, the tower could only be accessed from the outside. Its brass key had disappeared, but Barbara remembered a second key from earlier times, hidden close to the entrance. Today, it was either find the key to the forgotten tower or destroy the door, since Number 23 on Miguel's estimate for renovation read:

23. North Tower: ? (we couldn't get in)

Lars looked up to see Barbara carrying a pair of scissors and a travel mug. She meant business and said so. "While you've been hanging out here in the grass searching, I noticed your hair is rather shaggy. You need a trim and I'm here to do it!" Lars sank back on his haunches and grinned. She continued, "A fresh look and twenty bucks saved. Besides, you need to look your best for a certain lovely lady."

"So, is matchmaking now part of your job description? I don't remember that detail," Lars chuckled. "I don't mind you cutting my hair, whatever you'd like, as long as I don't have to wear a suit. Except for Sundays, I've worn Levi's all my life."

234

"Same pair for most of it, no doubt. New Yorkers aren't like you beach-bum Californians. What would your mother say about that mop?"

"My mother?" Lars shook his head, answering matter-of-factly. "She left when I was two, but if she ever returns, I doubt she'll care much about my hair."

Barbara's face fell as she handed him the mug. "How did I not know that? Please forgive me."

"Of course I do. It's not as hard a subject as you might think. My dad forgave her and taught us to forgive. It was his life rhythm. And as far as hair goes, he and my brothers have always had long surfer hair. They needed a Barbara in their lives." He grinned.

"Boy, that sun is hitting me right in the eyes," came Barbara's quiet voice.

"You're softer than you let on, dear Barbara," said Lars affectionately. He gulped from the mug, expecting coffee, but the thick mush of spinach, Cayenne pepper, and some mystery ingredients burned his throat. Lars jumped to his feet, choking and sputtering.

"Hmm, too much pepper? Or do you not like figs? It's healthy, you know!"

"Coffee—just—coffee, please," Lars wheezed. "Please warn me next time!" Steadying himself against a fence post, he wiped his burning lips. Suddenly the post gave way.

"You found it," shouted Barbara, staring down at the lost key, tucked into a carved space at the base of the crumbled post. "It looks like someone already knew exactly where it was!"

Sure enough, the key turned easily and the door to the tower swung open on well-greased hinges. Inside lay piles of empty bottles, soiled clothes, candle stubs, and tattered blankets. The pungent smell of urine filled the air.

Lars shook his head. "Look at this. I'm trying to build a safe home base for our homeless friends, and this is where they've been all along—in our own backyard."

"At least we know where they've been sleeping. You keep doing this messy job of loving people right where they're at and they'll keep coming."

"But who are they?" He covered his nose and stepped inside. Everything looked communal and disposable.

"I'm sure I've served coffee to lots of them!"

"Do me a favor," Lars teased, "please try not to kill them with your healthy shakes though."

Barbara tried to hide her smile. "Haircut first, then we give this place a good scrub, then you call Miguel. You must look presentable for your meeting with Mrs. Scott and the others at the old house. Oops, I forgot a towel—be right back."

As Lars waited, his cell phone rang. It was Estelle, calling to share the details of her conversation with the surgical oncologist. As a pastor, this kind of call was not unknown to Lars, but that did not make it any easier. As Estelle told him the news, his heart broke for her and her children.

At the end of their conversation, he asked gently, "Can I pray for you, Estelle?"

"Yes, please, Pastor Lars," Estelle responded calmly. "And please pray for the children too, that they will be strong, and feel God's love and strength for them all."

The two believers shared a faith-filled moment on the phone as Lars committed Estelle to God's care and asked for his tenderness and grace in her life. Before she said goodbye, Estelle asked Lars to share her news with Barbara.

Lars couldn't help the tear that fell from his eye when he silenced his cell phone and slipped it back into his pocket. Though he knew God would somehow turn things for good—he always did—Lars ached for the difficulty he knew was ahead. He was glad for the physical work of cleaning the tower in front of him—to take his mind off his sadness, and to occupy his hands while he prayed silently for Estelle.

At 3:40 p.m., Lars pulled up to Judith's old family home, still pondering Estelle's call. Slowly, he climbed out of the driver's side window. *Why, God?* he kept asking, over and over. *Why Estelle?*

There were times when Hebrews 11 guided him as a bright light in the darkness. He grabbed the little Bible he'd stuck in the glove compartment of the Gran Torino and read the verses out loud to himself. "'Now faith is confidence in what we hope for and assurance about what we do not see . . .'" Again and again, he'd read those two powerful words, "*by faith*," followed by each person who'd faced trials and clung to God's promises. Did he have faith that God was still good even when Estelle's body was failing? Did he have faith that God had a plan for Montreal and his siblings without their mother? Did he have faith that God could bring joy out of such deep suffering and sorrow? He approached the house to sit on a wide porch step and think. Through a split up the side of a board, a stray daffodil bloomed.

It reminded him of his wedding day. She'd loved daffodils. There'd been daffodils everywhere, radiant as his bride's face—radiant, at least, until the moment she was to walk down the aisle. The violinist had begun "Ode to Joy," one of his brothers poked him in the ribs saying, "This is it!", and everyone stood in delighted anticipation. But she had faltered and then, without explanation, fled out of the church—and out of his life forever.

He'd been devastated, but in his loneliness, Jesus comforted him, and that powerful love now shone brighter through the cracks of his broken heart. By faith he'd chosen to believe God could and would turn all things to good. It didn't mean he suddenly understood suffering, or that there wouldn't be pain. It meant that God would never leave or forsake him. He clung to faith now, believing that God had a good plan for Estelle and her children. "By faith . . ." he repeated.

But what else was stirring inside him? By faith Estelle had responded in love to Anthony. She'd forgiven freely, withholding nothing, even though he'd not returned her love. Lillian had willingly forgiven Bryce and found freedom from it. Shouldn't his own forgiveness of his bride release him to a new chapter, to love again? Perhaps fear instead of faith had kept his own heart bound for all these years. It hadn't even occurred to him until now.

He put his Bible away and decided to explore the grounds until everyone arrived. Weeds rose to waist level along the brick walkway that led around the two-story Victorian. He ventured along the side of the house and into the backyard, meandering through castaway tires and trash. In the center of the yard was a gazebo, enveloped by branches of gnarled fruit trees. Weeds cascaded from a crumbled fountain. Beauty had once lived here.

Two cars pulled up. Lars headed back, along the side of the house. Suddenly he stopped short, having caught his foot in a metal ring stuck in the ground. He pulled his foot out, hopping for just a second. *How strange,* he thought before hurrying to the street.

Ebony Scott stepped up to the curb just in front of the house, while Sinclair helped Judith out from the back seat of the Town Car.

Ebony addressed the group. "Welcome. Thank you all for coming. Judith Greenville Harris, I need to establish this building as your privately owned property and your place of residence. Is that correct?" She removed a folder from her bag and began examining documents. Judith didn't answer, but rather stared at Ebony, who continued, "Let's go inside; please watch your step."

"*Greenville* Harris?" asked Sinclair under his breath.

Inside the entryway, an elegant stairway curved up to the second floor. Some of the steps were missing, along with many of the spindles and parts of the carved railing . Rotted floorboards and mice droppings kept everyone wary of exploring. "Judith, do you understand my question?" Ebony asked without looking up.

"Of course," began Judith. "But I know you. You're Ida Lenore's girl. You were four years old when last I saw you, remember?"

Sinclair swayed, then leaned against the door frame to steady himself. Lars came alongside him, but said nothing. Judith's eyes stayed fixed on Ebony.

"No, I do not." Ebony held her pen poised. "But yes, that was my mother." She looked down at the papers in her hand. "Let's continue. I have property estimates listed here. Unless you would advise otherwise, Pastor Gundersen, I think we can sell the property as is?"

"Ain't she around anymore?" Judith interjected.

"No, she isn't. Now we must stay on task. Pastor Gundersen?"

Lars turned to Judith. "Judith, do you want to sell this property?"

Judith nodded. "But poor Ida. I didn't get to say goodbye. Did you live with family after the hotel?

"Judith, back on task please. We can do this smoothly, then move forward." Ebony answered sharply.

By now Sinclair's face was pasty white. In a barely audible voice, he excused himself from the group, refusing Lars' arm offered in aid. Lars watched him disappear out the door.

"I don't care about this house. It's full of sad memories . . . except the notes . . ." Here Judith furrowed her brow. "Where are the notes?" She gazed up the stairs and all around her, lost momentarily in her own memories.

Ebony hurried her along. "That's wise, Judith; the money from the sale will help pay for the apartment we have for you and for your daily needs."

Judith signed the electronic documents on a handheld device, then looked around. Before heading out, she gave Ebony a fleeting glance. "Your mama, tell me, when did she die?"

Ebony was silent as she fumbled in her bag for her key fob, which fell onto the sidewalk. Lars picked it up, placing it into her trembling hand. Ebony answered in a husky voice, "Last year."

Judith tucked her hands up into the sleeves of her coat and wrapped her arms around her body. "I would have liked to talk to her one more time. So sorry, so sorry."

"Thank you, and I'll be in touch." Ebony nearly fled past Judith, and in less than a minute, sped away from the curb.

Lars asked Judith, "Would you like to walk around the place one more time, before we go?

"No, only if I could find the notes . . . but I just can't remember . . ."

Much to Lars' relief, Sinclair suddenly appeared on the step, still pale, but steady. "Come Judith, let's enjoy some of those delightful sub sandwiches Bangji loves to make for us. Lars, will you join us?"

"No thanks," Lars answered, holding back a myriad of questions, "but I'm free later to talk."

Sinclair gave the slightest nod of his chin, then led Judith out.

Judith mumbled, "Those notes and . . . if only I could remember . . ."

Lars lingered on the steps for a few more minutes, marveling at the expansive home which surely had once been magnificent. Suddenly, he heard a strange chirp from under the gables, followed by a flash of orange descending from the sky. A pair of robins flitted about their nest of twigs and mud, tucked into the corner of the porch ceiling. A thought occurred to him: *What a beautiful place to raise a family.*

On the way to his car he prayed, "God, please show me if this is the way to help Estelle and her children. Will you please do what looks impossible to me and make a way for this home to be theirs, but first clear away the sorrow and confusion? Amen."

75

Lillian

The flower shop was in full production. The joy of spring blooms had seized the hearts of Lillian's regular customers and new faces appeared constantly. The days zipped along, one into the next.

Jesse burst through the door of the flower shop, shoveling the last bites of some non-breakfast food into her mouth. "Man, are those the bouquets for the Swedish furniture store? Gorgeous! You did them so fast."

"Jesse, it's 8:10, been up since 5:00." Lillian smiled. "Thankfully my buying spree of tulips paid off. Now if we had our *own* yard, we'd have tulips and a greenhouse as well."

Jesse dumped her bulging purse on the floor, then ran to the bathroom. "Tiny bladder coming through!"

"I'm glad no one else is here with that outburst . . . and for another reason. I need to tell you something exciting and then, later, I'm heading to Estelle's to share the same news." Lillian withdrew the printout of Judith's house from the outgoing mail folder.

"Me too! Let me tell you my news first—it's huge!" Jesse finished in the restroom, then gulped water from the faucet.

Lillian laughed, wishing she had a photo of Judith's house to go with her announcement. "Well, unless you've suddenly decided to jump ship, this is potentially *huge* for you as well. Business is thriving and I'm letting myself dream, but you go first—I can wait, Miss Drama."

"No drama here! I just choose to express myself in real time, as opposed to bottling everything up inside, then coming unglued." Lillian shot her a look. "Sorry . . ." Jesse pulled several books from her bag.

Lillian slipped the printout back into the folder. "Books? You read books?"

"I happen to love books—you don't know *everything* about me!"

Lillian began tucking the vases side by side in a box on the floor. "True . . . but before you start, just know, we may get interrupted. I asked Sylvia to stop by—"

"Oh man. Then my first huge thing has to wait, because there's this other really big thing I was going to tell you later, but Sylvia might be here for *forever* and I've got to meet Nolan after work. It's the ring and key thing. You know, the Anthony Mullenix thing?"

Lillian's smile melted away. "Wait, what?"

Jesse grabbed her apron, tying it carefully over her pooch, then fluffing her shirt over it. "I can't really answer without blabbing it all."

Lillian lowered herself onto her work stool. "Jesse, anything connected with Anthony Mullenix is dangerous. When you say *a thing*, you make it sound like a simple errand; nothing's simple with him. Please explain?"

"Okay, okay. It started the day the urn broke, I mean the day *I* broke the urn—well, before that, but that's when it got really bad."

Lillian and Jesse were deep in conversation when Sylvia tapped on the door, fifteen minutes before opening. "I'm here to talk finances . . ." She stopped mid-sentence, then looked from one to the other. "What's wrong with you lovely ladies? You look as grave as, well as a funeral, no pun intended." She started to laugh, but stopped herself. "Oh my, something really is wrong. I've got all the time in the world." She checked her watch. "At least the next thirty minutes, while Charles buys dog food. What's wrong?"

"Oh nothing, we're fine. Just sorting, right Jess?" Lillian tried to catch Jesse's eye. "Let me just get my list of bank questions, since that's why *you* came, Ms. Sylvia."

She peered over her glasses. "Hmm, do I smell a story? Jesse, I'm silent as the grave—oops, there I go again. I'm silent, I assure you. I'm dying to know your story."

Jesse shrugged. "As if I could say no to you!"

Lillian tried again to caution her. "Jess, I don't think . . ." but Jesse had already plunged headlong into her story to Sylvia. Lillian led the way upstairs. "Come on, I'll make tea. I've only got ten more minutes before opening, but you two can take as long as you need."

A few hours later, Lillian tapped on Estelle's front door. She'd hoped to share the idea of the house, but new questions about Anthony trumped all else. Lillian kept asking herself, *How can a simple thumb drive, hidden in the safe of a hotel room, be so important? Should Jesse risk meeting Nolan at all?* At least she'd thought to bring something delicious, special soup from Subs 4 U. Bangji had insisted, "Make new mother eat jook—chicken, rice, and herbs from my greenhouse to make her strong."

Estelle pulled her inside. Lavender was asleep in her Moses basket and Aurora lay next to it on the floor. "Aurora was *reading* to her sister," Estelle explained, "but please share whatever you were excited about on the phone."

"I will, soon, but something more urgent has come up." Suddenly, the words caught in Lillian's throat. No matter what was going on, this was still the husband Estelle had loved. "It's—it's about Anthony."

Estelle led her to the table. "If you're worried about me hearing this, don't be; I know my husband has done horrible things. It's now about protecting the people around him—whom he can hurt—that matters most to me. What has he done?"

"It's something from the past. Jesse and a friend have evidence against him hidden in a safe at the Garden Hotel."

Estelle nodded, but her eyes were dark pools of concern. "Anthony loved that hotel, but when I first met him, it was called the Greenville Hotel. Is his crime connected to it?"

"I don't know, but they believe their friend, Dwyer Ignatius, was killed over the evidence. Iggy, they called him, was Anthony's event coordinator."

Estelle leaned her elbows on the table. "Whatever they think they've got on Anthony, I'm sure he knows, unless . . . is it a necklace?"

"A necklace? No, it's a thumb drive. Why do you say that?"

"Oh, never mind, go on."

"On it are some documents relating to extortion throughout the La Maison hotel lines. Jesse wasn't very clear—but I think it shows a payoff, maybe?"

"Yes, extortion through illegal gambling rooms. I was there at the hotel openings. I sang at them all when I toured. He'd get gambling rooms going, then staff them. I feigned ignorance, but people disappeared in that high-stakes world. Do you know if Iggy died or just disappeared?"

"He died in a fire with several others, in the McPherson building—a building Jesse thinks Anthony owns—but no one can find any legal connection to him." Lillian saw the anguish in Estelle's eyes. She pulled off the lid of the jook, allowing the aroma of ginger and cilantro to fill the kitchen, then handed Estelle a spoon. "Shall we pause while you eat?"

Estelle stared at the spoon without seeing it. "Of course, arson . . . but just because you don't see the legal ownership thread doesn't mean Anthony isn't pulling the strings. He never does the dirty work; people disappear yet his hands stay clean. There was a time when the risk was exhilarating to me. So evil. Then I began having children and it was like I woke up! I ran, leaving everything behind, including money—I refused it. It was made by ruining lives." Estelle finally took a bite of the soup.

"How horrible." Lillian shook her head.

"Pure evil, yes, now go on."

"Okay, so Maria Ignatius, Iggy's wife, worked for the Garden Hotel. He handed off the thumb drive to her and she hid it in the safe before Iggy sent her and their children to Mexico."

"So, this thumb drive has just been sitting there in a room safe?"

"Yes. Iggy planned to use the thumb drive himself as evidence of Anthony's fraud, but then he became fearful Anthony suspected him of betrayal and had to hide it somewhere. That's why he passed on the responsibility of retrieving the thumb drive to Nolan."

Estelle sank in her seat. "Of course, just the kind of theatrical nonsense Anthony would incite, making them think he knew nothing, but using it to his advantage—vintage Anthony." Estelle reached across the table for Lillian's hand. "My brilliant husband obsesses over ideas to bring people down and shame them. And everyone is under surveillance. Anyone who had anything to do with this plot, he'd get rid of in an instant! Not directly of course—remember, always clean hands. Whatever this is, too many people already know. Tell them to stay far away!"

"Jesse's only job is to get Nolan the key and a ring, then he'll take care of the rest. He just couldn't have any evidence of their plan on his body."

Estelle let out a deep sigh. "Yes, of course. But my husband constantly says that he always knows everyone on the chessboard. The thing is, no one on the board is protected on either side; everyone is his pawn."

Lillian shuddered at hearing the reference again. "One more thing: I'm afraid Jesse told Sylvia too."

"Then you'd better go. Stop Jesse and Nolan and tell Sylvia to keep quiet. Oh—and does Lars know anything yet?"

"I'd planned to call him on my way home; I will!"

They embraced at the door and Lillian hurried off.

Lillian's head was pounding as she stepped back inside the shop. She hadn't been able to reach Lars and it was Barbara's day off. *I'm just one little woman,* she kept saying to herself. *I can't handle all this.*

Jesse called from the counter, "Hi! I didn't have a chance to deliver the vases to the Swedish furniture store because I got you several new customers *and* did a quick walk-in arrangement. Aren't you glad?" Jesse spread out the books. "Now I want you to see what I'm studying—got these from my mom—then I'll head out shortly."

The titles read: *Adoption and You: A Guide to Choosing an Adoptive Family, The Gift of Adoption,* and *My Birth Mom and Me: A Collection of Adoption Stories.*

Lillian slipped out of her jacket. "Just a sec. Let me get something for my headache. And I talked to Estelle; you mustn't go to the Garden Hotel tonight."

Jesse flinched. "I'm not ready to talk about that. For now, I have an announcement. I've decided to place my baby for adoption and I need your help."

Lillian rubbed her temples, feeling the tension rise. "Jesse, focus—this thumb drive thing, it might be a set-up—" She searched Jesse's face. "Wait, what? You mean *me* adopting your baby?"

Jesse laughed. "You? No, your life's great without kids! I can't imagine *you* as a mom." Jesse opened the book between them. "Can you just go with me here? I got all of these from my mom. Eventually, I want you to help me choose: married, a dog, maybe one spouse stays home, the perfect couple, no kids from before."

Lillian reached for the next book on the stack. Suddenly she noticed a library stamp on the book she held. The pounding inside her head increased. "Wait. So, what *does* your mom think?"

Jesse's face hardened. "Loves the idea." She stacked the books, hastily reaching for the bag. "All this cool stuff came from her maternity ward." She grabbed at the book in Lillian's hand, but Lillian held it tight.

"This is a library stamp; these are library books, Jess!"

There was silence between them.

Jesse exploded. "So what! So, my mom doesn't know I'm even pregnant! There, I said it. Who cares? I just need a little help from you, okay? She gets fried over a clogged toilet, the cost of coffee, two glasses of wine." She raised her hands then dropped them to her sides.

Lillian raised her voice, "And you can hide your pregnancy for how long? I'm sure she already knows! You tell her nothing, yet risk your life over strange situations that need more thought!"

"No, my mom's too stressed to hear about anything out of her controlled world to notice details. I can't tell her anyway, I can't! What do you think? She's gonna smile and calmly accept my pregnancy? She'll probably drop dead of a heart attack!" Jesse thrust her hands out. "You have no clue what I'm dealing with! Your mother was probably calm and reasonable. My mom's a wreck, like, ready to shatter. I have to protect her!"

Lillian lost it as the vice grip of her headache tightened. "My mother? As if you know anything about her, or me even!" Lillian tried but couldn't quell the flood of words. "And your mom? Protect her from what? From a daughter who obviously can't keep herself out of trouble? From a daughter who lies? Who thinks she knows everything about everyone but is so self-centered *she's* clueless? Why is she a wreck? Because she knows you better than you think. She's a wreck because of you!" Lillian slapped her hands over her mouth. "Oh, Jesse."

Jesse froze. She was white as a sheet. She backed away from the counter and fled out the door, slamming it behind her.

Lillian ran after her calling, "Jesse! I didn't mean it, I'm sorry! And you mustn't go—" Several people were chatting outside of Ben's shop and someone held the bakery door open for a group, while passersby wove in and out of the lingerers, clogging the sidewalk. Lillian backed up against the trunk of the Norway maple to text Jesse with elbows jostling her as she did:

Don't go to hotel
call Estelle
Says it's a trap
tell Nolan

She ran back inside and flipped the shop sign to *Closed*, but realized by then it was too late to follow. Jesse was gone, lost in the sea of pedestrians.

Lillian scooped up her keys. In her haste she almost tripped over the box of vases on the floor. "Perfect," she said aloud, "an alibi to get into the hotel lobby!" Carefully she backed out the door, balancing the box. Out in the narrow alley, a delivery truck was parked diagonally, unloading large bags of flour and sugar to the bakery. Her van was completely blocked!

While waiting, she quickly cleared out one of the narrow upper cabinets inside the van, extending along the side of the van, but the box of vases was too wide for it. All the while she kept calling Jesse, but to no avail. Finally, after fifteen long minutes, with a screeching of wheels, she sped out onto Lowell in the direction of the Garden Hotel.

76

Nolan

Traffic blared, horns honked, and tempers flared. Rush hour. Pungent fast food, busloads of commuters, sprays from the car wash, smokes at the gas station. Darnell's coral Pinto at the curb. Nolan snatched the ring and key from Jesse's hand. Her kiss brushed his cheek, surprising him. Sliding into the back seat, a wilted wave and a split-second look from her tearful kelly-green eyes. Darnell hit the gas, off in a cloud of smoke.

Dashing through alley shadows, back against the service door of the hotel. Sweat blurring his eyes, Nolan slipped inside unseen. Weaving through laundry room steam, billowy sheets, ring exposed, the contact handed him a door card. Silent sprint to Room 17. Green light access, darting through to the safe, key clicked open. Heart thumping in ears, poised hand to grasp thumb drive. Safe door swinging wide.

Empty.

77

Lillian

illian sped through the turn lane, barely making the yellow light and slamming on the brakes as she entered the Garden Hotel parking lot. Partially hidden behind dividers of lush trees and perennials sat three police cars! She made a hard right and hit the gas, launching over a low barrier separating the inn from the parking spaces of a restaurant. *Could I be any more obvious?* she thought, letting out the breath she'd been holding.

Behind the restaurant, her van was shielded from the hotel chaos. She jumped from the driver's seat and, without even closing the door, raced to the corner of the building. From her vantage point, she spied two policemen standing beside a broken hotel room window.

Trembling, she rushed to the van's back doors, then drew out the box of vases. They rattled in her arms. *Where is Jesse?* she kept thinking as she pushed with her shoulder to shut each of the double doors.

"Ma'am," came the stern voice of a police officer at her elbow. She jumped. "Sorry to startle you, but have you seen anyone in the parking lot since you got here?"

"No, sir," she answered, quelling her own questions she wished to ask about Jesse.

"Will you please show me the contents of your van?"

"Of course," Lillian set down the heavy box. Every nerve in her body felt suspended, like her shoulders, which seemed to sit at ear level. She pried both handles open as the officer hoisted himself up.

After only a few seconds he hopped out, saying, "You'd better go, but I'll accompany you to the lobby with those vases, if you're quick."

Lillian shoved them into the van and slammed the doors shut. "No, no, that's fine—I'll come back later!" She hurried to the driver's seat, hoping the officer didn't see her burning cheeks.

Back on the road, not even sure where to go, Lillian felt the tears streaming down her face. "Oh, Jesse, where are you?" she whispered.

Suddenly the side hatch of the overhead storage bin flew open, hitting the ceiling with a crash. Lillian swerved as her eyes darted from the rear-view mirror to the road and back again. Then, like an explosion, a person burst out from the narrow bin and rolled to the floor.

"It's okay!" he called out. "It's me, Nolan West! Jesse's fine—just drive!"

Lillian, gripping the steering wheel, began threading through traffic. "Where's Jesse? Did you get the thumb drive—and—how in the world did you fit into that upper bin?" she asked breathlessly.

"Jesse's home, she's packing up to leave. Drop me wherever. Been hiding since I was a little kid." He was crouched behind the passenger seat now, as if ready to leap out at any moment.

Lillian knew what Jesse would want her to do so she told him, "I'm taking you to the back lot of the church. I'll call Pastor Lars and explain. He's trustworthy."

"Yeah, I know—just get me away!"

"So—did you get what you needed?"

Nolan shook his head. "Someone betrayed us or the Boss set a trap—probably both. Cops think I'm an armed robber."

Lillian grimaced at the blood smeared across Nolan's arm and said, "There's a first aid kit in the low cabinet behind you. Did you go through the window?"

He found the box, then answered, "The only way out."

Lillian's van lumbered over the cracked cement of the old church driveway. Lars had answered her quick explanation and plea. "I'm glad you called; I'll take care of him—now breathe—all will be well."

She drove forward as Lars indicated, slowing down just long enough for Nolan to slip out and disappear through the brush. Lars jogged alongside the van and squeezed her shoulder as he promised to call later. For a brief second, she put her hand over his. It was reassuring to realize someone stood with her. Through her mirror she saw him turn toward the bushes where she'd last seen Nolan.

78

Sylvia

Sylvia folded sifted flour into her second bowl of batter while the standing mixer swirled heavy cream into fluffy peaks. At the ding of the timer, she withdrew a golden cake from the oven, filling the room with the aroma of vanilla. *Raspberries, kiwi, blueberries . . . hmm, what's missing for my filling?* she thought, examining the cutting board. *Of course!* She whipped around and dug into the fridge for a carton of strawberries.

The door chimes sounded. "I'll get it!" she announced, zipping through the kitchen. "Sinclair, are you still here?" She peered into the empty drawing room, just off the foyer, where she'd last seen her brother. Charles was off for the evening.

At the door stood Lillian, looking pale. Sylvia drew her inside and said, "Why, hello! I've been so nervous for this whole kit and caboodle with Jesse and Nolan that I've calmed my nerves by baking—well, my nerves are still frazzled, but doesn't my kitchen smell divine? Come sit at the island and tell me what you've heard."

Sylvia poured glasses of sweet tea and pulled up a stool beside her. Lillian began, "Thankfully, there's not much to tell. Estelle advised them to stay away, and even though I didn't get to warn them, they're both safe . . . though I'm still waiting to hear from Jesse."

"And that means . . . ?"

"I think she's safe, but I don't think she would let me know. Jess and I had an argument before all this went off. She always needs time to cool down . . . but this time I'm worried."

"I see, and she stormed away? I understand that girl—mountains and valleys with little in between." Sylvia nodded. "Anyway, back to the thumb drive of documents hidden in the hotel. I'm thinking one of those documents is the deed to the Garden Hotel, don't you think?"

"Um, well, I don't really want to know . . ."

"Oh my, I do! In fact, I started investigating it the second I got home. The hotel changed hands twenty years ago, but I can't find out exactly who owns it. There are no public records about the transaction whatsoever! That in and of itself is a great mystery. But does this involve Anthony Mullenix?"

"Again, I'm only here to say that Estelle wants us to let the police handle this or just leave it alone."

Sylvia tapped her chin. "Hmm, so did they deliver the thumb drive to the police or leave it?" Lillian glanced down at the sprig of mint in her glass. Sylvia waited for her to look up before continuing her cross examination. "Oh, I see, so they didn't get the thumb drive?" Sylvia moved closer to look directly into Lillian's eyes. "Ah-ha, the safe was empty! I knew it."

"Oh please, Ms. Sylvia, keep that to yourself! Without this thumb drive of documents, we have nothing against Anthony, but it's probably safer."

"And without anything to show Mr. Mullenix's illegal dealings, he will use the children and their mother in his pursuit of power, with no red lights to stop him. We must do something!" Sylvia jumped up from her stool.

Lillian's face was urgent. "Please, Lars is helping. There must be a logical way, if not this way, to protect the children when Estelle . . ." Her voice trailed off momentarily. "Right now, for Nolan and Jesse's sake, can we please keep this quiet between us?"

Sylvia sat back down and sighed. "All right, I forget that about you. You're ever so careful and that's exactly why Estelle trusts you, as does Jesse . . . or did. You have my word. However, you must keep me informed! And, as a side note, I have advice for you about your row with Jesse."

Lillian took a sip of tea. "Seriously, I need it. You and Jess have an understanding."

Sylvia heard something in the hallway. "Pearl? Is that you?" she called. "That's my pet; she may be looking for me. Anyway, *understanding*, you say? We do. And long ago, I had the same intuition with Sinclair, but that fell apart and is my great regret. I can't get back the lost years."

"I . . . I see."

"Our rift involved a precious possession, but the loss of relationship was priceless. Would you like to hear my story?"

Lillian looked at her watch. "Yes, I have a few more minutes."

Sylvia stared out the dining room window, trying to draw the distant memories in close. All those years ago, she'd hushed up the whole situation, fearing Sinclair would be in trouble with the law, or that his best friend's reputation as a jeweler would be ruined. She'd tucked her sad loss away in her heart. "It involves a Kashmir sapphire necklace that Father gave me when I was a debutante."

Lillian set down her tea, clinking the counter. "A necklace?"

A bark from the foyer startled them, then in trotted Pearl, a white standard poodle, who promptly dropped gracefully at her mistress' feet. Sylvia continued, "Yes, it sparkled blue, as bright as the sky is today, with diamonds encircling each stone. Father had originally commissioned it for our mother, created from rare gems found in the mountains of India. After she died, he saved it for my special day, his gift to me when I turned eighteen.

"Let's see, it must be about twenty years ago now, when we were in our forties, when the terrible situation occurred. I'd called our jeweler, Isaac, to make an appointment to adjust a loose prong. The necklace's velvet box had been sitting right here in the kitchen, where we are now, when Sinclair appeared. I'd hesitated, as you well understand, when he offered to do the errand for me. His cavalier drinking had increased over the years, causing my trust in him to decrease! I thought to myself, *Surely nothing can happen to my necklace in transit; the jeweler is his dear friend.* But the necklace never made it to the shop, according to Isaac, the jeweler. And imagine, I heard nothing—not a thing—from my brother until he staggered through the door, at 3:00 a.m., totally drunk!"

"The next morning, I let him have it, threatening him with every form of punishment I could imagine if he didn't find my necklace! My questions were fiery arrows. But, instead of being sorry, he was edgy, angry, and distracted! He stormed out, and for every practical purpose, that was the last face-to-face moment we had. He solved our fight—and whatever else was going on those days—by pouring his life into the gutter!" Sylvia held her fist to her chest. "He was dishonest, no doubt, but I broke our bond with my fury and unforgiveness. It's only recently, you know, and through your help also, that our relationship has been restored."

"What became of the necklace?"

"It remains a mystery, but in my heart, I've forgiven him and chosen to let it go." Sylvia suddenly smiled, feeling a bit embarrassed. "You know, sometimes I go on and on, but this must've been bubbling inside me for a purpose. Though this might seem rather an extreme story for what may be a simple argument, I hope you'll think of it as encouragement. I urge you to repair your conflict with Jesse as soon as possible."

Lillian had already risen to her feet. "Thank you. I am going to try!"

Sylvia turned to her island of partially made cream cakes. "Tomorrow I'll come by with some of these; by then I'm sure you'll have good news to share about Jesse!"

"I hope so," Lillian smiled, then walked to the door as they said their goodbyes.

Pearl barked again from the kitchen as Sylvia closed the door. It was strange to see her usually silent companion in such an anxious mood.

79

Sinclair

Sinclair could hear the whirring of Sylvia's industrial mixer from the far corner of the basement. As long as his sister obsessed over the perfect balance between fruit and custard in her cream cakes, she wouldn't dream of leaving the kitchen, nor would she realize he'd been home all along. Lillian had been gone for at least an hour, but their conversation played over and over in his head. His body still ached from eavesdropping in the cramped quarters of the hall closet, but his heart ached more. He missed Isaac like the pain of a wound not healed. He'd never known Sylvia and Isaac had spoken the day he stole the necklace, but the new questions that arose in his heart, he now forced from his mind. Something more urgent gripped him. The thumb drive may have been lost, but the evidence it contained was not.

Refusing to allow guilt to paralyze him, he drew a tarp from the final file cabinet of a bank of fifteen, untouched for decades. It seemed funny to him now that, in the midst of his years of self-destruction, he'd had the insight to keep records of everything he'd ever done as a lawyer. A cloud of dust enveloped him. He sucked in an enormous breath, like the outgoing tide before a tsunami and blew out an explosive sneeze. He froze, but the roar of the mixer continued upstairs.

"If only I'd had the wherewithal to date these files," he muttered, fingering through the top two drawers and finding nothing. Something scurried along the floor. "For Pete's sake, this is getting—" Suddenly, his heart seemed to miss a beat. With trembling hands, he withdrew a three-page document from the Stratford public records office, created twenty years ago. It was the quitclaimed deed to the Greenville Hotel.

As he flipped through the pages, he remembered the feeling of relief that notarizing the deed had given him so long ago. In exchange for the necklace, and the simple act of notarizing the deed transfer, Anthony Mullenix had promised freedom from his exorbitant gambling debts. As a lawyer, he had not asked the details of the deed. Anthony had asked him to notarize it, so he did. He hadn't imagined the path of self-hatred on which this freedom would take him. Two signatures stared back at him now: Judith Greenville Harris and Anthony Mullenix. He sank to the floor and held it to his chest. *My dear, my dear . . . it was your hotel. How could I have done this to you and not remembered?* He stared at the pages again as he gripped them. *I can do nothing about the necklace, but I must do something about this!*

Across the floor above him and to the stairs leading to the basement came the sound of footsteps. Moments later, a door burst open, spreading light in a broad circle onto the shelves filled with fall's canning. "Let's see, I need apricot preserves and lemon curd . . ." came Sylvia's voice. "Did I leave this light on?" She peered into the dimly lit corner where Sinclair stood perfectly still. "Odd indeed," she continued, then clicked off the switch, leaving the spacious basement black as a starless sky.

80

Lillian

At 9:00 p.m., Lillian flipped off the lights in her shop and headed for the stairs, but a rapping at the back door stopped her. Under the porch light, eyes puffy from crying, stood Jesse. Lillian yanked the door open and embraced her. "Jesse! Oh Jess—you're all right! I've been worried sick! I was awful to you . . . then, when you wouldn't answer my texts or calls—even though Nolan said you'd gone to your mom's, and I talked with Sylvia—I still didn't know what to do! I've been waiting, you've been silent, it's been awful!"

Jesse smiled weakly. "This is a first—me not able to get a word in. I'm okay, but I've got to go. Nolan told me it's too risky to stay." Out in the alley, Roxanne waved from behind the steering wheel of their idling car. "My mom wants to meet you real quick, but I said I'd be a minute. I'm sorry you were worried, but I had to deal with myself. You—what you said to me—you were right. I told my mom about the baby and all that . . . I broke open, spilled out a lot of heavy things I've never said . . . and so did she."

Tears stung Lillian's eyes. "That's amazing, Jesse, but I hurt your feelings, and totally came unglued—like you said I do. I didn't mean to; I'm so sorry."

"Don't be. I was so mad, but I had to hear it."

For a moment, the million things Lillian wished to say wouldn't come. Finally, she simply offered, "Should I tell Montreal and Estelle goodbye for you? And Lars?"

"Yeah, I love those guys so much," Jesse's voice became hoarse, "but you don't think Estelle will . . . will be gone when I come back?"

"I don't know, but don't worry, we'll keep in touch."

Just then, Roxanne hurried out from the car. "Hey there, I'm Roxanne and thank you for being such a good friend to my girl. I—uh—wish we'd met before, but thanks for everything and for keeping watch over her and the baby, my grand-baby." She stepped up to the door and hugged Lillian.

"You have a wonderful daughter."

"I sure do. Now we'd better go. We're heading to my brother's in Ohio, but I must be back for my shift tomorrow night. Come on, Jesse, time's up."

Lillian squeezed Jesse's hand. "Don't you worry. Nolan will be fine; everything will be fine. You'll be back—though how will I ever get along without you?"

Lillian felt tears again as Jesse hugged her one last time, then rushed to the car.

Lillian watched the taillights disappear. She stood there for a long time, then finally slipped back inside, careful to avoid the tiny new viola sprouting through the crack in the steps.

Instead of heading to bed, Lillian began puttering around her shop, finishing details she'd been neglecting for days. Her distracted mind could barely stick to a single thought. *What's wrong with me?* she wondered. Completely normal things, things she'd been doing for decades, felt foreign to her now.

Had she ordered the flowers for a wedding planned for summer? Had she thought more about financing the renovation of Judith's house? Where would she find the money for the initial repairs that were vital to living there? Everywhere she turned, responsibilities were mounting, but she was just one person—one little person, drowning in a sea of unknowns and complex relationships. They were beautiful relationships, but she felt herself becoming a chameleon, a different person depending on the need of the individual before her. She felt she'd lost herself in the needs of others, but who was she? A compilation of everyone else and their need? She felt lost in a new world where nothing made sense. *Go to bed!* she told herself. *The world will be fresh in the morning.* She didn't believe it, but there were only empty answers otherwise.

Lillian couldn't sleep. Her mind continued to race with even more torment-ing thoughts. She yanked her pillow up over her ear to silence the accusations. *Of course Lars didn't call, though he said he would. Of course Jesse's gone. Instead of house news for Estelle, I brought more stress. And what about Sylvia's necklace from twenty years ago as well . . . tell Estelle, or not? More stress?* Every good plan seemed to be turning to dust in her hands. The newly carved space in her heart that had felt so full of people to love and dreams to fulfill just a few days earlier now echoed in tumult and worry. And here she was alone, again.

Lillian tossed her pillow, barely missing the lamp. Mr. Blue Suede Shoes sat up to attention. "What are you looking at?" she cried, silently aching for him to curl up beside her. He sauntered from the room, twitching his tail in answer.

Reaching for her pillow, her hand grazed the surface of the trunk she'd had since childhood. It was a trunk full of memories. She paused, then, lowered herself down beside it, turned the key and opened the lid.

Two hours later, as the clock chimed midnight, Lillian sat like an island amidst a sea of old photographs and letters, spread out in every direction. Elvis serenaded her in the background, his voice bobbling every now and again, as the needle on her dad's record player skipped. She wept freely as she gazed at the last photo she had of her dad, mom, Jack, and Johnny, a month before the accident. The memories displayed opened the lock on her heart, allowing every sorrow she'd buried to surface.

She began to lay out a timeline of photographs, as accurately as she could recall, ending with the flowers—such ugly flowers, flowers someone had ordered for the funeral. Vaguely, she remembered the church and the organ playing dirges that made her feel even more alone. A crowd of grey faces, and handshakes and hugs that seemed only to add to the suffocating feeling in her soul. *Who'd been there?* She had no clear memories of the day, other than the urns—four in a row. She'd chosen urns because ashes seemed kinder than leaving the broken bodies of her precious family, lying cold and still, in coffins.

Lillian pulled another tissue from the box, blew her nose, and dropped it onto the little pile beside her. This is how it had been when she'd sat with Lars: piles of tissue, so many tears, so much regret, but what had he said? "Unforgiveness is like a festering wound . . . but forgiveness liberates your heart."

She wondered, *Who is there to forgive? The icy roads, the bad weather, the railing on the highway that couldn't hold their skidding car? Whom do I blame for their death?*

She caught her reflection in the mirrored door of the armoire. Lars' words came again, "Forgiveness liberates your heart, but only if you also decide to forgive yourself." Lars had sunk to his knees. He'd said her baby was with Jesus, in heaven, where there was no pain or suffering. *And what else was there? Something about grace . . . grace and healing.* She put her hands to her heart; it had felt so good to forgive Bryce and so good to imagine heaven.

The thought of heaven reminded her of Estelle. Estelle had also talked of Jesus on the night she'd asked Lillian about adopting the children. She talked about trust and death without fear. When Lillian said she had no faith, Estelle had answered that faith was before her, within reach. *And what else?* Lillian thought hard. *If I ask Jesus to show me who he is, he will. He's who I need most, with or without the children . . . with or without.*

Lillian pulled the comforter from her bed and wrapped it around her shoulders. She sank down on her knees and began, "Jesus, I'm not even sure you're real, but I can't bear this grief any longer. I've been carrying it around for twenty years and now there are more hard things with my friends, these friends I've come to love. I'm exhausted and it's all too heavy." Her voice cracked, but she was determined to find the words. "I . . . I can't understand how believing can help, but my heart aches." She held out her palms in desperation. "I see joy in Lars and peace in Estelle that makes no sense except for their trust in you. So, here I am."

She felt foolish but continued. "Help me please. I need strength to forgive my family for leaving me . . . and to forgive myself . . . for not going with them that day." The tears streamed down her cheeks freely. "Take these dark thoughts that I'm wrestling. If you can heal my heart, please heal it. Without Jesse, I don't even know how to face tomorrow, but without Estelle . . . I'm overwhelmed. I'm going to believe in you because . . . because I don't know what else to do. I can't do this alone anymore. I can't do life alone anymore. I believe you're real. Will you heal my soul and give me the faith Estelle said was within reach? I'm reaching."

When she opened her eyes, she found the moon shining through her window into her open palms. It spilled across her pillow as well and onto the laughing Elvis picture. The record, softly playing in the background, had come to the last lines of the last song, her favorite. "Blue, until you, made me new with your song, all the day long, then we swooned in the glow of the moon . . ." and then came the final phrase . . . "Blue until you made me steady and strong, all the day long, with your love, shining faithful and true."

"Love . . ." she whispered, "love, shining faithful and true." Though her pictures still lay strewn across the floor and the arm of the record player let silence take the place of the song, it didn't matter. Jesse would still be gone in the morning, Lars would be busy, and Estelle would be weak, but suddenly she knew she could face these things. Her desperate loneliness was gone. The heaviness that had always burdened her, even in life's best moments, was gone. She was free. The strangest thing was that, instead of reaching and grasping onto some idea or someone, she felt certain that, in some mysterious way, she was being held.

Her eyes fell on the book Benjamin had given her for her birthday. It lay on the shelf in her nightstand: *A Season to Bloom*. Suddenly it all made sense, like a grand, beautiful path opening before her. Tomorrow was a new day. She'd buy the house and fill it with love. The days to come might be fragile, but in her spirit, she wasn't alone anymore. She'd say yes to Estelle and the children, whatever that meant. "It's my season to bloom," she said out loud. She lay down on her bed, fully awake, yet thoroughly exhausted. She curled up, feeling peace envelop her, and fell into a sweet sleep.

Lillian opened her eyes five minutes before her alarm. She hopped out of bed. The day ahead was bright with possibility, and she wouldn't waste a minute. Brimming with thoughts, she desperately wished to talk with Estelle, but first she would run to see the house in person. Maybe Lars would meet her there. *I bet he will; I'll call him on the way!*

As she pulled on her running shoes, she glanced at her work clogs and thought, *Wouldn't it be funny to buy Hans a pair of matching floral ones? I do have the best neighbors!*

Downstairs she paused at the sky-blue door, then peeked inside. Birgitte was layering cinnamon rolls into the display case. She lit up when she saw Lillian. "Hungry?" she called.

Lillian laughed. "Just saying good morning, but absolutely, I'll taste one after my run." *We can try Julius' new coffee blend as well,* she thought as she clicked the door shut and headed out.

It took thirty-three minutes to run between her shop and Judith's house. She paced on the sidewalk, cooling herself down as she opened herself up to the potential before her. What a house! The chimney, gables, woodwork, and the gardens: she held her heart as she imagined the potential buried under years of neglect. This was her path, she knew it.

From a half block away, she heard the sound she'd hoped to hear: the Gran Torino roaring into the neighborhood.

Lars rolled up to the curb and swung the driver's door open.

Lillian laughed. "Impressive, but no more 007 slick exits through the window?"

Lars grinned. "Not for me, but if you want a lift home, you'll get a chance at that honor. Now the passenger door sticks." He laughed and stepped up to the house. "So? What's the word? Like it? I can't believe you thought of buying Judith's wonderful house before I told you about it!"

"Like it? No." She pushed the stray curls from her face as she looked from Lars to the house. "Love. Love is the word. I love it! And the garden is a garden of possibility."

Lars smiled. "And you said there was something else?"

"There is!" Lillian felt like she was going to burst. "It's Jesus. I . . . I found him . . . or he found me." She frowned, then laughed. "Oh, I don't even know how to say it except that I feel more alive than I've ever felt in my whole life. And whole . . . that's the word. I feel whole." Lillian stared into the eyes of the dearest man she'd ever known, and now that something, that twinkle, made complete sense. She knew his secret and it was growing inside of her: belief in someone, The Someone, Jesus.

Lars reached out his arms and drew her in. "How incredible and wonderful and every good thing!" Happy tears stung her eyes as she rested her cheek on his shoulder. She stepped back and slipped her hand in his.

"Come on," he said, with a bright smile, "let's walk in the *garden full of possibility* and you can tell me how faith found you!"

Lars made dinner plans for 6:15 at Subs 4 U. Estelle and the children had already arrived, and the Kitchen Sink sandwiches were in place when Lillian finally showed up. She squeezed in at the end of the booth beside Estelle and across from Lars. Florence handed her a drink while Sebastian plopped a big section of sandwich onto her plate. He left his seat at the other side of the table and slid up beside her. Her heart felt as if it was overflowing.

She turned to Estelle and whispered, "Are you excited about the house, now that you've had a few hours to think about it—since my call?"

"Oh yes, but I'm more excited about your faith!"

"Me too!" Lillian settled in, but as she gazed at Estelle's shining face, she also realized she hadn't touched a bite of her supper, even though Bangji had made her a serving of jook. Lillian reached for her hand.

Bangji appeared at the table with cups of oolong tea and straws. She pulled up a chair and proceeded to teach the children to shape the paper wrappings on their straws into snakes. Then they doused the paper snakes with droplets of water to make the snakes come alive.

Amidst their laughter, Sebastian leaned in toward Lillian and asked, "Have you ever wondered the color of God?"

"No," Lillian answered, "Have you?"

"Yes, I think he's black. He's every color he's ever made, up to the deepest shade." Lillian pondered this as she reached over his shoulders with a side hug. For a brief moment, Sebastian tapped his head with his fingers, then looked up at Lillian.

"No," he began again, gazing at each person sitting around the table. "I think God is medium brown, because when he looks around at every person he's ever made, he is in the center of them."

The center of them—yes, she understood perfectly.

81

Julius

A t the flower shop a few weeks later, Julius tapped on the back door, then let himself in. Lillian was just finishing with a customer. She smiled over her shoulder at Julius and mouthed, "Hold on," then turned to the next customer, who held a credit card in one hand and a hyacinth in the other. Two other patrons angled for spots behind him; one held only an order form. Julius eyed the notepad Lillian was using instead of her computer. "Would you like to set that right here?" Lillian said to the man at the front of the line, then addressed the others, "I'll be right with you." She turned to Julius and whispered, "I'm busy, come back later?"

"Got it! It's hard without Jesse; don't mean to distract." Julius fought the guilt welling up inside him. This was actually perfect; he could slip out without any extra fanfare or much explanation. "No problem, I'll give you a jingle from the airport."

"Airport? Where are you going?" Lillian asked, still trying to keep her voice fairly quiet.

"Paris, you know how I love Paris in the late spring."

"Let me just finish; it'll only take a sec."

Julius caught her elbow and leaned in close; he'd make this as seamless as possible for both of them. "I have to tell you one other tricky thing . . ."

Lillian shook her head slightly. "Not about my apartment, right?" Julius had agreed to rent her apartment as she moved into her new house. He had thought it a perfect plan; he could stay near Hope, and she would use his rent money to fix up the old house. But things had changed. He'd just say it, easy peasy. The sooner he left, the sooner she could find another renter.

"I can't rent it after all, sorry."

"No, no—not possible," she pulled her arm out from his hold, giving him her full attention, "let me just finish with my—" but the bell over the front door sounded. "Wait!" she called out, as the last of the three customers disappeared.

Mr. Blue Suede Shoes jumped up to examine the lone hyacinth. Julius pushed him off the counter and laid a hundred-dollar bill down in his place. "Sorry, this should cover those lost transactions. I must go; I just wanted to let you know in person, that's all."

Lillian ignored the money. "What are you doing? What are you even saying? I need you. All these weeks of figuring this out, you are a part of this!"

"I know, but it's complicated. I just can't. I'll take this trip, then I'll live at my sister's place on Long Island for a while."

Lillian's cheeks flushed. "What are you talking about? No! Of course, you're not going to do that. Focus. Listen." She began speaking faster. "You promised to rent my apartment. The loan for the house just came through. You get to be near Hope and I get to work on the house. That's *our* plan! Until things flow again, it's the only way I can afford this. I spent all my savings, Julius!"

Julius had to look away; her pleading felt torturous to his heart. "I know you'll find a solution, but my own plans have fallen through; it's too hard to explain. I'm headed to Paris. I can get my head on straight in Paris."

Lillian's green eyes were clouded with desperation, he tried but couldn't avoid looking into them. Panic rose in her voice. "Who's in Paris? No one, Julius! We're here—your people are here. We're here on this block, and I need you to keep your promise!"

"Our friendship's really important to me, but so is Hope's adoption—I must go." *Don't tell her, just get out. Save face, get out!* Julius stepped out the back door where he'd left his things.

Lillian followed him out where she grabbed his suitcase handle in one hand and his arm in the other. "No! You can't do this to me. You can't do this to Estelle and the kids. I need you, Julius, please tell me what renting from me has to do with your adoption. We'll sort this together. We're alike, you and me—isn't that what you thought!"

Julius pulled his suitcase away from her, its wheels caught in the cracked cement, crushing the little flowers blooming up through it. He tried to kiss Lillian on the cheek, but she refused. "I'm sorry. I have more people in my life than just you, you know! I have to follow the rules. Currently my situation is far from good!"

"Yes, of course." She let go of his arm. "But what if good is staying the course, Julius, even when it's painful? What if good is keeping *all* your promises? That's what good means to me."

"I can't . . . I'm sorry." He nearly fled down the steps, threw his case into the cab, then ducked into the back seat without looking back. If he did, he'd lose his nerve.

The taxi sped onto the street from the alley, swerving like a speed boat on rough waters. Julius ran his fingers through his hair as he leaned back in the seat. He removed the copy of Ebony Scott's document from his carry-on. "Crap!" he cried. "We were talking interior design, how is it legally possible to trap me like this?" He threw the document across the seat and swore.

"What?" came the taxi driver's voice as he looked through his rearview mirror. Julius shook his head. He tried his sister for the third time.

She called back. "What is wrong with you? You know I'm with a client! I'm in the hallway now—you've got two seconds!"

"Just tell me how to get out of this agreement—that's all. There must be a way! I can't leave Lillian like this. She's a mess—I can't handle it. She's counting on me living in her place."

"Exactly! And I don't want you to live with me either. Point is, you have no choice. How many times do I have to tell you—you signed a document you didn't read. You and Stuart separated. Ebony Scott now has every right to deny your adoption finalization; she has power over you."

"But she has no right to keep me from renting from my neighbors! And this document says I only have three options: either live in the same home with Stuart and Hope—which Stuart clearly refuses to accept, live with a relative, or travel. I can't, however, rent from Lillian or even give or lend her money. It feels like blackmail. How is that fair?"

"It isn't, but you're bound! We've gone over this," Gwyneth insisted. "Mrs. Scott's requirements sound absurd, but fighting them will jeopardize Hope's adoption finalization. You're at her mercy. For the *tenth* time, tell Lillian you're bound by your own stupid mistake of not reading what you signed. Tell her about your last home study appointment; explain how this suddenly came to light. You messed up. Tell her! This is the very thing that requires courage."

"Don't throw my own word in my face! This is different!"

"How so?"

"It just is. Everything's against me. I can't tell her; it's too embarrassing. What if it gets back to Stuart? Or Lucy? It's too risky for me."

"Yet you're willing to jeopardize everything Lillian needs, putting her livelihood and dreams at great risk? All because of your pride and fear of their bad opinion? How did Ebony Scott even know you'd decided to rent from Lillian? Whom did you tell? *I* didn't even know about it."

"I—I, uh, the day Lillian and I made our deal, I met with that excellent new coffee client, you know, the deal I said was too good to be true? He asked about my life. It was business; he was pleasant! How was I supposed to know?"

"The client backed by Anthony Mullenix? Julius, think! You talk to a strangely curious client who works for Mullenix, and the next thing you know you've become one of his puppet strings. You are under his power now. Come on, Julius, you have to be more careful."

"It's just not possible. How was I supposed to know? I'd never betray Lillian to Anthony Mullenix. It was small talk. Forget it, you're twisting this, trying to make me feel worse than I already do! If you can't fix this, then Paris is my only option."

"Paris can't fix this either. Only you can. Call me when you land."

82

Lillian

Florence finished reading her chapter a few minutes before the phone timer went off.

"Impressive," said Lillian. "You keep getting better and better—now hold on a minute." She maneuvered Lavender up to her shoulder, then crossed Estelle's living room to lay the baby in the crib in the corner.

"Set the timer again and I'll see if I can read a whole other one," Florence answered, flipping to the next chapter.

"Not tonight. I love hearing you read, but I need to talk with your mom before she falls asleep."

Lillian tucked Florence and Sebastian into their beds. Aurora had already fallen asleep in her blanket tent on the floor. Montreal, who'd been doing his math at Estelle's vanity table, looked up when Lillian entered. "Has she been asleep long?" Lillian asked him.

Estelle's cough interrupted him, but she didn't open her eyes.

"She just keeps coughing," Montreal whispered. They both stared as her shallow breath resumed. Montreal pushed his math book aside, then moved to fix his mother's blanket.

"Need some help?" Lillian asked. He nodded, grabbing his book. She added, "I'll make us cocoa. I'm pretty good at math—or at least I used to be. Two heads are better than one, anyway." Lillian shut out the light.

At 10:30 p.m., Lillian peeked into Estelle's bedroom, where she'd been sleeping peacefully for hours. Estelle's voice came softly, "Have I been out the whole evening?"

Lillian smiled. "Most of it. I did want to tell you something about Julius, but I'll share it tomorrow, if you're not up to it now. Tonight, you only missed seeing Montreal utterly outdo my math skills. What a smart dude."

"He is. It's your presence that helps most." Estelle reached for the light on her nightstand. Lillian moved to sit beside her. "*Dude*, you borrowed that word from Jesse. What do you hear from her?"

Lillian pushed aside a tray, on it was a pitcher of water and a bowl of untouched broth. "She's good. Now that she has space to rest, she's enjoying being pregnant. Said she loves eating everything in sight and wearing sweats all day. Her uncle's farm's refreshing, so, yeah, she's good. She's still also researching adoption."

"That's a hard decision, but she's wise for her age. Has it been three weeks since she left?"

"Four," Lillian answered with a sigh.

Estelle tried to sit up; Lillian adjusted her pillows. Once comfortable, Estelle responded, "It's hard to believe time these days; it feels too fast. But I need to tell you something too, about the necklace I mentioned long ago."

Lillian looked away, busying herself with straightening the comforter. She'd wanted to share Sylvia's necklace story for weeks but felt absurd, there was no way that this necklace could be one and the same. That would be ridiculous.

"What's the matter?" asked Estelle.

Lillian faltered, "Oh . . . uh . . . I was just thinking about something. Yes . . . please tell me about the necklace."

Estelle sank down in the pillows. "Let's see, you may actually need a cup of coffee for this story."

Lillian obliged, coming back with a steaming mug and baby Lavender, who'd whimpered from her crib. Lillian laid her beside Estelle, where she kicked and cooed.

Estelle began, "I was a young, up-and-coming jazz singer when La Maison hired me. I met Anthony and fell madly in love with him, but played coy, demanding constant demonstrations of his affection. I was exhausting, no doubt." She coughed lightly into her hand. "We were fire and ice, passionate or at war . . . if that makes any sense."

Lillian nodded as she sipped her coffee.

"Anthony shared little about his life, but I was as suspicious and manipulative as he, and I fixated on finding out everything. Gossip from the staff revealed that he'd been raised by a single mother who'd worked in the hotel, living on the premises while her son was groomed for management. Through his twenties, he'd scaled the ranks of the hotel, becoming indispensable." Estelle paused to sip water. "He'd bussed, then waited tables, and worked as a bartender. He was so suave. He soon gained an in with the back-room illegal gambling crew. His connections and their loyalty, garnered from the lowest rung upward, made an easy segue from open gambling tabs to eventual extortion. All done in secret." She smiled, ever so slightly. "When I met him, he was running the show, calling to account high rollers."

Estelle coughed again, then paused to steady her breathing before she continued, "One evening he came into my hotel room, holding a velvet box—I'd been given my own accommodations and he often joined me. That night he pushed me aside and demanded that I take the box and hide its contents in my closet safe." A cough caught Estelle off guard and turned into a coughing fit, awakening Lavender. Lillian scooped up the baby, waiting helplessly for the fit to subside. Estelle wiped her mouth with a tissue, then stroked the baby's back before continuing. "Where was I?"

"He told you to hide the box . . ."

"Right. I was not to open it. He promised to explain later, kissed me, and left. I opened the box. Inside was the most exquisite Kashmir sapphire necklace I'd ever seen." Lillian sucked in her breath. Estelle raised her eyebrow. "So, you're familiar with Kashmir sapphires? I only knew because my father came from a long line of jewelers and taught me about the rarity of certain gems. Have you ever seen one?"

"No, actually . . . but I imagine it was lovely," answered Lillian, in as calm a voice as she could muster.

"Yes, so lovely." Estelle put her hand to her throat for a moment and closed her eyes.

"Water?" asked Lillian.

"Yes, please." Again, she took a small sip, then resumed her story. "These weren't like ordinary sapphires; they sparkled like a tropical sea under blue sky. Each was oval, surrounded by strings of diamonds connecting them. I slipped the

necklace on and gazed at myself in the mirror. I was greedy to have it as my own."
She stared up at the ceiling, remembering. Lillian's heart raced with the realization
unfolding inside her but forced herself to stay calm.

"For three days he left the necklace in my safe. Amidst my mother's collection
of excellent imitation jewelry from her Elvis days, which she had handed down
to me, the necklace took center stage. Their fakeness grated on my nerves, even
though hers looked similar. I could think of little else but that gorgeous necklace.

"But one night, after a long set of songs, I'd asked him to join me for a night-
cap in my room. It was my birthday . . . our birthday, I should say." Lillian smiled.
"Instead of joining me, Anthony stayed at the bar, fawning over the big spenders
I knew would be gambling into the wee hours. I soothed my wounded pride by
soaking in a bubble bath, with champagne in my hand and the jewels at my neck.
So foolish." Lillian poured more water from a pitcher on the tray, seeing Estelle
struggle to swallow. Estelle forced herself to sip again. "When he finally arrived,
he sauntered into my room with an armful of roses, but when he found me in the
tub, wearing the jewels, his eyes blazed. 'How dare you,' he roared, then seized
the necklace and shoved it into his suit pocket before storming out." She paused,
as if lost in memory.

"Later, the staff told me he'd gone directly to a meeting with a beautiful
woman in his office. But the saddest thing was . . ." Here Estelle's face fell, and
an even greater weariness clouded her eyes. ". . . that his bodyguard at the time,
who'd gone with him into the office, disappeared a few days later. I'm sure it was
related. That necklace had to have been a payoff for someone's gambling debt, but
who was that woman? She was seen leaving and didn't return. And why did his
bodyguard have to die?"

"Did you ever see the necklace again?"

"No, never after that night, nor did I dare speak of it. But if it were ever found
by the police, I believe it would have provided enough evidence to break open
the whole illegal gambling ring." Estelle yawned, sinking a little deeper into her
pillows. "If only it had been found. If the necklace were ever to appear in his possession or be found by a trustworthy witness, it, combined with the thumb drive
evidence, would be enough to bring his criminal past to light . . . and enough to
remove his power over everyone."

Lillian searched Estelle's eyes. "So, you believe it's long gone?"

Estelle stared down at the baby. "From him, yes, but it's somewhere. A necklace like that can't go on the black market without detection. I believe that finding

just one of its Kashmir sapphire stones would be helpful, and useful, for negotiating with my fierce husband. Besides that, the value alone . . ." Her strained voice began to give way.

"If anything comes to light, he may be killed by those connected, I don't know . . . I don't want Anthony murdered. I want justice, but I want my children's father saved as well. I'm not sure if both are possible. Am I making any sense?" She blinked under heavy eyelids, then gazed at the baby.

"Yes, of course you are. Now I'll just put Lavender in her bed, be right back." Lillian felt relieved to leave the room, just to clear her mind for a moment. Could this possibly be the same Kashmir sapphire necklace that Sylvia had talked about? How likely was it that something so rare could be found twice in a small city like Stratford? Not very. She had to find out more.

When Lillian returned, Estelle asked, "Weren't you going to tell me something about Julius?"

"I was. He backed out of our rental agreement." Lillian bit her lip to keep her voice from failing. All these details felt as if they were crashing in on her.

"Oh . . . so you're worried about finances?"

"Yes. It's already close to impossible for a judge to choose me . . . but I may have ruined everything by purchasing Judith's house. I don't even have the money to cover all my expenses."

Estelle stroked Lillian's hand, then touched her Bible on the nightstand. "Nothing's impossible for God, and you haven't ruined anything. Neither Julius' choices, the courts, or even Anthony can stop God from making good out of these hard things." She tried to pick up her Bible, but Lillian realized it was too heavy under her great fatigue of the moment. "I've been meaning to give you this; it's my most valuable possession. The answers you need are here."

Lillian picked it up for her. "Oh please, no. I know how much your Bible means to you."

"Take it for safekeeping." Estelle spoke now with great effort. "I still have my father's. Mine has much written in margins and underlined, to encourage you now and when I can't anymore."

Lillian blinked back tears as she quietly climbed onto the bed next to Estelle. She held her for a long time, long after Estelle fell asleep.

83

Stuart

"Daaaaaaaaaaady!" Hope yelled from her bedroom.

"Hooooooope," Stuart called back, "Daddy's making pizza, what's up?"

"Daaaaaaaaaaady!" she yelled again. "Daddy . . . Daddy . . . Daddy . . ." she continued, as she skipped down the hallway and into the kitchen, wearing her purple tutu over her orange striped pajamas, which she'd worn all day.

He scooped her up and twirled her. "Do you just love saying that word?"

She broke into a flood of giggles, but when he tried putting her down, she clung to him whispering, "Daddy, Daddy, Daddy . . ."

"You—," he laughed, pulling her up to sit on his shoulders. "Just to be clear, with your chin on my head, not sure how I'm going to make this dinner."

Stuart leaned back in his chair, draining the last of his beer from the glass. There she was, his precious daughter, covered in pizza sauce and sound asleep in her highchair. "How did she fall asleep *while* eating?" he asked Serenity, who lay at his feet. Hope stayed asleep while he washed her face, wrapped her in her blankie, and carried her downstairs. He had something to resolve, and he might as well do it now.

They stepped out onto the sidewalk. The Norway maple in front of the flower shop stood silhouetted against the last rays of golden sunlight as the evening sky transformed from lavender into deep purple. The lights were still on inside Lillian's place, so he tapped on the door.

A wide-eyed Lillian answered, "Stuart, this is a welcome surprise! Want to come in?"

"Nah. I'll just say what I came to say. I've treated you rudely, and I've come to apologize."

"Thank you, but I don't think you've been—"

"No, I've been ignoring you, resenting your friendship with Julius. So, I'm clearing the air. I'm sorry."

"Oh. Well, consider it cleared then, thank you."

Stuart shifted Hope to his other side. "And Julius and me, we're done, but just to let you know, I'd never keep our daughter from him. And I think something's up with him. He intended to rent your apartment, not leave you high and dry. That's not like him."

Lillian shook her head. "You're really generous to say so, and in truth, I'm crushed. His broken promise is really going to hurt me."

"He's selfish."

Lillian nodded, but as Stuart backed down the steps, she stopped him. "Do you mind if I ask you a random question?"

"Shoot."

"I'm figuring out something new in my life—grace, actually—and . . . well . . . the name of your shop has always intrigued me."

He smiled. "It's a good story, but I'll tell you the short version." He gestured with his chin to the sleeping bundle in his arms. "Named after a neighbor. Bossy as hell, didn't follow the rule of 'mind your own business.' Kind of like Miss Ruby over there."

Lillian chuckled.

"She always had a coffee cup in her hand, like she wasn't leaving anytime soon. Saved my mom, my brother, and me from my abusive dad. He came back from war—PTSD and all that. But she got us out. Got him help too. Anyway, what else could I do but name my coffee shop after her?"

Lillian smiled. "That makes me feel like crying. That's really beautiful."

"That's part of why I came. I've been a bad neighbor and it's unacceptable. Every day I look at Hope, and I think I'm who I am because someone stepped in when my biological folks couldn't. I decided that if they could've done better, they would've. She was my example when I was a kid. You're doing the same thing, with Estelle's kids."

"That means a lot to me. Thank you." She stuck out her hand. "Friends?"

Stuart took it. "Friends and neighbors, yes."

84

Lillian

hen Lillian arrived at Estelle's apartment, the hospice nurse was just leaving. Lars was sitting on the couch between Sebastian and Aurora, holding the baby while he read. Montreal sat at the kitchen table, staring at his schoolwork, sharing space with a huge bouquet of roses. It was a somber crowd.

Lillian greeted the crew on the couch, then deposited a pastry box from Birgitte onto the counter. No one seemed to notice. "Hi," she said to Montreal. "Who brought the flowers?"

Montreal looked up through gloomy eyes. "Our father."

Lillian sat down. "So, uh, did he come?"

"Yup, stayed half an hour's all. Mrs. Scott's in there now, still."

"Still?"

"She came with him."

Lars spoke up. "I just ordered pizza, then, as I mentioned on the phone, I'll head out and be gone for a few days, but Bangji will help out." He nodded his head toward Estelle's bedroom door. "Florence has been sitting with Estelle for a long time, through *all* the visits. I think she's been waiting for you."

Lillian looked over at Lars and smiled. In the pressure cooker of this dark space, she felt his words wrap around her heart. She watched as he soothed the baby and jumped back into reading the picture book to the two eager faces impatient with his delay.

Estelle's bedroom door opened, and Ebony Scott's voice caught Lillian's attention. The spell was broken, and Lars' voice disappeared into the background as the social worker's cold instructions took center stage. "Thank you, Estelle, for talking through these delicate matters. I respect your request and will give my recommendations to the court. We'll decide amicably when the time comes, with the children's best in mind."

Lillian entered the bedroom. Ebony had turned to Florence, who sat in a corner rocker, thumbing through a book. "It was nice to meet you; you're a kind daughter." Florence didn't look up. As Ebony turned, she noticed Lillian, gave her a nod, and left.

Lillian lowered herself onto the edge of Estelle's bed. Florence left her homework on the vanity table and sat beside her. Lillian stretched out her arms to embrace her and Florence buried her head in Lillian's shoulder.

Estelle's voice was so weak. "You missed Grand Central, lucky you."

"Perhaps you need the sleeping car on the train at the moment?"

Estelle smiled, slurring her words a little. "How'd you know? Will the attendant come by with snacks on a cart? Will he wear a funny hat?"

"Tea. He'll come with tea, but I'll wear the funny hat and charge you a kiss for a sugar cube on the side," said Lillian, leaning over to kiss Estelle's forehead.

"Can I lay beside Mama right now?" Florence's voice was barely audible.

"Of course, honey," Lillian whispered back, believing Estelle was already slipping into sleep. Lillian laid an afghan over Florence, who cuddled in close to Estelle.

"Blue until you made me new," Estelle sang softly to Florence, her eyes fluttering open again. "Remember the story about the pretty blue jewelry Elvis gave Grandmommy when they sang that song . . . Mama's pretty blue brooch?" She sang softly again, "Blue until you made me steady and strong, all the day long, with your love, shining faithful and true." Estelle stroked Florence's face as her little girl's tears wet the pillow. "Will you sing with me, beloved?"

Lillian whispered, "I'll check on the others," and backed out the door, leaving them to sing their sacred duet.

Early the next morning, Lillian trudged down the alley toward the back door of her shop. She was blurry eyed from a sleepless night at Estelle's apartment, but she noticed a green army blanket hanging over the fire escape.

"Who's there?" she called, waking someone sleeping on a duffle bag. It was Judith. "Have you been here all night?"

"Hello, yes, but I don't mind. It was only for one night."

Lillian rubbed her eyes. "I imagine you, like me, need coffee."

A few minutes later, Lillian sat in her apartment kitchen and stared at Judith, who'd changed remarkably in such a short time. The dentist had made her a set of dentures, she'd had her hair cut, and she was wearing new, clean clothes. But even more so, the steady woman sitting across from her now wore dignity as her new identity.

Lillian set out bagels and yogurt, then handed Judith a steaming cup. "Is something wrong with your apartment?"

"Not at all. I just had to get away from Sinclair's hounding me."

"Why is that?" asked Lillian.

"He did something unforgiveable to me twenty years ago and I never want to see him again!"

Lillian sighed. "Twenty years ago? A lot seemed to happen twenty years ago! But didn't you just recently meet?"

"Friends recently, acquaintances for years, but he didn't know my whole name until Mrs. Scott read it at the house."

"Huh, well, I wonder if you wouldn't mind helping out with repotting while you explain your struggle with him. Time is really tight this morning."

Judith laid a saucer over her cup to keep it warm. "I'll drink that later, so I can help. Can I? Everyone always gives me a hand, but I'm never needed."

Lillian smiled. "Yes, please. These days, I need all the help I can get!"

Down in the shop, Lillian hauled in several stacks of pots from the back, directing Judith to do the same. She placed two bags of potting soil alongside several flats of herbs and flowers, then planted the first pot as a model for the rest. Judith warmed right up to the process. Lillian twisted her hair into a bun at the base of her neck, then handed Judith a hair tie of her own. "I imagine you had no idea I'd put you to work like this."

"I love it. I used to work really hard at my family's hotel."

Lillian stared. "Your family's hotel?"

"Yes, the Greenville Hotel—well, now the Garden Hotel—you know the one, down the road? It belonged to my family, and then me—until Anthony Mullenix took it."

Lillian blurted out, "Wait! What do you mean?"

"I gambled; I drank. My life was a mess. My hotel, my family legacy, I used it all to cover my debts." Judith kept planting like their conversation was completely normal.

Lillian shook her head slowly. "Wait a minute. So, Anthony took your hotel?'

"Anthony took it; Sinclair made it legal. He notarized it in the back room without ever laying eyes on me."

"And you agreed to this? Anthony settled your gambling debts with your hotel deed? Oh Judith, this makes my stomach churn." At the same moment Lillian put all the pieces together. *Sylvia was right. Iggy must've found Judith's hotel deed and copied it onto the missing thumb drive!*

"Yes, my hotel. Mine and my folks, but they'd died by then. I had a horrible uncle," Judith shuddered. "He kind of ran it too, but because of what he'd done to me, I didn't care about losing it as much as you'd think. I cared about liquor and gambling." Judith broke hardened soil away from the roots of several herbs, then carefully pressed them into the pot.

Lillian stood up and moved right next to her and sprinkled fresh soil around each herb. "This breaks my heart for you and I'm not sure if anyone's ever cried with you over this, but I feel like I could. Gambling debts—I guess I understand they could be high, but to lose everything over them? How did he do it?"

Again, Judith spoke matter-of-factly as she slid another empty pot over to fill. "I signed a quitclaim document in his office, for a bottle of bourbon and compliments. I owned the hotel free and clear, so he needed no bank approval. I was a sucker for smooth talk and Mr. Mullenix was a charmer. Sinclair was under Anthony's thumb too and says he was forced to do it to cover his own debts."

Was Judith the beautiful woman in Anthony's office that Estelle had heard about? Carefully she prodded, "Was Estelle singing jazz in the hotel at the time?"

Judith wiped her hands across her forehead, leaving a smudge of soil on her perspiring brow. "You'd think I could remember that don't you, but I can't. Sometimes it's like I'm missing chapters in my life book. Some things are clear, some ain't—aren't—but I'm slowly remembering."

Just then a pounding at the back door made them both jump. "It's Sinclair, I know it!" cried Judith, suddenly in flight mode. "I don't want to see him."

"Upstairs, go upstairs. Drink your coffee and wait for me," answered Lillian, trying to calm her own flustered voice.

Sure enough, a very weepy Sinclair stood at the back door.

Once inside, the wailing began. "Whatever Judith says, it's true. I'm a horrible person! I'm the guilty lawyer who notarized the quitclaim; I was the one who stole the report from public records. I didn't see her, but her name, I'd forgotten her name. I'd forgotten I even had the document." He paused, breathless under the torrent of his pent-up confession. "I, I brought her the deed, I tried to show it to her, and ask her forgiveness but . . ."

Lillian steadied herself against the wall. Jesse's words about bottling up emotions, then coming unglued, replayed in her mind as it raced. *What about your sister's necklace? Where does that come in?* She felt like screaming at Sinclair that this was all too much. *I don't want your chaos in my sanctuary!* She didn't want Judith's either, but here they both were. These troubled friends had run here for help.

But with all these pieces coming together, with the evidence in hand, maybe it could help expose Anthony and help her adopt the children. But it was all so overwhelming! *Could they have been witnesses to Anthony's crimes? Would they even be reliable? Would anyone believe them even with the deed?* She forced down the hope rising in her. Where was the deed now? She had an uneasy feeling.

She drew Sinclair into the back room and set him down in the comfy chair. "I have no idea how to process this, but there's a hurting woman upstairs. I think you care very much about each other. And, if I understand you right, and she is able to forgive you, the deed can serve as the real evidence against Anthony."

"Yes." Sinclair wouldn't look up, but wrung his hands instead. "It would have. I believe a copy of the deed was on the thumb drive Nolan couldn't find. But even my copy is gone now too."

She examined his troubled face. "What do you mean?"

"It *was* evidence, but I slipped it under Judith's door last night, along with my confession. I didn't realize she wasn't there. When I got there this morning, someone had forced her door open, and the deed was gone." He dropped his face in his hands.

"Scoot over," Lillian said with a sigh, perching on the soft arm of the chair. "We need Lars. Now go home to Sylvia's and stay put. I'll keep Judith here for a few days; she'll talk when she's ready. When Lars comes home, he'll have a plan, I just know it."

Sinclair gave Lillian an unexpected hug and did as she said. She locked the door behind him.

"At least I hope he'll have a plan," she said to herself, and headed upstairs.

85

Miss Ruby

Aurora yelled from the stool on which she stood at the counter of Learn 'N Play Daycare.

"I'm not a baby! I wanna go home!"

It was 6:30 p.m. and everyone else except the youngest Mullenix sisters had gone. Lavender cooed from a bouncy seat on the floor beside Miss Ruby.

"You most certainly are not a baby. Why look at what a fine, fine job you did getting that stool to the best yelling spot in my daycare." Miss Ruby grabbed a stool. "If I climbed up right here, not near as many people would hear me."

"You're too fat to climb on that stool," Aurora mumbled.

Miss Ruby laughed and walked over to the mirror in the dress-up center. "You think so?" She adjusted her glasses as she twirled in front of it. "I think I just need me a new pair of pants, that's all—these got a bit snug in the wash. Did you know I used to be a ballerina?"

"No, you didn't," Aurora scowled.

"I did so!" Miss Ruby carried her stool over to Aurora and sat down next to her. "You learn a lot about people when you talk with them. You know what else?" Aurora put her fingers in her ears. "It's okay to feel mad right now. And I don't even mind that you spoke unkindly to me. It hurts to be mad inside—so sometimes that mad's just got to come out. Let it out, I don't mind. I'll stay right here beside you. I get mad too."

Aurora took her fingers out of her ears. "What do you have to get mad about?"

"Sometimes I'm mad about my husband."

"You got a husband?"

"Sure do, wanna see how handsome he is?" Miss Ruby grabbed her bejeweled wallet and pulled out a photo of a man in a wheelchair. His arms were strapped to the armrests.

"Why's he in that?" Aurora asked.

"That's why I'm mad sometimes. Howie broke his back when we were young. He's paralyzed. That means he can't move his body, only his head. When it happened I yelled and cried a lot. And one other sad thing was we couldn't have kids. But guess what we did, we started this daycare. And you've seen that some of my kids here have wheelchairs just like Howie. If that hard thing hadn't happened, I wouldn't have had so many precious children here to love!"

Lavender began to fuss. Miss Ruby scooped her up just as Lillian rushed in. "I'm sorry, I'm so late. Here I am girls! Thank you, Miss Ruby."

"Not to worry, I like sitting beside Aurora. We were having a good talk."

Aurora hurried to button her sweater, saying to Lillian, "I can do it myself!" When she looked down, she saw that her mismatched button job had left the sweater askew. Aurora burst into tears. Lillian knelt beside her until her tears subsided.

"Do you need them to come tomorrow too?" asked Miss Ruby.

"I—I don't know," Lillian answered.

Miss Ruby touched her arm. "I'm on call for you and the kids 24-7, whatever you need."

86

Lillian

B y the time Lillian and Aurora returned to the flower shop, Lavender had fallen asleep in the car seat. Upstairs, Lillian greeted Judith, who was working a crossword puzzle, then headed to the bedroom. She gently laid the baby in the center of the bed.

"Why's she here?" Aurora asked crossly.

"Shhh, she's staying with me for a while. I know you remember Judith." Lillian offered to help Aurora with her sweater, but she refused, yanking it off and dropping it onto the bed. Lillian picked it up.

"Oh, look here, here's the problem: you thought this pin was a button," Lillian explained, looking closer. "What is this?"

Aurora bent her chin down, then peered up through a scowl. "Grandmommy's brooch. Are you gonna tell Mama?"

"I, um, well, I think your mama would say she's proud of you for telling me the truth and that's enough. Let me just put it here on the nightstand, so your sweater's easier to button when we head to your house in just a bit."

"Mama would want me to have a cookie right now," announced Aurora loudly, skipping from the room.

Lavender awakened and let out a sharp cry. Lillian scooped her up, but she only cried louder. Aurora peeked through the doorway. "She needs the blue song, and I need a cookie."

"You may get one—on the top shelf." Lillian began singing and Lavender snuggled into the crook of her neck. She could hear Aurora pushing the chair up to the pantry shelves. Then she heard her hop down and run to offer a cookie to Judith as well.

At 2:00 a.m., Lillian awakened, unsure of her surroundings. Estelle's bedroom came into focus. She reached for her coffee cup and lifted it to her lips, swallowing the contents: ice cold and comfortless. She pulled her aching body up from the wooden rocker in which she'd fallen asleep. Curled up in a fetal position, amidst a tangle of blankets, Estelle dozed fitfully in her bed. Lillian removed a basin of vomit from the nightstand table where Estelle's father's Bible sat. She stood motionless for a moment, staring at its worn cover. "Where are you God?" she asked. "Where are you when the kindest woman I've ever known is suffering? Why don't you help her?"

In the kitchen, Lillian washed out the basin and scrubbed the coffee ring from her cup. As the suds rose under the faucet, angry tears streamed down her cheeks. She wiped them with the dishtowel, then set the tea water to boil. Out of the corner of her eye she saw Sebastian, sprawled across the couch, sound asleep, but inches from sliding to the floor. She hoisted him up from the edge, then spread Aurora's fuzzy purple blanket over him.

He awakened and rubbed his eyes. "Hi," he said, sitting up. "What are you doing?"

"Making tea."

He scrunched up his face. "Are you crying also?"

"Yes, I guess so."

"Oh. When I was crying, Aurora sat beside me. She brought me her blanket. Want to sit beside me?" Sebastian pulled the blanket up to make room for Lillian. It was like the morning Estelle had asked her to adopt the children. Lillian wiped her eyes with the dishtowel as Sebastian nestled his hand into hers. "It hurts on the inside of your insides, doesn't it?"

"Yes," Lillian answered, remembering. "Sebastian, do you recall what I said about Emma's aunt, that not everyone who has cancer dies of it?"

"Mama a'ready told me stuff." Sebastian's lip quivered, as he went on. "But you're staying with us when Mama can't, aren't ya, Lillian?"

Lillian pulled him in close. "I'm doing everything possible to be here for you and your siblings, no matter what—I'll help in any way I can."

"Mama says when she asked God for help, he sent you."

The teapot began to whistle, and Lillian went to pull it off the stove.

A faint voice called from the bedroom, "Lillian, is that you?"

"And me, Mama," Sebastian called softly back, jumping up from the couch. He paused mid-motion, fixing his eyes on Lillian's.

"Go," she whispered. "I'll stay out here a bit, then I'll bring cocoa for you and tea for me and your mama."

As the tea steeped, delicate swirls swept through the water, transforming it into the most beautiful shade of medium brown.

87

Anthony

Name. An-thuh-nee : Latin origin, meaning "highly praiseworthy" and "priceless one"

The following morning, in the heart of the city, Anthony Mullenix glided through the lounge of one of his hotels, patting backs of well-dressed patrons, saying, "Hello, great to see you, enjoy." But his mood was sour. That morning, splashed across the front page of the newspaper, was his photo, along with the five other hopeful candidates in the mayoral bid. The caption read: "Race opens up, who will declare candidacy?"

All the other candidates had included photos of their families. All except him. At the bottom of the page was a stunning photo of Estelle from the night of the gala. Its caption read: "Are Anthony Mullenix and his wife at odds? New Yorkers want to know why." He'd had the papers removed from the lobby; nevertheless, everywhere he went, he fielded the same questions.

What would they have said had the current photos been published? The ones he'd bought for a quarter of a million dollars? Photos of his sickly wife, his new baby born in a car, surrounded by her solemn children. His cell phone vibrated in his coat pocket. He passed through the rest of the lobby unrushed, then ducked into his office.

"What?" he answered Finch, drumming his fingers on his desk as he listened. A smile spread across his face. "She's where? Really. This could not be more perfect."

From a locked drawer he withdrew a manila envelope, then slipped through inner hallways and stairwells down to the parking garage. Several of his men were there, waiting in expectation. "The press is salivating today; keep them busy," he said, leaving his entourage behind and climbing into his Corvette. He sped away, maneuvering through several back alleys.

88

Lillian

L illian ran the thirty-three minute run to the house. Numbers flooded
her thoughts. Estelle's apartment lease ended in three weeks and without a renter, Lillian could cover her own expenses only up through the
first of the month. She arrived at the house and paced, her breath and heart-
beat still fast.

For the hundredth time she asked herself, *What do I do? I need a renter and
I need money for the mortgage, and I need to be stable so the social worker will
even give me a chance. I can't possibly get custody of the children. There's no miraculous deed or necklace. What do I do?* She'd had a million questions for Estelle
the night before—painfully practical ones—but no answers had surfaced. And
with Judith still at her apartment, she felt she had another fragile soul who
needed her.

"Hello, I thought you'd be here," came a voice behind her that made her
jump. She spun around to find Anthony and only a few meters away was his black
Corvette; it must have purred up to the curb without her even noticing. Anthony
continued, "I guess you're at an impasse Ms. Bloom."

"I have no idea what you're talking about," she stammered, avoiding his eyes.

"How sweetly naïve. The hospice nurse says any day now. It's breaking my heart, but Ebony Scott has our paperwork in order. It's laughable—you versus me in civil court. I almost feel sorry for you."

Lillian stared at him. "Don't. I'm doing what Estelle asked of me, and it's what the children want."

"Not *the* children, *my* children. And children are children; they don't know what they want. Besides, you and my wife have brainwashed them. My own wife, whom I love, who won't even support me!"

"She wants the children to be loved—I love them. You only came once to see her *and* them. Ebony Scott certainly saw that they fear you."

"*Who* says they fear me? And that I don't love them? Exactly how long have you known my wife?" Anthony raised his eyebrows. "What has she told you about our tumultuous marriage? Her obsession with opulence? Her years of chasing fame? You've known her less than a year, hearing only what she wants you to hear."

"She's told me everything," insisted Lillian, in a louder tone than she intended.

"She has no filter; her reality and fantasy are fused. You, however, are very private—a wise trait—and that's the real reason I came." He handed Lillian the manila envelope he'd brought. "This is about your original family, not mine—and *your* livelihood." A shudder ran up Lillian's spine; reluctantly she took the envelope. "Your family could've been saved. Has anyone ever told you that?"

"How do you know? You're making this up," she said, beginning to tremble.

"Oh no. Since their accident, the road's been widened and aluminum safety rails added. Why? Because the curve was dangerously sharp, and that section of road had no appropriate signs or railings. The road management team had forgotten them. Negligence! Also, there was an unnecessary detour; the ambulance was delayed by a miscommunication. Again, negligence! All these years, the state has concealed their neglect from you. You'll see proof in the photos. However, considering your current state, I suggest you wait until you're alone to examine the graphic pictures. It will be rough on your lovely eyes."

Lillian crossed her arms, holding the envelope to her chest. "That's ridiculous. The rescue crew did the best they could—nothing would've changed. You don't care about this. You're just trying to distract me from—"

"From what? Don't you know everything's connected? If only you'd seen the photos before. If you'd known the negligence, you could've had justice and closure *and* been financially stable long ago, but it's not too late. Many were to blame. You deserve payment for your grief."

She shook her head. "Grief is not a commodity. Nothing would've changed the outcome then. This is now. You should be worried about Estelle and your children, like I am."

Anthony laid his hand on Lillian's shoulder. "Don't you understand that this is for them too?" He spoke softly now. "I know your pain and need for closure—I never knew what happened to my father. Wouldn't you like to see the last photos ever taken of your family? Consider litigation as an investment in your future happiness."

Lillian shook her head. "This has nothing to do with you—please, just leave."

"You have no family and you're scrimping along. Can you even afford this," he frowned as he looked at the house, "this pit of worthlessness?" Lillian followed his gaze. "What does next month look like for you?" He chuckled. "My lawyers can help you with litigation. We want the same good thing—we're alike, you and me. You get your finances in order, then I'll allow you to continue your relationship with my children."

"Why would you do this for me? What's the catch?"

"Because of my big heart. My children are mine, of course, but you'll be in their lives. I'll get you back on your feet and we all win, especially my children, who love you. You *want* to be on my side." Anthony backed away. "However, if you deny my help and fight me for custody, not only will I destroy you professionally, but you'll never see my children again. Your way is impossible—my way is the only way."

"Estelle says nothing is impossible for God." Lillian's sentence dropped to the ground like a stone.

"Did you really just say that? How embarrassing for you. You don't believe that. Power, money, and information, all that makes nothing impossible for *me*." He was almost to his car when he added, "And one more thing, not only does Ebony Scott have ample reason to convince the court of your deficiency, but she has her own past regrets she harbors. Think hard about my offer. Without it?" He scanned the property while holding his fingertips together, then released them. "Poof! Everything and *everyone*, gone!"

Lillian's cheeks burned and her heart ached. She held tightly to the envelope as she watched Anthony's car glide down the street. He waved through the window, saying, "See you in court."

89

Stuart

The last customers headed for the door as Stuart hung up his apron for the evening and let Kevin off early. Hope lounged against Serenity's paws, admiring her finger-painting masterpieces, laid in a row on the floor. "Nice work, Missy-Lou; you had quite a time at daycare," commented Stuart, squatting down beside her.

Hope jumped to her feet, held Stuart's face in her little hands, and said, "Hope not Missy You! Daddy's Missy You!" then broke into peals of laughter.

Stuart rose to lock the door but hesitated at the sight of Lars through the window, descending the steps of the bus with a carry-on thrown over his shoulder. Lillian appeared, hastening toward him from the direction of her shop, but stopped short to hide her flushed cheeks in her hands. Transfixed in the delight of seeing one another, neither seemed to notice the pouring rain. Down at Stuart's feet, Hope tucked her hand into his. "All right Hopie-Lou," he said, "bedtime is officially delayed; we have a special assignment." Stuart opened the door and called outside.

"Hey, you two, come in out of the rain. Need a hot drink?"

Lars frowned, examining his watch. "You're closed, aren't you?"

"Tonight's our late night," answered Stuart, winking at Hope.

Lillian breathed out in relief. "Thank you! This way we can have a moment to catch up by ourselves. Bangji's got the kids covered in the apartment."

They followed Stuart's lead to the best table in the house, with eyes glued to each other. "I'll be right back," said Stuart, scooping up Hope and sprinting upstairs.

In his kitchen, he found the special bottle of wine he'd been saving for his and Julius' anniversary. "Repurposing," he said to himself, grabbing glasses and cold pizza from the fridge. "Our homemade creation; bet they'll love it," he told his smiley helper, who grabbed her fishy crackers before following him back down to the shop.

Hope ran to their table with her snacks while Stuart discreetly flipped the open sign to closed, then seamlessly uncorked the wine and set a glass before each of them, close enough for their hands to touch.

". . . you can't even imagine how much more happened, but I'm sure you're too tired to hear," Lillian was saying. "Now, tell me about your trip."

Lars thanked Hope for her crackers, popping a few in his mouth as he set her on his lap. "Trip? Was I on a trip?" Lars joked. He looked into the uplifted faces of the two women surrounding him. Hope put her hand on her mouth and giggled. Stuart fought to hide the joy he felt rising as he glanced over and saw Lillian's face warm to Lars' twinkling eyes. "I need to get caught up. Tell me the rest," Lars said as he patted her hand and then gave Hope a hug before setting her down.

Stuart reached for Hope and took another look at Lillian's face. Her eyes met his and stared at his knowing gaze. He quickly slipped away, tray in one hand and Hope's cheesy fingers in the other. *Don't break the magic, Stuart,* he said to himself.

A few minutes later, Stuart set cloth napkins, small plates, and reheated pizza before them.

Lillian finished her sentence, ". . . on the fire escape all night, under an army blanket, just so she wouldn't have to talk to him about all of that!"

"She's been through a lot, that Judith, but all night outside. . ." answered Lars, shaking his head.

Stuart blurted out, "Who's him? You mean Sinclair?"

Lillian responded, "Yes, can you believe that?"

Stuart chuckled, "Oops, sorry to interrupt . . . proceed, I'm invisible, just serving pizza."

Though they continued to talk of serious things, a deep peace enveloped them. Stuart caught himself leaning against the counter, the cloth to wipe the counter suspended in his hand. To behold Lars and Lillian, with the whole world pressing in on them, yet finding each other's rapt hearts in the midst, was almost too much for him to bear. His own heart ached for this warm intimacy of emotion, but the privilege of seeing it unfold before his eyes inspired his soul nevertheless. *And they don't even know they're living a love story,* he thought.

Just then, Stuart realized they were praying, with heads bent and hands held. He tiptoed off to find his precious daughter curled up with Serenity on the rug by the window. The rain had ceased, replaced now by bright moonlight spilling over the broken sidewalk. Bangji's husband, Quon, was just passing by on his evening walk with their little dog. His eyes swept across the well-lit coffee shop, meeting Stuart's with a perplexed expression. Stuart raised his shoulders and tipped his head toward the pair. Quon nodded vigorously, with a smile stretching across his face as his dog pulled at the leash. Stuart bent down and lifted up his sleeping princess.

Lars commented as they pushed their chairs in, "I'll walk you home, but I just thought of one more thing to ask about Estelle's story."

"Of course, there's so much to it. And I still want to hear about your trip," Lillian said, taking his arm.

Lars beamed at Stuart. "You made this evening happen. Thank you, friend."

Stuart stroked Hope's head, rocking her slightly to keep her from awakening. "Oh no, it was all you."

90

Lars

Lars felt the warmth of Lillian's arm interlaced in his as they walked together in the cool evening breeze. He was nearing the end of his traveling tale after strolling around the block with her. They were almost at her shop, standing beside the Norway maple and under the glow of the streetlamp. He still longed to linger and searched his mind for questions he could ask to avoid saying good night.

"This will be a painful week; how can I best come alongside you?" he asked, bringing up the inevitable. He watched as Lillian's face suddenly clouded. He moved them toward the bench but, once they stood before it, spied the rainwater puddling at the back.

"Oh," she said, silently gazing at it as if she were really seeing something else. "I don't think I want to think about what's ahead." She dropped down onto the bench, right in the biggest puddle. With a tiny shriek, she jumped up and examined her soaking wet behind.

He smiled and sat right down on the puddle himself and they laughed at their cold, wet, matching soakers. He felt like he could sit in the muck and mud of the whole wide world if only he could be beside her. She drew off her coat to sit on, offering a section to him. Gently, he swung his arm around her shoulders and, as if they had done it a hundred times, Lillian tucked into him, pulling her legs up under her. The sounds of the city evening became their music as they both sat very still, not wishing to break the spell of peace.

"If only we could stay just like this," she whispered.

"If only," he answered.

A distant siren howled. The sound of a car door locking, a shout a block away, laughter following, all of it dancing around the quiet huddle of the two on the bench, soaked with rainwater.

Lillian sat up, resolution in her lovely face. Lars looked at her soft green eyes, inches away from him. She'd changed so much since the night he'd brought the pie on her birthday, allowing her heart to break for so many who'd come to her with their needs. Yet despite everything, she had such a new, beautiful hope.

A passion welled up inside him and, reaching for her face, he found the distance to her lips and gently kissed her. In all of his life, nothing equaled this startling feeling of dizzying joy and terror. Yet Lillian's delight folded right in as if echoing his longing. The surprise of their joy bubbled up and they separated with great laughter.

"Wow!" Lillian said. "I didn't know preachers could be such great kissers!"

Lars felt his face flush. "Me neither."

Lars walked her to the door where he watched her disappear inside with a smile that seemed like it might never fade. Back at the bench he gathered his things, but suddenly felt the discomfort of his soaked backside in the cold breeze. He glanced up into Lillian's living room just in time to see Judith's laughing eyes watching him through the window. He put his finger to his mouth in a shushing gesture and she gave him a cheerful nod back.

But why did he shush her? He didn't want to be quiet about this tender space he'd uncovered with the beautiful florist with blonde, dancing curls and laughing eyes. He didn't want to be quiet about the stirring of his soul.

With one last glance at the warm light streaming over the lonely bench, Lars stepped off the curb. The rain began again, pitter-pattering in puddles along the street, a melancholy song preparing him to shepherd his growing little flock in the days to come. Joy and sorrow mingled in his heart but for now, he thought, *I will rest in the joy and surprise of our walk home from the bus.*

"'Peace I leave with you; my peace I give you . . .'" He whispered his favorite verse as he walked into the night.

91

Lillian

Estelle laid her hand on Lillian's. "Will you help me touch . . . their faces?" Lillian and the children gathered around Estelle while Lars stood at the foot of the bed, cradling Lavender.

Lillian lifted Estelle's hand so that it rested on hers. Each child put their face up to their mama so she could caress their cheek. Sebastian held his eyes shut with his fingers but couldn't stop the tears. Florence pulled his head onto her shoulder. "It's okay, you can cry."

His whisper was as loud as his regular voice. "But then everything's too blurry and I wanna see. I don't wanna forget how Mama looks."

Estelle smiled weakly. "Son, you won't forget . . . and I won't forget . . . your wonderful face, either. God saves all . . . our memories . . . tears, and prayers in heaven."

Sebastian opened his eyes and the tears streamed freely, wetting Estelle's hand. "I don't want 'em stored in heaven; I want 'em here in my head, for always, and I don't want you to leave us."

Estelle breathed in a shallow breath. "I know. I wish . . . I could stay too," she said weakly.

Aurora's lip quivered. "What are you gonna do without us in heaven?"

Estelle's eyelids seemed almost too heavy to lift. "I'll—I'll be with Jesus . . . and maybe I'll sing . . . with my mother . . . but I'll also wait for your stories . . . I'll wait all your long, good lives." She paused to catch her breath. ". . . to hear all the beautiful things . . . you'll do. And I'll be so glad . . . that you're my children . . . and I'll be proud of each of you, always . . . every day of your lives."

Montreal caught Lillian's eye. Up until now, Lillian had been able to hold back her own tears, but he broke through her strong façade. As her eyes welled up, she glanced at Florence, who was wiping her red eyes with her sleeve. Lillian lay Estelle's hand gently down on the bed and wrapped her arms around Florence's shoulders.

"Lars," said Estelle, fighting the drowsiness that had begun to overpower her, "will you read . . . read Psalm 139 . . . to us."

Montreal opened his grandfather's Bible and held it out for Lars, who began,

"'*O Lord, you have searched me*
and you know me.
You know when I sit and when I rise;
you perceive my thoughts from afar . . .'"

As Lars read, the room seemed to stop, timeless in the hazy light seeping through the closed curtains.

"'*You discern my going out and my lying down;*
you are familiar with all my ways.
Before a word is on my tongue
you know it completely, O Lord.
You hem me in—behind and before;
you have laid your hand upon me.
Such knowledge is too wonderful for me,
too lofty for me to attain.
Where can I go from your Spirit?
Where can I flee from your presence?
If I go up to the heavens, you are there;
if I make my bed in the depths, you are there.
If I rise on the wings of the dawn,
if I settle on the far side of the sea,

even there your hand will guide me,
your right hand will hold me fast.'"

They had all moved closer now, shoulders touching shoulders, as if they were all connected. Each one of them had a hand on Estelle. From her head to her feet, she was enveloped in love.

"'If I say, 'Surely the darkness will hide me
and the light become night around me,'
even then the darkness will not be dark to you;
the night will shine like the day,
for darkness is as light to you.
For you created my inmost being;
you knit me together in my mother's womb.
I praise you because I am fearfully and wonderfully made;
your works are wonderful,
I know that full well.
My frame was not hidden from you
when I was made in that secret place.
When I was woven together in the depths of the earth,
your eyes saw my unformed body.
All the days ordained for me
were written in your book
before one of them came to be.
How precious to me are your thoughts, O God!
How vast is the sum of them!
Were I to count them,
they would outnumber the grains of sand.
When I awake, I am still with you.'"

Lars looked up from reading. Montreal leaned over and kissed his mother's brow. "Thank you," Estelle whispered. Lars laid Lavender in the bed beside her.

"My children . . . I love you." Estelle whispered, then she closed her eyes and took her last breath.

Summer

Noun. sum·mer : the second season of the year, from June to August in the Northern Hemisphere, between spring and autumn, when the sun is bright, temperatures climb, and nature flourishes

Earth's kind gardener, the summer sun, spread her glowing warmth upon the streets of Stratford. Under a dazzling blue sky, she coaxed the timid herbs, lemony sorrel, rosemary, and thyme up from the city garden beds, where sprinklers splashed the thirsty soil. Lapping cool water from a dripping spigot, a stray pup wagged his tail, then barked at a bee buzzing past his nose. Smitten by the summer sun's rays, a patient gardener rested in his folding chair, then lifted his face, daydreaming of fenceless fields.

Around the corner, steel drums and a flute serenaded craftsmen setting up booths to display wares on Lowell, where orange cones blocked off the street. Heaping baskets of plump produce competed with aromatic artisan bread and towers of savory cheese as the street fair gained momentum. Two friends sipped Italian soda while fanning their faces with borrowed plastic menus beside an artist painting kitten whiskers on children's flushed cheeks. A little boy gazed reverently at his green dragon tattoo, proud to be matching his father. For a few coins, a woman doled out balloons from her multi-colored bouquet to eager hands, her investment into the delight of summer's wistful days.

A sweaty child leaned over a bench to share a lick of Rocky Road from his sister's cone. With a splat, the drippy double scoop landed under the deep shade of the Norway maple. In answer to the wailing child, a fluffy cat pawed the glass from inside the darkened flower shop, tilting the sign that read *Closed for the Week*.

92

Julius

Standing at the window of his Paris penthouse hotel room, Julius fingered the tassels of the silk drapes that pooled on the floor by his bare feet. Bags of vintage flea market finds lined the wall, and several linen shirts with tags still attached lay in a heap on his unmade bed. Leaning on the velvet chaise was a crystal chandelier purchased at his favorite antique store. *No roof of my own, yet I've bought a chandelier,* he mused.

He sipped the coffee from his otherwise untouched breakfast tray, then pressed the voicemail arrow on his phone, yet again, to hear Lillian's voice repeat the most sorrowful message of his life. *How can Estelle Delacroix be dead?* he asked himself, staring with unseeing eyes out over the familiar streets of his favorite city.

He scrolled through the photos on his phone: Stuart and Hope, Storm and Lucy, Montreal and the rest of the children with Estelle on the day of their pastry "rain check." His favorite photo of Lillian was from the day she scooped up an armful of brightly colored fall leaves that had piled up on the bench just so that Montreal wouldn't have to work so hard, though she'd have never admitted it then. Returning to her phone message, he fought the desire to numb his emotions, to keep from feeling the pain creeping through the cracks of his broken heart. He stared at the phone icon. *Call her, call her,* he urged himself.

Immersed in the tug of war raging in his mind, a tap on the door startled him. "Sir," came the muffled voice of an attendant, "your masseuse is waiting to do your Shiatsu massage."

"Yes, yes of course," he said, shaking his thoughts free, "send her right in." He hesitated as he looked down at his phone, then clicked out of voicemail. ". . . and afterward, I need a fresh breakfast tray and . . . my personal gallery tour arranged for this afternoon . . . and . . . a list of plays and concerts happening this weekend. Actually, forget the list; just book me for something each night . . . if you'd be so kind."

93

Lillian

The immediate days following Estelle's death seemed innumerable to those whose hearts had been broken. Tears were shed by the gallon and hours passed in slow motion. The emptiness echoed in Lillian's heart as she fought against the weeping that ensued each time she looked into the eyes of one of the children. Lars' presence comforted everyone as he listened, held them, prayed, and read Psalms from their grandfather's Bible.

All the dear friends and shop neighbors brought meals and cards, games, and anything they could think of to bless the children. Their loving-kindness was like nothing Lillian had ever known. Jesse phoned several times daily, just to hear everyone's voice and to weep alongside them. She longed to speak with Julius, but he never took her call; finally, she just left a message.

Estelle had decided weeks earlier that she wanted a celebration of life in Sylvia's garden. Sylvia had taken it upon herself to arrange the exquisite party according to Estelle's wishes. When Lillian arrived with the children on the afternoon of the gathering, they saw that nature itself had done the decorating. Every flower in Sylvia's garden was in bloom while butterflies and birds flitted everywhere. It was an extraordinary sight. Sebastian explained to anyone who would listen that God was giving Mama his own special bouquet and birdsong music.

A few days later, summer vacation was in full swing and Bangji told Lillian that even in sadness, the children needed fun. At her request, Lars led the way from the main chapel, carrying every broom he could find. Lillian followed, holding the baby, while the children balanced subs, root beers, and a basket of socks. Bangji came last, hurrying along the flagstone path, with a whistle around her neck. There were no weeds to clog their procession, nor keys hidden under fence posts. Standing before them was the stately renovated North Tower, the first finished project on the property. The former library and study had been transformed into two studio apartments above, and below was an expansive community space.

Lars opened the door to a circular room lined with curved benches and windows extending to the ceiling. Along the side stairs leading to the upper floors, Barbara appeared, holding a tray with the remnants of a meal. She winked at Lillian before slipping outside. Lillian in turn searched Lars' face. He gave her a slight nod as he stepped into the sunlight streaming across glossy floors, then addressed the children. "Here it is. Miguel and Gabriel said everything's ready."

"Ready for what?" asked Aurora, kicking the doorstep.

"Ready for fun—it's a gym. Until we get basketball hoops and equipment, Bangji invented a game to celebrate summer."

"Sock hockey," Bangji explained. "You, Aurora, goalie—you and Sebastian." She pulled painter's tape from her pocket and set to work making goal lines.

Florence set the basket down. "Can we go home, please?" Her eyes welled up with tears. "I don't feel like celebrating. They might take us away from you soon. This won't be fun; nothing's fun anymore."

Montreal set the sandwiches on the bench and whispered, "Shh, Bangji's just trying to help. At least we can pretend it's fun."

Lillian stroked Florence's cheek. "Ebony Scott allowed me to stay with you this long. That was good, right?"

Lillian and Montreal's eyes met. She knew he could see the worry in her flushed cheeks. He interjected, "Why can't we come with you to court? It's about us. We told that man what side we're on."

Lillian lowered herself onto the bench. "Ebony Scott knows what you want. I'm trying to figure out how to proceed. I want what's best for you."

Bangji pulled on tennis shoes and instructed everyone else to slip into socks. She tied blue scarves to Florence and Lars' wrists and handed yellow ones to Lillian and Montreal.

Montreal slid in close as Lillian knotted his scarf. She spoke softly. "Montreal, the problem is, if I try to go up against your father and he gets custody, I may never be allowed to see you again. If taking a side means losing you children altogether, I won't risk it."

Montreal frowned. "I think you should fight for us. Mama used to say that God always has something up his sleeve. I'd say back, 'And God has mighty big sleeves.' It was our joke, kind of, but Mama'd say it to help me not be afraid."

"I guess I feel afraid now." Lillian regretted her words immediately.

Montreal tied Lillian's scarf to her wrist. "It's all right. We have the armor of God, right? That's from Ephesians, in the Bible, in case you haven't heard about that stuff before."

Aurora tied a yellow scarf to one of her braids and grabbed at Lillian's hand. "You get me."

Lillian looked around. "Oh wait, I forgot Lavender's bouncy seat."

"Bangji already planned for baby," said Bangji, fishing a linen cloth from the basket of socks. She wrapped it around her tiny frame and motioned for Lillian to hand over the baby. Expertly, Bangji secured Lavender to her torso; the baby's bright eyes peeked out from her perch. "And you can take this now; save for later for court." Bangji fished out an envelope from her apron and handed it to Lillian. She then turned to everyone. "Now, games begin!"

That evening at Silverstone Apartments, Lillian kissed the children good night, then walked with Miss Ruby to the door, saying, "Thank you so much for staying over. I'm sure I'll be up late at my place, poring over everything for the court. I'm so glad I won't have to study this material around them. I—I don't want them worrying."

"I know and I'm delighted you asked me; I just love these little troopers."

"What time would you like me back?" Lillian asked as she headed out the door.

Miss Ruby responded, "Take your time in the morning; I'll bring them over to my daycare around lunch, where the big kids can help me. I don't think Aurora will mind comin' over, seeing as how I promised she could name my new goldfish."

"Good, that might take until dinner anyway," answered Lillian, smiling half-heartedly as the door clicked shut.

She checked her bag to be sure she had the letter from Bangji and Anthony's manila envelope. Earlier that evening, she'd hoped to have a moment to talk to Lars about Anthony's plan, but they'd had no time. *How have I still not shared Anthony's idea with him?* she asked herself, wondering if she'd pushed it from her mind on purpose.

While waiting for the bus under the light of Archie's Convenience Store, Lillian read over Bangji's letter to the court again. It had been the surprise of the day. Her words glowed with details of Lillian's care for Estelle's family. Bangji had garnered character references from fellow shopkeepers and clients. Her eloquence as a former judge, translated by her daughter, an English professor at Lafayette College, inspired Lillian's waning confidence.

The doors of the bus swung open and Lillian stepped inside. Lost in thought, she jumped at the sound of her cell phone.

"Hey there," came Lars' concerned voice, "I just got off the phone with Bangji. Are the kids near you?"

Lillian slid into a seat. "No. I'm on the bus, heading home to study what my lawyer gave me." She stared down at the letter in her hand. "Why? Is something wrong with Bangji?"

"She's fine, but while we played hockey, the health department showed up at her place." Lillian blanched. "The inspector said there was a complaint of rats. Quon was in the back. Of course, it's false; they probably planted the dead rat, but Bangji worries her letter's obsolete now and may hinder more than help."

Lillian drew her hands to her face. "What?! This is all so awful. It's like quicksand everywhere we step. I'm going to lose the children forever, unless—unless I do what Anthony says."

"What do you mean? What did he say?" Lars sounded panicked. "Of course not! He's too dangerous to be trusted."

"We can talk more tonight. But I have nothing to offer the court, nothing of substance. I doubt I'll find anything helpful in the material I'm reading."

"Even if you find nothing, God is still in this."

"Where?" Lillian choked on her words.

"In the details, we'll find him in the details. I'm meeting with Sinclair and Judith shortly, then I'm free later to talk."

"Well, that's good news, anyway."

"Yes, absolutely," answered Lars with feeling. "We can meet either at your place or the chapel."

"Chapel's fine. I'm just so, so worried."

"I know, but don't lose hope and I'm here beside you every step of the way."

Lillian tucked Bangji's letter away and said goodbye, feeling the warmth of his voice lend peace to her spirit. But, as much as she tried, she couldn't stop thinking about Anthony's envelope. *Can there be something good somewhere in it? Could this be God's plan?*

Finally home, Lillian set a cup of coffee on the dining room table between Anthony's envelope and her court folder. She reached for the lawyer's material but had no desire to read it. She stared beyond the papers to Anthony's envelope. His words still haunted her: "If only you'd seen the photos before. If you'd known the negligence, you could've had justice and closure *and* been financially stable long ago, but it's not too late." Who was she kidding? He saw right through her. She missed her family. She ached for the children. How had she come to the brink of financial collapse? Anthony's words tempted her. "Wouldn't you like to see the last photos ever taken of your family?" And then, "I'll get you back on your feet and we all win, especially my children, who love you."

"Stop talking," she insisted, getting up from the table. She turned on some music, but the songs sounded jarring. In the kitchen, she searched for something to eat, but her pantry was empty.

She sat back down. Her coffee was cold. She wondered, *If I agreed with Anthony, and received compensation from my family's accident, wouldn't the children be better off? And they could visit. Visit. Would he let them visit? But then we wouldn't be a family. Family.* She held her hands to her head to stop her thoughts from unraveling. *Should I look at the photos of my family?* She shook her head. *Isn't that the last thing they'd want? And what would Estelle say?* She closed her mind to the question as she ran her hand across Anthony's envelope. *Perhaps it won't hurt, just to take a peek.* She loathed the thought even as she accepted it.

In slow motion, she picked up the envelope, then withdrew the contents. Her stomach churned at what she was about to see. *I can't ever unsee these*, she thought. As she hesitated, her fingers ran across an odd protrusion at the bottom of the back page. It was a tiny envelope stapled to the accident report. She could see the white margins of the photos at the center of the papers, but she avoided them. *I'm stalling*, she scolded herself, as she flipped over the envelope and pulled the staples from it. She shook out the contents into her hand. "What in the world?" she whispered, with her heart in her throat, "My mother's locket?"

Lillian opened the locket and stared. There were the familiar smiles of her parents on one side and her sun-kissed self and brothers on the other. She was Florence's age at the time and her brothers were Sebastian's. Lillian sank down in the chair as tears welled up in her eyes. *These are my favorite photos. The EMTs must've saved them from the scene for me—EMTs just like Al and Joe—twenty years ago. My mother was wearing this locket when she died.* The tears streamed down her cheeks. *These are the pictures I was meant to see. God is in the details!*

She fastened the locket around her neck, then looked from Anthony's packet to her lawyer's folder. She furrowed her brow remembering another phrase from Anthony's lips. "You deserve payment for your grief."

In a whisper, she repeated her answer from that day: "Grief is not a commodity." She shoved the packet, unseen photos and all, back into the manila envelope and said again, this time with a clear, strong voice: "Grief is not a commodity, and . . . *and* I will not only see the children again. I'll be their adoptive mom, because," and this time she believed it, "nothing is impossible for God!"

Clarity seized her, like the piercing light of dawn when the sun first appears on the horizon. She grabbed Anthony's packet and flew downstairs to the old brick fireplace. With loud clinking, she removed the empty mason jars from inside of the hearth, then tossed the envelope where they'd stood. She grabbed twigs as kindling from a bouquet, then tore through the armoire drawers to find matches. She lit all four corners of the packet and within seconds a flicker became a bright flame.

A worried meow sounded from behind her as Mr. Blue Suede Shoes approached. She scooped him up, buried her face in his fur, and watched until the flames blazed through everything until only ashes remained. Ashes again. She breathed in a new thought. *No one can steal my good memories. Even if I have to dig deep to remember them, even if there's sadness around them, they're still good.* The locket held good memories, as did her heart—so many good memories of Estelle. She would not give in to despair, not in these final days when she needed to fight for the children. Anthony couldn't steal her hope. "God has very big sleeves!" She repeated what Montreal had said. She answered the passion stirring inside her: *Now, I'll fight for new memories with my new family!*

She jumped up. It was late. Surely the meeting between Judith and Sinclair in the hearth room was done; she had to talk with Lars!

Lillian threw on her jacket, then raced across the street, corner to corner, and over a carpet of perfectly laid grass shimmering under lights lining a walkway. Her steps faltered at the sight of Anthony's signature benches, four of them, encircling a wide grouping of brightly colored playground equipment . . . all brand new. A red, white, and blue ribbon attached to a newly planted tree fluttered in her face. She stopped short to brush it away and it fell to the ground. Dotted across the park, each tree bore the same campaign token with his slogan written across the white section of each ribbon.

"No! I'm not having it! You were doing this in my neighborhood as Estelle lay dying! This is not your park—this is the children's park and my park!" she yelled as angry tears stung her eyes. Suddenly she found herself running from tree to tree, ripping off each ribbon.

At the last tree, the knot was too tight. She yanked at it with all her strength, even biting at it with her teeth, pulling so hard that the ribbon carved a line in the bark and tore at her hands. It finally snapped and she fell backward. As she stared at the pile of ribbons beside her on the ground, the tears streaming down her face were no longer from anger. She buried her face in her hands and began to sob. All this time she'd held the children, listened to their sorrow, and told them everything would be all right. But Estelle was gone. She wasn't coming back, and it was as if someone had cut off Lillian's right arm. She had no idea how to live life without Estelle or do what must be done to follow in her footsteps.

A voice at her shoulder spoke now, though she hadn't even heard Judith approach or sit down beside her. "I know how it feels to lose your best friend. Mine was my mama," she said, wrapping her arms around Lillian. "I've been alone a long time, until you stepped in, you and this whole community, and now I'm here for you."

94

Montreal

The next morning, Montreal stood at the window of the Silverstone Apartment scanning the street. Behind him, Miss Ruby was in the kitchen bouncing Lavender, who hiccupped and sniffled; she'd been crying for a long while.

"Montreal, I'm afraid Lillian isn't coming until later. I told her we could meet at the daycare after lunch. Lavender will be fine; she's just not used to me yet," explained Miss Ruby.

"I, I called her," Montreal answered, without turning around.

Just then, Lillian appeared on the sidewalk outside, wearing yoga pants and a sweatshirt, with her hair in a messy ponytail. Montreal had never seen her so bedraggled, but her face looked bright and determined. She plowed through the door so quickly, Montreal had to jump to the side in order to avoid being squished.

"Oh! Hi, sorry about that—I came as fast as I could!" she exclaimed, sweeping him into an enormous hug. Then, with one arm still around his shoulders, she pulled him along with her, crossing to the kitchen.

As soon as the baby laid eyes on her, she squealed and reached from Miss Ruby's arms. Lillian caught her, enfolding her in kisses.

Miss Ruby chuckled. "You've been missed!"

A smile appeared on Lillian's exhausted face. "Thank you for telling Montreal to call me. I had no idea how rough it was for you. I'm so sorry!"

Montreal avoided Miss Ruby's eye, but he could see her looking at him. Lillian continued in a rush, "I'm afraid I was sound asleep; can you believe it? Judith and I talked long into the night, then Lars checked in on us after his meeting with Sinclair was finally over. I fell into bed in the wee hours—but never mind, I'm here now!"

As Lillian kissed and rocked Lavender, she started clearing a few cups from the table, then opened the fridge. "I feel bad your night was so rough. Let's see, should I start breakfast?"

Miss Ruby examined Montreal's face from behind her heart-shaped glasses. Sheepishly, he caught her eye, just in time to see her wink. "Sure! And you can't believe how tough my night was. Imagine, me with all this experience, having such a hard time! Glory be, these children are more work than I could have imagined!"

Lillian peered over the open fridge door, looking from a beautiful fruit and blueberry muffin tray to the newly set table. "Oh, gosh, forgive me." She glanced around at the orderly surroundings, then, under a furrowed brow, asked, "So, Montreal told me Sebastian and Aurora refused to go to bed last night? Did I understand that correctly?"

Montreal felt the sting of his conscience, "Actually, I, uh—"

Miss Ruby interrupted, "They're all very strong-willed children, but you're here now, so all is well." She gave Montreal another wink and grabbed her overnight bag. "My thoughts will be with you today, and tomorrow's plan still stands for me to keep the children while you're in court." Montreal watched the worry cloud Lillian's eyes. Miss Ruby kissed her on the forehead. "Do not let worry steal the joy of today. We're all rootin' for you!"

Miss Ruby touched Montreal on the shoulder as Lillian poured orange juice and whispered, "I'm good at keeping secrets and I'm glad, not mad, that you called her."

Montreal folded his lips in and blinked back the tears that tried to betray him. "It's our last day."

Miss Ruby gave a quiet nod, then disappeared out the door.

After breakfast, Lavender fell sound asleep in Lillian's arms. Sebastian pulled his chair over to the two of them and began lining up blueberries along the side of the fruit plate, humming a tune. Florence grabbed her book, then returned to finish her cocoa, sitting close enough to touch shoulders with Lillian. Aurora sat on the floor at Lillian's feet, wrapped in her blanket, quietly reciting possible goldfish names. "Bubbly-boo, Mermaid-face, Gill-face, Floaty, Fred . . ."

The doorbell broke the sweet suspension of time that Montreal alone felt he was guarding. He hurried to answer. There stood their landlord with a couple beside him. He took off his cap and mumbled, "Sorry 'bout your mom, kid, but these folks just need a quick view of this space before they sign the rental agreement."

Montreal clenched the doorknob and swallowed down the words screaming up through his throat. He could feel his muscles tensing and a wave of anger surge through his body as the reality of pending loss crowded in on him.

Lillian appeared at his elbow, still holding the sleeping baby. Placing a gentle hand on his shoulder, she calmly took charge. "Hi there, Roy. There are four more days left in this month, and you'll owe us Estelle's deposit when we vacate this spotless apartment at that agreed-upon time. Until then, respect our privacy." She didn't wait for an answer, but merely clicked the door shut.

"No one can ruin this day!" Handing Montreal her cell phone, Lillian breathed out a long sigh, then straightened her shoulders and said, "Call Lars; tell him we need four kites. We'll bring snacks, pick up some yummy food, and meet him for a picnic at the new park in an hour! Oh, and grab that football I saw in your room."

Montreal stared over at his sibling. Florence had dashed into the back bedrooms and come back with a quilt and sunscreen. Sebastian was filling a brown paper sack with apples, carrots, and graham crackers while Aurora stuffed a matching grocery bag with her princess dress-up cape, gown, and sequined slippers. She frowned at Montreal as he watched her. "My cape flutters in the wind when I run!" she explained fiercely, then gathered up her own blanket and stood by the door, ready.

Lillian chuckled. "We'll have a wonderful day! Then tonight Miss Ruby will stay with you one more time. Be sure to be extra nice to her, will you?"

Florence frowned. "To Miss Ruby? Who said we weren't nice? We like her!"

Montreal glared her way and shushed her.

The day was one of the best days Montreal had ever had. After kite flying and a touch football game coached by Lars, they'd gone swimming at Stratford Community Pool, then ordered pizza and watched a funny movie at Lillian's apartment. Sebastian and Lars made heaps of popcorn while Lillian taught Florence how to make blended lavender lemonade.

Lillian whispered to Montreal at one point that he could accompany her to court. Somehow the idea of being there made him feel less nervous about the outcome. But for now, Montreal pushed tomorrow from his mind. Whatever happened, they'd chased joy and found it today!

Before taking them to their apartment, where Miss Ruby waited, Lars had prayed, "Lord, we don't know what to do, but our eyes are on you. Please guide us and open our hearts to understand your plans, and please God, we need a miracle tomorrow, thank you. Amen."

Miss Ruby phoned just before they left. Montreal watched a new burden settle over Lillian as she answered, "A subpoena? Of all things. I know your heart, regardless of the answers you'll have to give tomorrow. I'll ask Birgitte to watch the children in the morning so you can get to court." But when Lillian silenced her phone, Lars was there with a hug for her, and Montreal too.

95

Anthony

Anthony stood at the wall of windows in his office overlooking the New York City skyline. He touched a screen and blinds descended from the ceiling, making a soft, whirring sound.

"What's that?" came the anxious voice from the other end of the phone.

"My blinds. You're jumpy over nothing; get ahold of yourself. All you need to do tomorrow is grant me custody of my children—*my* children. There's nothing difficult about this."

"Difficult? What do you think is happening here? Some game? You're playing with fire," came Judge Rolland's sharp voice.

Anthony pulled at his cuffs. "No fire, just simple facts. When have I ever let you down? You're protected here, and my success means your success."

The judge continued, "Here's a fact for you: every single person affiliated with Lillian Bloom adores her. She's become a local heroine, so don't assume you have all of Stratford's support. Just wait, my courtroom will be packed with ordinary people who believe she's something extraordinary. Those kinds of people turn assumption on its head. And in case you missed it, your eldest son will accompany her."

"Montreal?" His son's name caught in his throat. "How do you know this?"

"Are you questioning me? It seems your guardian ad litem isn't as malleable as you thought. I've heard she's just granted Bloom's request for your son to be in court tomorrow."

"I'm not concerned," Anthony scoffed. "In fact this is a good thing. My son will be reasonable and obedient and I don't expect anything but respect from him. This is a formality, with publicity included; the outcome is secure. Now go relax and get your mind off the stress in my private club. I'll let them know you're coming."

Judge Rolland retorted, "No, I'm planning on being fully alert. I'd suggest you do the same; your pride makes you careless."

"I am never careless, everything is under my control. Give me support for my platform and yours will remain undisputed. I need my children alongside me. Your wise assessment of the situation in my favor will benefit you later. Now, goodbye; see you tomorrow."

Anthony was about to hang up, when Judge Rolland interjected, "Speaking of disputing, she rescheduled her appointment in Lafayette, correct? And she followed through with it—correct?"

"Yes, Jesse did, long ago. Do I ever miss a detail?"

"You'd better not have, this time," Judge Rolland barked, then hung up.

Anthony opened a drawer and stared at the latest photo of Jesse, obviously still pregnant, but he had nothing on Nolan West. He'd been hidden so well that Anthony's spies couldn't find him. Anthony set his jaw. "Loose ends, just loose ends to be dealt with," he said to himself.

There was a light tap on the door to which Anthony responded, "Enter." Ebony Scott stepped inside, but when he offered her a chair, she politely refused. "How can I fix whatever is bothering you?" he asked.

"You can't, because I finally understand," she answered, lifting her chin slightly in apparent defiance, but the beads of sweat appearing on her forehead betrayed her confidence. "I'm here to say that I know what you did to my mother. I know it was you, not Judith, who destroyed her. She didn't sell the hotel out from under everyone; you forced her hand."

Anthony smiled. "And hello to you as well. Please don't allow dark thoughts into this glorious day—the day before my paternal rights are restored."

"Anthony, you need to listen to me."

"Is that so? Please, share your concerns. Just don't forget your place."

"You—you lied to me. I didn't understand Judith's responses to me at the house, so I searched through my mother's old journals. I finally found what really happened," she said, trying to steady her rising voice.

"You exhibit amazing self-control. And how gracious of you, trusting your mentally ill mother's ramblings from decades ago. What would anyone else expect from a kind daughter—so kind that you believe her when no one else will."

Ebony pushed her braids behind her shoulders and drew in a breath before saying, "I know what you did. You stole the hotel—you ruined her and her colleagues' livelihoods, just so you could line your pockets and cover your tracks. Judith was the victim, not the villain."

Anthony laughed. "Villain? Nice. There's no villain here, but there is a very bold woman who chose euthanasia for her miserable, insane mother not long ago. I'll have to check my records for exact dates. Who would imagine that Stratford's most compassionate, respected social worker," here he paused to straighten his tie in the mirror, "would choose to kill her own mother? Publicity from that slight error in judgment would destroy your integrity and your livelihood. Like mother, like daughter?" He pulled on his suit coat. "I don't think so. Pour yourself a drink on the way out. You look like you need one."

Ebony rubbed the back of her neck. "I don't drink, remember?"

"Of course, but you should. You're obviously a bit tense." Anthony stepped in close and she flinched. He laughed again. "Oh, sorry to disappoint. Just getting the door for you; you were in the way. Don't be tomorrow."

She shook her head ever so slightly, then left.

Anthony turned to the mirror again to straighten his lapel. He was wearing black today, since all must see him as the grieving widower the evening before court. Tomorrow he'd dress in light grey, as the youthful, loving father who would eventually be mayor.

He took his private elevator up to the penthouse suite, then gazed down at the courthouse steps. The press was buzzing in early anticipation of tomorrow's well-publicized custody case. The tragic New York Cinderella story would finally be resolved through him gathering his children into the fold. A week of talk-show interviews had shored up his story of Estelle's mental illness and the misguided florist's reputation of irresponsibility.

It thrilled him to no end that hidden behind the court pillars would be the signs—a hundred of them, written in blue and red, that stated his motto: *Building community begins by valuing every individual* - *Anthony Mullenix.*

His only regret had been the children's absence when he was to exit the court-house in triumph. Now, however, Montreal would be the perfect visual for his well-orchestrated life. Perhaps Ebony Scott wouldn't need to pay for disloyalty after all. Her little tantrum was a ripple in his calm sea.

96

Judith

Name. Joo-dith : Hebrew origin, meaning "the praised one" and "woman of Judea"

Standing under the moonlight of Lillian's back step, Judith pressed her fingers to her temples, wishing to settle the confusion welling up in her spirit. Her message for Lillian felt urgent, but the details remained somewhat foggy. Sinclair's confession the night before had unearthed a slew of forgotten memories she wished would've stayed buried. She'd decided to forgive him for notarizing the deed, believing Lars at his word that forgiveness brought freedom. In truth, she felt lighter in her spirit; holding onto anger against Sinclair had been exhausting. However, in his own processing, Sinclair's incessant talking had driven her from her apartment tonight, where he'd finally fallen sound asleep on her new couch with his shoes still on—of all things. She'd slipped out without him noticing.

She tapped on Lillian's back door, ashamed of coming at such a late hour, but her brimming recollections respected no timeline.

Lillian's weary face peered around the door. "Judith," she said through a yawn, "come in. Help yourself to anything; I've got to sleep." She locked the door behind them.

Judith followed as she explained, "I have to tell you something."

At the couch, Lillian brushed her hair from her face and curled up in one corner, against the cushions. "Shoot. I'm all ears, unless I fall asleep."

Judith stared down at her hands. "I have new old memories filling in the missing information in my mind and in my story, and in Sinclair's."

Lillian leaned forward. "Does Sinclair know?"

Judith shook her head. "He keeps talking, I can't get a word in edgewise. Besides, I wanted to tell you first. Can I—get something?"

"Of course," Lillian answered, stifling another yawn.

Judith made a beeline for Lillian's bedroom, then returned, carrying the brooch. Holding it up to the lamplight, it sparkled in dazzling light blue. "I saw this on your nightstand when I stayed with you, and it reminded me of something from my past. Suddenly today, I remembered what it was!" She set it down, then gripped Lillian's hand and whispered in a hoarse voice, "Sylvia's necklace! I know where it is—the one Sinclair told me and Lars about—I, I stole it from Mr. Mullenix!"

Lillian sat up straight. "Wait, what?"

"It's crazy, I know!" Judith held her cheeks. "Mr. Mullenix left me alone in his office, alone with the bourbon and the guard at the door, like I said. That's where I found it! I heard him say, "Let her get drunk, then throw her out!" as he left. I'd just lost everything, and he'd promised to take care of me. So, naturally, I searched everywhere for something valuable to steal and the necklace was in his jacket pocket!"

The women stared at each other in mutual astonishment. Lillian pressed her hand. "Oh, my word, Judith, keep going! Then what?"

"So, I, uh, let's see . . . I shoved the necklace into my bra cup—my outfit was pretty slinky so that was my only spot—and I grabbed the bottle I was drinking, plus another one I found. The guard ducked into the office after I left, so I disappeared as quickly as possible." Judith scrunched up her face saying, "Think, think . . ."

"It's okay; just let the memories open up slowly," urged Lillian, a bit breathless.

"So, that night my uncle was at the house instead of our hotel. I thought I'd just tell him what I'd done, sort of out of spite, but I was terrified. He was always mean and I was pretty drunk by then. I don't know what I did instead, that's the problem." Judith dropped her head into her hands and started rocking. "I'm so dumb. But I also keep seeing my mom's notes in my head; she used to write love notes for me and I saved them all, somewhere in the house. I know I finished the bourbon then I left. That's the last memory from that night."

"And the necklace?"

Judith shook her head. "I can't, I just can't remember what I did. It's all foggy but I know I didn't take it from the house. So, it's there—or was there, maybe with the notes. I can't remember."

Lillian wrapped her arms around Judith's shoulders. "You'll remember—I believe you will! There's been so much rough news lately, like everything's against us. I've been tempted to give up, I'm ashamed to say, but now you're here, with good news. Thank you!"

"That's why I came. You need that necklace as evidence in court by tomorrow!" Judith stood up. "Without something, Mr. Mullenix will win—so I'm here to help us win!"

"Yes, you are!"

"I'll go to the house right now and find it."

"Oh, no, you don't!" Lillian pulled Judith back down to the couch. "We'll figure this out with Lars' help in the early morning. We'll search the house, and we can ask Officer Jensen to come along for protection. Our time will be tight, but it's too dangerous to go alone in the dark. Let's get some sleep now. The fact that the necklace may be in the house restores my hope." She squeezed Judith's hand. "Now to bed immediately. Let's pray you remember exactly where it is as you sleep!"

At 3:00 a.m., Judith awakened with a start. Suddenly, just as Lillian said, she knew exactly where she'd hidden her mother's precious notes—and where the notes were, the necklace was! She crept past Lillian's closed door, shushing the cat, who pawed at it. *This is my deal; it's for me to solve,* she thought. She headed downstairs, but before slipping out the back door she held up something she wanted Lillian to have. *Where can I put this envelope for safekeeping?* she thought, eyeing Lillian's purse. Rummaging around in a catchall drawer, she found a pencil and a sturdy flashlight. She scribbled on the envelope for Lillian's purse, then on a sticky note for the counter:

Don't worry, I remember where I hid it. I'll be back soon, Judith.

Outside on the back step, she impulsively called Sinclair and left a message on his voicemail. "Wake up! Wake up and meet me right now at my old house. I think I know where your sister's necklace is—I hid it in the ground! Okay, so, bye."

Judith ran most of the way, darting between shadows under the pale moonlight, stopping only a few times to catch her breath. When she came to the property, she pressed her back against a wooden fence, trying desperately to gulp enough breath to fill her lungs. *Too loud!* she scolded herself, when a rustling in the bushes alerted her to something. Without waiting another second, she ran to the far side of the house just beyond the washroom door and squatted down by the steps. Frantically she patted the sparse grass and dirt beyond them, inching along, until finally her hand touched the metal ring protruding from the ground. Quickly, she pulled away the rocks that hid the seam along the house, that, in the daylight, would reveal the door to the root cellar. She pulled with all her might, and, to her amazement, the cellar door gave way.

Judith shone the flashlight onto the rough, whitewashed walls and ceiling of the cellar. Old bins lay empty, except for one that contained a few canning jars and tools. Along the back wall, dusty but intact, were sweeping lines of twine she'd strung to hold her mother's notes, attached by clothespins. She let out a gasp, then immediately clamped her hand over her mouth. Hot tears stung her cheeks. She hardly knew what they were, it had been so long since she'd wept. *Oh, to read just one note,* her heart cried, but she refused to pause.

She searched the walls for the smallest hint, then in rushed the memory. The second empty bourbon bottle sat beside a whiskey cask in the corner. Judith reached down inside the barrel and felt around in the dust until her hand rested on the cold, hard, unmistakable shape of the Kashmir sapphire necklace. She brought it into the light, dangling it before the flashlight beam, marveling at its beauty.

Suddenly, something smashed down on her skull. Excruciating pain riveted her mind, blurring her eyes and ringing through her ears. Chaotic voices echoed around her, shouting, "Grab it!"

"Is it real?"

"Is it what she said?"

Someone tore the necklace from her hands. The flashlight flew from her grasp as her face hit the dirt floor and the door above her head slammed shut. The flashlight beam was strong, but to Judith everything went blank.

97

Lillian

Lillian jolted awake. "Stop, danger!" she called out. Her nightmare had returned, but this time, instead of the four members of her family walking along the quaking road, holding her lost baby, it was the Mullenix children, with Lavender. Running to save them, as jagged asphalt slabs jutted up through the ground, was Judith, but her voice was drowned out by a huge pounding gavel.

Lillian sank back onto her pillow and rubbed the tears from her eyes. Fighting a wave of fear, she shook herself back to reality. There was hope, faint as it felt, because Judith's bizarre story aligned with everything else. She repeated, "Nothing is impossible for God and God is in this."

She climbed out of bed and headed for the kitchen, clicking the door shut behind her so as not to disturb Judith with the whir of the coffee grinder. She'd awaken Judith shortly, after her first restorative mug of coffee. An hour and a half was all they had to scour the old house before Lillian's responsibilities set in; it would have to be enough. Hope stirred inside her. Estelle wouldn't give up—even in the eleventh hour—and neither would she.

Back in her room, she slipped on some comfy clothes, then settled onto her bed to soak in the peace and quiet. For just a few minutes, she'd do what she'd intended ages ago: find encouragement from Estelle's Bible. Reaching for it on the nightstand, she accidentally knocked the brooch to the ground. She felt around the floor for it, then tucked it into the pocket of her sweatshirt.

A light blue ribbon already marked Psalm 139, the beautiful passage Estelle had asked Lars to read on her last day. It was curious to see that instead of little phrases and highlights here and there, as she'd expected, the phrase "search me" was circled several times, then random words were underlined in light blue ink. From there she read, "Discern," "my," "path," "search," "before," "you," "lay your hand," "upon it," "attain it," "inward parts," "hidden," "secret," "in your book," "precious," "thoughts," "search," "see," "lead," "in the way."

What? she thought. *This looks like an intentional message.*

Her phone broke her concentration. On the other end, Sinclair's voice was urgent. "I'm at the old house. The ambulance is on its way and so is Lars to get you. I found Judith in the root cellar; she's terribly injured! She's barely coherent but keeps asking for you! She was searching for my sister's necklace."

Again, fear grabbed at Lillian's throat as she drew Estelle's Bible close to her chest and raced through the hallway. Guilt seized her mind. Yet again, a beloved person for whom she'd committed to care had disappeared from the safety of her own home. *How could this be?* Downstairs, she shoved the Bible into her purse then pulled on her clogs, just as the Gran Torino roared into the alley.

Hans stomped out his morning cigarette and ran over to the car window, just ahead of Lillian. "What's happening?" he cried.

"It's Judith. She was attacked. She's with Sinclair, conscious but badly injured," Lars quickly explained, as Lillian climbed through the window.

"What the devil?! Go—go! I can help! Birgitte is already replacing Ruby with the kids, as you arranged, but I can get Montreal—I'll bring him to the courthouse!" answered Hans, waving them off.

Lillian thanked him as Lars pressed the gas and sped through the alley toward the house.

The paramedics were already lifting Judith onto the gurney as Lars drove up over the curb. Lillian rushed to her side and took her hand. "You're here," came Judith's weak voice, "like last time. I . . . I blew it again."

Judith's hair was matted with blood on one side from a cut above her left eyebrow. Lillian stroked her hand, saying, "Oh, no, you didn't; you were helping me. Remember how much I need your help?"

Al, the paramedic, interjected, "Lillian, we gotta go!"

"Of course," she said, trying to back away, but Judith wouldn't let go of her hand. She looked to Lars for help.

"Don't leave me," Judith cried as the EMTs lifted her bed onto the truck.

Lars hugged Lillian, saying, "The courthouse isn't far from Carson Memorial. You'll have time to get ready in the courthouse restroom—just text me the clothes and things you'll need. I'll sit with the kids over breakfast to settle them before meeting you there with your things. Between Hans and Birgitte, everything will be fine, so don't worry."

"Why wasn't I watching over her?" said Lillian, getting into the ambulance.

"You were there for her then, and you are right now. See you soon!"

As Lillian sat in the hospital waiting room, she mused over Florence's need to make order, even to the point of changing out lightbulbs and batteries. Lillian had purchased fresh supplies purely for the sake of an emotional distraction, but because Florence had taken charge of the shop, Judith had had a strong flashlight at her fingertips. It was the flashlight's beam, shining through the slim cracks of the cellar door, that had alerted Sinclair to Judith's presence. "God in the details," Lillian whispered to herself, trying to hold back tears at the thought of Florence and each of the children. *How can I live without them?* she thought for the millionth time.

After lamenting over the missing deed and now necklace, Sinclair had tried to compensate by explaining complex court procedures for every possible scenario, but for all his help, her hands remained empty of evidence of Anthony's fraud.

Judith received the diagnosis of severe concussion and would stay overnight for observation. Finally, with a neat line of stitches in place along her brow, the ER doctor announced that she was stable. Lillian whispered goodbye, then walked to the courthouse to expel her nervous energy, arriving sooner than expected.

Just as she sat down on a bench to wait for Lars, who'd bring her fresh clothes shortly, Jesse's face appeared on her cell phone on FaceTime.

"Hi!" Jesse exclaimed. Lillian felt her heart warm, just seeing Jesse's face.

A man walked in through the double doors as Lillian answered, "Hello, Jesse, so good to see you. I can't talk now. People are arriving, but I will call later."

"You betcha! Just wanted to check in! Me and this little dude . . . did I tell you my baby's a boy? Dang cute on ultrasound! Anyway, we're thinking about you and I'm eating all day long to calm my nerves for you!"

"Good, you do that. I'll call later, love you, bye." When she glanced up, the man had stopped short and was staring at her as if he'd seen a ghost. Just then Lars appeared through the double doors with an armload of everything she needed. The man hurried away.

In a whirlwind, Lillian changed, fixed her hair and makeup, then shoved her soft clothes into a sack. As they entered the courtroom, Hans joined them with Montreal in tow.

"Hi," Montreal sputtered, standing awkwardly.

"Hi back, I'm so glad you're here," she answered, forcing her voice to sound upbeat. She embraced him quickly before leaving to thread through a few people milling around and find her place at the front. Lars, Montreal, and Hans sat directly behind her. As Lillian peered over her shoulder, the room swelled with many recognizable faces of friends, acquaintances, clients, and fellow shop owners. Lillian put her hands to her heart, warmed by the solidarity all around her.

She tucked a strand of a curl behind her ear as she stole a glance at Anthony. His lawyer spoke in low tones, but quieted when Anthony waved his hand. A hush fell over the courtroom as the bailiff called out, "All rise." Lillian was surprised that Judge Rolland wasn't the bold, confident man she'd expected to see. He looked antsy and troubled, buried in a robe too large for his stature. Slowly it dawned on her: he was the man from the hallway. She bit her lip: it was Jesse's words that had gripped him.

The bailiff then announced, "Judge Richard Rolland presiding. Please be seated."

Lillian looked over her shoulder to see that Hans had already tried distracting Montreal with a game of hangman—but Montreal sat bright and alert, focused on the situation unfolding before him. He smiled at Lillian and gave her a thumbs up. At that very moment, her phone dinged. She fumbled to silence it, feeling her cheeks flush.

A long-awaited text from Julius lit up her screen:

Loads of luck today. Wish I were there. Paris is grand but I miss you.

Everyone sat down as Judge Rolland addressed the room. "Good morning, ladies and gentlemen. Calling the case of Anthony Mullenix versus Lillian Rose Bloom. Are both sides ready?"

The attorneys answered affirmatively and gave their opening statements.

Friend after friend sat on the witness stand, answering questions from the opposition, unwillingly guided into destroying Lillian's character. Through tears, Miss Ruby was required to relay the details of the disappearance of Aurora. She explained Lillian's immediate response as running down the street, leaving Florence, whom Miss Ruby had never met, in her care and requesting she refrain from calling the police.

But amidst the painful cross-examinations, there was dear Benjamin, catching Lillian's eye with a gentle nod of support. Quon sat by Stuart, both at the edge of their seats: an unlikely pair cheering her on in quiet solidarity. Sylvia and Charles were close to the front, with Sylvia peering at the judge through her withering stare as if this might subdue him.

The last person to be sworn in was Ebony Scott. With perfect poise and confidence, she relayed her recommendation to the court. Anthony leaned back, crossing his arms, like a well-seasoned coach watching the last play of the game, ending in a touchdown. Ebony looked from him to Lillian as she left the stand, but Lillian saw something she'd never seen in that beautiful face. She thought it was regret. A slight hesitation caused Ebony to slip on the second step in her high heels. She grasped the railing, barely saving herself from falling to her knees.

Judge Rolland scanned the silent crowd, asking if there were any more witnesses. Lillian followed his gaze, blinking back tears as she did. No one said a word, but Lillian felt her weary heart bolstered by all the dear faces of people she'd met over the past year. Slight waves, nods, and eyes full of compassion greeted her from every corner of the room. She swallowed the lump in her throat as she acknowledged their kindness with a sad smile. When her eyes finally met Montreal's, he leaned over the railing to give her a quick hug.

As he did so, Lillian noticed that Lars had passed a note to her lawyer, who in turn asked Judge Rolland for a fifteen-minute recess. The judge pounded his gavel, adjusted the collar of his robe, then retreated to his chambers. Immediately the courtroom was abuzz with chatter.

Bangji, who'd been notably absent from the witness stand, approached Montreal. "Come," she insisted, "I brought you food." She squeezed Lillian's shoulder as he reluctantly followed her out.

Lars hurried over and grasped Lillian's hands. "I'll go grab Barbara and Bill in the back to pray with us. I just felt like we were all holding our breath and needed a pause to think. Sinclair said our lawyer could ask for a time-out if we needed one."

Lillian watched Lars disappear down the aisle and then caught Anthony's glare across from her. To avoid him, Lillian lowered herself into her chair and grabbed her purse as a distraction. She found relief in discovering she still had Estelle's Bible. As she withdrew it from her purse, a partly crushed envelope appeared alongside it. *I don't remember this*, she thought, as she laid it at her side, then opened the Bible to Psalm 139. In this unexpected moment, she examined the mysteriously underlined words again, which had nagged at her mind since seeing them earlier. This was an odd gift of space to investigate the message that had eluded her all morning. Again, she read, "Discern, my, path, search, before, you, lay your hand, upon it, attain it, inward parts, hidden, secret, in your book, precious, thoughts, search, see, lead, in the way."

Instinctively she flipped through all the Bible pages, then examined the front and back covers. Inside the back cover, the inner lining had been snipped at the edge. She pulled at it and the entire flap lifted easily, revealing a thin piece of paper. Inside was a letter penned in Estelle's lovely handwriting. She looked around. No one was paying attention to her as she sat hemmed in within the railed-off area. So, she began to read.

Dearest Lillian,

First, I love you. And I'm so thankful for the way you love my children. When you read this letter, I hope you'll find help in what I share. The night I explained my past with Anthony, I neglected to explain an important detail. You may remember me mentioning that I came from a long line of jewelers as well as musicians. You may also remember that Anthony left the stolen necklace with me for several days before taking it.

During that time, I realized that, by some miracle, the imitation sapphire gem in my mother's brooch from Elvis was the perfect match to one of the Kashmir sapphires in the necklace. In my hotel room, I switched my fake stone for one of the real ones. If you still have the brooch, which I've prayed God would preserve for you, know that it holds one of the real Kashmir sapphires. It is worth around a hundred thousand dollars and is evidence of my husband's extortion.

Without the entire story of the necklace's past, it may not be enough for the custody battle, but I am praying now, on this side of heaven, that everything will fall into place. Perhaps even the thumb drive evidence will return to you and then you'll have what you need.

I'm not sure if we still pray for our loved ones when we finally meet Jesus in heaven, but I do know that with or without me, Jesus is praying for you. And God is good. He's with you and my children right now, this very moment. Know that you are precious to me and I believe you'll find a way to adopt my children. It is my only remaining earthly desire, besides my husband's salvation.

With all my love, always,
Estelle

Barely breathing, Lillian slipped her hand into the paper bag sitting at her side and pulled out the soft jacket she'd been wearing. As if in slow motion, she withdrew the brooch she'd unwittingly stuffed inside her pocket hours earlier. She felt as if she were frozen in time and space. Her heart raced, yet she dared not move, as if doing so would break the power of this incredible miracle. She leaned back in the bench, staring at the exquisite gem, sparkling now more than ever in her hand. Her other hand rested on the curious envelope that had fallen out of the Bible. *Is this something more?* Lillian thought as she held it up. Slipping the brooch back into her pocket, she withdrew the papers from the envelope. Scribbled in pencil was a note:

Lillian,

> *Sinclair stuck this under my door before I left for your house, not after. I took it without telling him. Whoever broke in got nothing. Please keep this safe.*

Judith

With shaking hands, Lillian opened the folded pages. It was the quitclaimed deed to the Greenville Hotel!

Lars appeared at her elbow with Barbara and Bill. "Sorry, getting through the crowd was harder than I thought it'd be. Here we are, we've got five more minutes, ready to . . ." Lars' words died on his tongue. "Are you all right?" With trembling lips, Lillian tried to speak but couldn't. She handed the letter, the document, and the brooch to Lars. As he read, a smile spread across his face and his shining eyes welled up with tears. "Oh, Lillian!" he exclaimed, "It's the miracle we've been waiting for!"

At that moment, Sylvia appeared, tucking herself into their little huddle. "From my vantage point," she announced, "things do not appear to be going well; what can I do?"

Lars laughed out loud. "As a matter of fact, there's been a miraculous turn of events, and you're part of it." Lars called Lillian's lawyer over and in hushed tones explained everything. When the court resumed, their lawyer requested a meeting in the judge's chambers.

98

Judge Richard Rolland

Name. Ri-churd : English origin, meaning, "strong in rule,"
Name. Raw-lahn : Frankish origin, meaning, "fame of the land"

I n his chambers, Judge Rolland laid Estelle's letter on the walnut table, between the brooch and the hotel deed. He set his reading glasses down, then folded his hands and stared at the two opposing lawyers, the only other people present in the room. He ignored the sweat accumulating at his brow that dripped down along the back of his ears to the collar of his white shirt. He brushed his hand in the air for one of them to begin.

Lillian's lawyer nodded. "Your Honor," he began, in a voice that grated on every nerve of Judge Rolland's being, "this newly uncovered evidence proves that Anthony Mullenix operated an extortion ring connected to illegal gambling. Estelle Delacroix Mullenix's personal account, in letter form, gives solid proof of her just reasoning behind her desire for Ms. Bloom to gain full custody of the children. There's ample evidence here through the hotel deed, jewelry, and the obvious tampering with public records. In addition, we have multiple eyewitness accounts of his illegal activities, use of bribery, manipulation, and violence to promote his agenda, all of which can be called to the stand in light of this substantial evidence—and that is only the tip of the iceberg! His former lawyer is gathering more information even as we speak."

"Enough!" stated Judge Rolland, hardly able to focus on the droning. He motioned for the other lawyer to speak.

Anthony's lawyer leaned forward. "Your Honor, I ask you, what kind of evidence is this? Is this even real? How'd this suddenly appear? This is a straightforward case that is moments away from your appropriate ruling in my client's favor. I ask you to dismiss this so-called evidence immediately. They're stalling and I see no reason to continue wasting the court's valuable time."

Judge Rolland pounded his fist on the table. "And you have nothing to counter this evidence?"

Anthony's lawyer frowned. "Not at the moment, but if you'll give me time to speak with my client, I'm certain—"

"Time?" interrupted Judge Rolland. "You talk of wasting the court's valuable time, yet you're doing that now. You have nothing to oppose this evidence." He ignored the slight tremor in his fingers as he repositioned his glasses onto his face, then pushed the letter and document aside. He closed his hand over the brooch, squeezing it until its pin pricked his skin. He quelled the impulse to smash it against the wall. Hiding disdain from his voice, he recited the only ruling possible. "I've decided to seal these proceedings in order to protect the children. To extend this case with layers of evidence and more witnesses would only hurt them, and allow my courtroom to become a mud-slinging battlefield. My job is to protect the most vulnerable among us. I've decided the verdict. You may be excused."

In stunned silence, the lawyers stood up to leave. As they approached the door, Anthony burst in, followed by the court security officers calling for him to halt. Judge Rolland intervened, saying roughly, "I'll handle him, thank you. Give us a minute."

As the door clicked shut, only the two of them remained inside the chambers. Anthony exploded, "What the hell's wrong with you? Get out there and finish your end of the deal! The crowd's getting restless."

Judge Rolland seethed as the venom of hatred surged through his veins. In a voice barely audible, he spit out the words, "Get on your knees!"

Anthony laughed. "Me? On my knees? What is this?" Judge Rolland crossed the room and reached for the door. Anthony held up both hands. "Whatever, okay! What's this, some ritual?" He lowered himself to the floor.

"This is you begging me for mercy." The suffocating claustrophobia of Judge Rolland's newly found power seized his chest. He fought to breathe through the intricacies of this decision wrought with potential to destroy his own life. He cast the evidence onto the floor in front of Anthony. Estelle's letter floated in the air before fluttering to the ground. "You missed a few details after all, along with *the* detail that involves me."

Horror rose in Anthony's eyes as he scanned the letter. Clenching his jaw, then crumpling the letter in his hand, he paused, momentarily paralyzed. Then, finally, in a monotone voice, he asked, "What do you want me to do?"

"Submit. Today you lose your children. I will grant custody to Ms. Bloom and you will no longer pursue them; however, you will pay her the alimony you owed your family for the years you neglected them. And whatever you've done with that necklace, find it and return it." He took a deep breath. "You will not hold Jesse or her child over my head, nor will you cause her any problems. I will allow you to run for mayor, but the evidence of your past will remain sealed under my supervision. If I mysteriously disappear, everything you've ever done will be known." He stopped for a moment, looking down at the now quivering Anthony Mullenix. "Remember this stance. You are bowing to justice, and every act of injustice you've ever done dangles like a noose in my hand before you. Your casual lies are now burning coals under your bare feet on your path ahead. Get up and get out and humbly receive far less punishment than you deserve."

99

Lillian

Judge Rolland waited for silence in the courtroom. With all eyes fixed on him, he shifted in his seat, then announced, "This court, after thoroughly investigating both sides of this custody case, with the best interests in mind for Montreal Mullenix, Florence Mullenix, Sebastian Mullenix, Aurora Mullenix, and Lavender Mullenix, grants full custody to Lillian Rose Bloom, with the termination of rights therein of their father, Anthony Mullenix." He stated the next steps to be followed, the date and time, and pounded his gavel. The entire room erupted in shouts of joy as everyone applauded, jumped to their feet, and hugged each other. The distinct whoop resounding over the crowd came from Stuart, but Hans also shouted out his own celebratory cheer in Danish.

"How on earth?!" Lillian blurted out, with the full force of the miracle coming to light. "They're mine? We're a family?" She was laughing as she spun around to catch Montreal, who'd scrambled over the railing. Lars drew his arms around both of them, kissing them while laughing and crying at the same time.

With shining eyes, Montreal looked from one to the other. But then, he loosened his hold and slipped out of Lillian's embrace. He ran across the room to his father. Then, wrapping his arms around Anthony's waist, he said, "Thank you, Father. Mama would've been proud of you."

Anthony froze in silence. Lillian's eyes met his and she was sure she saw traces of those same soulful eyes his son had inherited. Unguarded, in that split second, there was a hint of something else, something that could be.

Anthony walked down the courthouse steps, through the frenzied blur of reporters and the hired crowd, then up to the podium. Lars, Lillian, and Montreal made their way not far behind him, pausing to shake hands and receive hugs.

Lillian's lawyer ran over to slip the brooch into her hand saying, "Judge Rolland says you may have this for safekeeping."

"Please, thank him—and thank *you*!"

When the people outside realized what had actually happened, they clamored for interviews and photos. But Lars was quick to draw them behind the pillars, past the signs, where they were hidden from view. Standing only a few yards away was Ebony Scott, awaiting Anthony's speech.

Anthony raised his hands to silence the crowd. He dabbed his eyes with his pocket square. "Hello and welcome. Your support is invaluable to me as I face the result of a difficult decision, one I was reluctant to make. These last moments of concession in court came at a great cost to me, but as a selfless act of love that will benefit my children. I've decided to model the truth my dying wife whispered to me in her last days, that every child needs both a mother and father, two adults always available to raise them. I've allowed Lillian Bloom this privilege of partnering with me on their behalf, but I will strive to be available for all their needs as they arise, as a watchful guardian. Sometimes the greatest act of love is giving the ones we care about wings to fly."

Montreal stared up at Lillian with a frown, "Did Mama really say that?"

She answered, "Your father is surprised by this outcome. You may need to filter a few of the things he says. He's processing the best he can today."

Montreal shrugged. "Mama said stuff like what you're saying all the time. Got it."

Anthony continued, "I've chosen to allow Lillian to do her part in their lives, just as we all do our part to value every individual in our community, whether neighbor or friend. In the end, we're all family. Parents must sacrifice to benefit all children. And you know me: I'll always fight for the most fragile among us. Whether it's the homeless or homebound, together we will build a better community filled with grace, honesty, and compassion. Thank you for believing in all that's good in me. I am humbled by your companionship on life's magnificent, though sometimes painful, path . . . I mean journey."

Lillian watched as Anthony played the part of the perfect politician, gesturing from behind the podium.

"As we move forward in these days, I'm turning my face to the joy of serving you as I prepare for my next role as your mayor. My heart is full of gratitude that you stand by me in victory over my children's future and the joyous future we all share as invaluable members of our great New York City community! Please join me in my campaign! I'll see you all again soon! God bless you!"

Ebony Scott stepped out of her shoes and leaned against one of the pillars, folding her arms as she sighed. Lillian glanced at Anthony, then looked back at Ebony and saw her tense up her shoulders. Ebony glared at Anthony, who was blowing kisses out to the applauding crowd and cooing at a baby nearby. As if out of a stupor, Ebony dropped her arms and shook her head, then turned just in time to catch Lillian's eye. Leaning down to grab her shoes, she hesitated. Lillian smiled and Ebony drew near, putting her hand out first to Montreal. "Congratulations on getting the outcome I know you were hoping for," Ebony said stiffly, looking up at Lillian and Lars. "I'm sorry I represented you poorly today," she said as she dropped her shoulders, "but I want you to know from here on out, you have me as your advocate, cheering you on." Again, Lillian felt the tears stinging her eyes. Ebony smiled and added, "You're going to be a great mom to Montreal and his siblings."

Ebony shifted from one foot to the other. Lillian answered, "Having you as an advocate will be invaluable, thank you."

Ebony swept her braids across her shoulder, then leaned down to put her shoes back on. "You're welcome. We'll be in touch." Glancing over her shoulder at Anthony, she turned back to the little group, smiled, then walked away.

It seemed that no one had noticed the coolers overflowing with sodas that lined the stone wall near the campaign signs. A paper taped to a pillar read, *Take one in celebration!* Montreal pointed to them. "Does that mean us?"

Lars answered, "If they're for anyone, they're certainly for you! I don't see why not; your father meant for people to enjoy them."

Lillian had already FaceTimed home with each excited kid's face now crowding into view on her cell phone screen. Birgitte was laughing and clapping in her infectious way at their joyful clamoring, and sang a festive song to Lavender in

Danish. Lillian could barely see them through her eyes blurred from happy tears. She could hardly even get a word out except to laugh with thankfulness from a deep joy flooding her soul. Montreal handed her a soda, but it slipped from her hand, crashing onto the cement. *Wham!* The lid shot off into the air, and orange soda rained over each one of them.

"CAP-SNORT!" Montreal exclaimed.

"CAP-SNORT!" the children called back through the screen.

Lars looked at them quizzically, shaking orange soda from his hair. Montreal laughed as he licked his fingers then explained, "Lillian and I have all sorts of fun stuff to teach you now. Right Lillian?"

Lillian was just saying goodbye to his siblings. "Love you too! We'll be there to hug you and kiss you and scoop you up in just a bit! Bye for now!" She clicked her phone off, then asked, "Fun stuff? Take the lead, I'm ready!"

"Yeah, cap-snorts, Elvis back-up dancing, more colors like happy, you know—and you'll teach us blooming stuff too?"

Lillian laughed. "Not sure who's best at the blooming stuff. It was you, way back in the beginning, the boy on the orange bike, who leapt into my life. And I'd say it's you who's been teaching me to bloom all along!"

100

Lars

Warm light shone from the bedroom window of the chapel rectory, Lars' tiny house at the corner of the property. It was midnight, and inside, Lars was on his knees to pray.

"Thank you, God, for your mercy in court today. We stood back and watched your miracles unfold, even to the tiniest detail. Thank you for Estelle's letter and for preserving the brooch, for our lawyer and the judge's ruling. Thank you for Estelle's courageous example of living in faith and for honoring her request by protecting her children. Please transform Anthony's hard heart, for his own sake and for theirs. Guide Lillian as she mothers them now in this new season and comfort them even as they still grieve their mother. Thank you for saving Judith's life and for answering our need with your abundant hidden mysteries. Thank you for that sea of ardent encouragers, some I've never even met, who came to support us. Thank you for your truth and grace over our lives, covering all our past mistakes with the sacrifice of Jesus' blood over our sin. And thank you for these precious children and for beloved Lillian. I surrender my own deep desires to you in this. I ask for your guidance of my own heart. Amen."

Several weeks later, having paused the chapel renovation, Miguel and Gabriel's crew had already begun transforming Lillian's vision for Judith's old home into reality. Under the canopy of blue sky, yellow beams of sunlight bathed the old house and yard as it waited expectantly for all that would come with new life ahead. The grass, soft and thick, was prepared for coming picnics. The bountiful leaves of the fruit trees blanketed strong branches, ready for climbers to dwell in secret places. Flowers in all imaginable colors soon would bloom for the shop and the table.

At the far corner of the yard, Quon, Bangji, Florence, and Sebastian were repairing the dilapidated gazebo. Sitting on a lawn chair was Judith, now fully recovered, holding Lavender, who drank hungrily from her bottle. Lillian and Aurora spread paint chips on a blanket for each child to pick their own room color. Montreal walked over to where Lars was throwing debris into a dumpster. Holding up his green paint chip, he asked, "What do you think?"

Lars answered, "Green, the color of new life—it's perfect!" He pulled off his gloves and put his hand on Montreal's shoulder. "I have a question I've been meaning to ask you, that has a lot to do with that color. Since you are now Lillian's oldest son, how would you feel if I asked her to marry me?" Montreal dropped his chin down and covered his eyes with his hands, then shook his head. Lars said in a worried tone, "I'm so sorry I asked. I see it's too soon for you to handle my question. We can talk about this in time."

"No, no," Montreal choked out, "it's really cool, the best, coolest thing. I didn't mean no . . . I just . . . it's just I never thought we'd all be a family—but I really hoped we could."

Lars laughed but tears were in his eyes. "That's the same thing I've been hoping!"

Just then Lillian appeared, holding a handful of paint chips in different shades of yellow. "Hey, you two," she said, looking down as she fanned them out. "I was wondering if you'd help me choose a living room color. I believe it must be the color of happy!" Peering from one to the other she frowned, "Why are you both crying . . . and smiling? Are you all right?"

Montreal nodded to Lars and whispered, "Do it now!"

"Now?" Lars mouthed, "I didn't exactly . . ."

Montreal laughed, "Not yet, hold on!"

Lillian stared at them. "Will someone please tell me what's going on?"

Montreal called out as he ran toward Judith. "Hey, Flo, Sebastian, hurry up—come here, Aurora—drop all of those colors, come here!" He scooped up Lavender from Judith's arms and ran back, then made everyone stand in a row before turning to Lars to say, "Go ahead, we're all ready."

Lillian's bewildered face peered up into Lars'. He answered, "Uh, not exactly as I'd planned, but here goes nothing!" He sank down on one knee. Lillian gasped and dropped the yellow paint samples she had been holding. They fluttered to the ground like petals.

"Lillian Rose Bloom, I think I've loved you since the minute you refused to eat the slice of birthday pie; I just didn't know it. So," here he looked at the kids, "if it's okay with everyone here . . ." Florence's dimples had never looked so deep under the smile she tried to hide. Lars gazed up at Lillian whose cheeks flushed with delight. "Though I have no ring. . ." Aurora zipped over and handed him the elastic feathery ring she'd been wearing, then hurried back in line. "Thank you, Aurora. Okay then, with this ring . . ." Sebastian gasped, finally realizing what was happening. Lars stared into Lillian's eyes, "I'd like to know if I might have the most glorious privilege of being your husband, and joining you in this beautiful family standing before us."

Lillian reached her arms out to Lars. "Yes, yes, yes!" she exclaimed to the cheers of joy all around. The children piled in close as Lillian and Lars wrapped their arms around them in a loving family embrace.

Epilogue:

Two Years Later

Under the gables of Judith's childhood home, on a speckled egg tucked in a nest, a crack appeared. "Tap-tap," went a beak as it broke through the shell, revealing damp feathers on the head of a newborn house finch. Mama Bird sang her song of delight as Papa Bird soared above in a red burst of pride.

Below the nest, down through the attic library, past the children's bedrooms, then swirling out the kitchen windows, that same new-life joy enveloped the entire Gundersen household. For today was wedding day!

With a baby on her hip, Lillian opened the greenhouse door. Bangji, carrying a bucket of herbs, hurried down the brick steps. "Hmm," said Lillian, closing her eyes as she breathed in the fragrance of mint and lavender, "where will you put these?"

"Serving platters must be beautiful!" Bangji waved a bunch of chamomile under the baby's chin. She giggled as the delicate blossoms tickled her nose.

"To think that you and Quon built us this greenhouse, now filled with bounty!"

"We were happy to do that for you," said Bangji.

Lars popped his head around the corner. "How do I look?"

Lillian kissed him and said, "Handsome as always. I adore that linen suit, but not sure about the tie. Is it choking you?"

"Thanks for reminding me—it's off as soon as the ceremony's done."

Bangji pulled her glasses from her apron to fuss with Lars' tie and pocket square. "Now you look very good." She nodded and headed for the kitchen.

Lars pulled Lillian and the baby close, then scooped up the wriggly toddler at his feet. Together they admired the garden, bursting with blooms and joyful activity. Water danced from the fountain, the perfect spot for the exchange of vows to come. On the grass, at the end of each row of white chairs, Aurora and Hope finished tying silken ribbons. In the gazebo, a huge farm table stood under the old garden chandelier. Tendrils of ivy and million bells spilled over its sides, while blue-faced violas peered out from the center. Just below it, Sylvia held a piping bag of frosting before the wedding cake, while Florence pointed out each spot another toddler's finger had poked.

From the back porch, the aroma of fresh rolls wafted through the air. Birgitte, holding an immense basket, yelled something in Danish to Hans, who was having a smoke amidst the hydrangeas.

Stuart approached with a coffee carafe in each hand. He held them up. "Ninety-six ounces in each, and two more to unload. The blend for today: complex, with floral notes and spice."

"Perfect," laughed Lillian, "set them beside the cake. Is Julius here yet?"

"Haven't seen him, but Lucy just arrived and Storm's looking for Montreal."

"I'll find him," replied Lillian.

"And I'll check on Ben," said Lars, heading for the apple trees, where Benjamin was rehearsing his sonnet.

Midway up the stairs, Lillian met Miss Ruby, who addressed the baby. "I was looking for you, cutie-pie. Miss Ruby wants to introduce you to Howie!"

Lillian answered, "I'm so thankful you've come. Is Howie pleased with the ramps?

Miss Ruby beamed, "Fabulous! Miguel is a miracle worker."

At the top of the stairs, Lillian found Montreal and Sebastian with the door to the bathroom wide open. Soapy water filled the sink as Montreal rubbed jam from the cuffs and collar of Sebastian's white shirt.

"Birgitte's jam tarts?" Lillian asked.

"She needed a poison taster." Sebastian brightened at the question.

"Of course she did," Lillian agreed. "Better run; Storm's looking for you boys. We're about thirty minutes from starting."

Lillian tapped on the master door. "Come on in," called a muffled voice.

Standing before the full-length mirror was Jesse, with her curls cascading over her bare shoulders and onto the lace of her wedding gown. Roxanne, with a hairpin in her mouth, finished pinning a crown of blush roses to the veil on Jesse's head.

"Jess, you're gorgeous," said Lillian.

Jesse embraced her. "And I feel like it too—that all started with you."

Roxanne gazed lovingly into her daughter's face. "You've been beautiful since the day you were born."

Jesse dabbed her eyes. "Oh Mom, you're the best—and you always told me; I just forgot to listen for a few years. I love you both so much—but no more mushy talk or my makeup will smear again!"

Roxanne turned to Lillian. "We've already had to fix her mascara once from tears, and mine as well, at the extravagant gift Ms. Sylvia left on the vanity in an envelope. It's enough for a down payment on the tiny apartment they wanted to buy!"

"How glorious! I'm so glad you're not secretly living in the North Tower," Lillian smiled. They all laughed at the thought.

A hush fell over the guests as Raymond Dreyfus lifted his violin to his shoulder while Luminous sat like a statue at his feet. "Ode to Joy" filled the garden air as Jesse tucked her arm into Sinclair's, the fatherly figure who would give her away.

Judith took the little ringbearer's sticky hand to help him down the aisle. It was little Benjamin, who looked from his adoptive parents, Rosie and Michael Estevez, to his birth mother, Jesse, then took off running toward the cake, squealing in delight at the chase. It was the groom, Nolan West, who finally caught him mid-stride and set him into Rosie's arms. The guests erupted into laughter.

Along the front row, Lillian gazed at all six of her children. Aurora, who sat beside her, asked, "Can I hold our baby?"

Lillian laid the baby into Aurora's arms. "Did this crazy moment make you want to calm baby Stella?"

Aurora's eyes became wide. "No way, this kind of crazy makes me want Stella to calm me! She's just like Mama was, only really pink."

"Yes, a bright star, just like her namesake, Estelle. And you, sweet girl, are becoming more like your mama every day, too."

Montreal bent over to ask Lillian, "Does it make you sad that you and Dad," he stuttered, "I mean Lars, had such a simple wedding with just us kids?"

Lillian leaned in. "Our wedding couldn't have been more beautiful: it is you children and Lars—or Dad, I love hearing that—who matter most to me. It was only your mama's presence that was missing, but I see her in all of your beloved faces."

Lavender scrambled off her chair and ran to Lars with outstretched arms. He scooped up the toddler and, with eyes twinkling, looked from his family to the crowd. "Welcome, one and all, to this family celebration!"

At the edge of the cheering guests, as the bride and groom swept down the aisle, Julius found his empty seat beside Lucy and Storm. He cleared his throat, then whispered to Lucy, "I bought you a house."

"That's certainly an original excuse for being late. You missed the *entire* wedding."

"No, I really did!" he countered.

"Of course you did, because you haven't quite figured out how to keep your promises." She whispered back, with her eyes fixed on the wedding party's shining faces.

"Ouch," he laughed. "They'll be fine; they'll love my gift. But I really did buy you a house."

"Why?" she asked.

"Because I want you close; I want another chance to be a real dad to Storm," answered Julius, resting his ankle over his knee.

Lucy raised her eyebrows. "And why did you buy us a house without asking, no matter how honorable your intent?"

Julius leaned over. "Storm, what do you think?"

Storm pushed a stray lock of hair from his face and looked at his mom. Lucy's expression softened. "You don't have to answer right now, son."

"Good," he said with a grin. "Whatever happens, I'd like a basketball hoop—and a dog!"

Julius watched Storm take off across the yard in search of the kids and asked Lucy, "What will it really take to win that boy's heart?"

"You're going to have to figure that out—on his timeline."

Just then, Hope appeared at Julius' side and tugged at his coat sleeve. "Hey, Papa, want to get some cake with me?"

Julius grabbed her hand and smiled. "I do! Let's be first in line and find the biggest pieces we can!" He gave Lucy a slight wave as he headed to the gazebo with Hope.

In the kitchen, Birgitte mopped her brow with a dish towel as she squinted through the window at the depleted cake table. "Hans said he'd buzz right back from the bakery with something—but that was long ago! That man!" she exclaimed to Lillian.

"The cake line has dwindled, so no need to worry. I'm heading out now with more lemonade," Lillian consoled her. "I imagine there'll be just enough for everyone."

At that moment, Hans plowed through the kitchen door with two trays of cinnamon rolls, one cool and the other piping hot. In his apron pocket were a pack of doilies and an icing bag bursting at the seams. "Hero to the rescue, better than cake," he said with a wide grin as he kissed his wife's rosy cheek. He set the hot tray on the kitchen island, while Birgitte swept away the other from his hands and headed out to the grass. He followed with the icing bag poised.

Lillian closed her eyes as she leaned over the steaming tray to breathe in the tantalizing aroma of cinnamon. A rush of memory overtook her. "Our fortieth birthday," she said quietly to herself.

As she opened her eyes, there was Montreal, on the opposite side of the island. "Need help with . . ." he stuttered. "the lemonade . . ." He'd caught a whiff of the glorious aroma as well. He lifted watery eyes to Lillian. "Mama's favorite . . ."

Lillian blinked back her own tears as she pulled two hot cinnamon rolls from the batch. "Come on, someone else can serve the lemonade. We won't waste this minute."

Montreal followed Lillian out to the sunny front porch. "Mama used to say that, same as my grandpa, about not missing a minute."

"I know. I remember; Estelle told me about how he'd wave from the porch. She didn't waste a minute either, and valued every person she ever knew. She saw us all as beloved, even before we knew it ourselves. I want to see people just as she did."

Montreal licked the sweet remnants of pastry from his fingers and said, "I do too."

Lillian smiled into his soulful eyes as the light of joy radiated across her face. "You already do and I'm learning from you."

About the Author

Grace E. Running-Nichols grew up in Southern California while spending several formative years in Norway. She is a Fulbright scholar, educator, wife, mother of eight, grandmother of three, and a prolific painter of walls (in every hue imaginable). Her writing journey began with fantastical allegories written for her young children in the early 90s. As her first published book, *The Color of God* grew over eight years as a product of love, sweat, and tears.

Grace lives in North Idaho with her family as she mentors, writes, and tries to herd the various cats, dogs, and other denizens of the household, in which each experience reveals a different shade of the Creator.

A free ebook edition is available with the purchase of this book.

To claim your free ebook edition:

1. Visit MorganJamesBOGO.com
2. Sign your name CLEARLY in the space
3. Complete the form and submit a photo of the entire copyright page
4. You or your friend can download the ebook to your preferred device

Morgan James BOGO™

A **FREE** ebook edition is available for you or a friend with the purchase of this print book.

CLEARLY SIGN YOUR NAME ABOVE

Instructions to claim your free ebook edition:
1. Visit MorganJamesBOGO.com
2. Sign your name CLEARLY in the space above
3. Complete the form and submit a photo of this entire page
4. You or your friend can download the ebook to your preferred device

Print & Digital Together Forever.

Snap a photo

Free ebook

Read anywhere

CPSIA information can be obtained
at www.ICGtesting.com
Printed in the USA
JSHW020909060922
30147JS00001B/133